WICKED PARADISE

ERIN RICHARDS

Midnight Muse

WICKED PARADISE
Erin Richards

Digital ISBN: 978-0991126408
Print ISBN: 978-0991126415

First Edition: August 2012
Second Edition: December 2013

PRAISE FOR
WICKED PARADISE

"Full of vivid imagery and an amazing plot, *Wicked Paradise* is a gem in the fantasy romance genre." ~*Long and Short Reviews*

"Wickedly sexy story! Ms. Richards has woven a lush tale of desire, betrayal, and mystery in *Wicked Paradise*. The story is a novel mix of fantasy and dystopian, with enough to satisfy readers who love either genre." ~Jennifer Shea, author of *Blood in the Stars*

"Wonderful combination of fantasy and romance." ~*WiLoveBooks Reviews*

"*Wicked Paradise* pushes all my romance buttons. And the writing is superb.... If you want a fun, frightening frolic through a steamy jungle while the fate of the world hangs in the balance, then this book's for you." ~Beth Yarnall, author of *Rush* and *Vindicate*.

"Overall, this story blew me away. Riveting, intriguing, and scenes so well written the reader feels like they are front and center in the middle of it all. This was a magical, sexy, beautiful adventure that I was glad to have taken a ride on. A job well done to this author, and I await and anticipate much more!" ~*Storm Goddess Book Reviews*

BOOKS BY ERIN RICHARDS

Psychic Justice Series
Chasing Shadows, Book 1
Twilight Rising, Book 2
Stealing Twilight, Book 3
Seducing Darkness, Book 4
Tempting Midnight, Book 5

Forbidden Legacy Series
Forbidden Thirteen, Book 1

Wilde Witches Series
Igniting the Witch, Prequel
Black Magic Rising, Book 1
Black Warlocks Prowling, Book 2
Black Curses Brewing, Book 3

Wicked Paradise

Young Adult
Vigilante Nights
Dragonfly Nightmare
Bittersweet Wreckage

See updated book list at:
www.erinrichards.com/booklist.htm

WICKED PARADISE

CHAPTER 1

The last day of Morgan's life dawned gray and dismal, absurdly appropriate for her looming death. Ten years ago, her Seer's Sight had foretold her death on this day, and her infernal Sight rarely failed her. She had told no one about the awful prophecy, not even her powerful sorcerer father. At twenty-two that day, she was prepared to pass on to the Afterlife.

Not that I have a bloody choice. With a catch in her throat, Morgan swatted the thinning velvet drapery aside. Gripping the cold stone windowsill, she stared out her window for the last time. Chills seeped into her as the morning sunlight lost its challenge to the thick fog ghosting the courtyard's scattered structures. The buildings on the hillside were almost invisible.

"Accursed fog!" She thumped a fist on her thigh. "Perfect day, perfect death." Icy jaws of anguish clamped down on her insides. *Damn the Fates.* Why had her Sight not revealed more about how she would die? In some small way, she had prepared for this day. Yet, who ever prepared for death? Her stomach knotted as questions kept pricking her like thirsty mosquitos.

She deliberately closed off her mind to her doomed fate, instead diverting her attention to the vision that had flung her out of a fitful sleep that morning. Who was the tall, handsome sorcerer in the vision who held her in his arms and danced with her on a moonlit beach below a lush jungle? Fire magic had sizzled between them, gyrating and tangoing together in perfect harmony. Was it merely a far-fetched longing her mind conjured up on her final day on Avalon? At least until the horrid foresight at the dream's end turned her tingles of desire into the stabbing pain of prophecy.

Even now, the foresight jabbed an ache behind her eyes, refusing to release its hold on her mind. The wild storm, the drowning wave, the unfamiliar man's desolation, and the swirling sea of despair as his internal fire winked out as water submerged him. She remembered pressing her lips to her dream sorcerer, giving him the breath of life until the ocean claimed him and he drifted away, a wry smile locked onto his face. Flailing about in the watery grave, she pushed against the murky currents to reach him, all to no avail. She had spied a spot of light clutched in his hand...and the face of horrendous malevolence met her gaze. Gleeful, howling laughter ripped her out of sleep and out of her vision, her body burning with desire, a cry of terror on her lips. Sweat-drenched, Morgan had awoken that morning shivering in her cold, lonely bed.

"I will never learn what the vision meant." She shoved away from the window and added peat to the embers in the fireplace. The instant she straightened from the slate hearth, the heavy door swung into the stone wall. Her pulse quickened.

"Morgan! Why are you dallying?" her father roared, barreling into her bedchamber. His long, graying hair flew in every direction, his blue eyes blazed with his ire until a hint of sadness flashed across them. "You were to meet me an hour ago." He rushed to her bulging packs and picked them up. "Come along. We have little time to waste."

"Sorry. I...I overslept." The vision flashed across her mind, touching upon the erotic chapter at the beginning, sending fierce heat to her cheeks. "Why didn't you send someone for me earlier?"

Her father gave her a bemused look, an infrequent flush working his weather-beaten complexion. As the High Sorcerer, not only did he have the ability to scry into the present and future, he had the ability to read thoughts. She always instinctively blocked her mind from his intrusions, and they had an unwritten agreement never to pry. At times, they both slipped. As in that moment.

For the love of purgatory, steal me away now. Morgan dipped her head, shoved her arms in her coat. Sweet hell, she had no reason to feel ashamed of idiotic dreams or her Sight. Besides, she couldn't stop her sleeping mind from going astray on its own. A hot throb grew in her throat and spread downward. She narrowed her eyes at the fire, wishing she hadn't stoked it.

"I was finishing a delicate potion," he finally replied, regaining his composure.

She hid a smile. Her father always lost himself in his herbs and spells. "Good morning, Gwilym." Using his given name was a long-accustomed habit from her sorcery training days. Most often, she used it teasingly. This time, only sorrow and wistfulness hung on her voice.

Morgan took her packs from him and slung them over her shoulder. He advised her a week ago to prepare for time away from home and duties on her birth date. He implied a lengthy journey, but divulged no more.

There was no need to say more—she already knew her fate.

Taking no chances, she packed her most cherished possessions, several changes of clothes, her finest herbs, and traveling food. If her prophecy came true, she would need these tokens of status for her journey to the Otherworld.

Her father approached and kissed her forehead. "Good birth day to you, my beloved daughter." Valerian wafted strongly off his tunic and she wrinkled her nose to stifle a sneeze.

"Thank you." Suffering his groans of compliance, she brushed a smudge of green powder off his sleeve.

He snatched her hand in his warm clasp. "Now come along. I have a gift awaiting you."

They left the castle and hiked briskly along the well-worn path that cut through the forest to the Sacred Stones. The woods closed about them, and unease chilled Morgan well before the cool air seeped through her layers of clothing.

"The only gift I want is for everyone to gain freedom from this island," she grumbled to herself, hitching her satchel over her shoulder to even the load. Would there be a safe place off this cursed island for every inhabitant who didn't know any better? The injustices of the old Gods and Goddesses who had forsaken Avalon left her with a persistent anger. Morgan stomped on a mushroom, pulverizing it into the thick forest mulch.

The trail narrowed to one body's span and Gwilym took the lead at a fast clip. Morgan nearly had to run to maintain pace, afraid to lose sight of him regardless of the well-marked path. Birds trilled and small animals scurried over sodden leaves and crumbling twigs. Forest noises increased the hammering of Morgan's heart. The pungent decay in the dense undergrowth added fuel to a new foreboding inside her.

"Father, why the haste? I'm sure my gift is not going anywhere. It's not as if we can leave this gods-forsaken land in my lifetime." *Maybe he prophesied that my foresight was a poorly disguised jest, and I will awaken from a bad dream under a glorious spring sun...dancing in the arms of my mythical lover.*

Memories of her morning's delicious dream infused her with torrid heat. *Again!* Could she not let her unknown dream lover go? For the sake of the Goddess, she was *the* High Druid Sorceress. She didn't need a man! She certainly had no need for what her nocturnal mind summoned and made her body covet.

"Morgan, hurry along. You will learn soon enough."

She kicked a pinecone into the woods, booting the visions out of her mind. Passion and love were not stars in her destiny. She'd resigned herself to that fact once she reached marriageable age and no man of proper bloodlines existed on Avalon. Her family and her people demanded she mate with one of equal stature. Instead, Avalon stifled her potential, her life, and her desires. Born too late in a fading world, little remained for her to do but perish with it. Exactly what her prophecy had predicted. *Bloody hell of a life.*

Losing sight of Gwilym, Morgan lurched forward, slipping on a fist-sized stone. She grabbed a prickly fir limb for balance. A squirrel crashed through a thicket to her right, shaking her tenuous foothold. Smoothing her hand over her stomach, she felt the childhood scars beneath her tunic. Inhaling deeply, the fresh scent of pine and fir helped quell her inane fear.

The jagged path took a turn up a sharp incline and the smothering trees thinned. They climbed a few steps higher until the trail leveled off. Primroses reached for the late morning sun at the forest's edge. Ahead, the fog grew lacey around the perimeter of the forest, and the morning brightened, cheering her mood somewhat.

"Why are you taking me to the stones? I certainly don't need gifts from you."

Gwilym uttered an odd humorless chuckle. "This is as much for me as it is for you."

The pathway's final bend carried them into the lush spring meadow at the hilltop. Morgan's breathing eclipsed the silence of the sliver of heaven. Brilliant sunshine bathed the crest, the sky as blue as the summer ocean surrounding the island. Wildflowers perfumed the air, swallowing the lingering odors of the woods and the remainder of Morgan's fear.

The Sacred Stones stood in a ring, thirteen statuesque knights guarding the meadow from the encroaching forest. Awe crackled in her magic core. Intact and unfathomable, the stones' energy spiked the air intensely. The surrounding land's energy was raw, unpredictable. Certain days of the moon phase placed the stone circle off limits to all human inhabitants. For caution's sake, Morgan shied away from the stones altogether.

Gwilym beckoned impatiently from the center of the behemoth pillars. Slow, deliberate footsteps carried her across the carpet of grasses and wildflowers into the ring beside him. Power engulfed her, raising goose bumps over her entire body, drowning her innate powers. Morgan touched his sleeve for reassurance. "Why are we here?"

He placed his herb stained hands on her shoulders. Pride replaced the sorrow that flashed across his face. "This is the first day of your destiny, my gift to you, to all the Druids."

"I don't understand. Why are the stones involved in my destiny?" Emboldened, she confessed her long-held secret. "I have seen my fate. I'm prepared to die today." The partial truth bumped off her tongue as her gut churned.

Gwilym smiled proudly, but his smile failed to stretch to his gray eyes. "Yes. The day marking your birth is also one of death." He grasped her hands in his cool dry fingers. "When your mother died at your birth, she foresaw your death and your rebirth at an indefinable point in the future."

Air lodged in her throat. To share a prophecy with the mother she never knew—a powerful seer—made her fate all the more real. She looked heavenward.

A lone raven circled overhead, hunting food for its young tucked in a nest atop the highest pine. The hunter issued a haunting, forlorn screech, knowing its offspring were ready to flee the nest for a life of their own. What did the bird of ill omen herald? Morgan shivered at the foreboding refusing to release her from its grip.

Shielding his eyes, Gwilym glanced up at the sun. His agitation rode the air so thick and heavy it bogged down Morgan's heart.

"We have little time. Listen to me." He squeezed her hands gently and rushed on. "Druid magic is dying off everywhere. Avalon holds the last sorcerers of the ancient blood."

Morgan sucked in her middle. She knew matters had worsened on Avalon, but she hadn't anticipated magic disappearing elsewhere. "How did this happen? How can we stop it?"

"It is more severe than our sorcerers losing magic to dying bloodlines. This loss worsens throughout time, contributing to mankind's devastation far into the future."

Morgan dug her heels into the grass. "Are you certain it was foresight?"

"You know my visions always come true in one form or another." He brushed a loose tendril of hair off her face. "Dead humans and animals litter an arid future land. Fresh water is tainted. Trees and foliage are dead. Buildings, monuments crumbled. A wasteland of death."

"I don't understand." She rubbed her forehead with her fingertips. "How did the loss of *magic* cause such devastation?"

"Fomorians, the gods of chaos and destruction, will rise again and multiply over the years. They will become a blight on the lands of the future, growing stronger from the magic in their paths."

Fomorians! The violent, evil beings who had oppressed the Tuatha dé Danann? "I thought Merlin slayed the last descendant of Balor the Fomorian King before he died. How can *I* help these future people if you have already seen their destruction? You know we cannot change the future."

"Even the wise and powerful Merlin was fallible. The future will happen and you cannot save everyone. The strongest sorcerers will fight off the Fomorian uprising. You can help the survivors rebuild, to start a new life free from further demon threat." Gwilym stroked her cheek lovingly. "Do you remember how Merlin rid Avalon of the strongest Fomorian from Balor's line? How he used Avalon's magic to bind it on a hidden island?"

Tentatively, Morgan shook her head once, her eyelids fluttering rapidly as the old tales jumped into her memory. "I remember the bards' tales. What does that have to do with me?"

"I have discovered a means for you to leave Avalon and fulfill your true destiny. Most notably, I have found a method for you to halt the loss of magic."

The vigilant raven let out a croaking caw above their heads, masking her horrified gasp. "Do you mean..." Stars wavered before her and her knees watered. "The magic necessary to keep the half-Druid, half-Fomorian—WindWraith—in its prison is faltering?"

"Yes." Gwilym's throat bobbed several times. "The shadow island bound to Avalon reaches far into the future."

Blasted blind Sight. "So I'm to *die* on Avalon, merely to be reborn to save an already dead world." Morgan wrung her hands, wishing to wring them around Fate's scrawny neck.

"Love..." Her father reached for her, but she backed away. "You will save our bloodline, our people now and in this future time. There is naught else we can do. It must be enough."

A hum began to radiate off one megalith sentry, moving to the next, until all thirteen stones created a low reverberation. Energy lifted Morgan's hair and it floated around her shoulders in a live mantle. Her powers ascended, pushing at her bones, muscles, skin, as if the stones tried to draw the magic out of her. Disconcerting in one respect, in another it felt right, natural. The noise grew louder and the tips of the pillars crackled, shooting tiny lightning bolts into the sky.

Hands cupping her face, her father stared deeply into her eyes. Unblinking, she felt the telepathic intrusion into her mind, a cool breeze whooshing through her skull. "Remember the old tales of WindWraith." She nodded. The dizzying effects of his spell trembled down her weakening legs. "They are true. Not the fables the bards made them out to be."

The whirling liquid depths of his eyes pulled her into the visions he invoked in his mind. A strong telepathic sending thumped inside her skull, dumping a library's worth of knowledge into her confusion. The horrendous story of Avalon's Shadow—WindWraith—bubbled to the surface. An icy shiver turned her blood sluggish.

How could *she* save the Druid sorcerers and their magic? Or the world? Would Father banish her to an unchartered island prison to die alone, or worse, to allow the oldest and most powerful Fomorian to murder her?

Morgan wrenched out of her father's hands, slammed her booted foot upon a spray of lupines. She inhaled the citrusy bouquet of the lavender-colored wildflowers, memorizing the scent. "None of this makes a lick of sense!" She wagged her head as if to fling off her father's imparted knowledge. It refused to budge, swirling chaotically in her already fuzzy mind.

Gwilym glanced at the sun, the lines deepening around his troubled eyes. He pulled her into a fierce hug. "Hear me out." Releasing her, his words flowed, giving her no time to voice her countless questions. "I possess enough magic to aid the Sacred Stones in sending you to defeat this malevolency, to mend Avalon's connection to the hidden island, thereby saving our magic. In so doing, you will be able to awaken that island and build a safe haven for those sorcerers who survived the Fomorian conquest. You can rebuild our ancient bloodlines." He touched her cheek, his callused thumb rough against her skin. "You will live a long life, which you would not otherwise enjoy on Avalon."

"Alone?" She wanted to grab his shoulders and shake the madness out of him. "Will I kill Avalon's Shadow by myself?"

"An assassin from the future, born from an ancient Druid bloodline that has survived time, will aid you. He stems from a bloodline that resists the Fomorian's bite or magic, much like our own."

She held up her hand, challenging him. "Did you foresee my...*our* triumph?" The words felt like jagged glass spitting out of her mouth.

"I foresaw your arrival on the shadow island and the island's return to life." The skin around his mouth drooped. "The rest was hidden from me." A salty breeze wrapped them in edgy silence amidst the increasing pops and sizzles the stones secreted. From the leather pouch tied at his waist, he pulled out a vial filled with opaque, greenish syrup and uncorked it. "Drink this."

Arms tight around herself, Morgan inched backward. Tears stung the back of her eyes. "You need me. Our people need me." Thoughts cascaded into her head, and her heart felt as if a sword was slicing it into pieces. "I'm to replace you as High Sorcerer." Her chest ached for the people of Avalon, the people of the world.

Remaining on Avalon was not an option for her, even if she lived another day. This task was her duty to their people. Now it made absolute sense why Father forced her to read the fascinating archaic tomes about ancient Ireland, Fomorians, demons, and their ilk during her final sorcery training.

Gwilym closed the distance between them. "Morgan, do you trust me?"

Without hesitation, she nodded. He was the one person she always trusted—the one who never failed her.

A tear spilled upon his weathered cheek. "Do you think I would not go in your stead if the Gods willed it?" Arm wavering, he held the vial out to her again. "Drink it. You will need the knowledge it contains to survive on the island, to understand your entire destiny."

Angry and confused, she plucked the potion from his fingers and downed the contents in one swallow. Morgan hurled the bottle with all her might, barely throwing it outside the stone circle as the palpable energy pushed against it. Deep grass buried the wretched vial as the bitter liquid burned in her throat. She coughed several times to clear out the awful taste.

He tied a stuffed pouch on her knife belt. "Take these charms and do not lose them. Strong magic fills them. Once you are on the island, you will understand their purpose."

The sun neared its zenith in the crystal blue sky. The air within the stone circle darkened as though a thundercloud blotted out the sun. Gwilym kissed her cheeks. "I love you with all my heart, my Morgan. Do not ever forget that."

She flung her arms around his beloved lean frame. "Please come with me." Inhaling deeply, she savored the scents of familiar herbs clinging to his tunic.

"I do not have your strength. The stones will kill me." Gwilym clasped her upper arms and his trembling became hers. "Our people will need me once your task is complete. I must train your cousin Ceri to take my place.

"The Goddess has willed your fate. Your mother died to bring you into the world for a great purpose. I don't see a greater purpose than this." He released her with a flourish of his hands. "Stay strong and do not be afraid. You will not be alone in this task, trust me."

Morgan choked down a sob. The great prophet told the truth. She felt it in her soul, and her father would never betray her. Given the chance, he would sacrifice his own life for hers many times over.

"You are the heart and soul of the Druids, my beautiful, courageous daughter." Gwilym kissed her forehead. "We will meet in the Afterlife, and you can prove to me how right I was." His thin lips spread in a wry, lopsided smile even as his eyes swam in tears.

Resolute, she gazed up through blurry vision into her father's beloved face. "I love you." She caressed his pale, dry cheek.

His shadow towered above the stones with the magnificence of his powers. A blue glow saturated the stone ring. The air sizzled and snapped. He raised his arms heavenward. Lightning bolts flared from the top of the pillars, merging with the force flashing in the cloudless sky.

A strange airlessness filled Morgan as if she soared above the ocean in her dream lover's arms, carefree and happy. Gwilym's tremendous magic flowed around her, through her, became one with her. The energy of the stones lit up her blood like flickers of fire.

In her emotional maelstrom, a sudden idea occurred to her. "Father?" she shouted above the din. "How will the Druid assassin get to the island?"

Wind blustered inside the pillars, and she heard Gwilym's baffling last words in her head. "His charm has already been cast."

"Cast? Whatever do you mean?" Morgan's words vanished in the tempest.

Her cherished father disappeared. The Sacred Stones melted into one sky-towering column of radiant starlight. An abyss of destiny devoured Morgan, her father's scratchy voice giving final instructions in her mind.

CHAPTER 2

Sunlight dappled through the canopy of trees, and Morgan squinted against the hazy light. A peculiar odor of fertile soil filled her nose as heavy heat weighed down her limbs. Disorder cluttered her mind like spider webs in an ancient, untouched forest. She sucked in air so warm and condensed it coated her tongue.

"Father?" she called softly, hoping she had suffered a nightmare to end all nightmares.

Harsh raven cackles and trilling bird songs were the only replies she received.

Dread blew away the cobwebs in her head, forcing her to open her eyes wide. A circling raven issued a warning caw. Surely, it wasn't the same raven that trailed her on Avalon? Morgan peered through the seemingly harmless woods, wary of potential danger in the dense interior. A sharp rock poked her buttocks, forcing her to roll onto her side into a heap of dead leaves and twigs. The bird's screeching pierced her ears, adding to her chaos.

"Bugger off, bird," she said, tasting her father's sour potion. She swished her tongue around her mouth, dredging up moisture to wash the vileness away.

The unfamiliar tropical woods gave validity to her father's task. *Wretched destiny!* His last words haunted her more than anything else she learned in her last hour on Avalon. With countless unanswered questions, her father plucked her parting questions from her as the maelstrom whipped her through the alternating fierce heat and intense cold of space. "Why didn't you tell me all this sooner? Will I ever return to Avalon?" she had hollered into oblivion before a suffocating weight pressed upon her and Avalon disappeared.

As she'd hurtled through dense air, his faint reply had echoed in her ears. "I sought a path to travel alone, leaving you here to rule. My Sight did not reveal to me until this morning that I could not go, that you had to travel alone." His voice had grown fainter. "You will live your life on the island. You cannot ever leave."

Recalling Gwilym's prophetic response sent her heart thudding against her chest. She was terrified of her new life sentence and her monstrous task.

"The demon's prison has become my own." Morgan hammered her fist on a clump of tiny leafed ground cover. She willed her heart's beat to steady and her lungs to process the molasses-thick air faster. Knowing her father's penchant for solving problems before they affected her, she believed he would have done all in his arsenal of magic to change the tide of destiny. She understood why he'd waited to divulge her mission until he had no choice.

Clasping her satchel and Gwilym's leather pouch, she rose to her feet. A breeze kissed her face, salty and sultry. Perspiration dotted her temples, dripped between her breasts. She stripped off her stifling overcoat and wadded it into her pack. Morgan shook the twigs and dust from her skirt. The loathsome jagged scars across her lower belly itched from the sweltering air.

Power rippled beneath the ground, flowed over her feet. It sifted through her fire and air magic, filled her with earthy energy. Pleasantly startled, she let it penetrate, calming and cooling. She felt as if she floated on a fluffy white cloud overlooking a tropical paradise that belonged to her, in her. She dipped in and out of luscious rain forests, fragrant meadows, dazzling waterfalls, all awakening on the air currents left in her wake. Arms outstretched to capture the unusual, welcoming energy, she laughed and spun in a circle.

The old tales, along with Gwilym's spoken and unspoken directives quickly plagued her momentary bliss. Unopened library tomes seemed to cram her head, throbbing behind her eyes. Except for the spells, recipes, and notations in the set of Mage's Book of Secrets passed down from one generation to the next, she never understood the tales and prophecies painstakingly handwritten in the leather-bound journals. Some were so old and jumbled they made no sense. Dejection slumped Morgan's shoulders, forcing her leaden arms to her side.

A shallow burrow of ferns in the woods caught her eye. She needed to rest and regain her sensibilities, to temper the magic roiling in the air, softly vibrating beneath her feet, becoming one with her. The island seemed to secrete power, similar to what she'd felt from the Sacred Stones. Pushing aside the lush foliage, she crawled into the viney nest.

"I may as well tie my wrists behind my back for all the will granted me in this life." She slapped a dead flower off its stem onto the ground. "No! I will not let it defeat me...not the most powerful sorceress on Avalon!" She wanted to laugh at the incongruity of her situation she was the *only* sorceress on *this* island. Exhausted, she leaned her back against a petrified tree stump. Her eyelids grew heavy in the blistering heat. A horrid memory hung onto the edge of her mind and she refused to name it or give it proper due.

Her body grew languid, and sleep came fast. The dream arrived quick and persistent...

Her dream lover guided Morgan over the misty meadow, her back molded to his muscled chest. His fingers danced across her flesh, scorching trails of fire up and down her body. They halted at the cliff's edge, Avalon's Sacred Stones holding silent vigil behind them. Molten lust deluged Morgan, leaving her boneless. Mesmerized, she possessed no will to resist the pleasure cascading over her naked body.

Desperate to feast her sight upon his face, Morgan started to turn in her dream warrior's embrace, but his arms tightened into iron bands, forcing her to remain immobile. The burning fingers of desire suddenly disappeared, replaced by the scraping itch of ice. Invisible ropes shackled her wrists to her sides, and her power rose defensively inside her. A howling, evil laughter floated up, filled her senses with wicked shards of darkness.

Oh, hell. This wasn't her dream lover!

Readying a spell, she wrenched on her magic. She managed to toss a ball of destructive Druid magic outward, bending it behind her. Her magic faltered, slashing into ineffective embers that evaporated on the humid air.

She struggled against the unyielding bands, drawing on magic that refused to cooperate. Malevolence seeped through myriad thorn pricks across her skin. An unseen force carried Morgan off the crag, and then released her. She drifted above the infinite aquamarine sea, the gentle spring winds carrying away her terrified screams.

A desolate landscape ate the vast waters, and fascination replaced her fear. Crumbled buildings crammed the arid land below. A golden spire remained standing, a stalwart beacon in the devastation. As she focused on it, grounding herself in the strange land, she began spiraling downward.

Panic clawed at her stomach. She never fathomed her life would end this way. As she beseeched the Goddess for a painless death, a fireball whizzed past her toward the cliff. Sailing through the air, she whipped her head around and watched the fireball strike a dark, cloud-like shadow on the meadow's edge on Avalon's cliff. The shadow wavered on the precipice, taunting and beckoning her at the same time. The fireball left a hole in its side, and the shadow demon's piercing screeches echoed off the Sacred Stones.

Spurred into action, Morgan assembled her inner powers. Fire balled into a crimson and amber sphere on her palm. Bitter sulfur, tinged with sweet Druid magic, energized her. She flung her arm back and hurled her blazing weapon. Another fireball from behind her raced to meet hers. The two deadly orbs struck the shadow, exploding in brilliant golden light. A gusty, angry howl split the air before the shadow dissipated into harmless wisps.

Morgan's body grew leaden. The ground sped toward her. Breath seizing terror overwhelmed her in a black tide. Seconds away from colliding with the tarnished gold spire, strong arms caught her from behind.

In an eye blink, they stood in a lush meadow surrounded by verdant tropical woods. Her savior's arms wrapped protectively around her, her back pressed against his hard body in a perfect fit. Relief wilted her against her real dream lover's chest, and she managed to blot out her near-death horror.

The air sizzled with their magic, danced together in synchronized rhythm. His fingers whispered across her skin, stopping before reaching intimate territory. Gasping, she clung to his muscular arm draped around her waist. The touch of his lips on the back of her neck sent shockwaves rippling across her shoulders. He showered kisses from her neck to her ear lobe, his hand splayed on her stomach, pressing into her as if he owned her. Her skin burned in the aftermath of his blazing possession, fire dripping off his fingers.

Without warning, his warm mouth retreated and his large hands spanned her waist. He turned her to face him, and she licked her lips in anticipation. Balmy ocean breezes stirred the air, swished her loose hair over his arms. Head dipped, she both feared and longed to gaze upon him.

With forefinger and thumb, he lifted her chin and her hungry gaze latched onto his face. Fair hair swirled about his head, mating with her black tresses. Gleaming with promise, his cerulean eyes held the ocean depths of summer in which she longed to soak her inflamed body. The uncertainty and angst rolling off him startled Morgan. She caressed the sculpted planes of his smooth, bronzed face, reached to slide her fingers into his thick hair. He caught her wrist, kissed her palm, his lips branding her skin with his heat.

A raven cawed overhead and landed on a palmetto next to them. The bird of oracles flapped its wings in invitation. A second raven dove from the sky and landed next to the first. Two sets of beady eyes watched, waited.

The warrior studied her as if to imprint her features into his memory. "Someday, little raven." He cupped her cheek in his large hand. "I will find you," he whispered.

Morgan blinked rapidly and the mists grew murkier. Her savior vanished, leaving behind two ruffled symbols of healing and death. The ravens cawed in unison. One flew to Morgan's outstretched arm. The other disappeared into the fog.

Disoriented, Morgan awoke, desire quivering in her middle. She fully expected to gaze upon the meadows surrounding the Sacred Stones, the man from her dream beside her. But her cocoon's hot, leafy shrubbery flung her back to the present on the strange island.

"Damnable dream." She wiped the moisture off her forehead. Or was it her Sight? Her Seer's Sight usually revealed itself in her dreams, but her Sight never left her feeling as if the vision was real, like the languid arousal tickling her middle, traveling lower. She snorted. "An event unlikely to ever happen to me."

A wild animal roared, the fierce sound flinging the vision into the quicksand of her mind. Her pulse quickened. Another tree-shuddering roar rent the air. Morgan swallowed a scream. She pushed forward to peer beyond her haven, hiding behind the wide leaves. Strong memories of a childhood trauma stilled her heart for several seconds. She clutched her stomach where proof of an altercation with a wildcat marred her skin. Her frantic gaze darted left to right, landing on nothing but the steamy tropics.

A loud scrabbling clatter in the brush to her left sent her leaping into the open. Morgan summoned her fire magic, but only sparks sputtered from her fingertips, dying before they hit the ground. She tried two more times to no avail. Traveling through time and space from Avalon to the island had depleted her magic reserves. Unable to stifle her cry a second time, she searched for refuge, deciding the nearby sea was safest.

"Save me from this madness. Send me to the Afterlife now," she muttered, feet flying toward the booming waves crashing against the shore.

CHAPTER 3

Ryan lunged at the wild boar, stabbing his wooden spear into the nasty beast. The animal squealed in agonized rage, sidestepping from the protrusion in its hoary body. It stumbled a few feet before sinking to its knees. Sometimes he hated using caveman ways to kill his food, but wielding magic wasted his power. On the flipside, he liked the exercise of thrusting, lunging, and jabbing the spear. It kept him in peak physical condition. The better to gut a demon he couldn't kill with magic.

The grunting boar gasped out its last breath. Smug satisfaction chased a hot breeze down Ryan's bare back, and his empty stomach rumbled in anticipation. Arms folded across his chest, he watched the beast convulse until it stilled. He swatted at the buzzing insects already drawn to the metallic tang of pooling blood.

Noon sunshine hammered him, drying the sweat on his brow. The sun magnified the pair of grayish-violet moons, and they hung brighter in the sky than ever. "Must be my lucky day." He snorted, flexed his arms behind his back, taking grim note at the hypocrisy of his life.

Spiky plant shoots poked through the thin soles of his leatherleaf sandals. Scowling, Ryan inspected his makeshift foot coverings. *Time to pick through my leather scraps and make a shoddy pair of shoes.* He eyed the boar with speculation.

"Why fucking bother?" His urban feet were growing

immune to nature's torments. By the time he figured out a way off this freak-show island, he wouldn't need caveman shoes any longer. The coven back home had scavenged a department store's worth of shoes and boots from the corpses littering the land. He had plenty from which to choose from.

The blood's coppery odor thickened in Ryan's nostrils. A year living among the dead made him immune to that, too. He nudged the boar to ensure it was dead. As he bent to yank out his spear, a wild shriek disrupted the island's incessant chorus of animals, birds, and insects. An odd prickle crawled across the nape of his neck, as though fate untied another knot in his lifeline, opening another freakish chapter. Tantalizing Druid magic edged the brackish breeze, sprinkled into his center of power, intensified the growling in his gut.

Multicolored birds flocked from the trees, flapping a swift getaway. Hidden animals scrambled through the jungle in all directions, snapping and thrashing the dense brush.

He'd lived on the island alone for two weeks, and it was the first time he'd heard anything resembling a human sound. Baffled and excited by the diversion, he tugged the spear out of the boar then sprinted in the direction of the scream.

It made sense that a new challenge cropped up that day. Earlier that morning, he'd sensed a change in the atmosphere, the presence of something untamed, of incalculable energy. All his senses had blazed with new life. After a restless night, he'd found himself mired in an erotic dream of a vivacious and beautiful sorceress from another time and land. It'd been so long since his mind filled with anything but death and annihilation, sorrow and sadness. Even now, hours later, the dream left him reeling. The bizarre sensation of the dream sorceress merging her magic with his had enhanced his desire. His pleasure had been so real, he'd awoken hot and sweaty, hard as steel, his fire magic bubbling inside his core. His body had thrown off a diffuse blue glow, which only happened when he wielded a certain kind of magic. Magic had simmered in the cool cave air, and he bristled with electricity from head to toes. Never in his life had he lost control of his power while asleep. It scared the hell out of him. Uncontrolled magic was easily stolen from the unwary. Losing control was too risky, and he mustn't ever allow it to happen again.

The dream still disturbed him, though. He'd rescued the sorceress from near death at the grimy paws of a shadow-shifter Fomorian. The bastard acted like it wanted to kill her. Or did it want to mark her and make her its minion? He scratched his jaw, returned his reverie to the dream's erotic ending, wondering why he'd voiced his wish to find her one day.

"What was *that* all about?" His snort turned into a wry chuckle. "Two weeks in paradise and I'm totally losing it." His hands clenched. He wasn't ready to admit to the sinking realization that the woman satisfied needs he never knew existed. They certainly no longer existed on a bleak, destroyed Earth.

"Who the hell is doing this to me?" Known for his impeccable level head, he sure as hell wasn't allowing the madness inspired by a damned dream destroy his already messed up life. He had enough to deal with just surviving each day.

Another eerie scream split the air, flinging him back to the present. Acrid fear floated from the woody depths, attacked his senses, gripped his soul. Ryan increased his pace. Twigs snapped to his left within a copse of sandalwoods. Loud gasps following the scream raked a nervous thrill up his body. As he shifted direction, he caught sight of midnight black hair flowing down the back of a curvy, petite woman. She crashed through dense shrubbery, shoving aside bracken to clear a narrow escape route.

Ryan raced toward her, sensing her panic in his blood. Afraid to startle her further, he called to her in a low, even tone, "Hey! You okay?" Her self-destructive fright propelled her further away from him into the unyielding jungle. If he didn't halt her, she'd end up shredded alive. "Stop," he yelled louder, gaining on her.

Not letting up on her relentless tear through the jungle, the woman swung her head around, her long tangled hair veiling half her face. "No, no," she cried, bursting through an opening in the vegetation, emerging onto a craggy clearing. Terror ravaged her pale face. Wild hair stuck to her temples, cascaded over her shoulders.

Too late, he recognized the false hilltop. He flung away his spear and dove for her ankles, missing her by a hair as she disappeared off the cliff. His chest slammed against a grassy knoll, the wind all but knocked out of him. The woman's deathly cries echoed in the cliffs bordering the cove. Her body hit the water, a muted splash squelching her screeches.

Ryan vaulted up and leaped off the hill into the churning sea. He bent into a dive, slicing through the dangerous water. The sea cooled his sweaty body, but didn't temper the heat of his fear. Or the burgeoning flames of hope. Whipping hair out of his eyes, he searched for the woman beyond the exposed rocks along the reef she'd missed by mere feet. Ryan dove under the water, shoving aside meandering seaweed, scanning the murky depths. He spied her small body floating toward the surface. She appeared dead, but Ryan knew she lived. His blood sang her tune. Magic ebbed and swelled around them, unstoppable even by his iron defenses.

With sure strokes, he knifed through the water and

caught her in his arms. He stood to his full height, the water leveling just beneath his chest, and carried her out of the sea. His searching gaze swept over the woman he'd seduced in his head during the night. Shock riddled him and she suddenly became dead weight in his arms.

"What the hell?" He whistled, tightening his hold on her before he dropped her. Kneeling on the beach, he cradled her slender, wet body to his chest, offering her the last of his body heat. As she lay limp and frigid in his arms, he scanned the length of her body.

"No blood. Good." Relief unclenched the fist around his heart. Seaweed knotted in her black hair, a dark blanket covering the pristine white sand. Fear stung his eyes and he pressed his fingers to the pulse in her neck. The vein beat life against his fingers. He pushed out another sigh. Thick black lashes flickered against her pale face. Taut skin stretched over high cheekbones, and her petite nose twitched above bow-shaped lips.

"You're safe now." He hoped she heard him. "I won't let anything harm you."

Tenderly, Ryan stretched her out on the damp strip of beach between the tide and the baking dry sand. Concentrating on reviving her, he forced himself not to stare hungrily at the clinging blouse accentuating her rounded breasts. Troubled by the physical awareness of the woman from his dream, he ignored the prickly confusion curling in his ribcage.

He positioned his palms on her chest and started resuscitation efforts. His mouth met her lips, and he wanted nothing more than to give her the life from his lungs, as she had once done for him—the day his sailboat capsized and a bizarre squall had tossed him onto the island. He hadn't recognized her at the time, had only felt a niggle of magic in her breath before oblivion claimed him. He believed it a hallucination. Until now. The vision pushed through his mind in a senseless stream. Was Fomorian black magic screwing with him?

Ryan brushed a speck of seaweed off her nose, his warm fingertips pressing into her cold cheeks as if to pop answers out of her mouth. For the first time since he'd sailed away from New Angeles two weeks ago for a safe day of peace on the Pacific, he might find answers to the million questions warring in his brain. "I won't let you die," he growled.

Unbelievably, the world had deposited this treasure in his lap when he believed he'd lost it all again. Vibrant and alive like the island he'd come to both despise for his loneliness and love for its lush life.

"Come on, breathe," he demanded. "Wake up!"

He pinched her nose closed, puffed air into her mouth. "Breathe, damn it."

His thumb caressed the creamy damp skin above her breasts, stroked over rough scars welting her flat stomach. Slow and steady, her heart tapped a triumphant rhythm beneath his palm. Her mouth compressed and she sputtered against his lips. Ryan gently turned her head to the side.

Salt water gushed between her ashen lips, and a final clearing cough heaved up her chest. Then her eyelashes fluttered up, exotic green eyes rounded wide. She croaked out, "By the Goddess, it *is* you!" Cringing against the sand, her face flushed. Frantically, she tugged at her soaked blouse, crossing her arms over her exquisite breasts. "What monster of insanity has invaded my body," she murmured in a voice he strained to hear—in a tantalizing British lilt.

She attempted to rise, but he held her down with a light hand on her shoulder. "Hold on. You're not going anywhere." The intense need to protect her from whatever sent her streaking through the jungle soared across his suspicion. To assess further damage, he methodically pressed his hands gently over her wet body. Her skin awakened, growing warm beneath his fingers. Expression wary, mouth gaping, she froze.

"Do you hurt anywhere?" He combed his fingers into her gritty tresses, picked seaweed out of the tangles.

Eerily familiar magic teased his power, infused his senses. He detected more than a mortal Druid's magic within her. It felt pure, from an ancient well of the earth's nascent energy. It surrounded him, flirted evocatively with the negligible amount of magic he emitted. Defensively, he threw up his internal shields, locking her magic out. Had a Druid or Fomorian placed a spell on him before he sailed away from L.A.? She might not be an evil being with magic like his, but was she Fomorian-wrought? Regardless, he couldn't drop his guard again for anything.

The blood thrumming in his body sang a different song, though. The mysterious woman represented a seedling's drop of moisture in the bone-dry hell of his life. And he wanted to lick every trace of water from her beautiful face and down her lush body, to hydrate the desert he'd become. The instinct to claim her roared through him in the blood rushing straight to his groin. The force stunned him. In a day's span, his life had flipped upside down, flipped again, and splattered him like demon-kill.

A flock of blue and white seagulls swooped overhead. Their shrill cries cut through his insane thoughts, scattering them into the ether. The young woman blinked cagey eyes at him. Blood electrified his nerve endings as he struggled to purge his lust.

He hadn't felt this aware and alive since...hell, ever.

CHAPTER 4

Time killed everything. Healing came at the end, because there could be no healing without death. Truly, he had all the time in the world to kill, to heal, to forget the sins of a millennium. Or did he? Laughter filled WindWraith's memory, an unwieldy noise that didn't penetrate the cave, remaining only in his mind.

WindWraith circled the inside perimeter of the cavern, loose ebony particles dripping off his form, filling the dead space. The bits sizzled, turned amber as they tumbled into the rivers of fire. Thin spirals of smoke evaporated as the lava incinerated the fragments.

The ancient being screeched and howled, pulling his expansive corpus into the shape of a man. His solid body was faltering and he must retain the deteriorating cells. Although his magical strength escalated, he also knew his memories were vanishing. Little remained of his early years as an ordinary Druid sorcerer. What remained were the dark years of adulthood, the black magic, the evil that encompassed him entirely. Without his memories schooling him, he couldn't breach the human bodies. Or the host body he desired most.

Holding his mass into a concentrated human shape, he cast a calling to the world that shunned him, to an era after the old mage's death—the great one who sentenced him to die. The veil between this island and Avalon was thinner than ever. It had grown so fragile the crystal barrier the bastard mage had erected around the island was disintegrating in tandem. The island's magic weakened, while WindWraith's power intensified. Soon his magical endurance would surpass the dwindling strength of the prison locks. Already, his magic leaked through a crack in the veil, latching onto the bands of energy connected to him, feeding the mind of the one who mattered most...the one who called to him from a great span of time and space.

For now, he allowed his mind to travel the distance to his homeland. Within a moment, his magic bounced against a powerful protective wall. Startled, his body splintered and he exerted force to maintain his cohesive shape. The heavenly magic he butted against contained aspects of home and infinitely more. Human perfection. Ancient Druid blood coursed through the body, possessing fire magic that excelled even his abilities in his prime. The unfamiliar body contained great strength, vast magic. It held a blood element absent in the other host bodies WindWraith had lured to his island prison. An almost perfect body tied to another unknown sorcerer of equal vigor, both created from the necessary elemental magic to return WindWraith to the living.

Excitement shimmied over WindWraith and he lost his tenuous tie to the land of his birth. Gray, stormy clouds shaped like arms extended from his body, and he heaved the leg bone of a long dead fire sorcerer into the boiling river.

"Useless!" The soundless scream tore a hole in his chest cavity.

The bone of his last sacrificial host popped in the fiery liquid before the river consumed every trace. The Druid's magic had empowered the man to travel between a future world and the island, but the weakling sorcerer wasn't strong enough for WindWraith's ancient spirit. The moment his soul invaded the fire sorcerer, he knew the sorcerer missed a necessary element of nature. The body had thrust WindWraith out faster than blood from a heart wound. It took a month for WindWraith to recover the energy he expended...even after absorbing the other magical elements from the weakling Druid. An hour to deplete the Druid's power. Two hours of fire-eating pain before the Druid sorcerer passed out, never to awaken again.

WindWraith had stored those memories into the small container he managed to bring to the surface and not lose to the entrails of time. He howled a blustery, screaming laughter that swept through the cavern, wafted up to the pinpoint of light in the high ceiling.

Life would be different from this time forward. He may have found the perfect host body. Of a certainty, he had also discovered another method to absorb the power he needed from the crystals without the melting radiance.

Strength had found him at last.

CHAPTER 5

Morgan watched the nearly naked man scrutinize her from soaked boots to wet, stringy hair. His expression shifted from fear to concern then from lust to wariness. Her skin tingled where he touched her, and the intense need to lay her hands upon his broad chest overwhelmed her to distraction. Surreptitiously, she pinched her thigh, feeling the throb radiate down her leg, proof that she wasn't dreaming...or dead. After all, she had foretold her death many moons ago. *Surely, the Afterlife didn't include near drowning, did it?* Throwing her predicament into the refreshing sea winds, she boldly assessed the sorcerer who had haunted her awake twice that day.

Silent, he traded stares with her, his square jaw tensing in an arrogant sun-bronzed face. Moisture clung to his forehead and cheeks, glistening in the sunlight beaming from a sky so clear and blue one would think she had indeed died and gone to the Afterlife. The man's strong, golden body hovering over her heated up her water-chilled flesh. Magic radiated from his warm hands, almost becoming one with her, a spark frolicking with her fire element. She had no doubt—he was real and her dreams had sprouted to life. Was he the Druid assassin Gwilym had mentioned? Is that why she dreamed of him? *Holy Mother of Satan.*

The magnitude of this new reality set her heart racing

again. Her head fell upon the damp sand. Her life had ceased to exist on Avalon and begun anew on a nameless, deserted island. Deserted, except for an unknown sorcerer—possible assassin—who appeared ready to pick her up and toss her back into the sea. Deserted, except for the world's oldest and nastiest Fomorian she had to hunt down and slay before it stole the powerful magic from her body and left her carcass for hungry island beasts.

As the sorcerer leaned over her, his vivid blue gaze flitted from her mouth to her eyes. "Are you okay? Did you hit your head on the rocks?" Lyrical and cultured, his deep voice held an odd accent, yet it echoed in her head with a pleasant cadence.

Despite his lovely voice, her head throbbed maddeningly. She recalled thrashing her forehead against a tree branch in her frenzied dash through the woods. Even the ache of traveling through space left a gnawing cavity in her entire being as though parts of her body hadn't fully aligned. Goddess alive, her insane notions made her sound like a human puzzle.

Wincing, Morgan scraped sandy, sodden hair off her face. She rubbed her temple, feeling a growing lump and the slow seep of thick, warm liquid. She eyed the crimson stain on her fingers. "I am well enough. Thank you."

The fair-haired man muttered an oath, brushed her hair aside to inspect her injury. Careful not to touch the scraped skin, he examined the rest of her head, gently sifting through strands of hair.

Recalling the reason for her mad flight renewed her shivering, although the baking sun wasted little time drying the salty water on her bare skin. The man's devouring gaze left her burning from the inside out and a deep flush crept up her chest to her neck. Her clothing clung to her in the most inappropriately disconcerting way that she felt naked under his scrutiny. The fine-grained sand beneath her suddenly felt like new fallen snow. She straightened her skewed tunic over her stomach, pulled the neckline up to her chin, covering the top of her exposed breasts.

His fingers softened on her arm. "You're safe from whatever frightened you." Without skipping a beat, he scooped her into his arms as if she were a child. Jarred against his solid chest, she gasped at his sudden movement. He cut off the retort forming in her throat. "You need to get out of these wet clothes. You're probably suffering from shock."

Morgan kicked at him, her heels hitting his solid thighs. "Set me down at once!" Weakly, she struggled against his unyielding arms.

"Settle down. I won't hurt you." Concern teased his gruff voice. "You're dead white and probably feeling faint, right?"

She did feel out of sorts. Remaining vigilant, Morgan halted her struggles, leaned her head on his iron-hard arm. Magic shimmered in her fingertips, and when she seized his forearm for balance, he jolted against her shoulder as if burned. Cool ripples slid down his bronzed chest as if to guard against her touch. Or to ward off the outlandish tale she had yet to tax him with, if indeed he was the mythical assassin destiny had paired her with. *Thank you, Fate, for not preparing two innocent sorcerers for a death-defying task.* Morgan fisted her hand until her nails bit into her palm.

Had she awakened only that morning in her bed on Avalon? Had her father truly sent her catapulting through space with a sack of charms, her magical powers, and her tired and waterlogged wits in tow? Her mind swam with myriad information, offbeat tales, and Gwilym's spells.

Regardless of her wariness, she felt safe nestled against the sorcerer's comforting warmth. Despite every instinct telling her to trust him, the prophecies, and her dreams, she wasn't ready to grant them their due. Prophecy oft-times traveled in directions least anticipated, or beyond interpretation. The pulse beating inside her blood was all the proof she needed. Prepared to die on Avalon that day, her most outrageous visions never predicted this outlandish outcome. Nor did all her dreams become reality. Wary contentment eased the dull ache in her head. For now, she allowed the stranger to carry her to whatever constituted a soft bed on this mysterious island.

"What are you called?" she asked softly.

"Ryan O'Rourke." The richest of bass tones vibrated against her shoulder. "Who are you? How long have you been on the island?"

Purposefully, he strode across a wide expanse of fine white sand along the lazy shoreline. He smelled of salt and spice, a tantalizing mixture of maleness. She breathed him in, culling the memory of him from her dream. Without having ever met him in the flesh prior to that day, she *knew* the arms holding her, the strong, wide chest pressed to her body.

Ryan's arms tensed around her. "Answer me."

Morgan focused on his face. "I beg your pardon. I am Morgan." She deliberately withheld her titles. Names and titles held the ability to control. She felt no need to grant him that much influence over her until he proved trustworthy. "I arrived today." What did he know about their destiny, or of the island? Not that she had uncovered the full extent of matters, the knowledge swam erratic circles in her head. She prayed her father's parting burst of telepathic magic would provide answers to her heap of questions. Until then, she would remain vigilant and uncover what Ryan knew.

Waves of dizziness swept over her, and she sagged deeper into the warrior's embrace. Was he from an undiscovered land, far into the future, as Gwilym insinuated? Maybe he stemmed from her time or perhaps a time in between. How did he happen to land on this island shrouded for ages under the long gone Merlin's powerful magic?

Sweat rolled down Ryan's temples, dripped on her arm, drying almost instantly. He carried her up a short, stony incline into the woods framing one side of the beach. The verdant woodland enclosed them and her heart flip-flopped. As though he sensed her agitation, his muscular arms tightened about her, mashing her breast against his chest. She dragged a shaky hand through the kinks in her hair, hoping he didn't feel the fire that kept blazing up inside her.

"Morgan who? What's your last name?"

"Last name?" Her jumbled mind rushed to decipher his words. "I am Morgan of Avalon." A Druid sorceress belonged to the Goddess, and therefore, she took no man's surname, choosing the names of maternal lineage.

He snorted. "Just Morgan?"

Indignation assailed her, but it was difficult to remain so while being carried like a babe. She feared her body would betray her further if she didn't put distance between them. "Please set me down." *Before I ignite an inferno in your arms.*

"Why? So you can nosedive off another cliff?" His fingers bit into her arm. "I'm not in the mood to rescue idiotic women again. Doesn't matter now, we're here."

Ignorant peasant! He pressed her face protectively into his chest, and she choked down her acerbic reply.

Slanting his shoulders, Ryan shoved sideways into a thick, leafy passage. Vines caught in her flowing hair and energy pinged her flesh. Morgan's fingers captured the flexible limbs, pulling them free. Her hand tickled as she wound up her hair in her fist. They emerged on the fringes of a magnificent grotto hidden by earthen walls, trees, and arm-thick vines twined together so abundantly the vegetation created solid living walls. A waterfall at the far end fed an alluring emerald pond. A narrow entrance to a series of caves opened to the left of the waterfall, partially hidden behind the sheet of fresh, sparkling water.

"Oh, my." Morgan's wide stare landed on one incredible sight after another. Flowers of every color and size sprayed the green grotto. Papaya, pineapple, and banana trees carried a whiff of fruit punch on the air. Palms, tropical grasses, ferns and other bushes enclosed the fresh water pond. Excitement whisked away her indignation. She would risk traipsing through miles of woods alone to find this tranquil paradise. "It's beautiful." She couldn't wait to discover the grotto's treasures.

Ryan grunted and carried her into the dry caves past a barrier of smaller waterfalls. Water trickled randomly down green and black granite walls, cooling the caves against the tropical heat. They passed the first cavern directly behind the main waterfall and walked beyond to Ryan's shelter.

Coarsely stitched furs lined a ledge raised off the solid packed floor. Embers glowed in a ring of rocks in the dwelling's center. Small fissures in the tall ceiling drew smoke out, allowing enough hazy light to see within the cool cave. Quartz veins streaked the stone walls, reflecting the stippled light. Other than a few rudimentary wood tools and tidy piles of Ryan's belongings, the parlor-sized cave held little else.

Finally, he relinquished his hold and set her on the furs covering the bed. "Sit tight and I'll patch you up."

Morgan probed the crusty wound on her head, satisfied that it no longer bled. "Do you have healing herbs?"

Ryan snickered. "I wouldn't know a healing herb from a marijuana leaf." He walked away to rummage among his things.

Morgan scrunched her face. "Pardon? I'm not familiar with mara...wanna."

"Pot, cannabis? The leaf people once smoked to get high. Before the cursed blight—" He clamped his mouth shut.

The "cursed blight" must be what her father had alluded to that caused the future's devastation. She buried the idea for another time. "High?"

Ryan turned slowly, a small cloth clutched in his hand. "Who the hell are you, Morgan *of Avalon?*" Iron edged his velvet tone. "And you damn well better answer my questions."

With a feline grace, he approached, his body seeming to dominate the space in the cave. He stood tall with a warrior's bearing. Wearing only a scanty loincloth crafted from a tanned animal skin, his flesh was as brown as the hide. Her eyes traveled from tapered hips to rippling stomach, following the narrow trail of gilded curls up his chest, to the black and green dragon and Celtic knots banding his upper right arm, finally resting on his strong wide jaw.

Morgan felt power coiled within him as if the dragon thrived beneath his skin. Yet, his magic caused wanton heat to spread upwards from the junction of her thighs. A confusing sensation she had never experienced in the presence of any man. She forced her mind elsewhere, stalling him. "Are there others on the island?"

"Just you."

Shock jerked her upright and she knocked her elbow into the rock wall. Stars wavered in her vision and she rubbed her tender arm. Either Ryan was the Druid assassin or he was WindWraith in disguise. Could evil Fomorian magic mimic Druid magic? Did he visit her dreams that morning to trick her or befriend her?

Ryan knelt and gently applied a wet compress to the

wound on her temple. Smooth against her skin, the finely woven cloth scraped over the stinging gash. Despite his gentle touch, she winced when he applied pressure.

His full, slightly chapped lips tightened in a straight line. "I reopened the cut to clean it. Do you have a headache?"

Irritating words and notions stuffed Morgan's head, but she assumed Ryan referred to physical pain. Already, fantastical ideas knitted together, sifting into the recesses of her mind. Hopefully, Gwilym's strong mind magic would soon shed clarity on the chaos and enable her to recall the various legends of Avalon's Shadow. *Later. I will dwell upon Father's irksome spells and wisdom later.*

Daylight leaked through the chinks in the ceiling, speckling Ryan in glints of light, bringing out the sparkles of curiosity in his ocean-blue eyes.

"I ran into a tree limb in the woods. I'll be fine." No sooner had she voiced the words than another swell of dizziness teetered her alarmingly on the ledge. She was unable to prevent her body from tipping toward the beckoning soft furs.

"Damn it." Ryan snaked an arm around her waist, supporting her back. "Lie down."

Gently, he helped her stretch out on the bed, then retrieved a waterskin. He dripped cool water into her mouth. It held a faint leathery taste, but she welcomed the refreshment, especially after sucking down a mouthful of salt earlier. And Father's putrid potion. Her stomach lurched alarmingly and she cupped a hand over her mouth. Breathing deeply, she managed to halt the weakness from encroaching further, hating how this island seemed to suck the life out of her.

"Thank you," Morgan murmured, waving the waterskin away. "My body...I must rest." *I must figure out what is real versus myth from the pesky ideas battling within my mind.*

The splashing, tinkling waterfalls lulled her bone-weary body toward the realm of dreams. She fought it, not wanting to sleep and give up her defenses to the stranger beside her. The last thing she needed was to show additional frailty to this man. Who knew what torture he might subject her to if he discovered her vulnerabilities? If he were Avalon's banished Fomorian, what tricks did he play on her? The only demons Morgan had ever confronted were in Father's old texts. Sprinkling deceptions and lust upon innocent victims like birdseed, Fomorians and demons before her time hoodwinked even the most powerful sorcerers. Even Merlin had succumbed to their trickery, hence the island prison the old mage had created for the one evil being he failed to destroy. Did WindWraith now inhabit the handsome stranger sitting before her?

"You need dry clothes." Ryan moved to his stacks of belongings and returned with a black garment. "You can wear my T-shirt." He held the garment toward her. "Do you need help changing?"

Heat surged up her neck, and she wagged her head violently. Goddess help her, her internal fire magic would burn her alive on this forsaken island hell. *Yes, that's how Fate decreed I would die today! Death by the flames of mortification.* The last thing she wanted was for Ryan O'Rourke to view her nakedness. Morgan took the T-shirt, and he turned his back to her in a surprising gentlemanly action. Hastily, she tugged off her damp tunic and leggings without leaving the cover of the furs. Her clammy chemise clung to her breasts. Without a second thought, she eased it off and shrugged into the black garment. The shapeless T-shirt draped to her knees, wonderfully smooth against her cold skin. It smelled fresh with a faint lemon fragrance. Morgan threw Ryan a curious look. Lemons and water created a purifying cleanser. What man or creature knew such womanly things?

"Are you hungry? I have pineapple and leftover fish." Rustling sounds wafted over as Ryan dug into his food supplies.

Morgan wrinkled her nose. Despite having lived her lifetime on an island surrounded by oceans full of sea creatures, she hated the taste of seafood. *He must be evil if he likes seafood*, she mused half-heartedly. "Thank you. I'm not hungry." Propped on her elbow, she scanned the cave, absorbing evidence of human life. A sparkly object caught her attention above the bed by her feet. It looked excruciatingly familiar. Startled, she cried out, "Oh, bloody hell!" She bolted upright. Pain stabbed her head like a dagger, but she ignored it.

A rough niche in the wall held a silver circlet pendant, an amethyst crystal embedded in the center. Tiny runes inscribed the flat silver ring around the large uncut stone. The charm hung from a braided leather and silver chain cord. She grabbed it off the wall, her eyes narrowing as she closed her fingers around the all too memorable pendant. A strange mix of anger and bewilderment twisted the dagger in her head.

Ryan wheeled around. On wobbly legs, Morgan rose off the bed, raised her fist in his face. "Where did you get this?"

He shrugged. "Found it."

She blinked rapidly. "On *this* island?" *Was this what Father meant when he said the assassin's charm has been cast?*

Ryan braced his legs in a defiant stance. "What difference does it make?" He folded his arms across his chest, arm muscles bunching tightly. The dragon's tail twitched across his biceps.

"I made it as a child. How did you..." Shock choked off her voice. At ten-years-old, she'd crafted the charm for the one she hoped to love forever. Little good it did her on soul-sucking Avalon. At the time, she made it for an older sorcerer's apprentice she believed she loved. Before she gave it to him, a roving band of thieves ransacked the village and she lost the charms to them. Not long afterward, the apprentice disappeared, and she learned later that he had run off to Scotland before Avalon became inaccessible. Gwilym told her the boy was intended for another, that his path traveled in a direction never to cross hers again. She was too powerful for him. Too powerful for any man, it seemed. Longing and pain shoved the dagger into her chest.

The pendants were nothing but a child's fancies piecing together the old bards' tales. Too young to know what she was doing, she followed her mother's spell books. It didn't matter that she had skipped instructions for the spells she truly wanted in a series of rituals. In the end, she had imbued the amulets with a temporary binding spell, meant to entwine the magic of two Druids with matching pendants who invoked the spell. *Does Father believe we must bind our magic to slay WindWraith?*

Morgan sank upon the bed and scooted against the stone wall. She yanked the long tunic over her bare legs as far as it stretched.

Ryan's eyes deepened into swirling lakes of blue danger. In a blur, he closed the space between them. He bent over her, his large hands taking her shoulders in an unrelenting grip. "Where did you come from?" Flinty-eyed, his face looked carved from the granite surrounding them. "Who sent you here?"

Fire magic rose inside her and sparks dripped off her fingertips. "Take your grimy hands off me! Do you know who you are mauling?" How dare he treat her like a petty horse thief!

Suspicion radiated through Ryan's hands but he loosened his hold. He could easily snap her body like a twig, toss the pieces into the sea, and not spill a drop of sweat. *Demon or not, I will not cower before him.*

"Drop your magic, sorceress. There's no call for that. I said I won't hurt you," he ground out, a tic in his jaw visible. "You sure as hell don't want to cross my magic." Ryan leaned forward as if to force his threat upon her.

Best she calm him lest his earlier regard for her wellbeing turned ugly. "I mean you no harm. I have much to explain to you." She'd tell him only enough to accomplish her goals. Otherwise, Fate determined their next steps. Wariness stiffened her spine. Her own mistrust over this peculiar twist had a ways to go before it granted her a moment's peace. Reconciliation within her confused mind was leagues away on a road she'd have to traverse all too soon if the farfetched truths rising in her head gave any indication.

Ryan released her and held out a hand. "Give me the pendant."

Reluctantly, she dropped it into his palm. As he slipped the braided leather over his head, old memories stopped her heart for an instant, freeing it with a jerk. With dawning horror, she recalled the invocation of the charm's spell.

"No!" She jumped up and clawed for the amulet, her fingernails raking his chest. Crimson drops welled up on his skin, burning her fingertips.

Too late. The amulet held her touch. And the right combination to set the spell in motion. Her fingers prickled where his fiery blood turned sticky. Ryan sucked in his stomach and stumbled back. His tanned face blanched as the sizzling pendant burned into his skin. Aghast, Morgan stared at the tattoo the pendant began to create on Ryan's smooth, tanned skin. *Goddess, no! What is happening?* A temporary binding spell wasn't meant to mark the receiver. Her jaw hung open.

The stone blazed against his chest, blinding her briefly. The engraved runes on the circlet reflected silvery shadows on the cavern's dim walls. Cursing, Ryan slapped at the pendant. He yanked his singed hand away, grunting deep in his throat. The runes on the pendant's reverse side blistered the skin over his heart, branding him. The amethyst in the center of the amulet flared in shades from lilac to purple, tinting the rune shadows on the walls.

The crystal's tiny beams gleamed in Ryan's wide-eyed reaction to the magic she infused in the charm long ago. A grimace narrowed his glare, the amulet clenched in his white-knuckled fist.

No, no, no! She wasn't ready to bind her magic to a stranger. Who knew what mayhem he might do to her or her magic with access to it? *Father, why didn't you tell me about the charms and their role in my destiny? Where is this information in my head?* She wanted to scream and curse her father and the ancient Druids for giving her the blood to create the wretched magic now tormenting her existence.

A new hunger streaked through her veins, diverting her internal tirade. The vibrant rush of Ryan's magical essence sank sweetly beneath her skin. She clutched her throat, incapable of stopping the now familiar tingles of the desire she'd felt in her dreams. Unable to deny the compulsion, Morgan brushed Ryan's hand aside and kissed the singed tattoo, wrinkling her nose at the stench of charred flesh. As her mouth circled the tattoo, her tongue trailed a cooling path to assuage the ring of fire. Not a muscle twitched in Ryan's body, and his dangerous, dark gaze never left her face. She recited a spell to heal his blistered skin. Flicking her tongue over her lips, she tasted him, relishing his salty sea tang in her mouth. She had the unnatural urge to taste all of him with her lips and her tongue. The friction of the T-shirt against her hardening nipples sent fiery feathers tumbling through her middle. Being so near him, she was unable to shut the floodgates of arousal that had opened in her morning's dreams.

Ryan remained immobile, but he grew hard against her

stomach, the pressure bouncing Morgan from her drowning senses to her impending task. Power roiled inside her in anticipation. She must continue the binding ritual. No other choice existed. Her eyes stung, and she blinked away tears.

Averting her sight from his tented loincloth, Morgan knelt. Thank the Goddess she'd never completed all the spells on the charms as she had intended. She'd maintained a modicum of modesty and hadn't read the entire series of spells in her mother's spell books that started with the magic binding...and ended with a mating ritual. She gulped down the dry lump in her throat, fanned her face with her hand.

Ryan grasped her upper arms, tried to lift her to her feet. "What the hell is going on? What did you do to me?"

"It's a temporary tie to my magic." She shook off his hold.

"Temporary!" He flicked the hot amulet off his chest, holding it away by the cord. "You call this temporary?" Steam practically blew out of his nose.

"Do not resist, or you will die if I don't temper the magic," she bit out. Without the spell's next step, her powers would blaze through him like a rampant firestorm, eating at him from the inside out, eventually leaving behind nothing but bone dust. If he didn't first kill himself from the tortuous pain. Or kill her to break the spell. She may not trust him or even like him, and she loathed the fact that he had access to her magic if she let him, but she wasn't a killer. Not yet, at least.

He straightened, seeming to recognize her candor. His muscles flexed down his torso in a ripple. She took his hand, and his fingers curled instinctively around hers. Without losing another second, she uttered the ancient protection spell. The lump forming in her throat receded, and she started the binding spell, hesitated. More tears welled up.

It was not right, not time to bind herself to a man in any way.

Regardless, the words surfaced. She fingered the water from her eyes. Ryan's stony gaze was riveted on her face, watching, waiting, fighting his emotions. She wanted to wrap her arms around him, wanted him to hold her. She wished him to know about her dreams and his presence in them, for him to tell her the why of it all. But her head warred with her heart and body. It berated her, told her to walk away, to think, to rationalize her actions. She wrung her hands, fisted them at her sides. Her mind frantically tried to unearth a way out of her predicament. There was no nullification for fleeting spells designed to run their course. She stared at the brand on Ryan's chest, a very *permanent* binding. *Ignorant sorceress!*

Words tripped out in an unstoppable whisper. She didn't feel the bond, but she would have if Ryan joined in the ritual and bound his magic to her. A tiny thread existed between them now. He'd feel more as the days progressed. She'd feel little to nothing. Perhaps it was for the best, until she figured out how to annul the spell.

The words were said, the Goddess appeased. Tears streamed down Morgan's cheeks. Nothing ever happened as planned in her life. She failed at dying as she'd prophesied. She had a wealth of knowledge scattered to the winds in her head. She had a vicious creature to kill and an uncertain future on a deserted island, magically tied to a hardened stranger, no less. The idea that she was bound to this man in a way she thought never to occur overwhelmed her, and she rubbed at the increased thumping in her temples. As time passed, Ryan would sense her magic and even delve into her strongest emotions, one step closer to his ability to actually use her magic to supplement his own. Worst of all, the bond could mask his true feelings toward her, leaving her mired in a relationship based on deception.

At least Morgan was certain of one thing. The amulet spells only bound Druid sorcerers, and none other. Ryan O'Rourke was no Fomorian. Morgan closed her eyes.

"Little raven?" Ryan's constricted voice intruded upon her mental dance of pity.

She whipped her head up and stood ramrod straight. Little raven? Did he know she'd dreamed of him calling her that? Had he shared her morning's dream? "You called me that in a dream." She pressed her fists into her stomach.

"I know. I was there." He touched her lips with trembling fingers. "From the time you breathed air into my lungs as I was drowning, to this morning when I rescued you from falling to your death at the hands of a shadow-shifter."

CHAPTER 6

The peculiar resonance of home spooled through the air. WindWraith whipped about, sniffed the familiar reverberations, tasted it on his tongue, relishing the sizzle of magic. He hardly recognized the sweet bite of Druid sorcery. It had been an eternity.

Breathing it in, he filled his shattered being with the remnants of a stolen life. Magic waltzed through him, ancient and memorable, watering the burnt sprout of humanity buried so deep he did not know if enough life existed in it to grow again. The long-forgotten sense of longing splintered his spectral shape into fragments. He yanked his form into a sphere, wallowing in the odd prickles of desire, a sensation he once hoped never to forget, or thought never to experience again.

Dropping to the comforting cavern's rocky ground, he spread out in a mottled gray blanket across the rubble. He stretched out a tentacle and tentatively touched the ebony stone platform on the black granite altar. The blood-red crystals had died off long ago, bled dry until they were black.

Thin fingers sprouted from his arm-like appendage. They gripped the edge of the stone bed, flowed into tiny fissures deep inside the pillar until his fingers brushed the first layer of untainted stones. Crystals burned his fingers and he howled in pain, folded in upon himself, reducing his corporeal form by half to preserve his strength. He nearly withdrew his melting hand from the stones. Perseverance won out, and he soaked up the energy, fed his malevolence.

Once he grew accustomed to the pain, he spread out on the ground again, undulating softly over the gravel. Buried energy vibrated beneath the island, rippled across his form. The island's energy had hidden far within the earth's farthest depths, inching deeper and deeper until he no longer touched or sensed it. Until this moment. The island pulsed in the tip of his finger. Undercurrents of power created a new echo across the ground, surprising him.

Fresh, vibrant power had awakened the island, a force equal to the mage who had caged him in this prison long ago. Strong magic he could use for the escape he'd waited centuries to gain. Remembered pleasure tore blustery cries from him, howling up to the top of the spire. Excitement blossomed from that seedling embedded inside him.

Tsk, tsk. He always had access to the island's various energies. However, this new energy proved distinctive. Unsullied, luminous, fed through the gems buried throughout the island—other crystals he was unable to touch or draw near without suffering grave loss to the cells of his finite form. The more energy he soaked up, the blacker his soul became until the earthy force smothered it completely. The stones had destroyed his human form until nothing remained but particles. Evil shards that coalesced and did the bidding of the mind he managed to retain.

He surveyed the dead crystal cavern he called home. Nay, not home, a temporary respite from the ignorant, small world that shunned him. A prison meant to destroy him. He blew out a whooshing laugh, fueling the fire burning on the river's surface at the far end of his sanctuary. Triumph replaced the heart no longer beating inside him. It pounded a steady rhythm of ecstasy through the diminutive part that remained human.

In response, a human skull screamed at him silently

from across the bubbling pools, its mouth a gaping maw of teeth.

WindWraith's fingers burned. Particles of his shape disintegrated. He held onto the buried crystals, depleting their magic, conquering the island at its own defensive tactics. This slight contact was all he could afford and he needed the energy boost. Needed it to locate the being that possessed such power to awaken the island he threatened into sleep eons ago. The one being that whispered across the twilight of his dreams, and lent him hope. The pure and ancient body from his homeland that promised to take him to the decaying world of the future, where he could exact his revenge on those who lived off his sacrifice.

Oh, yes. The world would finally welcome him home and rejoice at his second coming.

A glorious second vessel had arrived on his wicked paradise.

CHAPTER 7

Shockwaves rolled through Ryan, but the bombshell to his system was unable to crush the yearning Morgan's touch incited. He sure as hell couldn't hide the evidence behind the snip of leather covering his groin. Ignoring his outlandish desire, he coiled his fingers around Morgan's wrist and glowered down at the ring of strange symbols and the crystal that continued to shoot beams of lavender. Pain receded as her healing lips rasped over his burning skin. The bond he'd sensed to her in his dream, to the brink of lunacy, became real. A tangible thing he touched in the prickly air between them, smelled on her pale, creamy skin. Fragrant and airy, her Druid fire tangled with his fire magic bursting up to dance with hers.

She leaned into the rich, raw energy and shuddered from the impact. Power rumbled beneath the ground, washing pure, aromatic earthiness over him. Desire stoked his internal fire. As Morgan finished her whispered incantation, he felt her power's invitation, like a vault door unlocking. With a mental kick, he prodded the door wide. Elemental air and earthen power spattered inside him. Defensively, his innate magic quashed it, but not before ten seconds of paradise streamed in his blood.

Ryan's jaw tightened, his shock yielding to anger. He managed to slam the door shut on her magic, hiding the key in a cranny of his soul. "What did you do to me?"

The amulet's gem flared brighter, casting a faint glow

in Morgan's eyes. Who was this sorceress who made his tightly wound body lose control?

Morgan tipped her head back, looked him square in the eye. "The amulet is one of a matched pair. I possess its mate." In a sudden fluid movement, she leaped up, her mad raven eyes darting about the cave, growing frantic. "I lost my packs in the woods." She rushed past him toward the cave opening. "We must retrieve them." He caught her arm and she twisted against his hold. "Please." Her agitation crinkled the skin across her forehead. "I will explain on the way."

Annoyance bit him, but Ryan held his tongue. Not wanting to let her out of his sight, he kept his clamp on her wrist. Somehow, that slight contact eased his freakish longing for her. It proved that she was real, not island magic tricking his mind. He needed to touch her more than anything he'd ever needed in his life, for more reasons than he cared to admit.

"Cart me off to the Fomorian hideout and toss me in as breakfast," he murmured under his breath.

"Pardon me?" Morgan's eyebrows peaked.

"Nothing," Ryan growled. He hooked a waterskin over his shoulder, snatched up a short spear and knife. He wanted to snag his dead boar if an island predator hadn't already poached it. The anticipation of roasted boar meat set his mouth watering. Ever since he'd spied the angry beast two days ago, he'd been ravenous for fresh pork. Hell, anything resembling the meat he used to eat before the Fomorian blight destroyed animal life on Earth was a boon to his constantly rumbling stomach. Already, after two weeks, he'd gotten used to eating on a regular basis again after a year of scarfing whatever scavenged food his coven found in their travels from one hideout to another in New Angeles.

In jittery silence, he led Morgan out of the grotto.

Holding the branches of the leafy shrubbery aside, he guided her through the hidden entryway. Cloying flowers and grasses permeated the air, caught in Ryan's throat. Uncertainty spiked the syrupy aroma on his tongue.

Leaves clung to Morgan's hair and he reached to pick them out. Her eyes followed his movements, narrowing as if he meant to strike her. Slowly, he feathered his fingers down her silk smooth cheek. He wanted to touch every inch of her, just as he wanted to do from the moment she invaded his dream. Now, she stood before him in the flesh, wearing his T-shirt, alluring as hell. So very alive, he feared turning his back on her, afraid he'd find his fingers touching air, his eyes gazing upon a mirage.

"Did you tell the truth about the dream? You spoke to me." She shook a finger at him. "What did you say?"

Did she honestly believe they hadn't shared the dream? Druid or not, dream connection or not, she was pure trouble, and he had a difficult time burying his paranoia. He also had a tricky time reconciling his lack of trust with his desire. For the first time in his life, he wanted to believe in someone he simultaneously desired. There was a first time for even that, right?

On impulse, he bent his head as if to kiss her. A hairsbreadth separated their lips, and he breathed in her fresh, shallow exhale that contained her entire essence blowing into his soul. He nearly yielded to his hunger and tasted her pinched lips. Easing back, she flipped her hair over her shoulder, and he met her insolent expression. Lust arced through him, stunning him with the blow to his system. Hell, he never believed dreams came true. Especially in the life he led, and certainly not in the last two nightmare years.

Until now.

"I said I would find you." His lips grazed her velvety cheek. "When my work was done," he whispered in her ear.

Her hand landed warmly on his chest, holding him back. Despite her attempt to restrain him, he doubted she'd put up a fight if he wanted to take her now. She sure as hell hadn't resisted in their dream, not that they'd gone beyond touching and kissing.

"Damn." He gritted his teeth. Dreams weren't real! The sorceress radiated strong magic, paving her way into his head, his heart, even his soul. A simple task for a Fomorian toying with its prey. She was probably a plant to deter him from his duties. The witch would carve out his heart and feed it to his enemies if he surrendered to his cravings. He refused to falter. He owed it to his people who counted on him to lead them to a safe new existence on the hellhole Earth had become. His life had no room for love. Desire, yes. Love? Hell no. He scrubbed a hand over his face, trying to erase his insanity and figure out what to do about her. Second on the agenda was finding a way off this freak-ass island.

Ryan released her wrist and jerked away. "Let's go. Start talking." He threaded his way through the jungle maze, not waiting for her to follow.

A briny ocean breeze fluttered leaves and branches above their heads. Palm fronds rasped together like sheets of paper. Morgan's crunching tread eclipsed the myriad island sounds.

"I'm waiting." Impatience lay heavy in his tone.

She let out a frustrated sigh. "I fell asleep in the meadow at home this morning and woke up in your woods this afternoon."

Ryan smirked. "You were joking about Avalon, right?"

"I wish that I were," she mumbled more to herself.

Ryan's keen sense of hearing wrenched the words from the air. He stopped short amidst a bed of blooming vines sporting multihued leaves. Sweet and heady, exotic perfume overpowered the thick jungle odors the refreshing sea winds discarded.

He tugged a burnt orange flower off the vine and spun around. Morgan stood so close he plowed into her. Ryan slipped his arm around her waist, and she leaned into him, clutching his forearm for balance. He wanted to push her away and run, wanted to pull her into his body and never let go.

Ryan stuck the flower in her hair, lodged the stem behind her ear. "Don't lie to me," he whispered in her ear. "I'm a Druid Master Sorcerer of immense power. You don't want to toy with me." He licked her ear, savoring her sweet salty taste on his tongue.

Berating himself, he jumped away and drew a flame from his power core. Fire magic flared up, surging fiery power into every fiber of his body, the main elemental magic flowing through him. It streamed outward, forming a bright bluish white globe on his palm. He erected an invisible protection shield around them. Moving backward a few steps, he launched his flaming ball at the trunk of a mature sandalwood tree. The tree exploded in a shower of bark and limbs. The fireball cut down two more trees until Ryan withdrew his power, ending his show of destruction.

Confidence and pride dampened his molten magic, sending it to rest inside him. Most fire sorcerers barely managed to decimate one or two trees at a time. Ryan had the ability to raze a small forest if he chose. For now, he'd reserve his strength in a small exhibition of ego, with a subtle warning to the enigma standing beside him.

Morgan fisted her hands at her sides. The last sparks of magic fizzled outside their cocoon, and she plowed through his impenetrable shield as if wading through a scant inch of water.

"What the—?" Mouth ajar, he checked his intact protection spell, double-checked it. How'd she walk through a barrier no one has ever penetrated? The strongest

Fomorian had never breached his shields. Frowning, Ryan stroked his chin, eagle-eyed her, contemplating her strength. What the hell kind of magic did she wield?

Undeterred, Morgan stomped to the first damaged stump. Gray smoke billowed in angry spirals from the ruined trunk. Limbs and branches littered the ground. She swished an arm in the air, and white puffs of smoke floated away on steamy air currents. "Can your magic do this, Druid *master?*" She sneered.

Ryan cocked an eyebrow, regarded her in silent amusement. The sway of her glossy hair glistening down her back transfixed him, drew his gaze to the curve of her hips. He gulped down the air lodged in his throat. Again, he wondered how this wisp of a girl held power to rival his own. Where had she come from?

Morgan waved her arms over the stump, as though stirring the contents of a cauldron, chanting unintelligible words that sounded like Latin. She stepped out of the way, and the tree reformed its sundered pieces. Within seconds, the sandalwood stood intact, its mighty branches shivering in the breeze, leaves rustling an eerie song of joy. His eyes widened, and he smiled appreciatively. She returned his admiration with a thunderous frown.

They measured each other warily until the noise of large, flapping wings overhead stole Ryan's attention. Hairs lifted on his scalp. He craned his neck, scrutinized the clear sky, saw nothing out of the ordinary. But the unmistakable omnipresence of evil, which so far had kept its distance, zoomed toward them. The air shimmered and darkened. The ground trembled as if a herd of boars raced past them. The day's heat gelled oppressively, and he tasted vileness on his tongue with every inhalation.

Upon the first step Ryan took into the jungle after hacking out a lungful of water on the beach two weeks ago, he'd recognized the presence of evil, so familiar to him. He'd been around enough Fomorians and demons all his life to know the island was home to an ancient, formidable creature. The specter made itself known in devious ways. A feeling here or there that encroached upon Ryan's sixth sense, or a flicker of light and shadows. It hadn't taken him long to smell Fomorian stink—the rot of flesh—infesting nearly every cranny of the island as if the paradise was a breeding ground for evil.

Ryan dug further into his memory. The one other time he'd heard the fluttering wings was when he neared starvation and cast a spell to kill the speckled brown and gray bear whose fur lined his bed.

Too late. He now realized that magic attracted the evil like death to a vulture. Heat drained from his body, and his power sank into a lead ball in his gut. His protection shield disintegrated. Now, he understood the source behind his sluggish magic whenever he left the grotto. Back home something rare in his blood prevented the Fomorians from drawing upon his magic or marking him. During the two weeks he'd spent on the island, he'd felt a trickle of loss. He'd chalked it up to the peculiars of a foreign land. If he contained full magical energy, he could've uprooted the trees, rather than hack them to stumps.

"Morgan!" He bolted toward her, flailing his arms to catch her attention. "Stop!"

Up to her ankles in wood chunks and splintered limbs, she halted before the second decimated tree. Arms outstretched as if to blast him, she spun toward him. "You dared to kill living trees in a reckless fit of bravado, so do not tell me to stop my restoration spells."

Ryan plunged through brambles. "Hold up, Morgan. Please!"

Ignoring him, she bent over the blackened tree stump and swirled her arms in a circle.

The giant bird-like flapping drew closer, more insistent,

heading straight toward them.

Unusual pain wrenched Ryan's heart. "Damn it." He lunged, grappled her around the waist, and slung her over his shoulder.

Outraged, Morgan shrieked, kicked, and beat her tiny fists against his butt. He jogged behind a rocky outcropping, set her on her feet, his palm planted over her mouth. Her breasts lifted and fell with each breath against his chest. The huge wings flapped louder. The sooty, looming specter took shape in the very spot he'd cast his magic. It grew to twice the size of a warhorse, an undulating blob of gray evil devouring the air and light in its path.

"Quiet, okay?" he said in her ear.

Head bobbing, her eyes sparkled in an odd mixture of awe, anticipation, and fear.

"Let's go. No magic." He gave her a stern look, his aggravation wrenching on his arrogant heart. "Our magic drew it to us."

"It is WindWraith. Avalon's Shadow." Morgan cupped her hand over her mouth. "It needs us to feed upon."

The foggy spirit encircled the first restored tree, enshrouded it in inky air. It practically luxuriated in their residual Druid power. A crooning sound drifted out of the dense cloud.

"I will need your aid in killing it," she decreed decisively in a low voice.

Kill it? Ryan regarded Morgan with renewed speculation. Earlier, he questioned whether she was linked to the evil spirit he'd sensed here. Her shaking body refuted any such collaboration. Even so, he still wasn't convinced he could trust her. A mystery he'd unravel later, once he got them out of the jam he'd created.

He took her wrist and tugged her into the heart of the jungle, away from the specter sniffing at their leftover magic like a Fomorian one step behind its next minion.

CHAPTER 8

Sucking in deep breaths, Morgan tried to crush the terror thickening in her throat. The Fomorian—WindWraith—was truly in their midst! Everything her father told her was true. Until that moment, she hadn't fully believed the ungodly myths.

Earlier, when they left the grotto, she let herself drift along with the rhythm and currents of the contradictory soothing and jagged-edged island. Her heart resonated with the land and it resonated with hers, drumming in harmony. Part of her wanted to accept the possibility that she had indeed died and was floating in the Afterlife. Now, she knew absolutely that her father's plan and Fate's will was in full-scale attack.

The Fomorian's evilness had smothered the island for over a century. Only now in the wake of ancient and modern magic uniting to restore its vitality did the island return to life. Only now in the creation of an ancient and modern bond could Morgan and Ryan destroy the evil once and for all.

Countless ideas stuffed Morgan's head, stirred a cacophony of myths, prophecies, and truth. Not only had Gwilym transferred his Sight to her through telepathy, his potion crammed her brain with his complex knowledge collected over decades of reading people and places, present and future. Morgan slapped her hand over her mouth, stifling her outraged screech at Fate for dumping her into this dreadful position. Mostly, she'd rather die than let Ryan O'Rourke sense any weakness if he heard her cry like a terrified ninny.

Leafy foliage closed in upon her, and her intestines knitted into tight stitches. A squeeze of Ryan's comforting hand helped quash her inane fear of the woods. She locked away her unsettled emotions and concentrated on his relentless tirade against the hampering vegetation. He steered them around the rougher branches and vines. Other plants softly flayed her bare legs, tickling rather than stinging, easing rather than thwarting her passage. Curiosity warmed over the frozen fear in her chest. How did an island have a heart and pulse like a living being? Speculation opened her senses to a newfound wonder.

A high-pitched screech behind them grated on her ears, similar to an owl's cry on a silent night. It put to rest her crazy ideas about the mystical island. Morgan and Ryan remained mostly hidden within dense thickets, under shelter of rainforest trees. Landscape patterns appeared familiar. They passed the magenta orchids she accidentally trampled earlier that morning. The bed of grass on which the traveling stones had deposited her was also nearby.

Another thundering shriek pierced the air, gaining on them. Ryan began running, tugging her behind him. Her legs pumped twice as fast to keep up with his long, fluid stride. Instinctively, Morgan's defensive powers stirred, air fanning fire magic from her scalp to her feet. Ryan stopped abruptly, his handhold crushing her fingers. She smacked into his side, flung her arm around his waist for balance, her fingers slippery on his sweaty torso. He radiated body heat that had less to do with the sweltering air than with the electricity between them. The natural union of similar magic, the puzzling bond of magnetism.

He pivoted around, unfathomable emotions darkening his face. "Drop your powers," Ryan said in a low snarl.

"You're drawing it to us."

Forcibly yanking on her power, it rammed into her, staggering her against Ryan. He caught her in a loose hold, and she eased away, straightening her twisted tunic, preparing her mind for the inevitable. She knew the evil shadow wasn't strong enough to escape the island. Not yet. However, she was losing more magic to it than the negligible amount expended to sustain her link to Ryan. Her power sank to the dungeon of her soul, seething for liberation. Morgan's stomach churned with the unsettling sensation meeting her fear. Not since she was a child novice had she felt such fright without access to her protective powers. She hated the awful emptiness, the inability to wield magic as natural to her as breathing.

Ryan's expression softened. He knew what it cost her to surrender. And he'd always maintain a slight sense of what she felt. The brand on his chest and the binding spell ensured that connection. Another thing she loathed at the moment. She stared at the intricate Celtic knots design stamped onto her leather boots. Knots infinitely easier to unravel than the ones tangling her mind and body.

Strong gusts stirred the trees and bushes. They rustled in amplified tempo, warning of danger. Invisible wings beat the air into a cyclone. The fog-like wraith was almost upon them.

"Run." Ryan gently pushed her in front of him. "Keep to the right."

She tore off in the direction he pointed, heedless of the limbs and plants lashing her arms and legs, snagging her clothing, reaching for her and trying to cling. Was the island also afraid of the Fomorian?

"There's a path down the cliff you flew off earlier. It leads to a naturally shielded cave." He nudged her from behind, his hand firm in the hollow of her back.

Tornado howls grew deafening. Morgan tripped over a

crumbling log, and Ryan grabbed her waist from behind to prevent her from planting her face in a prickly bramble. Hot and solid, his hands pulled her against his slick torso. *Wretched jungle! You wasted no time to push us together again.*

"Thank you." Waning energy forced her to wheeze out the words. Before she lost all her stamina and wilted to the ground, Ryan picked her up, cradled her to his chest. His heart pounded against her shoulder, his internal fire wrapped around her, turning her muscles to mush. "Is it much farther?" She gave into his strength. *So be it, island. You've had your say for now.*

He shook his head. "I'm sorry," he muttered, shame flirting with his arrogance in the downturn of his mouth. He veered to the left and headed down a short, steep incline. "I shouldn't have been a power-tripping jackass."

Morgan scrunched her forehead. A powerful donkey tripping? She choked on a laugh, coughing for lack of air. She quickly expelled what air she did possess when he took a long jump across the rocky cliffside. Instinctively, she locked her arms around his thick neck. *Propriety be damned.* It was either risk clinging to more of his warm, enticing bare skin, or tumble down the craggy cliff. Hardly much of a choice.

Ryan leapt three more bone-jarring steps down the incline and released her on a flat granite ledge overlooking the cove she'd unwittingly fallen into earlier. She flattened herself against the cliff face and clutched Ryan's arm, her fingernails digging into his skin. Not that she feared heights, she merely didn't care for the bitty span of rock beneath her feet, all that separated her from another harrowing plunge into the sea.

"The cave's below us," Ryan explained without missing a breath, as though he'd taken a stroll along the shoreline.

"Did it follow us?"

He smiled smugly. "It can't. The crystals protecting the grotto also protect this cave and its perimeter." He pointed out the triangular area of protection.

"What crystals? They hold magic?" Morgan tilted her head. "Are there great quantities of them?" Maybe they could use the crystals to rid the island of WindWraith. An excited idea bloomed. The crystals must be the source of the stones in their amulets!

"The island is plastered with them. I haven't figured them out yet." Ryan shrugged his broad shoulders, a challenging demeanor about him. "Maybe you can shed light on them."

Gwilym's potion worked its magic in her mind, and Ryan's dialect became clearer. Her thoughts still felt like unopened books, but she was distinguishing concrete knowledge in bits and chunks. At least Ryan spoke a common tongue. For the most part. The power tripping jackass phrase still puzzled her. The idea seemed to suit him. She stifled a snort.

"In fact," Ryan lifted his amulet to eye level for closer inspection, "this crystal looks like it came from the same source. There's a bed of purple stones behind the grotto's caves." A grunt sounded low in his throat. "I'll be damned. I never linked the two." He studied the amulet's reverse side. "You made this?"

His eyes darkened in that intense gaze Morgan now recognized as mistrust. He had no reason to trust her, but she'd soon change him of that absurd notion. She must. It seemed Ryan O'Rourke, Fomorian assassin—she thought no less of him now—was part of her destiny.

"Yes. I'll explain once we reach refuge." Morgan peered over the precipice and her stomach somersaulted. She saw only a descent into the rocky sea below. Toppling off cliffs wasn't a feat she ever cared to repeat. "How do we get down there?"

Ryan stepped to the rim of the rocky platform. "I'll jump down first, then you."

She pinned him with a grimace. "Easy for you to say. I'm a High Druid Sorceress, not a raven."

"Yeah, well, I'm an assassin, not an extreme survivalist." Ryan faced her and lowered away from the ledge, disappearing from view. "Come on."

Morgan inched her leather-shod feet toward the edge. Panic welled up, mocking the last of her good sense.

"Get on your knees, and work backward until your legs dangle. I'll catch you."

Morgan backed up, butting against the rock face. "I can...not."

"It's a short drop. You'll be okay. Trust me." Concern replaced the impatience in his tone.

Fueled by both his empathy and his entreaty, her determination kicked in. Show of strength became her new motto, even if she didn't feel it inside. She inched toward the edge and crawled backward until her ankles left the solid surface.

"Don't look down. Focus forward."

Morgan followed his advice. Within seconds, his hands encircled her legs, and he grasped her waist to tow her into the safety of his muscular arms. Her feet met rock, and she twined her arms around Ryan's waist, burying her face in his chest. He stepped into the cave entrance, dropped to the ground, holding her on his lap. Hugging her tight, he rested his chin on top of her head.

It was easy to relax with Ryan's warmth gloved around her. His quickening heart against her cheek stabilized her own erratic heartbeat. The stone in his amulet glowed strongly—from her nearness, his urges, she didn't know. Closing her eyes, she blocked out everything except the truth of her destiny and the reality of this man. *To the Goddess with my show of strength. I'm a woman, not a warrior. He won't like me if I proved too powerful to him.* Bloody hell, she acted as if he wanted her!

Her mind drifted to that morning, waking safe in her bed on Avalon, her body in pained-pleasure from her frightening and passionate dream. The dream where her longing met Ryan's desire in harmony, where life seemed simple, love appeared natural. Where distrust and recklessness never visited.

A skittering awareness on her backside sent her pulses racing again. Ryan's fingertips caressed her back, his hands angling toward her hips. Automatically, she curved tighter into his body. Security and warmth tinged with heart stopping desire cloaked her.

"Morgan," he whispered against her hair. "It's all right now. We're safe." He touched her almost reverently, disproving his earlier suspicion.

She had the wildest urge to touch every inch of his bare skin. Something she'd never done to any man, nor ever wanted to until Ryan appeared in her dreams. Heat suffused her face and she fought the inappropriate and poorly timed urge. Instead, burning with need, she lifted her head and touched her lips to his full, warm mouth experimentally, something she'd wished to do since the moment he became real. He responded, pressing his lips to hers, first softly, then demanding, forcing her lips apart. She rested her hands on his wide shoulders. He made a harsh sound in his throat and slanted his head, the tip of his tongue breaching her parted lips, his lips soft yet firm on hers. Quivers started at the base of her spine and raced along her nerves. She opened her mouth wider and his tongue darted in. Her tongue met his, caressed it, tasted the lingering pineapple he'd snacked on earlier. Ryan poured himself into the kiss as if starved, and her own hunger liquefied her entire being. His ice melted into the warm pool her body had become.

Desperate for air, she freed her mouth and drew a shaky breath. Ryan's hand slipped down her arm, until his fingers brushed the side of her breast, not taking extra liberties. The heat of his fire magic burned through her muscles and bones. She smothered a moan, aching for him. Craving a love so long denied her.

He kissed the curve of her neck, worked tiny kisses up to her ear, leaving a path of fire where his lips devoured her flesh, his harsh breath fanning the flames. The roughness of his whiskered jaw rasped along her skin. He nibbled her bottom lip, ran his tongue over her lips, until she parted her mouth. Again, he accepted her invitation and speared his tongue inside. Hypnotized by his kiss, her lips tingled, her mind clouded. Their tongues danced in an everlasting waltz.

Excitement poured over his sweat glistened face. But doubt flashed behind his need and his massaging hands on her back froze. His eyes had gone wild, like a stormy midnight sky. Morgan wanted to rip off her tunic and rub her moistened skin against Ryan's slick body, anything to keep the contact of skin on skin. Passion spiraled through her, melting her magic into molten drops. Finally, he tore his mouth off hers, and she fell into his wide, sharp eyes.

"Holy mother of the Gods." He sucked in a sharp breath.

Gasping, she slumped against him, dazed in body and mind, in a way she had no words to describe. Silence stretched long as they held each other, evening out their breathing, slowing their wildly beating hearts. The last she remembered before tumbling into a bottomless sleep was Ryan carrying her bone-weary body into the gloomy cave, gathered close against his trembling body as if she were the last woman on Earth.

CHAPTER 9

WindWraith gave chase, zooming after the trickle of Druid magic flavoring the swampy air. He lost sight of the fleeing pair in the overgrown jungle.

"No!" he howled, the word slamming through his form. The half-Druid Fomorian remembered how to voice his mind, even if silence reigned in the external world. But he remembered. He felt. And if he did not discover a living vessel to host his leftover humanity, he would lose it all to the ravages of eternity. The death sentence old Merlin pronounced upon him would be fulfilled, his long imprisonment a waste.

WindWraith wasted nothing! He gave no quarter to any Druid sorcerer, or any other human. The Outerworld owed him a life. It owed him immortality.

The Druid man he'd sensed several times prior to that day and the mysterious new woman hid within the jungle. WindWraith halted to gain his bearings, pulling his roiling mass into a cohesive shape. He adopted the form of a black lion. Ruffling mane, swaging tail, omnipotent growl. Dense midnight black fur, bloodstone eyes. His powerful, solid body raced into the low-growing brambles at speeds his disjointed, expansive form failed to achieve.

Tearing through the jungle, he cut down the foliage in his path, strewing bits and pieces of greenery behind him. He zoomed across a narrow creek and lifted off his hind legs to fly over a quartet of dead crystal boulders. Wind fluttered his mane, fresh Druid magic sizzled on his tongue. Magic as ancient and potent as the magic he had tasted, nay, possessed, many lifetimes ago. Residual energy deep within the blackened rocks filtered into him, aiding his strength, sending him flying through the brackish jungle air.

The island secreted a new power that day. It languished on the air in tentative pockets, testing a newfound boldness, easing out of a deep hiding. Oddly, the island paradise acted less intimidated by WindWraith after many years docilely hiding to avoid being raped of its power. WindWraith roared out his glee, as if *he* had everything to do with rousing the island back to life.

Not wishing to ensnare the couple, he maintained a narrow distance behind them, enough to gauge their magic and origins. And to discover how the two together had awakened the slumbering island. How the woman preserved ties to his homeland and held the ancient blood of his era. How had the couple arrived? They hadn't traveled through the gateway he'd manipulated the few other useless sorcerers through to land on the island. Was there another gateway? He'd searched every cranny of the island and the perimeter waters as far as the crystal barrier and never discovered another portal. Had the earthquakes opened one? Better still, had the quakes destroyed more of the brilliant stone barrier, the outer lock on his prison? The barrier old Merlin thought WindWraith too weak to destroy.

Drawing upon his former powers, he shifted into an eel shape and slithered into a crevice in the rocky cliffside, his color morphing into the hues of the cliff. He watched the man and woman rest on the rocky ledge, assessing each other. He stretched out a feeler one foot, two, three. Dazzling sunshine flooded him with fuel from the heavens. Crystal power pricked at him, and singed holes in him, eating away irreplaceable cells. Enraged, WindWraith squealed in pain and whipped his feeler back into his rocky haven.

The Fomorian studied the electrical pulses in the air around the couple. The man hid his magic well, though not completely. Easy to detect, the fire in the Druid's blood was a perfect complement to the Druid fire in WindWraith's magical makeup. Yet, the man seemed overly strong to be merely a fire mage. Another form of magic existed inside him. Not water, not air, not earth. WindWraith's confusion rippled along his coiled length. A possible vessel, the young, strong body he desired most of all.

The woman, though. Ah, she represented a perfect magical counterpart. Ancient Druid blood flowed strong and thick in her veins—fire, air, and earth. WindWraith must get closer to determine her particular strengths. She may be the ideal vessel. On the other hand, she may be too strong for his magic, a nigh impossible, yet thoroughly intriguing conundrum.

Weary of his idleness, he pressed his powers to the ground, setting in motion another battle of wills with the island.

CHAPTER 10

Ryan spread a thin hide over the length of Morgan. She snuggled into a mattress of droopy fronds and moss leftover from his last exploration. The crinkling beneath the spongy moss made enough noise to wake the dead, yet she slept on. A fierce need to protect her swept through his very center, battling his resolve to remain wary. Overwhelmed by his heightened emotions, he inhaled slowly, bolting her unique bouquet inside his senses, a light floral scent that permeated her hair despite her saltwater dunking.

Unable to tear his sight off Morgan's serene face, he clenched his thighs, preventing his hands from touching her. His body thrummed from the control it took not to wake her and resume what they'd started. It'd been so long since he'd had a woman, scarce and precious in his ravaged world.

At first, he believed his dream of Morgan was demon-wrought, meant to divert him from hunting Fomorians or finding a way off the island. He hardly remembered the last dream he'd experienced living in the remains of Los Angeles—New Angeles. All he remembered were the nightmares of the fighting, the Fomorian's poisonous bite, death's wreckage, the razing of nearly every living, breathing thing across Earth's barren lands.

The dream they'd shared had been different from any other he'd experienced, though. He'd felt what Morgan felt, shared in the sensations of her arousal. So real, it confused and excited him all at once. It made him believe in a future, while he wondered if she represented death. Future and death were the two beliefs that kept his people sane as they resisted the deathly bite of the Fomorians that killed off most of humanity.

The recollection of a shadow-shifter he was sure was a Fomorian flirting with Morgan, exerting its false claim upon her in their dream, inundated him with white-hot jealousy. No one had the right to touch her! Not even in his dreams.

Shock shoved his spine ramrod straight. What the hell? She didn't belong to him. He pounded his fist on the ground. What the temptress did to his senses wasn't a good thing. She could weaken him, make his heart feel things he didn't want it to feel, didn't know how to feel.

He stole one last glance at Morgan's bewitching face, and left to sit on the ledge outside. As he swung his legs over the smooth lip, the treacherous, endless sea riveted him. Ryan stabbed his hands into his snarled hair. "I can't let her get to me."

Morgan and his overwhelming attraction to her went against everything he believed in, everything he'd trained for since birth. As the most powerful Druid in North America, descended from centuries of dominant sorcerers, his people depended on him to protect and lead them. They expected him to make the proper choices for their wellbeing, especially in a treacherous post-apocalyptic world. That included introducing anyone into his coven who posed a potential threat. Paranoia had become common sense among his people when very few humans remained who weren't ensorcelled by the Fomorians.

Even in his dream, he'd sensed a veil of danger shadowing Morgan. Had his enemies planted her to distract him from leadership? Why not? The Fomorian Horde had tried every game in the playbook to bully him. They'd infiltrated his coven once, killing several guards, stealing magic from those he trusted most. The more magic the bastards stole, the closer they traveled to their goal to turn Earth into the ultimate Fomorian playground...including a massive breeding ground for strong Druid-Fomorian freaks.

But his people weren't newbies at fighting evil. All pagans born with innate magic had been on the frontline of attack for several years before the Horde Wars. Druids, witches, and warlocks weren't able to mass a united offense to defeat the growing Fomorian population. The day after he sailed away from the California coast, he was expected to enter into a pact to merge the remaining Western and Eastern Druid covens of North America. As much as he hated the merger, it was critical to fight off the attacks. To help the rest of the human race survive, if anything remained of it.

For those reasons, he refused to allow entanglements to deter his purpose or his responsibilities to those who counted on him. The raven-haired beauty embodied everything he fought against. Ryan groaned deep in his throat, shook off his tangled thoughts. *Damn it!* In his twenty-six years, he'd never experienced such a war between his head and heart. A death dirge had strummed inside him for so long he hardly recognized the life budding in his blood, bones, and muscles.

Mesmerized by the flat sea stretching to the ends of the bizarre, foreign world, Ryan watched the sun dip into twilight, an amber oval floating on the sapphire surface. He'd lose his incentive to find the dead boar if he didn't get his ass in gear. He had only a small cache of dried food buried in the cave. Who knew how long they'd need the cave's crystals to protect them? Especially since that bastard shadow-shifter now knew of Morgan's presence on the island.

Ryan checked on Morgan, brushed silky, dark wisps of hair off her pale face. He gathered his gear and climbed up the shorter length of the steep cliff wall, using the footholds he'd marked when he first discovered the cave. Tracking was one of his innate Druid talents, but he dared not use the minute magic necessary to invoke it even when shielded from outside detection. He also wanted to preserve his magical energy and prevent the Fomorian from stealing more than it'd already filched from him. He'd be damned if he became a midnight snack for the bastard and desert Morgan to its evil clutches.

Ryan poked his head over the top of the crag and scanned the encroaching jungle. Although he sensed a faint trace of the Fomorian, the cliff-top appeared safe, and he hauled himself onto level ground. Sprinting into the jungle, he stomped off his irritations on crackling twigs and leaves carpeting the jungle floor. Twin moons lit up the twilight sky, and the sinking sun in the eastern horizon deepened the shadows in the jungle. After two weeks on the island, it still amazed him how ass-backward this land was from the world he knew.

He hoped Morgan knew something about their mysterious location, one of a million other questions begging for answers. Least of all, why he felt as if she were winding through his soul, why he felt her magic. He'd never experienced such a strong connection to a woman—or anyone, for that matter. And he'd never wanted anyone so bad, so fast.

With raw needs, just like any other man, Ryan had known his share of women before the Horde Wars. He never sought them out. He gave them what they wanted and sent them on their way. A few returned for more, hoping to break his shell, to win the heart of a man known for his cold, calculating distance. The temptress in his mind, now in his life, defied even his basest needs. All he wanted was to explore every inch of her delicious body with his hands, his mouth, his tongue. When he'd kissed her, and she flicked her tongue against his, he drank her taste into his soul, locking it deep to draw upon later.

Renewed aggravation trod up his back, anchoring, suffocating. Finding a way home was a top priority. Unable to lose sight of that, he understood he couldn't act alone. Once they discovered a way off the island, Morgan's magic was crucial for his plan to work. Even if it meant he never touched her again, he needed her.

And they sure as hell were *not* killing that Fomorian.

Ryan was taking the bastard home with him.

CHAPTER 11

Jumbled images peppered Morgan's mind. The spent greenery underneath her crinkled, and she focused her sleepy eyes on shimmery gold flakes veining the granite wall to her right. Rustling sounds across the dwelling startled her into full consciousness. Reality slammed into her. Time to face the Druid assassin, a murderous Fomorian, and a bizarre island destined to do them all in—despite the syncopated heartbeat she'd felt lying close to the ground, or the cool, calm reverberations that had lulled her to sleep. *Thank you for the wonderful birthday gift, Father.* She heaved the bed covering off, sending it flying across the cave.

"You're awake." Ryan closed the distance between them. He crouched beside her, hooked her hair behind her right ear. He checked her head wound, his long fingers lingering on her cheek.

Mistrust oozed across her stiff shoulders. She scooted against the stone wall, stretching the borrowed T-shirt over her knees, hiding her bare skin along with her chaotic emotions. Bewildered by Fate's slap in the face, she needed to step back, to erase her moment of weakness when *she* kissed him.

"It's not time to play shy with me." Ryan returned to the other side of the small cave and picked up the discarded hide.

"I cannot do...what you want." Her body ignited,

betraying her mouth. She fisted her hand on her stomach.

He folded the hide into a small square and shoved it into his pack. "Who said I wanted anything? You sure as hell didn't mind my touch last night."

"You certainly didn't give me much choice," she accused lamely, beating down the heat of her own regrettable act in the seduction.

His eyebrows peaked. "No?" He sneered. "Are you saying you didn't like it? Sure as hell fooled me."

Alas, the problem. She loved it. It was difficult to hide how he made her feel when she initiated the kiss and melted against his body. The intensity of her pleasure in his arms, her lips pressed against his, scared her. Binding spell aside, Morgan should not trust this stranger. She picked at the bedding, crumbling dried fronds between her fingers. "Are we safe?"

"Yes." Ryan strutted out of the cave where a small fire burned in a circle of stones on the ledge. "I have something for you." He returned to the entrance. Firelight framed his silhouette in the inkiness of full night. Her rune-marked satchel and the small leather pouch Gwilym had given her dangled from his hands.

"My belongings!" She jumped up and snatched the bags from Ryan's outstretched hand. "Thank you." Pleased, she gave him a wide smile. "I can return your T-shirt. I have clean garments."

"Keep it. I like it on you." His voice held a smile, though shadows concealed his face.

Morgan liked the T-shirt, too. The softness of the unusual material caressed her skin and offered her a sense of familiarity in a world where nothing belonged. "I will keep it until you want it back." She refused to admit to herself that the shirt now held Ryan's faint smell, spicy and male, thoroughly beguiling.

Taking her bags, she slipped cross-legged onto the

rustling bed. "I have a gift for you, too."

"According to you, I already have something of yours." Ryan gripped his amulet.

"Indeed." Morgan rolled her eyes. She burrowed into her leather satchel and tugged out her herb pouch. Myriad aromas wafted from the bag, some bitter, some sweet, all smelling of home. "This will help with your...problem." Her gaze rose to his loincloth, held for a meaningful moment, continued up his sculpted chest to his overconfident face, to the one tiny dimple, more like a frown line, on the side of his left eye. His fair hair hung loose, framing his tanned face. Earlier, he'd tied his hair in a leather thong, and his rugged handsomeness was captivating. Now, with his deep golden hair flying free, mystery in his sparkling eyes, a smile flirting at the corners of his full lips, he was breathtakingly beautiful. A palpable entity in the air, his magic was at once wild and tame, ancient and fresh, soothing and aggravating. A boon to her powers, she welcomed the intriguing meld.

"Only one thing will heal that problem." He crossed his arms over his chest, the bulge growing beneath his skimpy leather garment.

Ignoring him, Morgan plucked out a worn suede pouch. The pungent aroma of ground kava wrinkled her nose. Stifling a sneeze, she pulled the drawstring secure then held out the bag to him. "Sprinkle the herb in boiling water and steep it for a few minutes. It will help...er...restrain your enthusiasm."

Cynicism settled across the tight lines of his lips. "What if I don't want my *enthusiasm restrained*?" He squared his shoulders, held his hand over his crotch, barely touching, proving a point.

Morgan's mouth went powder dry. She swallowed to build up fluid to slake her cotton stuffed throat. "It's your choice," she managed to choke out as she tossed the herbs to him.

Catching the tiny pouch, Ryan chuckled. "You're an herbalist? Could be useful here."

Returning to the cave's interior, he grabbed another lumpy sack heaped against the wall across from Morgan. Back against the wall, he settled down, a respectable distance between their physical bodies. However, their magic frolicked together in the air in shimmers, a visual enhancement the crystals in the cave created. Dust motes sparkled in all the colors of a rainbow, giving rise to a small joy in Morgan's precarious new life.

"My fresh kill was gone. This is all we have to eat."

Warily, she watched him pull dried strips of meat from a coarse leather sack and offer one to her. Her stomach had been growling at her since she'd awoken, and she eagerly accepted the meal. Traveler's fare wasn't normally fit for a High Druid Sorceress, but a necessity she often enjoyed on a dying Avalon. "I have foodstuff in my bag."

"Save it." Ryan heartily bit into a jerked-meat strip. "We may need it later."

Morgan took a bite of the jerky. Surprised, she chewed slowly, enjoying the spicy, wild taste on her tongue. "It's good. What is it?"

"Some sort of deer. Things on this island aren't the same as home."

"Where is home?"

"New L.A."

Morgan frowned in an attempt to ferret the definition out of her cluttered mind.

"Los Angeles, California." As though she held the long-lost Excalibur, Ryan stared at her. "You don't know where that is, do you?" In a blur, he lunged across the small space between them and clutched her shoulders, pressing her against the rock wall. "Who the hell are you?" His face hardened like a war leader charged with enemy interrogations. Or like her father when he failed to find his beloved magic book containing several lifetimes of spells.

Her powers rose, not that she felt threatened by him other than his deplorable manhandling. "Unhand me," she scolded. "I will not be subjected to your abuse. I see your father did not teach you the art of gallantry." A sharp protrusion jabbed her shoulder blade, and she pushed forward, forcing Ryan to ease his pressure.

Disdain flashed across an odd hatred in his eyes. "Then give me something to bite, other than your neck." He let her go and sat back on his heels. "You're a High Druid Sorceress from England, Ireland, wherever. Big deal. You're no different than the sorcerers—" he clamped his mouth shut.

The spicy dried meat sank to a solid ball in Morgan's belly. Did he mean that Druid magic or sorcerers still prospered in his age? Was Gwilym wrong about the annihilation of humans in the future? Had she misunderstood him? Why else would Father subject her to this miserable existence? For the sake of binding her magic to a bigheaded assassin? Dying on Avalon sounded more tolerable.

"We're not going anywhere until you spill your guts." Ryan scooted to the opposite cave wall and resumed chomping on his jerky.

Spill her guts? The ball in her stomach expanded, and she frowned at the deer meat in distaste. Did Ryan intend to kill her? Impossible. It had to be more future jargon.

Would he believe anything she told him? A decisive frisson shimmied down her spine. She'd reveal more as their mutual trust developed, if she lived long enough. Or if she didn't stick her dagger into his heart first.

She slipped the jerky into a pocket of her satchel and hugged the supple leather bag to her chest, her last remaining possessions from home. A lifeline to a lost existence. "I'm from the island of Avalon, Britain, centuries before your time. I'm the highest born sorceress left on Avalon. Our bloodlines stem from the joining of the magical *Tuatha dé Danann*—children of the Goddess Danu—and the Celtic Druids. We are the magical arm of the Druids. Many call us the Ancients."

A sneer tightened Ryan's lips. "And I'm the long lost President of the defunct United States." He snickered. "You can do better than that." He stretched out his long legs, crossed his ankles.

She twisted the satchel's ties around her fingers. "I don't know of whom or where you speak. I'm telling the truth. The Druids of my time were born with magic that rises from within," she patted her chest, "tied to the earth, sky, fire, and sea."

"The same as Druid sorcerers of my time. Born with origins to the Celts with innate magic, many have ties to the elements, which strengthen our internal powers." Ryan cocked his head, eyed her critically. "You still haven't given me concrete evidence."

Ire weaved inside her, trickled into her voice. "I didn't choose to travel through time and space to land on this ageless island any more than you did. It is our destiny, like it or not."

Silent, Ryan ate his meal, glowering between bites.

Encouraged by his willingness to hold his tongue, she told him the tale of Avalon's Shadow. He at least deserved to know about the monster they faced. "During the great Merlin's time, a Druid sorcerer, part Fomorian, pillaged the lands, draining magic from every sorcerer he encountered. It is written in history that some Fomorians never left Ireland after the *Tuatha* conquered them. The *Tuatha* drove the Fomorians into the sea, but the remaining Fomorians were the spawn of humans, Druids, other races, and were able to hide among us." Morgan focused on his stony face. "WindWraith commanded elemental air and fire magic, but practiced black magic, magic of the Fomorian gods of chaos and destruction. Some called him Avalon's Shadow because he lurked within shadows everywhere. Little was known about him, few ever laid eyes upon him. Unable to kill WindWraith, Merlin feared the black sorcerer's potency would surpass his own. He tricked WindWraith and reduced his corporeal body to a shadowy air form, leaving the beast on the edge of death. He then banished WindWraith forever to this hidden island to prevent him from gaining additional power."

Despite Ryan's incredulous look, he remained silent. She continued, "WindWraith's malevolence and Merlin's magic prevented anyone across eras from discovering this island." She unclenched her hand from around her satchel's strap before it fell asleep. "The island maintains a connection to Avalon. It pulls energy from Avalon to hold Merlin's magical barriers in place, to protect it from detection or invasion, and to bind WindWraith to it until it died. My father believes the Fomorian has found a way to steal nourishment from the island and to chip away at the barrier. In turn, the island is pulling more magic from Avalon to maintain the walls and locks. Merlin didn't anticipate WindWraith's ability to live so long without access to human energy. Killing it will restore magic to Avalon. Destroying it will also lessen the spread of evil that has grown from my time to yours."

Ryan flicked his hand in the air. "How will that help my people? My world has already been destroyed."

Morgan cricked her neck, her curiosity about Ryan's world besting her judgment. "Tell me about your world, your era."

He opened his mouth and shut it, seeming to battle an impulse to speak with a need to hold back. "Let's just say that Fomorians apparently survived throughout millennia and have already immersed my time in evil." He gestured at Morgan. "This is your fairy tale, not mine."

Morgan spit words out as if muck caked them. "WindWraith is trapped on this island until it can consume enough power to break down the protective barrier on the ocean floor. Now that I've seen and sensed the Fomorian," she gulped hard, "I believe it needs to possess a corporeal body to escape. It has lost most of its solid form." The old fantastical tales had haunted her all day. Voicing them loosened the tightness in her shoulders.

Ryan clapped his hands, smiling cruelly at her. "Bravo. Your imagination could fill a whole new library to replace what we've lost."

Wrath flared into her power center. Morgan silently intoned a sending spell. She sent images into Ryan's head of a foretelling she experienced two weeks ago. At that time, her Sight made no sense. Now she understood its nature.

The scene revealed Ryan sailing away from a gloomy, barren world, and washing ashore on this island. She also shared a moment from his childhood, a memory he had locked away in the farthest recesses of his mind. That particular image froze Ryan's body. An instant barricade encircled his mind, forcing her intrusive transference out.

"I'm sorry." Her lower lip trembled.

Ryan fisted a hand against his other palm, cracking his knuckles. The sound grated along Morgan's nerves like a knife on crockery.

"Sorry for what? For breaking into my head?" he asked in a composed voice. "For knowing I didn't care if I died in the squall? Seeing my screwed up childhood? Seeing how my father suppressed my magic when I defied him? Witnessing me reduced to begging on my knees in front of the bastard and agreeing to his terms in order to get a break from the torture of not having my power?" The dragon tattoo on his arm quivered as if preparing to launch itself at Morgan.

"I'm sorry for everything." She sighed loudly. "I'm a seer. However, my ability sometimes includes perplexing and disturbing visions of an unknown past."

"That's supposed to make me feel better? If you saw that much, you saw what's left of my hellhole of a world."

His frosty glare held the demeanor of a boy whose dark secrets had fallen into enemy hands. She shoved aside her packs and claimed the space between them. Tentatively, she touched his arm, then gave him a reassuring squeeze. His muscles jumped beneath her hand, resisting the compassion she offered.

"My gifts don't work in such a manner. I see only what the Goddess allows." She shrugged. "There is always a purpose behind my visions. I can't always comprehend them at first, but ultimately they serve to enlighten or aid those in need."

He shrugged her hand off his arm. "I don't want your sympathy." The glare he gave her was as icy as his voice. "Duty prevails over my life." He straightened his spine against the cave wall. "My parents were the most powerful Druid sorcerers on Earth in *my* time. They married for the specific purpose of creating dominant sorcerers. I was born and raised solely to replenish our dwindling population in a world that believed we were a bunch of tree worshipping ritual priests. Those Druids haven't existed in over a century. Few people believed in or understood the lost magic of the Druids and our ties to the elements." A dark, wintry expression formed lines around Ryan's eyes and mouth. "All my father cared about was proving the world wrong, creating a dominant race. There was no fucking love in my family." His fingers dug into his thighs, whitening the depressions in his tanned skin. "Once my father discovered how powerful I was, all he wanted was to raise me to be his successor. To do that, I had to garner the respect of our people in the only way I knew how—killing the Fomorians and their spawn hell-bent on annihilating our magic." Ryan's body quaked with anger. "I earned his grudging respect. The day I killed a Fomorian he couldn't touch, I earned his fear. Duty is all I know, all that matters." Bitterness spiked his tone.

An oppressive air descended upon them. Morgan wiped the perspiration off her brow, unsure how to respond. She knew all too well the prevalence of responsibility in a ruler's life, evidenced by her luckless presence on the island. At least she hadn't died on Avalon as she long expected, she thought wryly.

Ryan's mask softened, and his shoulders hunched forward. "Did you mean Avalon, like in King Arthur?" Curiosity glinted in his eyes.

She smiled in fond remembrance of home. "Yes. My great-great-grandfather was a child when King Arthur died."

Ryan searched her face for truth, lies, she knew not which. "Explains a lot."

Irritation skittered down her back. "Excuse me, but I—"

He held up a forestalling hand. "I only meant that you talk and dress differently."

"Oh." Her lips curled up in a tiny smile.

"You're not," a flush worked up Ryan's neck, "Morgan le Fay, are you?"

Morgan flicked a dismissive hand. "Heavens no. She exists in my lineage long, long ago. Many women of power in my family have been named after her."

Another weighty silence draped over them in the small space. Morgan plucked her damp tunic away from her breasts to give the air a chance to cool her moist body. Leisurely, Ryan's gaze traveled from her face and downward, stopping at the rounded neckline baring the top of her breasts.

Licking his lips, he asked, "What magic do you possess?" Hoarseness toned down his usual forceful voice.

A flicker of anxiousness conflicted with the gleam of lust in his eyes. A cheerful swirl fluttered in her stomach. The little devil on one shoulder wanted to prolong his obvious discomfort and show him her abilities. As she opened her mouth to stall him, a rolling swell shook the ground beneath them. A loud rumble erupted below the Earth's surface.

Terror grappled the bit of contentment Morgan had begun to claim. "What's happening?" she cried.

"Damn," Ryan bit out. He hauled her to her feet and shoved her toward the cave opening. "Get out of the cave!"

CHAPTER 12

Rocks and clods of dirt clattered to the ground, tumbled into growing piles. Thick dust zapped the air from the cave. Morgan stumbled toward the entrance, fighting the shaking ground, feeling like a sailor on a storm-tossed pier. She halted in the opening, peered through the dust cloud at Ryan.

He rushed to gather their gear. "Get out!" he hollered over the clamor of shifting terrain.

Frozen in place, she feared the rocking island would pitch her off the narrow ledge to her death on the reef below. She searched the cave walls for a handhold, hugging the entrance walls instead. Crystal laced gravel cascaded in a dry waterfall down the walls. The rear of the cave avalanched toward them in a deafening roar. A tide of earth blanketed their makeshift bed.

Ryan clamped his hand on her arm. She pivoted to face him, but her eye caught the bag of charms her father had relegated to her protection half buried in rubble. *I will not give up this easily!* The wretched island would not win before she had a chance to right the wrongs against Avalon and her people. The leather pouch lay a few feet from the opening. Morgan wrestled against Ryan's steadfast grasp. Another rolling rumble belowground sent him lurching off balance, forcing him to release his clamp on her arm.

"Get outside!" he snarled.

Ignoring him, she mangled a shielding spell and ducked

back into the shrinking cave. Grit filled her mouth and she gagged. She crawled to the stuffed pouch, regardless of the sharp stones poking into her bare knees and hands.

"Morgan!"

Vaguely, she heard Ryan cursing, felt him grab her ankles and his fingers slip away. He made it safely outside, and her heart pitter-pattered in relief. Undeterred, she stretched forward, snatched up the pouch containing the seeds to grow life on the island.

Grime coated her nostrils. She closed her stinging eyes and flattened her body against the rough cave wall, feeling her way toward the entrance. Pebbles pelted her, bouncing harmlessly off her thin barrier of opaque air. The collapsing cave edged toward her inch by inch. Only her elemental magic kept it from claiming her completely.

Morgan squinted into the gritty air, her sight drawn to a sliver of predawn moonlight in the blocked cave opening. A thread of panic coiled in her middle. "You will not win, island," she said. "I didn't put my life at risk to have it dashed away by the likes of you." Winding down her panic, she tossed out more air and earth magic to slow the cave's destruction.

"Morgan! Can you hear me?" Ryan's anxious voice penetrated the blocked entrance.

"Yes," she yelled through a raspy throat.

"Is the cave still collapsing?"

She sucked in dust and gagged. Spitting, she managed to croak out, "I'm holding it back." She had only a few moments to maintain her shields and retain enough power to enlarge the hole. Her magic stores had sorely diminished since she'd arrived on the island. Either the journey had depleted her or the magical resonance she shared with the island was draining her. Whatever it was, she needed a full day of rest to return her powers to peak strength.

"I can't blast through the rocks without endangering

you."

"I can get out. Step away. Give me a moment." Power swelled inside her. Sweet elemental fire and air met her innate energy and ascended to the surface, drenching her with strength and exhilaration.

A glow leaked out of her, surrounded her. Fire and air magic waltzed together like lifelong partners. Dense air contained the earth while she prepared a destructive fireball. Golden lightning collected on her right palm, and she shot a fireball forward, blasting a small hole in the rubble. Two more followed, widening the opening enough to squeeze through.

The moment she reached the other side and felt Ryan's hands grab her, she released her barrier. Rocks obliterated the cave, and the ground shuddered from the force. Clouds of dust dissipated above their heads into brown puffs floating across the ocean.

Ryan stepped in front of her, his chest pinning her against the cliffside. His magic encircled them, sheltering them from further danger of falling particles. A vein in his neck pulsed dangerously. The fire in his eyes crept over her body in a wash of heat.

"If I give you an order, you damn well better obey me." His mouth tightened in a stubborn line.

She clasped her hands together to prevent the wicked impulse to slap him. Obviously, he was accustomed to giving orders. However, she didn't suffer orders from any man, whether king or peasant. Not even her father resorted to ordering her about unless she allowed it. *Which, obviously, happened more often than naught, you dolt.* Despite the outlandish desire tickling her insides from the sheer proximity of Ryan's nearly naked body, she certainly was in no mood to allow it from this man.

She scowled, wishing like mad to escape his overpowering body. "You are not my king. I take orders from no one."

Ryan inched closer, pressing his grungy chest to her filthy tunic. His eyes burned sapphire—not from anger, but with a fearful and joyful lust. Ryan grew hard between them, an iron rod digging into her stomach. Even in moments of danger, his body responded to hers in arousal. A strange satisfaction rimmed the pleasure dripping into her lower torso. She cupped her mouth to hide her smile.

Ryan's jaw squared. He inched away until they no longer touched. "You will do as I say," he commanded in a strained tone. "I know this island. You don't." He gave her cheek a brief stroke then snared his fingers in her grimy hair. "When I tell you not to use magic, I mean *no* magic. Next time, we might not have the protection of the crystals to keep that bastard wraith away."

Morgan licked her lips and grimaced at the metallic, chalky taste of dry soil. Had men not changed throughout the ages? Did they all suffer from a head overflowing with arrogance? "I would be dead if I had not used my magic."

"You wouldn't have needed to if you'd listened to me." Palms flat against the rocks, he braced his arms on each side of her shoulders. Caged in place, only a pinch of sultry air separated Morgan from Ryan's powerful body. "What was so important you had to risk your life for?" He flicked his hand at the small sack she held to her side.

She contemplated the worn leather bag. Seconds before the cave-in, a solid thread of knowledge struck her mind, as if she had read a chapter in one of those intangible books crammed into her skull. An effect of her father's slow-working potion. Now she understood what she must do with the charms. An important task her father had left unsaid, at least verbally.

The knowledge of what her father had done nearly turned her knees to water. Gwilym never betrayed himself the thief of the amulets, but he knew how much magic they contained and the incomplete spells she attempted upon them. A powerful sorcerer such as her father knew how to unravel even the strongest spell and either extinguish the spell or change it. By the Goddess, he had crafted a beckoning spell, which turned her temporary binding spell into a permanent bond. *Holy mother of Satan.* Did that mean she had bound Ryan's magic to hers until one or both of them died? Would the spell diminish over time? A sick feeling pinched her stomach.

Morgan squeezed the pouch, clinking crystals and silver together. The amulets were definitely the triggers to bring Ryan's surviving people to the island. She must never lose them. Rescuing these unknown lives was worth risking her own over. Regardless, she possessed more than sufficient magic to remain safe in the cave while she retrieved the pendants.

Not sure if Ryan would believe or understand the purpose of the amulets any more than she did, Morgan formed an innocuous answer. "I have little left to me in this life. At least let me keep what I do have."

Ryan's brow smoothed. "I hear you." He sifted his fingers through kinks in her hair, caressed her neck. "But I don't care if you're queen of the demon spawned world. From now on, you do as I say." He detangled his hand from her hair and fingered the pouch. "Nothing is worth risking your life over. You don't know this island. Dangers abound in every crevice, least not the volcano on the island's northern tip that probably just cursed us."

That sick tightness began to unwind in her stomach, leaving her reluctantly relieved that Ryan knew of these perils. She owed him respect in this matter. Until he acted stupid again. She was beginning to understand the gist of the power tripping jackass phrase.

Morgan opened her mouth to acquiesce, but he cut her off. "We need to get back to the grotto before full daylight."

Sunrays peeked over the western horizon, elongating and purging the last stars in dawn's sky. Crystals planted in the cave's exterior winked in the rising sun, casting flickers on the stone walls.

"Why the hurry?" Morgan slapped the grit off her bags and secured the pouch to her knife belt. "Is the grotto safe?"

"Safe enough. I've planted crystals around the outskirts, and there are tons embedded in the caves." Ryan dropped his arms and eased aside, affording her a view of the white-capped aquamarine sea beyond. "The shadow-demon feeds off sunlight, seems to avoid night."

"Yet, the vibrant crystals stop it? You would think it had found a way to draw power from the crystals to increase its own if it can feed off that blasted orb sucking the life out of me." As if to prove her point, she swiped grainy sweat off her upper lip.

Ryan shrugged. "Doesn't appear that way."

"You seem to know much about WindWraith."

"I've studied it." Ryan shrugged. "There's not a helluva lot to do on this island alone after a day of exploring."

Morgan touched the ruby eye of his dragon tattoo, trailing her finger to the dragon's wings disappearing into Celtic knots around his biceps. Ryan's arm muscle spasmed beneath her fingers, either excited at her touch or battling against it. "You're not alone any longer," she whispered, her treacherous longing laughing at her common sense. Her finger tickled from touching the tattoo, and she rubbed it against her lips, wishing to taste dragon fire.

Why did she feel such desire toward this wretched man? She had just met him! She smoothed out the furrows in her brow, rubbing sense into her rebellious mind, trying to erase the idea of putting on her amulet and allowing Ryan to bind his magic to her.

Everything inside her longed for Ryan's touch, despite the nagging vision of his past she experienced crawling through the cave. Gulping down the lump in her throat, Morgan shoved her conflicted feelings to the no-man's land in her mind.

Ryan growled low in his throat and spun away. "Let's go," he said gruffly. "Time's ticking." He slung their satchels over his shoulder and nudged her in front of him. "Start climbing. There are plenty of handholds." He gave her a reassuring rub in the small of her back. "I'll be right behind you. There's no chance of you falling."

His tenderness alleviated a corner of Morgan's concern. At least he was a gentleman in some respects. The rest remained to be tested.

"Stop at the top, so I can shoot out feelers in case WindWraith's hovering about."

She took hold of a fat root above her head, stuck her foot in a crevice, and began climbing. "No magic," she said sarcastically.

"I'm a tracker," he drawled. "I know how to shield my tracking magic—even against that bastard demon."

Wide-eyed, Morgan stared at him over her shoulders. He did indeed possess great magic to rival hers. "My magic was shielded," she added as an afterthought.

"You weren't shielded. I felt your magic."

Surprise raced down her legs, jolting her foot. She slipped and banged her knee against a boulder. Pain shot through her leg muscles, and she gritted her teeth to kill her cry. Ryan braced her ankle, steadying her.

"Of course it was shield—" She bit down on her tongue. He'd always know when she used her magic, whether shielded or not. A powerful sorcerer normally sensed magic in the air when emitted, but their partial bond gave Ryan awareness of her magic even when shielded.

Don't tread there. He will know soon enough. "Earlier you asked what magic I wield." She stretched up to grab a small rock protrusion, muscles tightening in her sides. "I have elemental and innate magic abilities. I can draw from the land's elements and use them without notice. I have studied with the best teachers to learn how to use all my magic."

"The only thing your magic is good for now is to tame WindWraith." Ryan smacked her buttocks softly, his large hand lingering hot on her right cheek. "Now zip it and get moving. I need a damn bath."

They arrived at the emerald grotto unscathed, each lost in reflection and wary of the other. Sunlight snuck through the chinks in the canopy of trees overhanging the heavenly site. Morgan shook leaves and twigs from her hair, drew in a deep breath of flowery heat. Despite the sweltering hike, the return trip had revived her. She pivoted around and absorbed the grotto's enchantment. A pleasurable feeling of welcome and acceptance inundated her.

Various tree species—palms, ferns, coconut, bamboo, oak, and mahogany—intertwined with flourishing vines. Shiny and matte leaves of bright green, dark green, and every color in between gave tribute to the grotto's adopted name. Multicolored flowers rioted along the outer fringes of the pool. Many varieties Morgan did not recognize. Some appeared familiar, but their colors and sizes were dissimilar to those in Britain. Bold blossoms in blues and purples larger than Ryan's hands put together grew out of lily-like stems near the waterfall. Morgan had never seen the like. The island's heart centered in the vibrant grotto, anchoring her there. In no other place did her magic resonate with the earth as fully as it did in the grotto. Not even on Avalon.

"I think those only grow here." Ryan's voice bounced her back to the present.

She turned to him, smiling wide. "They are magnificent. Do you know what they're called?"

"You're the botanist, not me."

"No. I know mostly of plants that aid in spells, healing, and cooking." Soil encrusted roots drooped from her raised hand. "Like this soaproot. I have never been this grimy." *Except when I had to catch the piglets from last year's litter and tripped over that beastly sow.* Ryan didn't need to know the mundane tasks Avalon's demise forced upon her. Fortunately, those tasks left her prepared for her new life on this island.

His gaze strolled indolently from her face to her lower legs. Fierce heat whirled up from Morgan's feet and she stood as if she were a broodmare on display to the highest bidder. Not the most pleasant sensation if one dwelled on the idea. She rubbed her nose, feeling it elongate and fur sprout. Trading stares with the powerful warrior standing before her, Morgan shoved the impressions out of her mind, letting heat bathe her cool edges.

A frown painted Ryan's face. "Your knees." He squatted and rolled up her T-shirt to the bottom of her thighs. "Why didn't you say something?"

She glanced down. Blood and dirt caked her knees. Soothing aloe bits stuck to her scraped skin. No wonder she hadn't felt pain with the healing aloe mysteriously clinging to her. "That happened when I was crawling in the cave. I hardly noticed." The island's healing heart encapsulated her, shivered over her knees. She literally felt the scraped skin knitting together.

Ryan suddenly scooped her up like a babe and strode toward the pool.

Indignation arose in her stomach, trouncing her leftover energy. "Put me down!" She kicked out her legs. "They don't hurt." She slapped her hand ineffectively against his shoulders.

"Stop it or I'll spank you." Mock severity masked his face, his playful mood shocking Morgan into silence. He deposited her on a slate slab alongside the waterfall. "Don't move."

A loud sigh escaped Morgan, and she gazed longingly at the enticing water. Dappled sunlight lit the waterfall, and the cascading sheet sparkled like gemstones feeding the pool. She looked forward to slipping in and sloughing the fiendish day off her skin, out of her hair, after she indulged in Ryan's ministrations. She was so used to healing others on Avalon that the idea of someone caring for her caused a gentle, cheerful stirring in her heart. And the notion of the powerful sorcerer touching her sent her pulses racing. *Not again!* Evidently, the island had tricked her body to beat her head into submission in all matters concerning Ryan O'Rourke. A frustrated groan slipped out.

Ryan returned with a cloth and a hollowed coconut brimming with water. He cleansed the dried blood off her knees. Diligently, he picked out each speck of debris, tossed away the aloe bits, a perplexed look on his determined face.

"I have a healing salve in my bag. I'll use it after I bathe," Morgan offered behind closed eyes. She leaned so far back on the boulder, she was practically prone. Drowsiness overcame her, and her limbs grew languid.

Silence greeted her. Morgan thought Ryan had left, and when she opened her eyes, she saw him drop his loincloth to the ground in front of her. For the first time, she glimpsed him fully without the leather garment.

Startled, Ryan froze, staring down at her upturned face, as if waiting for her to say or do something. Without an ounce of embarrassment, her gaze crawled up Ryan's suntanned torso. Rivulets of sweat cut through the dirt coating his skin, striping him like a tiger. Her senses ravished his flat, rippling stomach, his powerful chest, the crusty edges of the rune tattoo. Her brand. His lips parted, revealing a hint of straight white teeth. His smile spread to his eyes, deepening his dimple the slightest bit. She internally tramped down the twist and pulse of desire staging a scorching comeback south of her stomach.

Ryan's half-lidded eyes held an immeasurable promise. She reached out and touched his wrist, barely conscious of licking her dry lips or of her hard nipples straining toward the sky. He stroked his thumb across her palm, and electricity arced up her arm. Not another muscle stirred in Ryan's body until the caws of two swooping ravens tattered the tense silence.

He groaned. "You're killing me." With that, he spun on his heels and dove into the pool.

The waterfall masked the splash of his body hitting the water and the pounding of her heart in her ears. Morgan swung her head back and laughed, the first time in what seemed ages. She reveled in the influence she held over this man of immense strength, who stirred feelings in her she desperately wanted to explore. Little did he know he was killing her, too.

She propped her elbows on the smooth stone, unable to take her sight off his magnificent, sun-worshiped body. His muscular arms knifed through the water as strong fluid legs scissored the pool's length. Despite her renewed exhaustion, arousal sprawled from her middle and sprung a need she never knew existed until she met Ryan.

The magnitude of her feelings for him inundated her and dismay quickly hammered her longing. The other vision she suffered during the earthquake flooded back. The fleeting image of Ryan making love to another woman— Lauren Blackwell—on the altar of a crumbling church on the night they announced their coven pact was like a knife dicing her heart into pieces. Lauren Blackwell, a Druid leader in her own right, was worthy of her claim on Ryan. What did the horrid vision foreshadow?

A jealous hatred ignited in her chest. From her earlier scanty visions of Ryan's life, she recognized his fierce loyalty to his people. "Defend and lead," was his motto. He would find a way to return home for their sake, leaving her on the island, alone as she always envisioned herself on a dying Avalon. In time, maybe her father's beckoning spells might bring her a man she could love. Or maybe love simply wasn't part of her destiny. Wistfulness pricked her heart as she stared at Ryan's strong, beautiful body standing erect beneath the waterfall.

The raven pair cawed loudly, diverting her troubled contemplation. The birds landed on a straggly oak branch above her head. One alighted above the other, then fluttered down to perch beside its mate, scooting together until their wings tangled. Were the birds destined for one another? Did the island bring them together? Morgan's thoughts clouded. "Get lost, you mangy featherheads."

CHAPTER 13

An owl hoot interrupted the serenade of chirping crickets and croaking frogs in the grotto. Not a breeze stirred the humid air. The relaxing sounds of life combined with the plummeting waterfall loosened Ryan's stiff muscles. It had only taken him a couple of days living in paradise to realize how much he missed the bursts of nature he experienced in his busy reality before the Horde Wars destroyed all plant and animal life. Now, he never wanted to live without the sight and sounds of a precious world protected from the blight. If he found a way, he'd love to bring the covens to the island. As it was, he hadn't figured out how he and Morgan landed there, where they were, or if other islands like it existed.

Taking his nightly check around the grotto's perimeter, Ryan's thoughts centered on Morgan. He couldn't fathom knowing her anywhere but on this idyllic isle, possibly the last piece of the proverbial paradise pie. In their dream, they had met in a verdant meadow. If what Morgan said about traveling from the past was true, she had never seen his destroyed world, and it gladdened him. She didn't belong in that hell. She belonged to the island.

His heart twitched, and he wheeled away from his reverie to collect firewood from the stack outside the alcoves. Thick stone kept the caves cool from the sweltering heat, but at night, they got downright chilly. If it were just him, he'd not bother with a fire.

Morgan slept on, regenerating her powers, while he made do with a few hours of fitful sleep on the cold, hard-packed cave floor. When the fire died down, he revived it and prepared a meal for when Morgan awoke. He forced himself not to stare at her willowy body cuddled on his bed. He fought the overwhelming urge to climb into the furs and bundle her softness against him, to let her soft curves smooth his hardened edges.

While she slept, he brewed tea with the herbs she'd given him. Hell, he couldn't walk about 24/7 with a perpetual hard-on. The cool waters of the pool hadn't slaked his demented thirst for the sorceress either. He'd even tried to swim off his frustrations to the point of exhaustion. No luck there. The useless tea relaxed him little more than a beer.

"Damn it all to hell." He knocked his neat stack of kindling into a heap, wanting to knock out his idiot brain cells. Too bewitching, too distracting, he'd let her get to him when they had a boatload of things to discuss. He sensed Morgan had withheld vital information during their conversation in the destroyed cave. Ryan wanted to get to the bottom of it after she awoke, before he acted on his crazed impulses to seduce her, losing his mind in her totally.

He hefted the crudely split wood into the cave, tenting pieces inside the fire ring. Blowing on the embers, he coaxed flames to life. Ryan snuck a glimpse at Morgan. The bunched furs at her side revealed the outline of her breasts, barely concealed by a sheer gown. Her rosy nipples strained against the material, and the warmth flowing down to his groin reignited the fire in his body. An instant hard-on put an end to Morgan's impotent herbs. Nothing was strong enough to dampen his internal fire for her. "Damn it." He knocked his fist on the wall. "Get your shit together, man."

As if feeling the weight of his lust upon her, Morgan's

eyelids fluttered open. She rose up on one elbow, pulling the fur over her chest, a shy smile tilting up her dry lips. "Did I sleep long?" She yawned, visibly battling to keep her sight fixed on his face, rather than sliding lower to the bane of his existence, which stood at attention, unfortunately, at her eye level.

Disgust ran through Ryan at his foolish lack of control. Morgan knew how she affected him so it was useless to hide it. "It's evening."

Fire licked at the wood, brightened the cave. Flames and shadows tangoed on the walls, and the memory of the rune images mirrored on them screeched back. In the day's events, he'd forgotten the displays of power and the amulet's spell. The brand on his chest tingled, causing him to recall Morgan's lips soothing his skin. He groaned aloud and twisted away from the sight of her shapely beauty taunting him. He almost summoned his fire magic to kill his longing, something he'd only had to do as a girl-crazy teen.

"Are you all right?" Morgan's small hand settled on his arm, alabaster against the black tattoo—his family's crest—circling his biceps. So wrapped up in stomping down his arousal, he hadn't heard her move off the bed.

"Yes. No. Ah, hell!" He shrugged his arm, dislodging her fevered touch, turning around to face her. "What did you do to me?" He balled the amulet in his fist. "Why did this brand me? What do these symbols mean?"

"They are rune marks."

"No kidding." He sneered. "I figured that out." He grabbed her slight shoulders, his eyes practically bulging from their sockets. "What do they mean?"

Firelight blazed in her eyes, reflecting her caginess. "They are of little consequence." In obvious avoidance, she wrung her hands, shuffled her feet.

"You made the damn thing, so they must mean

something."

She swished a hand in the air. "Fanciful words I strung together as a child." She broke away from his loose hold. The back of her knees hit the sleeping wedge, but she held her ground, hands on her hips.

He knew she held back—felt it in the minuscule clamp on their bond. Like a bird dangling a worm in front of its hungry mate and then gobbling the worm itself. Morgan narrowed her eyes with a mad raven, beady look that turned him on more than any look should.

Feet spread in a defensive stance, he towered over her as if to force his dominance upon her. "Why did the amulet burn into me? What kind of magic was it?"

"Does it still hurt?" She pursed her lips. "I have a healing balm that will help."

"It doesn't hurt." Ryan edged closer to her. "Why did the amulet draw my attention in a stormy sea before my boat capsized? Why did I clutch it when I washed up for dead on this gods-forsaken island? Why does—" Ryan was unable to ask her why his magic leapt alive and danced around his heart whenever she was near, or why the amethyst gave off a hum when lust raged through him. The barely perceptible din annoyed the hell out of him because it never ceased. Why did her magic touch his? Why did he sense some of her emotions? He shouldn't feel this way! Magic like this didn't exist. Although he'd read about ancient Druid magic, binding rituals and the like, they'd disappeared centuries ago. Fomorians burned every book they got their grimy paws on after the Wars. His people managed to hide several caches of history books in the consecrated churches, but nothing he read explained Morgan's spells.

It didn't matter. He'd escape the island soon, return to killing evil and protecting his people. Those obligations called to him every minute of every day. Unable to wipe away his frown, he snagged his hands through his hair, scratched his scalp.

Morgan rested her delicate hand on her dagger belt. "All will be made apparent when the Goddess wills it."

Ryan laughed scornfully. Maybe he ought to toss her a piece of her avoidance pie. "I want *you* to make it apparent for me." Gently, he captured a handful of her long, silky hair and wound it loosely around his fingers.

Anger stained her cheeks. "I cannot." She clamped her fingers around his wrist—barely able to reach half its circumference. "Unhand me, or I will be forced to use magic on you."

Energy spiked between them, raising the hairs on their arms to dance in the slight breeze kicked up by the heat of the fire.

A wicked smile split his mouth. "No magic," he warned in a low voice. "You don't want to risk WindWraith's attention. Who knows how long my crystal barrier will last. If it actually works."

"You jest with me." The hesitation in her voice clouded the irritation in the set of her jaw.

"Try me." He smoothed her flyaway hair, his thumb stroking her neck. Dipping his head, his lips caressed the tip of her satiny ear. "You say you cannot tell me, but I think you mean you *will* not tell me." He licked her lobe. The rune brand on his chest stung. His crystal gleamed brighter, hummed louder as heat spread from his center of power, southward.

Morgan inched backward with nowhere to go. He wound his arm around her waist, preventing her falling on the bed. He recognized yearning in her darkening eyes, and his blood smoldered in response.

"Where did you get those beautiful, expressive green eyes?" His mouth brushed over hers. Her lips parted in anticipation but he resisted the temptation.

She collapsed into his bracing arms. As he leaned down, she molded her soft curves into his hard body. "From my mother," Morgan breathed out on a whisper. Her voice was like wind chimes in a cool ocean breeze.

Emboldened by the little noises in her throat, he nuzzled her neck, alternately nibbled and kissed a path to her ear. Sucking her lobe into his mouth, his tongue tantalized it before he slid his mouth ever so slowly across her jaw to her plump lips. Her floral scent coated his senses like aged whiskey.

Morgan whimpered in an endearing way that spun his world out of control. He touched his tongue to her soft lips. When her lips parted this time, he crushed her mouth with his, possessing it, staking his claim to her body. He thrust his tongue into her inviting warmth and explored languorously. She moaned as her tongue met his in a mating frenzy. Power bloomed, sizzled in the air, whispered in his blood. Shock slammed into him, and he almost sank to his knees, a boneless mass of electric nerve endings.

Without breaking the kiss, Ryan tightened his hold on her, where not even air penetrated. Linking her arms around his neck, she pressed one hand to the back of his head. Her short fingernails bit into his shoulder. He reveled in the pain, wanted it and more as long as she inflicted it with her touch. Her round butt filled his hands and he kneaded the soft flesh. Their kiss became frenetic, and the heated, velvet interior of her sweet mouth unraveled him.

Ryan eased her onto the furs. The sorceress's fiery power streamed into him, pranced in and out of his magic, spurred them on. She thrust her hips against his, and pained-pleasure ground his hardness into her yielding curves. He sucked in his stomach, gasped. It drove his ferocious need, and he had to hold himself back from not tearing off her clothes and burying himself deep inside her. Quivers spooled through his taut muscles as he fought for control. She smelled so good, fresh like a morning meadow, just as he'd imagined in their dream.

Beyond reason, Ryan eased back and peeled Morgan's gown up over her breasts. A ragged groan escaped him at the glimpse of the milky-white breasts and dusky rose peaks. His feverish gaze raked the length of her naked body, and he grew so hard, he thought he could drill through the rock walls. Gods, she was beautiful perfection.

Unspoken misery bloomed across her face, and she languidly tried to hide the four scars on her stomach. With light fingertips, he traced the white welts one by one, loathing the thing that caused the pain tinting her face red.

He rested his forehead against hers. "You are beautiful," he whispered, smoothing his hand over her scars. "Every inch of you."

Light swirled over her pale flesh, kissing it with the color of fire. She trembled beneath him, her eyes fixed on his. Her fingers feathered over his rune brand, her touch a balm to the stinging pain. Eons crawled by while they died and were reborn in each other's eyes, until passion compelled him to press his lips to hers in another kiss, tender and hungry at once.

Contact with her silky skin sent currents of desire over him, the friction igniting his natural fire. Her eyes rounded in awe, and he gasped. No one's magic had ever incited his fire magic. Ryan had never experienced the range of sensations, both physical and emotional, that he experienced with Morgan. And he feared his inability to resist her. Hell, he didn't want to resist. It maddened and excited him at once. Part of him wanted to explore and challenge those feelings until the day he died. He locked away the dissenting part of his mind and tossed away the key.

Morgan sifted her hands through his hair, raked her fingers across his scalp the way she did in their dream. He burned so hot for her he thought he'd combust. Her breasts mashed against his chest and her heart drummed in perfect sync with his. Aching to enter her, he untied his loincloth, letting it drop away from his hips. He spread Morgan's velvety legs and wedged himself between her knees.

Her hands froze on his chest, her entire length tensing beneath him. "Ryan, no," she pleaded in a small voice.

An uncontrollable inferno raged within him. "At least let me pleasure you." He lowered himself over her, but she pushed harder. A mix of fear and frustration brought back the gentle celadon depths from the darkness of her lust-filled eyes.

Curiously, Ryan studied her. She caused his natural fire to blaze in ways he was dying to investigate. Reluctantly, he bolted her enticing magic out of his body. He refused to do anything she wasn't ready to do. But if he didn't at least sample her, he'd send a torrent of unrestrained fire magic into the air, which would only cause him to burn harder for her when it met her magic. "Let me touch you, kiss you."

Hesitating, she chewed on her bottom lip, brushed her moist lips across his, and nodded.

Electricity sparked in his body. He braced himself on the furry bed to support his weight. Morgan trembled hard in anticipation, an encouraging whimper the final enticement he needed. He licked a path around one stiff nipple, then the other. His hand moved to the upper slope of her breast, then underneath the satiny smoothness. He filled his hand with one breast, suckled the other nipple, bringing her to a writhing frenzy.

Ryan raised his head, drank in her loveliness. Morgan combed her fingers through the hair at the nape of his neck. Goose bumps crept over his skin in the wake of her delicate touch. He lost himself in the depths of the power and longing he saw in her eyes. The power she held over him, the beginning of his total undoing.

His mouth captured hers in a long slow seduction. Morgan opened her mouth, and he slipped his tongue inside, enjoying her sweetness, tasting their destiny. Their kiss became fierce and demanding as her tongue stroked his in a frenzied duel. Her soft breasts crushed his chest, inciting and inviting.

Before Ryan lost it completely, he ended the kiss and rose between her legs. They both gasped for air. Morgan's breasts heaved, her hands curled at her sides, face flushed and beckoning.

Ryan kissed the flowery sweet skin between her breasts, flicking his tongue over each pert nipple, unable to escape his panting groans. Then he kissed and licked his way down her stomach, dipping his tongue in her navel. He planted soft kisses on her scars and she quivered against his lips. Her hands twined in his hair, holding his head against her stomach. He chuckled low in his throat. Lust flowed hot in his veins as he tongued the white ridges of scarred skin, wanting to heal them with his touch.

"Ryan. Ryan! Oh, that tickles." She squirmed beneath him, his name on her lips in her exotic accent sending him off the rails. He smoothed his hand down her hips, his fingers reaching into her wet heat, his erection throbbing for his own release. Not yet, it wasn't his time. He swallowed down a groan.

"Oh Goddess! Ryan," she whispered in a throaty voice.

He lifted his head to see her face. Her eyes hazed over, her cheeks crimson and moist. "Fly for me, little raven." His heart panged with an unfamiliar emotion. A gush of magic escaped him and covered them both in gooseflesh.

Morgan rocked and cried out, clutching at him. The brand on his chest burned a hole in him, and her magic raced to ice the sensation. Suddenly, his internal magic shield cracked, and her power poured into him, mating with his. Her release seized her, and her body convulsed violently, her screams resonating in his head.

Gasping, Ryan slumped into the wall, trying to purge the pain of his lust, breathing in the essence of heaven. It wasn't enough. It would never be enough until he had Morgan in all ways. In that moment, he realized that whether or not they left the island, he wanted everything she had to offer him. The realization staggered him, rasped up his back in a cold wash.

Morgan eased away, her breasts rising and falling with each gasp. A tremulous smile stretched her mouth. Reaching forward, he dragged her onto his lap, her legs straddling him, wrapping her into his embrace.

"Let me pleasure you now," she said on a warm breath in his ear, her tongue darting behind the exhale. She nibbled and kissed a path down his neck to the hollow of his throat. She nestled his iron hardness within the heat of her thighs and rocked against his length.

He was about to ease his own pulsing need when reality smacked him. Icy fury and resentment rained on his heat. "No!" he roared. Neither Morgan nor his people deserved his selfish pleasure. Damn the consequences to his body and heart. Gently, he rested her on the furs and clambered off the low bed. Rummaging through his stack of clothes, he found a pair of denim shorts and tugged them on.

Ryan turned, masking his expression. Pain blanched Morgan's love-ravaged face. He wanted to die on the spot.

She rose from the bed, crumpling her gown over her breasts. Resolve shifted across her mottled face. "You do not want me," she stated simply.

"No, it's not...hell, yes I want you." His gut lurched. "You have no idea—" *I've never wanted anyone the way I want you.* He scrubbed his hand across his face, wishing to mop his confusion away so easily. "It just cannot be."

"Because I'm a powerful sorceress from another land, another time?" Her voice rang flat and resigned to her fate.

Softening his gaze, he replied, "It has nothing to do with who you are."

"Then enlighten me," she challenged, giving him her black, mad raven glare.

He considered his words carefully. "It's about my duty to my people. I...we...must find a way off this island. I have a life to return to, people to help, Fomorians to destroy." He hung his head. "Fucking, lifelong duty," he grumbled.

"Will you tell me about your responsibilities to your people and your world?"

Ryan warred with the wish to tell her everything versus nothing, spoiling their time together in paradise. All too soon, he must return to that harsh, oppressive life of fighting, running, and hiding. A long pause ensued before he heard the faint rustling of clothing. Ryan lifted his head. Morgan wore her gossamer gown, arms folded over her breasts.

"Why were we sent to this paradise prison?" His step ate the distance between them.

Morgan squinted, regarding him coolly. "Someone must kill WindWraith before it steals more of Avalon's magic, escapes this island, and completely annihilates both our worlds. She gave him a slow, appraising look. "We were sent to this island to destroy the creature. Together we can defeat it."

Disgust curled Ryan's lips. "Who sent us? Who but our worst enemy would do that to us?"

Morgan's bare soles swept the hardened ground. Their mixed floral and spicy aromas clung to her. He inhaled through his mouth, trying not to let it suck him in again.

Ryan felt a single tremor pass down his spine. "Tell me, Morgan. Who?" He moved a step closer.

Embers in the fire ring threw off a pitiful glow in the

darkening cave. Too dark to see, he felt her spark of defiance, the twinkle of challenge.

"My father," she finally said. She sent a vision into his head, showing her father telling her, verbally and telepathically, about her obligations to her people and Avalon. Once again, Ryan saw WindWraith's identity and its ages-long path of destruction. She cut off the horror show, depriving him of the ending. Morgan tightened her arms around herself, guarding her body from his venomous look.

"You set me up." Power leapt inside him with angry flashes of lightning along his nerves. He stalked out of the cave and didn't look back.

CHAPTER 14

The revulsion that stormed across Ryan's face as he stomped out clearly revealed the meaning of his words. Morgan didn't need a time-traveling interpreter to decipher them. She pushed out a heavy sigh. His reaction wasn't unforeseen. She still hadn't resolved the enormity of her destiny in her own baffled mind. Especially, when only two days ago, she thought her life was over. *This second chance at life isn't my idea of a birthday gift.*

"He'll return when he calms down." Certainty fluttered in her chest. "To carry out our hellish tasks." Then what? How much more did she dare reveal without alienating Ryan further or making an utter mess of matters? When should she tell him there was no escape from the island? At least not for her. Would he believe that Fate brought them together? Would the next binding spell join their magic forever as ancient tales foretold? What if she had mistakenly set in motion the other flawed amulet spells? Cold reality seeped into the marrow of her bones and she trembled under its weight. Old magic lived in her father, in herself, in the archaic spells, even here on this timeless island. Many of her father's dire predictions had transpired, and she had no reason to doubt his other foresights.

Unbidden, the memory of Ryan's gentle touch and the intensity of his fire coursing down her body weighed upon her. Her heart had almost taken leave of its wits and begged him to take her fully, when her head had already told him no. Bloody hell, she mustn't falter again! That is, if they managed to slay WindWraith and live another day. She threw up her hands and forced her mind to mundane tasks. After all, she had a home to establish, with or without a moody demon assassin.

Morgan added two logs to the embers, coaxing the fire to life. Flames licked at the wood, creating phantom dancers on the walls, sparkling off veins of quartz mapping the stone. Shadows rolled and rippled, overlapping one another like lovers in embrace.

A depression in a russet-speckled boulder across the cave twinkled in the water dripping down the walls. Firelight glimmered on the shallow bowl's surface from the bottom of the puddle as though lit from within. Curious, she walked to the roughhewn bowl and peered into it. Diffuse amber light swirled in a wild pattern until water formed a solid amber circle.

Vibrating with excitement, Morgan knelt on the ground, careful not to disturb the liquid. On Avalon, without proximity to a natural body of water to scry with, she used a scrying bowl, but any puddle or container sufficed. The amber color and the swirling pattern belonged to her father's scrying footprint. Was it possible to communicate with him from this world?

She concentrated on a calling spell. Harmonious air, fire, and earthen energy soared to her fingers. Morgan uttered the divination and swished the water, magic sparking from her fingertips. The shallow depth clouded, and then the water stilled. Tendrils of steam spiraled into the air. She held her breath until the water cleared and her father's beloved face materialized, a specter rising from the stone.

Tears slid down her cheeks. "Father, is that you? Can you hear me?"

"Darling daughter." Gwilym's faint voice wavered. "I

wondered how long it would take you to figure this out."

"Why didn't you tell me?" she berated, slapping the wetness off her cheeks.

"I did not want to give you false hope. I honestly wasn't confident you could scry from that world to Avalon. But I see the island's magic is strong and aiding you."

"Oh, Father!" Unable to restrain her happiness, she raised a triumphant fist. The light in the depression dimmed and she rushed on. "There's much I need to know. I'm glad you're here for me." She touched the bowl's rim, wishing she could caress his weathered face.

His expression sobered. "It may not always work if your powers are faint or the island's energy is depleted. Or the link severed."

Morgan refused to allow his caution to trump her joy. Ever since her vision before the earthquake, she dreadfully wanted to know more about the charms. Now she'd gain answers.

"The spell will not last. You must talk swiftly."

She slanted her head, squinted. "Did you steal the crystal amulets I made when I was a child?" she accused not too sternly.

"I put them away for you." A wry smile spread Gwilym's mouth. "I'm sorry. However, you instilled powerful magic into them. Your spells would have failed miserably if the intended recipients did not receive them."

Morgan fingered a lock of hair off her knitted brows. "There were no intended recipients for the trinkets." Except for the special one she created—the one now strung around Ryan's neck.

Gwilym's voice lowered. "You did not understand the spells you used or the prophecies attached to them." He coughed and the water dimpled. "You used ancient beckoning spells for lost lovers, a healing spell for despair and broken hearts." Water rippled the fringes of his head, his white hair a floating halo.

She had little time left. "And a magic binding spell," she added, her shoulders knotting.

"A potent binding spell." Creases deepened on his wispy brow. "Not simply to bind magic and certainly not one to play games with."

Morgan disregarded the chagrin rebelling in her gut. "Did the crystals come from this island?"

"Ah, Daughter." Pride spilled from Gwilym's tone. Tiny waves in the bowl increased, and his voice grew fainter. "The crystals washed up on Avalon after following the path of magic that ties the islands together. I had visions of caves embedded with crystals on your island. Pure and immense, I knew the crystal magic was meant to aid you in your fight against WindWraith. I knew you and your warrior belonged on that island, to that island.

"Eventually, other sorcerers from the future will discover the island to aid you in rebuilding our ancient bloodlines and carry on our magic."

"Do you mean people from Ryan's time?"

"I suspect so. The land of his time has been devastated, has it not?"

"I don't know for certain. I've been the one to open the doors of disclosure. He has yet to reciprocate." The water swirled, paling his face. "Hells fire," Morgan cursed under her breath. She cast another scrying spell, attempting to hold onto him longer. She touched the water and he disappeared.

Pain bolted through her head, and she rocked back on her heels. A small dose of air magic helped her focus, diminishing the pressure in her skull. Gwilym resurfaced, a ghostly visage tinted in amber.

Morgan rubbed her hands on her thighs, trying to quell her persistent agitation. "What other spells did you add to the amulets? You said a potent binding. I already know the magical binding is permanent. Can I annul the spell?"

"Not if you've fulfilled both steps and bound each other's magic. Do you wish to nullify it?" His voice grew dim. "The only way to sever a complete bond is death."

Morgan had already feared his answer. "What other spells?" she asked weakly, gripping her tunic's hem.

Father sputtered weakly. "I gather this information has not come to light in your head?"

"No, Father," she spat out in exasperation. "Can you just tell me now?"

"It is a soul mate binding spell. Once you've bound your magic, if you...make love, you will be bound in all ways. Unless either of you are tied to another, that is, or the spells reject one as unfit for the other."

Morgan gasped, blinked rapidly. "Did I transfer that spell to the amulets? I thought I had failed."

"Your magic is strong, love. You did not fail."

"Goddess save me from my own stupidity." She rolled her eyes.

"Don't you dare demean yourself. You set in motion Fate's chain of events."

Numb, she sat back on her heels. Before he vanished again, they quickly discussed the dissolution spell to break Ryan's tie to her magic and other bits of magic lore. Morgan's scrying spell dissipated, and she contemplated her father's parting words. Gwilym had added magic to the amulets to blend her spells properly and to ensure a linked path to the mystical island. In due time, Morgan must scatter the amulets from the sack her father had given her on Avalon in the sea and let Fate, with a dash of magic, take charge. The stones served to draw those sorcerers of ancient Druid blood, worthy of creating new life on the island. Each amulet matched another, binding their destined recipients at an indeterminate time in the future.

Mists would always hide the mystical island from time

and space. Once Ryan and Morgan destroyed WindWraith, those sorcerers destined to populate the island would find their way there once they met their greatest despair in a life that no longer had meaning. Or in their final moments before death claimed them.

Gwilym's colossal task crowded her mind. She stood on shaking legs and walked to the bed, wilting onto the rumpled furs. Ryan's lingering scent created a sharp jab in her chest. Morgan beat her fists on her thighs. No feeling sorry or yearning for him! For Goddess's sake, she was a powerful sorceress. What need had she for a dangerous Druid assassin who belonged to another?

Gwilym's words reverberated in her head defiantly. Prophecy and the binding pull of magic had carried them to the island. Despair. Fate. Desire. If the island offered its enchantments to others, Morgan and Ryan more than deserved them, since they'd sacrifice the greatest to make it happen. She refused to let duty get in the way of taking what she wanted. Not this time. Not ever again.

Ryan mentally kicked himself for not snagging his knife or spear. He plodded deep into the jungle on a narrow animal path from the northwestern side of the grotto. A creeping vine curled around his ankle and he mashed the purplish leaves into the ground with his heel. He halted to gather his bearings, swiped the sweat off his forehead before it dripped into his eyes.

He'd jogged off his fury, but a renewed surge juggled the iron balls hardening in his gut. Sluggish trickles of water lured him a few yards to the left where he found a mossy rivulet slithering through the undergrowth. He followed it until it widened into a freshwater stream. He drank his fill, washed the sweaty grime off his chest and arms.

"Damn it." He flung the twig he'd used to clean his teeth into a clump of pampas grass. "Every time I turn around...ah, screw it all." He lay down on a smooth patch of ground, pillowed his head on his arm.

Stars twinkled brilliantly in the indigo sky. Towering trees obscured the eastern moon from his position on the ground and granted a slice of the deepening night to the stars that called to his magic. Ryan intoned a silent calming spell, his body slurping up an infusion of fuel from the cosmos. Renewed turmoil quickly resurfaced in his head, tightened the vise on his heart. The calming spell was wasted and he blew out a heavy breath.

"Used and abused again. Damn it." Was he doomed forever to lead at the disposal of others? Never given a chance to call the shots in his life? He'd thought all that crap ended with his father's death. Thanks to the Fomorian horde that'd picked off his people one by one before the ultimate wave of desecration, his father's death merely signaled the beginning of a worse hell.

All Ryan had ever wanted to do was track and kill evil. Not lead. He'd craved power and danger, and protected his people well. So how could he not reconcile his abilities and wishes with what Morgan's father set him up to do? He just didn't want others manipulating him and playing tricks to get him to do what he did best. Confusion drummed a frenzied beat in his temples. *Hell, it's not like the old sorcerer could've sent me an email.* Ryan snorted. He thrust his arm over his eyes, blocking out the western moon moving into his field of vision.

Tepid air played over his bare chest, ruffled the T-shirt stuffed in the waistband of his shorts. Drowsy, he emptied his mind of all but one thought, the one person who never left him alone. After his stern admonition about not leaving the grotto, he was certain Morgan remained there in safety. He let that belief tempt him to relax.

No sooner had his eyes closed when he felt the infinitesimal swoosh of evil in the lazy breeze stirring the fern fronds by his head.

A suffocating presence engulfed Ryan, anchored him in hardening cement. The shroud undulated, changing from the density and heat of lava to the heavy, wet pressure of boiling syrup. Air whooshed out of his lungs and Ryan struggled to breathe. His eyelids glued shut, and he was unable to budge a muscle or touch his magic. Horror clawed at his heart, squeezed it until he thought the organ had burst. He heaved in air denser than tar. The smothering pressure around him expanded until it felt as if his bones were breaking, his internal organs imploding. Writhing on the mossy ground, he screamed from the choking, blazing agony tearing his insides to shreds. How had the creature breached the safety of night?

The terrifying thought of Morgan left alone on this island hell was the last thing his mind grasped before a solid inkiness filled every cavity of his body, stealing his last lick of air.

Ryan didn't return that night, or the next morning, worrying Morgan. Yesterday, he'd warned her not to leave the emerald grotto. Once they set foot away from their haven, they became easy prey for WindWraith, especially in daylight. Heedful of Ryan's cautions and from her own altercation with the Fomorian creature, Morgan feared leaving the sanctuary. Ryan wanted his privacy, and she'd grant it to him. She knew to the bottom of her soul that he'd never intentionally desert her for long. He seemed to know the island's perils, and was more than capable of defending himself. Regardless of the danger, if he didn't return by the next morning, she'd start searching for him.

Concentrating on her other problems, she sifted through her jumbled thoughts, searching for a plan to destroy WindWraith. After an hour of theorizing, she unearthed partial plans with negligible chances of success. Morgan rubbed her aching neck and raised her head.

"A solid plan will reveal itself when Fate decrees it." Confidence pushed out her distasteful thoughts of WindWraith, and she hoped a better idea might crop up while she went about her work.

Morgan tidied the cave, and then went out to explore the emerald grotto. To her delight, she found several herbs useful for healing and cooking. She labored over the course of the day, constructing a bamboo drying rack, using reeds to lash the pieces together. Then she hung cinnamon, ginger, cloves, and periwinkle plants above the fire to dry.

Fond childhood memories comforted her as she shimmied up coconut, papaya, and banana trees. She was thankful the boys on Avalon taught her how to climb trees after the...incident. Hastily, she reburied that particular nightmare. Her young friends had played tag with her, swinging from tree to tree as boys were wont, taking unfair advantage and winning every time until she learned to climb like them. And learned to use her air magic to launch herself from tree to tree.

Morgan hacked at bunches of fruit with her dagger, dropping them into piles on the ground. Once she returned to firm footing, she attacked the fruit with the eagerness of a starved orphan. Her stomach rippled in ecstasy with each bite. "You can eat your lousy dried fish, Ryan."

Morgan ate until her stomach felt ready to burst, then resumed exploring behind the caves. She stumbled upon a mass of freesias peeking out between ferns, and excitement sped up her heartbeat. Magenta and snowy blooms spread twice the size of freesias in Britain. The sweet, strong perfume permeated the air, reminding her wistfully of the scent she adored once she'd discovered it was her mother's favorite flower. Morgan gathered handfuls of the flowers and bundled them into the cave. She prepared freesia and vanilla soap for herself, clove and sandalwood soap for Ryan. A late afternoon bath left her smelling like a garden, almost making her forget the twisted fate that had turned her life upside down.

Sapphire night blanketed the grotto, and a sea of diamonds twinkled in the velvet sky. The northern moon shadowed the southern moon, casting twin reflections on the pool's black surface. A haunting melody of burping tree frogs and chirruping crickets spread over the tranquil air. The island music reminded her of summer nights on Avalon, and with a pensive frown, she walked into the caves.

The lonesome night compelled Morgan to dwell on unforgettable things. She lay on the furry bed, aching with an emptiness she knew not how to fulfill. Firelight bathed her with a tawny tint and stroked her skin in comforting warmth. Her hand curled around her amulet. Part of her yearned for her amulet to meld and flare together with Ryan's, uniting their magic. Would the spells also unite their hearts and souls as prophesied in the spell books? Morgan longed for the gift of love the shadow moon island promised them. They both deserved it after they accomplished the horrifying task forced upon them in another selfless act of duty. Their greatest act.

Yet, she knew it was wrong to think such thoughts unless Ryan renounced his other life and accepted his true future. It was wrong to think such thoughts when he may ultimately leave her or the final spell rejected them as soul mates.

CHAPTER 15

A clumpy presence stuffed the crevices in Ryan's skull. A fierce surge of power escaped him, and WindWraith ravenously slurped up his magic. Never had Ryan experienced complete incapacitation of his power. At the rate the bastard demon drained him, that time was a short jump to permanent midnight.

He sucked in shallow breaths of fetid air, focusing on the essence of evil enshrouding him. The air element was prominent and stronger in WindWraith than any other Fomorian he'd encountered. The increasing tangible mix of elemental fire stolen from Ryan and Morgan made an impact, though. Ryan concentrated on untangling the black magic thread by thread. It was easier to kill a powerful Fomorian if you weakened its magic before the killing blow. First, he needed to know what that magic encompassed.

"Why per chance do you believe it is your body I desire?" The feeble, broken voice of a man who hadn't spoken due to a long coma slinked into Ryan's mind.

Shock roared through him, causing him to bang his forehead against the wavering shroud. Fireworks exploded in his head, blinding him. Quickly, Ryan shuttered his thoughts, but he was unable to banish the sinister specter pressing into his brain in his moment of weakness.

"You can suck on me all you want, but you'll never be strong enough to possess me." Ryan's vocal cords had frozen, but he placed emphasis on the thought in his mind—using the same communication method the Fomorian practiced.

"You have the strength of two men, the strong body I desire. You are the body that will carry me as a king into realms I long to visit. Nevertheless, you are not the single source of food on this island. Nor the sole body," WindWraith replied, his voice smoother, an arrogant sneer now evident.

"What realms? Not that you can escape this island."

"Are you certain of your convictions? Mayhap you fail to grasp the methods to escape the island, eh? I have endured a millennium learning the secrets of this land, jarring the locks on the doors, absorbing the wellspring of elements. Waiting for one like you."

"So you've found a way to escape. You can pass through the crystal barrier. Big fucking deal. Where will you go? Back to Avalon? Like there's any magic left for you. You'll go back there, snack on the few remaining sorcerers, then die because you won't have enough magical energy to sustain your body." Fomorians didn't necessarily die without access to magic, but Ryan was baiting WindWraith, trying to get it to cough up its plans.

"Your delusions are amusing. I might fancy your enticing body after all." WindWraith brushed a hand over Ryan's growing erection, wrapping airy strands around it.

Ryan stifled a groan, forced his anger to freeze his arousal. False desire trickled into him as WindWraith stroked him up and down, hard and gentle, slow and fast. Ryan chomped down on his bottom lip, tasted blood in his mouth. He refused to give in to the son of a bitch.

"Your world calls to me," the Fomorian intoned. "I believe your people will welcome me with great fanfare when *you* return to them."

He sucked in thick air, choked on it, fought the blood pounding in his groin. WindWraith's relentless seduction continued, damaging every iota of his control. "You have no ties to my world. You'll never get there in my body."

The hand stilled on Ryan. "How do you suppose you wound up on my island? Do you not fancy that this land has ties to both your world and the world of your lovely sorceress?"

Ryan's heart thundered in his ears. The evil protrusion clamped tight around his erection. "How will you get to my world?" The thought came out strangled. Blood coated his mouth as he clenched his teeth and bit the inside of his cheek. He focused on the question, needing to know the answer so desperately he'd sacrifice his dignity for it.

A punch to Ryan's gut knocked what little air he managed to consume out in an explosion of breath. Pain jarred through his torso, and he began hyperventilating, sucking in tar thick air. He waded into the morass of oblivion, fighting off the darkness threatening to murder his last fragile breath. He concentrated on the magic seeping into him to slow his racing heart. The Fomorian's stinging, pulsating magic replaced his dwindling fire element. It leached into his power's wellspring, and he latched onto a nucleus of exposed magic, quickly registering WindWraith's magical footprint in his mind. From that trace, he knew without a ghost of a doubt that WindWraith wasn't strong enough to subsume him. Relief kick-started a stream of confident endorphins in his blood stream.

The coffin of water and lava squeezed him, entered his pores. His heartbeat slowed, skipped a beat, then another, nearly stopping. Ryan flirted with total incapacitation, painfully struggling to hold onto a smidgen of elemental magic regenerating inside him. An eternal void beckoned. Just as he was about to grasp it, his cement coffin began disintegrating. Sultry air zoomed over him, more refreshing than any cool sea breeze, and he heaved it in.

Flung awake, Ryan found himself lying on the grass

where he'd fallen asleep. The lingering effects of WindWraith's virtual rape left him weak, sore, soaked with sweat. The sun rising in the west burned the last stars to ash in the brightening sky.

Wind howled and screamed around Ryan. Cloudy wind blustered within the trees and plants, surrounding him. Not attempting to move closer, WindWraith encircled him from a few feet away, a ghostly form shaped like a freakish giant of a man. Ryan bounded up, steadying his rubbery legs against a tree trunk. He erected a thin fortress around himself. Drawing from the residual magic, he sprinkled starfire on WindWraith and lumbered through the splintering cloud into the jungle.

Strength returned to his legs and he eased into a slow jog. With quick glances over his shoulder, he saw small blobs of WindWraith following from a distance, forming into the shape of a wolf. The spotted wolf rushed up on him, growling and nipping at Ryan's heels, then backed off for another rush forward.

Ryan raced north of the grotto toward the eastern shore, the closest cliffside he knew held crystals buried within it. The area around that particular cliff had supplied his biggest score of brilliant gems now lining the grotto's perimeter.

The jungle lashed out at him, and he pummeled the dense overgrowth. WindWraith grew farther behind the closer Ryan approached the cliff. By the time he stumbled and rolled down the shallow end of the grassy, rocky facade, WindWraith had disappeared. Relief swept over his drained body. He continued his trek down the cliff until he spied the edges of a depression partially hidden by boulders and a hodgepodge of plants. Energy sizzled in the air, flooded him with adrenaline, and buzzed in his eardrums. He shoved aside palmettos and tall grasses to reveal a cave entrance. Faint light glowed around a bend in the dark tunnel, the source of the intense energy hissing around the opening.

"This wasn't here last week," he said, his throat scratchy. He sank onto the hard-packed dirt inside the cave opening, completely hidden from outside view. He slumped against the tunnel wall, his mind spinning in excited circles.

Rubbing his jaw, he studied the cave entrance. Did the demon cause the earthquake? Was that what he meant by jarring the island? Were the earthquakes breaking down the crystal barrier around the island?

"If he escapes, that SOB could annihilate every human and Fomorian left in the world." A slow grin spread Ryan's mouth wide. No question about it now. The demon was more powerful than any other he'd encountered. It had the vital magic Ryan could use against its brethren back home. He knew WindWraith was exactly what his people needed to shift the power to them.

The hardened lava felt almost pliable against his back compared to WindWraith's steely body bag in his vision. He squeezed his eyes closed, shutting out the horrifying nightmare, reveling in the disclosure the idiot Fomorian unleashed in Ryan's mind.

Once he investigated the cave, he needed to head back to the grotto. To Morgan. He wanted to see and touch her so badly. His body buzzed with the need to hold her, to make sure she was safe, alive, and real.

They had to take WindWraith down soon, or there was no telling what torture the creature had in store for them. "I need your magic, Morgan." Using his T-shirt, Ryan scrubbed the sweat and dirt off his face. "Once I draw that prick to me, I'll need her to weaken it and hold it in thrall while I..." He chomped down on his tongue. The first rule of demon hunting: keep your thoughts to yourself and shield your mind.

"Bring it on, bastard." He slammed his right fist into his left palm.

CHAPTER 16

"Mor-gan." A forlorn voice whispered in Morgan's head. "Morgan!" The urgent wail chased her out of a fitful sleep.

Jerking upright, she shivered in the damp cave. She slipped the fur around her and eased out of bed. Embers barely glowed in the fire ring, and she rekindled the fire, trying to identify the suffering and loneliness riding the air. Was Ryan hurt? WindWraith playing games? A dream or her Sight? It was difficult to discern on this island.

Morgan repacked food and medicinal herbs in her satchel. Her fingers grazed the amulet buried on the bottom. She drew the pendant out, feathered her fingers along the silver and leather braid. A twin to Ryan's amulet, it had identical rune marks, the amethyst created from the same cut and dye. She touched her lips to the stone, and then slung the cord around her neck, tucking it beneath her tunic. "You're never coming off. I can't lose you." The pendant represented hope.

In long-legged strides, she left the cave, buckling her dagger belt around her waist. She listened intently for the voice on the air, discarding the various sounds of the awakening jungle. Determined, she jogged along the grassy rim of the pond to the grotto's hidden doorway, the morning's dew not getting a chance to dampen her boots.

"Hello." The childlike voice floated like a butterfly in her head.

Hairs rose on the back of Morgan's neck. Was a child on the island? Fighting branches and brambles, she nudged through the obscure opening to the grotto, shoving her way to the other side. Absently, she dashed at leaves stuck in her braided hair. Her fear of the woods and charging animals left a vague jitter in her belly.

The frightened voice called again. Hesitating no longer, she raced into the jungle toward the sound, barely aware of the path the jungle cleared for her, easing her passage. The awakening island's life force energized her blood, fed her sure steps into the woodsy depths.

Muggy air grew more oppressive the farther into the jungle she ran, pungent and syrupy on her tongue. Acrid grasses, mosses, and a bevy of floral fragrances besieged Morgan's nose. A mix of ripened pineapple and bananas set her stomach to growling. The ripe vegetation and the land beneath her feet felt alive, thriving with vitality and magic. Latent earthy energy pervaded the air. The ground vibrated with it. Flora and fauna swayed rhythmically. Her elemental powers had heightened and her bizarre ties to the sentient island were strengthening. Regardless, from the moment she left the protective grotto, she felt WindWraith steal her magic, drip by drip.

Morgan halted and rubbed her arms. Despite the morning's growing heat, cool island power crept beneath her skin, chipped away at her fear. Did she really derive power from the island, or did someone or something play tricks upon her? She had no desire to test it with magic and alert WindWraith. Peacefulness settled over her, her taut muscles relaxing as she rushed forward, listening intently for the beckoning voice.

Chattering animals distracted her. Parrots trilled in answer, warning her. Morgan saw no living beings, only the dynamic, multihued jungle. She hopped across a narrow brook. Clear water bubbled over smooth river stones before it switchbacked deeper into the jungle. Sweat already trickled down her temples. The pesky raven pair circled overhead, cawing at her as if to warn her back to the grotto.

Morgan froze and clasped her throat. Musty soil and fauna aromas created mayhem with her senses. An animal chittered to her left, and she spun toward it. A monkey screeched to her right. A large animal crashed in the bushes and howled behind her. She whirled to face it. Nothing. Sounds encompassed her, taunting, beguiling. Fear clawed at her, ratcheting up the drumming of her heart against her ribcage. Mentally reaching for her powers, she prepared to unleash it at the least provocation.

"Hello! Morgan!" the voice cried to her left.

Cold perspiration coated her skin. She continued forward, pushing aside thick layers of fronds and vines, still unable to drive a hole through the jungle maze. Circling the small enclosure, she tried to force an opening in the greenery from one spot to another, but the jungle trapped her. Even the path that led her to the clearing had disappeared into an impenetrable wall of vegetation. Overwhelming thoughts paralyzed her as she stood stone still in the center of her verdant cage.

The island's power fed her magic, oozed energy into her core. Her magic became a living entity, without her drawing upon it. Exhilaration pumped through her, and she tussled with air and earthen energy that pleaded for liberation. Desperate, she used her powers to demolish her fear and focused on the new earthen energy churning into her elemental magic. Could she use it to break out of her jungle prison?

An animal roared, a strangled lion sound, on the other side of her prison. So near, she smelled the beast's odor, thick and sour on the stagnant air. It smashed down bushes trying to tear apart the living green barricade. Although she sensed its manic hunger, it remained invisible to her.

Old nightmares escaped the closed pockets of her mind. The scars on her stomach stung in remembrance. The animal rammed the hedges hard and fast. It stopped and bellowed its anger, and Morgan feared it gauged its strength to tear the hedge into slivers. Again, the beast butted into the enclosure. Plants ripped from the ground and the animal uprooted a sapling.

Her heart roaring in her ears, she scanned her cage for a tree to climb if needed. "Hells fire," she whispered. The sky held no place to hide either.

She yanked out her dagger and readied it in her right hand. The animal's vicious growls and booming crashes into the fence seized hold of Morgan's fear. Immobilized, she felt another fresh flush of earthy magic float up from the ground. A beefy, thorny vine fluttered and popped free of the hedge near the spot the animal battered. Morgan held out her left hand and sent a billow of air toward the vine. Another vine snaked out of the ground and joined the first one. The vines slithered over the hedge. The creature's angry roars turned into squeals of pain. Eyes closed, Morgan envisioned the vines squeezing the beast, thorns tearing into its flesh. Blood fed the vines and they roped the animal into submission, tying it to thick branches along the green fence.

Stuffing her dagger into its sheath, Morgan shot a cord of invisible fire at the shaking barrier. An earsplitting bellow of agony stormed the air, sending the remaining nearby animals scrambling deep into the jungle and birds flapping high into the sky. Mewls erupted from the beast and it thudded to the ground, snapping dried limbs beneath its body.

"Morgan!" Ryan hollered.

"Ryan?" Her liquid knees deposited her onto the trampled grass.

"Stay put." Anxiety muffled his voice.

Morgan sat on her heels, drawing deeply of the calming sea breeze now refreshing the jungle. Her heart stuttered with each inhale. *Calm yourself. You're safe.*

The jungle receded like waves off a rocky beach. Seconds later, Ryan emerged between two palmettos. He stopped beside the dead creature, now visible as the jungle gave way. The thorny vines unwrapped around the animal and snaked into the undergrowth, the ground soaking up the crimson drops. She glanced with sick interest at the grotesque animal, dimly wondering if they could make use of its hide, or if she even wanted to.

"Holy mother of the Gods." Ryan stared at the strange gray-blue beast. He walked to her in what seemed like slow motion. Kneeling, he gathered her close. "Are you okay?"

A sob climbed up her throat and she managed to nod.

Ryan examined her face. He spared her a second to witness the concern wrinkling his brow before his mouth claimed hers. He kissed her hard, his tongue demanding, his touch sending tingles across her scalp. He folded her into his arms, his body consuming her, a balm to her overwrought sensibilities. Their kiss gentled and Ryan eased away, leaving an airless fire smoldering inside her.

He smiled wide, cupping her face in his large hands. "You scared me to death." His voice hitched. "I thought you were a goner when I saw that beast."

"I'm well." Morgan tightened her arms around his waist, her heart swelling.

"Did you kill it?" Ryan stroked her hair, his fingers snagging in her braid.

She chewed on her bottom lip. "I used magic."

"I didn't feel it, and I was just outside that...whatever the hell jungle thing that surrounded you." He surveyed the area, his lips twitching.

"It felt like a wealth of magic, but I only used a thimbleful." She sighed against his chest, glad that he'd returned to her safely. "I feel alive, overflowing with power."

Ryan pulled her up with him as he gained his footing. "It's the island."

"What do you mean?" She narrowed her eyes at the nearest reaches of the jungle.

"I'll tell you later." He dropped his arms and stepped toward the dead beast.

Panic crept into her. "Ryan!" She grabbed at his arm. "Don't leave me."

He twined his fingers in hers, molding her against his side. "I'll never leave you like that again."

Ryan slipped his other hand to the side of her neck and kissed her softly. His touch dripped a drugging need into her middle, and his kiss was a long, slow possession, leaving her gasping for more, for a promise. She felt an awakened response deep within, her promise giving way to the hypnotic grin on Ryan's face as he drew apart.

Breathless, she smiled at him shyly. "That's not what I meant."

He chuckled. "I know. I have so much to tell you, to show you." He tugged her braid teasingly. "First, we need to work on your fear of the jungle."

"Was it that obvious?"

Ryan crooked his thumb over his shoulder in the direction of the dead animal. "Was that what scared you when you flew off the cliff?"

Grimacing, she glanced at the bluish, hairless animal, a bizarre cross between a bear and a lion. She rubbed her chafing scars. "I believe so."

"I've been hunting that bastard for weeks. It's been chasing off other animals, making it harder to hunt fresh game. It killed a winged horse past those trees." Ryan pointed at a copse of small trees behind a cache of lava rocks.

"A winged horse?" Morgan blinked rapidly. "Are there others?"

"A small herd lives on a meadow up island."

"I must see them one day."

"You will." Ryan's arm tightened around her waist, squeezing out her residual fear.

Her gaze lingered on the carcass, darting off to survey the jungle that saved her. "If we live long enough," she whispered. "Thank you." She stretched up on her toes and kissed his cheek.

"For what?" He shrugged. "You did okay on your own."

"I didn't hear the animal stalking me." She shuddered. "Your magic made the jungle protect me."

The steely muscles of his body quivered against hers. "That wasn't your magic?"

"What?" Morgan swiped a hand over her damp upper lip. "It wasn't yours?"

Ryan swept his arm in the air. "Did you feel threatened by the jungle?"

She reflected upon the incident, forced herself to search beyond her normal fear of the woods. "No." Eyes wide, she held his gaze as though her life depended on it. She wasn't sure how to explain her impressions to Ryan since she didn't understand what they meant. "When I left the grotto, I felt as if the jungle were alive, almost human. It seems to enhance my powers. I feel a part of it."

Ryan pressed a kiss to her forehead. "You're connected to this island. It changed the moment you arrived here. I felt it then, and it increases every day."

CHAPTER 17

Subtle and not so subtle changes had occurred since the day Ryan washed ashore, even more so since Morgan had arrived. He'd never forget the storm that tossed him up for dead on the mystical island, a land so vastly different from the continent he'd left behind. One bleak, gray moon had drooped in the northern sky in the middle of that fateful afternoon. The next morning, the moon radiated vibrant violet light. The following night, a second violet-gray moon appeared in the southern sky. The moons hadn't changed in two weeks. One day stretched into another, and he'd noticed formerly dead plants and trees leafing out with new growth, flowering plants breaking out in dozens of long-lasting blooms. Fruit ripened sweeter, more plentiful. Animals appeared more animated, livelier, as if preparing for a zoo party.

The day before Morgan appeared, hundreds of lightning bolts flashed across the sky. The moons and the cloudless sky deepened. The sun waned but didn't disappear. Salty ocean winds carried strong magic, purifying the air. Then Morgan appeared. Pure. Powerful. Beautiful. So alluring.

The island awakened with Ryan's arrival. It flourished for Morgan.

He shook off his puzzlement. Morgan opened her mouth to protest, but he hushed her with a finger over her lips. "The jungle protected you. Not me."

"Holy—" Morgan closed her eyes. "It's not my skewed

perception."

He cherished the feel of her in his arms, loved the extra rush of magic merging with his. While he was gone, he'd missed her like air, yearned for her like water to quench a post-apocalyptic thirst. His power had crawled sluggishly without her near. As much as he wanted to stand there and hold her, common sense prevailed. "Let's get out of here."

She held her ground, hand on her dagger hilt. "No. Wait."

Ryan clasped her hand in his. "I'll give you a lesson in fighting your fear. Then someday you can tell me why you're afraid of the woods."

She squeezed his hand. "Thank you. It's more than that, though. Something drew me here. I don't believe it was you or the jungle."

The ravens squawked at each other in a red oak above their heads. One bird swooped down and landed on the dead animal's side. It pecked at the carcass, not at all intimidated by them standing near it. The large bird twirled its head, bloodied blue skin dangling defiantly from its beak. High in the oak, its mate cackled, seeming to scold the fearless one.

Ryan surveyed the jungle, deriving no tangible or magical evidence of Morgan's compulsory presence. He didn't sense WindWraith nearby either, and simply added one more item to the list of dangers on the mysterious island. Shrugging, he turned to her. "I don't think you have anything to worry about in this jungle. Not after what just happened. But fear is mostly in your head." Ryan tapped his index finger on her forehead. "Whenever you're afraid, stop and count to five slowly, take deep breaths, concentrate on the beauty around you. Think positive things." He laid his hand on her heart. The even thrum against his palm matched his own pulse. "Think of the magic you possess. You're stronger than any sorceress I've ever met."

His thumb caressed the side of her breast, his hand sliding down to her waist. Electricity jetted up his arm from the contact through her thin top. "Hell, I should be afraid of you." He chuckled.

She covered his hand with hers and pressed it to her heart again. "Thank you."

Lifting her hand to his lips, he pressed a kiss on the inside of her wrist. Terror had shot straight into his heart when he spied that huge beast bearing down upon her and the jungle sealing her in. He'd destroy any man, beast, or gods-forsaken island if a freckle on her face got hurt. He didn't think he could bear never seeing or touching her again.

Only half-alive without her, Ryan now recognized the persistent emptiness within him. The first moment he laid eyes upon Morgan, touched her, inhaled her, he knew she was the heart of the Druids, possibly the heart of his heart. She'd already bitten so deeply into his soul he never wanted to let her go. He'd protect her to the death. And he sure as hell wasn't leaving the island without her.

The brilliant sun neared its pinnacle, promising another roasting day. They rested for a brief time on a mound of silvery-green grass beneath an awning of oak branches. A soft breeze fluttered the trees and bushes, blowing the humidity into the jungle depths, soothing their overheated skin.

Curiosity warred with Ryan's overwhelming thoughts. "What put those scars on your stomach?" Anger chilled his voice knowing that something had hurt her. "Looks like a large cat or bear clawed you."

Morgan's lips compressed, her small fingers combed the grass. "When I was a child of six, my father went traveling, and he left me in the care of my aunt. My cousins and I were playing hide and seek in the forest and I got lost."

Ryan eased her between his legs, and she settled her back against his chest. He traced the rigid lines beneath her blouse.

"I couldn't find my way home. Eventually, my cousins gave up trying to find me and left to get help. Already scared out of my wits, I heard a crash in the bushes, and I ran blind. An animal stalked me. I didn't see it, but I heard it, felt it." She swallowed hard. "Twilight fell and I found a hollowed out log to hide in." Ryan kissed the top of her head and rested his chin on her silky hair. "I heard the roar of a large wildcat. I was terrified. I—"

He burned with the need to wreak vengeance for her. "Don't relive anymore." Ryan smoothed his hand over her stomach.

"It's all right." Morgan snuggled into him and patted his arm. "That was when my dormant air magic emerged for the first time. For hours, the cat tried to claw his way into my burrow, scratching me in its efforts. My unruly air magic tricked it, and the cat darted off hunting invisible prey." She gave a wry chuckle. "A search party found me in the morning, terrified and hungry."

"I'm sorry." Ryan wedged her closer, tightening his legs around her. She leaned her head on his shoulder. A temperate breeze ruffled her hair across his face, and he buried his nose in the crisp floral-vanilla fragrance.

"On the way home with the search party, I saw the raven pair for the first time. They never seem to leave me, always there whenever a significant event occurs in my life."

"Nasty featherheads. I'm sure it's just a coincidence."

"I disagree. I believe they're my totem animal, my lucky charm of sorts." Her fingertips danced along his arm. "There are those who believe my totem is a cat and that I'm a cat shifter because I bear its mark."

Ryan laughed. "And they think you possess the cat's

power and will overcome those who are weaker."

"Yes, that's exactly what they think! That's why I hide the scars, for the most part."

"Sweetheart, you had a traumatic experience, but you aren't a lioness or a tiger." Ryan's chuckle vibrated against her head as he kissed her. "At least not that I've experienced." He growled low in his throat and teasingly licked her neck.

She squirmed in his arms. "Do the marks intimidate you?"

"They make me want to lick your stomach." He kissed her ear lobe, blazing heat across her shoulders.

Morgan shook against him with a start, both hands clutching his forearm. "Did you hear that?" She wrenched out of his arms and jumped up, scanning the small glade.

Fire magic boiled up within him. "What?" He gained his feet, wrapping the straps of her satchel in his hand to use as a weapon.

"Someone's out there calling me. You didn't hear it?" She ran toward a slim path fading into the jungle.

"Nothing's there." Ryan reached for her, but she eluded his grasp. "We've wasted too much time already."

"No!" She threw up her hands, dropped them onto her hips. "It's hurt."

"Is that why you left the grotto?"

"I thought it might be you at first, but I distinctly heard a child's voice."

She strode into the jungle. Ryan caught up behind her, grabbed her hips to pull her back. "Might be a trap."

She shook her head, her glossy black braid swinging across her back. "I don't think so. Can you hear it?"

Birds shrieked, monkeys chattered, and small animals scurried in the underbrush. "I don't hear anything unusual." Unease crept up his backside like a slow crawl of fire ants. The air suddenly stilled, and his breathing eclipsed the jungle noises. Then he heard it, a muted whinny to their right. He pushed in front of Morgan and led the way to a low rise of lava rocks. Skirting the pile, he halted in another small clearing.

A tiny winged horse, its legs folded beneath it, nestled in a fortress of boulders surrounding a patch of trampled ground cover. The foal trembled, ears flattened against its head, wings scrunched to its sides. Ryan drew near its haunches and it growled. Morgan shoved him out of the way in her hurry to reach the foal.

"Don't go near it! The winged horses are mean beasts."

She snorted. "He's just a baby." She crouched and stretched her hand toward the black foal.

The winged horse scrambled toward her and buried its head in her lap. Ryan snorted in disbelief. Morgan lifted her head, her smile worth all the stars in the midnight sky. Her face gleamed with a new mother's joy. He flogged down his apprehension and watched her in awe.

"That must have been his mother you saw." Sadness swam in her eyes. "Oh, dear. That creature killed his mother when she protected the foal. Weakened from birthing, she could not escape."

Ryan's eyebrows slid up his forehead. "You speak to animals, too?"

"The foal and I seem to share a mind link." She smoothed the baby horse's charcoal hued mane and scratched behind its tiny fluttering ears. "This island does strange things to my magic."

"A psychic connection. Now what?" Ryan rolled his eyes. "Little raven, you're freaking me out."

An eerie, shrill whistle soared above the busy jungle music. The area dimmed as though a cloud sailed across the sun. Except Ryan hadn't seen one cloud the whole time he'd existed on the island. The darkening jungle started to blot out the clear skies.

Damn. "WindWraith's out there, Morgan." He reached for her hand. The winged horse shrank away and growled at him. "Let's go."

"We can't leave him here." Wrapping her arms around the foal's midriff, she tried to boost it up on its spindly legs.

Ryan gently eased her away and coaxed the animal to its feet. The foal hissed at him and edged against the boulders. After a few attempts, he got it to stand on its stick-thin legs, but its knees wobbled and buckled. The winged horse lifted its head with the most incredible dismay on its face. It grunted in frustration, and a white star-shaped patch on its forehead wrinkled.

Morgan rubbed the foal's head. "I'll use a bit of shielded restorative magic," she announced.

Without waiting for Ryan's response, light streamed thinly from her index finger. A palpable air current nudged the foal's belly, swirled around its haunches. The glow disappeared, and the animal stood stable on all four legs. Tail swishing, it took a few tentative steps, pranced, testing out its dexterity.

Ryan gave her an appraising look. "Close your magic off."

She smiled grimly. "I did."

He grabbed her hand and led the way, the foal trotting alongside Morgan. They headed toward the grotto, retracing her original path. Silent, she remained as close to Ryan as possible, one hand on the winged horse's neck.

A warm wind picked up, sweeping leaves and sticks into the air like tiny lost souls. Noon sunshine penetrating the tree cover dulled into the gloom of sundown. The Fomorian grew and expanded with the energy it zapped from them every moment they were exposed to its invisible tentacles. If what WindWraith had said in his nightmare was true, the island also fed it. If true, what was the island doing to Morgan? A band squeezed Ryan's chest.

They plodded forward, slowed by the encroaching jungle. Vines, living ropes of magic, twined and unwound around their arms and legs. The jungle tumbled into darkness to rival dusk by the time the first airstream of evilness prodded their backs.

Morgan scooted between two palms into another small meadow. "Will the jungle protect us?" The ominous emerald mass absorbed the colors of the trees and bushes. The jungle fell behind in shadows.

"Don't count on it. We'll need our magic."

A risk they'd have to take. It opened the door for WindWraith to suck out more power or possibly consume one of them completely if it had gained sufficient strength.

They guided the foal into a thicket, hiding it with fronds. Morgan patted its head. "Baby, stay here." She clasped his hand, her palm damp and shaking. "What shall we do?"

They had to raise their voices to hear over the creaking and whirling of increasing wind in the trees. Palm fronds rasped together. Leaves, dead and alive, swirled thick as a blizzard.

Ryan enclosed them in a shield until they were ready for defense. "I'm working on it," he yelled.

Morgan rose on her toes, her lips grazing his ear. "What kind of power do you possess? Can we combine our magic?"

He realized he'd never told her the extent of his magic. Or what he intended to do with it. How could he tell Morgan he didn't want the powerful, ancient Fomorian destroyed?

CHAPTER 18

Morgan sensed Ryan's hesitation in the muscle twitch under her hand. He tucked her into his side, his mouth at her ear.

"Elemental fire and," he hesitated, his nervous expression stilled and grew calculating, "ether."

Starfire? Something invisible crawled across her skin. No one possessed ether magic any longer, not even in her time. *Oh Goddess!* Ancient Druid blood ran through his veins, whether he knew it or not. Only an Ancient had the power to wield ether. Yet, she sensed he held something back, a puzzling innate ability within his elemental magic.

They traded bold, assessing stares, ignoring the dissonant noise raining upon them. Ryan's eyebrow peaked in a questioning slant.

"I command fire, air, and earth magic," she said in his ear, knowing her combination of elemental magic was nearly as rare as his ether.

Ryan's jaw dropped, and he rasped his fingers over his chin thoughtfully. At least they could combine their firepower to escape.

WindWraith wavered in a smoky cloud, alternately expanding and diminishing. The ghostly form encased them entirely. Venomous depravity plagued the air outside Ryan's barrier. Trees and vegetation undulated eerily in the chaotic wind. Vines shrank away, rolled into balls. Flowers closed and hid behind leaves. The island's intangible angst seeped into her bones. The winged foal whispered his fright in her mind. Evil penetrated through tiny holes in their cocoon, sipping air from the bubble.

"It has a strange mix of powers for a Fomorian, even if it is part Druid," Ryan said. "Fomorians in my time can shift into or possess bodies, but I've never seen a shadow-shifter like this."

"It has lived many years to develop such powers." An invisible spark struck Morgan's leg. "Now, Ryan!" Her fingernails jabbed his arm. "It's breaching the shield. Let's start with fire until we determine what it can do."

His eyes were ocean cool against his serene angular face, but his muscles coiled for a fight. The dragon tattoo tensed on his straining biceps.

"I'll have to dissolve the shield for maximum contact, then blast up with fire. You follow with a second blast," he shouted above the roar of seething trees and the shrill keening of the heaving cloud. "Then we blast together. Shut down your magic after each shot. Give it no opening to forge a bond."

She released his arm, readying her power. Malevolence thickened the air inside their fortress. More invisible sparks flew at Morgan, concentrating foremost on her, seeming to ignore Ryan.

Ryan's hair lifted like spider webs floating in the air. He dropped his invisible wall and thrust his arms toward heaven. A white ball turned to golden fire on his palm and exploded from his fingertips. He waved his arms in circles, encompassing the enormous evil shadow in his magic. Bullet-sized holes split WindWraith's mass where Ryan's scorching fire struck. The Fomorian howled, a deafening hurricane, determined to drown out the island's myriad sounds. The dense shadow bore down upon them. Air scraped Morgan's throat with every inhale.

Ryan flexed his muscles, preparing his inner body for

another onslaught. "Now!" Diffuse blue magic shimmered off him.

Morgan drew forth fire. Thrusting out her arms, she twirled her index fingers in circles, shooting one invisible bolt after another of damaging magic. They blasted alternating waves of exploding fire at the evil blob.

WindWraith splintered as if torn apart by wild beasts. Its bloodcurdling screams resonated throughout the jungle. Gale force wind knocked Morgan on top of a trampled fern, interrupting her concentration. She rammed shut her external door of magic but she wasn't quick enough.

A chunky black arm wrapped about her, separating her from Ryan, from the island. An invisible rope shackled her wrists. She cried out, but the sound died inside her. Horror paralyzed her.

Ryan shot spheres of fiery magic at the sundered parts of the evil shadow. Each mottled bit of evil detonated into white puffs and drifted away until the specks disappeared. He dropped to his knees before her shadowy prison. His lips moved, but the wind whipped his words away. Morgan no longer felt the island, and her links to Ryan and the foal had been severed. WindWraith's remains concentrated on her, arrogantly discarding additional threats from Ryan.

The Fomorian touched her like a familiar lover. Tongues of opaque air picked apart her tunic and leggings, and she was unable to raise a finger to stop it. WindWraith's seduction returned her to a state of arousal, preying on her memories of Ryan as though it held none of its own. She was defenseless to prevent her garments from disintegrating into useless threads, carried away on the malicious winds.

Ryan grabbed at the pulsating gray mass, yanking his hand away. His magic was useless without risking harm to her. She fought the seduction, tried to concentrate on escape. Light and shadows penetrated the gray void and

Ryan disappeared from view. She no longer felt her heart beating. All feelings but one left her body numb, although part of her mind remained alert. An indistinct windswept voice infiltrated her head, crammed it with ancient images, pagan rituals, and magic spells.

Air spiraled memories within her mind. Water swished ancient magic into the hurricane. Earth powers erupted, capturing the air and water greedily into a cauldron of information. The three elements swirled chaotically in Morgan's brain, bereft of one missing element. Fire.

WindWraith nipped her bare skin with a lover's mouth, fueling urges she battled. Her breasts tingled and her nipples ached. A smooth, fingerless hand tickled her scars, glided along her quivering stomach toward her thighs. Morgan thrashed on the ground, infuriated with her body's reaction to this foul creature of darkness, unable to end the maddening hunger fueling her blood. The Fomorian forced memories of Ryan caressing her to the front of her mind. It used those images against her, tricking her body. Confusion pounded in her head. She tried to push at the mass, but her limbs refused to move.

A male voice filled her mind, raspy with age, thick with conceit. "I once loved a powerful sorceress much like you," the voice held the distinct British accent from her land.

Avalon's Shadow. Talking telepathically? Morgan's throat closed on the words begging to tumble out.

"She possessed the fire magic that complimented mine. We were to wed and bind our magic in a powerful alliance. A perfect union. We planned to conquer the world together. Intended to love one another far into the Afterlife." His voice grew regretful. "Alas, she kept great secrets, and hid an element of magic, which she knew could destroy me if we were to mate and fulfill the binding. In the end, her lies and betrayals, her promise to her coven to steal my magic and kill me to increase her own strength, worked to destroy us both."

WindWraith's agitation pressed on Morgan's senses in a morass of anger, sadness, and guilt. Empathizing with his agitation, she finally found her voice. "Why did you want her after learning of her duplicity?" The pressure eased up, although WindWraith continued to caress her body. "She didn't deserve your magnificence."

A pleasurable sigh escaped him, almost as if he were grateful for Morgan's interest, preening for her compliment. "I loved her beyond reason. I long desired her for my wife. Our magic completed each other in ways no other could. We epitomized the traditional roles of the ruling High Priest and High Priestess. We had it all in our midst. Love. Honor. Happiness. Duty. Peace and riches. A multitude of subjects across the lands who loved us, begged for our union to return joy and prosperity to their dismal lives."

An air strap tightened around Morgan's throat as if she were the traitorous woman of whom WindWraith spoke. She gasped for oily air, gagged on the evilness clogging her throat. The band loosened and WindWraith continued.

"The night before our nuptials, she drugged me. The whore seduced me, instigating the binding ritual. My precious lover filled my body with her dark magic. Stealing the night from me, forcing me to crave sunlight in order to cleanse her impurities from my body just to live another day. Until the dark magic congealed again and the cycle began anew." WindWraith made an odd guttural scream of rage. "Little did I know until the moment of her betrayal that she possessed the one element unable to meld with my magic. She lied to our subjects, told them that *I* came from the wrong line of Druids. *I* sought to destroy them if allowed to live. She was the one spawned from a Sluagh mix, the foulest, manipulative demons of the dead. Even the Underworld rejected the vile creatures. She wanted to feed upon my magic to make her the most powerful being alive."

WindWraith's high-pitched snickers pelted Morgan's mind. "Alas, her plans failed. During the binding, my body cleansed her darkness, diluted her taint. Before I killed the betraying hag, I drew out the Sluagh bitch's magic and made it my own breed of power."

WindWraith's seduction magnified and his caresses became more intimate. Unable to halt her ecstasy, she cried out and writhed on her bed of ice. Visions of its former human body making love to a voluptuous red-haired sorceress stuffed her mind. Spread eagle, the Sluagh's wrists were tied to the posts of a massive sumptuous bed while WindWraith assaulted her naked body in ways Morgan had never seen. Cringing at the brutality, she tried to shutter her mind to the visions, but the door refused to budge.

"After I imprisoned her, I spent several fortnights loving her mind, body, and soul. Filling her with my seed over and over, making her beg for it time and again. Making her beg for a spoonful of magic to fill the empty cavities beneath her skin and bones. Forcing her to understand the error of her selfish ways. Not long afterward, her belly swelled with my child, and she vowed to be a good mother, truly promised to rule by my side, to obey me without abandon. The day she told me she loved me, and meant it, was her last day walking the earth."

Morgan watched the tortuous evisceration of the Sluagh, closing her mind's eye to the sickening slaughter. "What...what happened to the baby?" she gasped out.

"The boy lived." Pride filled WindWraith's voice. "My child is the most powerful of his kind on Earth. He goes by the name of Alasdar. My beloved son awaits me in a land prepared for my return."

Morgan's mind revolted as air tried to spread her legs apart. WindWraith probed her mind, body, and soul, searching for a way inside all three. The treacherous tale sent shockwaves through her head. One tiny seed of doubt floated in her consciousness, despite her unbearable rapture. She fixated on that seed, grew it, and sick revulsion blackened it.

Another seedling bloomed. A chink spread in her mind, separate from her brain's pleasure center. A second placating voice spoke to her, but she didn't understand the words. She stopped her delirious thrashing and focused on the calming influence, finally able to ignore WindWraith's relentless seduction.

Pure, radiant energy fused with her magic. The unfamiliar prickly power of stars. Elusive ether. Ryan's starfire.

Another pod of power burst within her, this time an earthy energy. Morgan's Druid senses instinctively raced to work with the allies, letting the two gifts of power fuse together. Combined energy expanded to mammoth proportions, ready to burst forth. The potency sizzled in her blood. She braided the three cords of power together, her intangible fingers numb and uncooperative. *Hurry, hurry!* she wailed silently.

Coarse tendrils of fog caressed her, hardening into a thick rod rubbing against her thigh, not taking further liberties. False waves of ecstasy throbbed through her even as she felt like she was crawling out of her skin. Fighting it, Morgan lost her concentration on the magic meld. The braid started unraveling, but ether rushed in and stopped it from breaking apart completely. A sharp stab in Morgan's chest returned her to her desperate task.

Without touching her further, but manipulating her mind, WindWraith continued to drag her into its false seduction. She used everything at her disposal to fight the coercion. Finally, the earth, ether, and her tangible combination of elements became one. An ocean of exhilaration and magic crested inside her.

Morgan flung out her arms, her constraints dissolving into a puddle of bitter nothingness. Wicked magic discharged from her, deadly in its intensity. Brilliant azure energy ruptured outward, shattering her evil shroud.

WindWraith disintegrated, scraggly black particles blowing away on a silent, rank wind. The acidic stench of evil assailed Morgan's nostrils. Her back bowed, her arms sagged to her sides. A massive energy surge evacuated from her body, ripping a shriek from her throat. Tortuous fire tore through her empty shell. She crawled into herself and waited for the emptiness to fill up and the pain to retreat.

"Be wary of those created from ether." An airy malignant laugh slithered into her mind.

Strong arms gathered her close, and she floated into the darkness of welcoming stars.

CHAPTER 19

Ryan gathered Morgan close, alarmed by her deathly face and chilled body. Pale light dripped from her fingertips, melted into the ground. Had his ether been too much? He rested two fingers on her neck. Her pulse beat slow but steady. Ryan heaved out a relieved breath, even though it took every ounce of self-control from destroying everything in sight.

Harmless slivers of WindWraith floated above him, pinging him like sodden snowflakes. Ignoring the disintegrating onslaught, he pressed his mouth to Morgan's in a gentle kiss. For the first time in his life, he wished he possessed his brother's empathic healing skills. Using his bond to Morgan and his tracking abilities, he swept his senses inside and outside her body. No existence of evil appeared to reside within her. The weight crushing his chest let up, and he settled her lifeless body on a stretch of mashed grass. He tugged off his T-shirt and slipped it over her shoulders poncho-style.

On unsteady legs, he lifted her in his arms. Ryan battled the relentless jungle and his lagging energy on his trek to the grotto. Halfway there, something furry bumped his legs and rage coiled in his gut. He twisted around, primed to annihilate the threat, and stumbled over the winged foal. Morgan nearly slipped from him, and his arm muscles burned as they joggled against her weight. A gnarled tree trunk took his weight.

"Move it," he grumbled as he stabilized his balance.

Unperturbed, the little beast nosed Morgan's leg, whickering fraily. Barring its teeth and flattening its ears, the foal's gold-flecked eyes rounded at Ryan. A pathetic growl rose in its throat.

"You little shit." Ryan nudged his hip into the horse. He resumed his hike, repeatedly shoving the foal into the bushes. "Get out of my way." Any other day, he'd laugh at the animal's weird loyalty to Morgan. But not when the woman he was falling for, his salvation, was possibly on the edge of death in his arms. The foal's devotion granted him the momentum he sorely lacked.

By the time he reached the caves, his arm muscles burned with tension. Although he'd carry Morgan to the ends of time, he was relieved to settle her onto the lined sleeping ledge. Careful not to touch her amulet, he removed it from around her neck. He covered her with the fur and combed her disheveled hair away from her pasty face.

"Morgan," he whispered, brushing his lips over her mouth, wishing to breathe life into her. "Come back to me." Tired and frustrated, he stared at her stuffed bag on the ground. What healing herbs might help? He racked his brain trying to remember anything useful his brother might have told him about his potions. Since healing wasn't his forte, he never retained the knowledge.

"Damn it!" He rubbed his neck, stomped over to his pile of clothes.

Ryan dunked a piece of torn shirt in the crude container collecting water trickling down the granite walls. Holding the cloth against her cold forehead, he quickly realized his mistake. Flinging the rag away, he snarled low in his throat. "She needs warmth, idiot."

It only took a few moments to stoke the fire and set several oak logs ablaze. As his gaze bounced from the drying rack to the tidy stores of fruit, he whistled in awe.

"You've been busy, little raven."

Herbs and flowers hung upside down from a drying rack near the fire. Tidy nooks along the walls held their respective belongings. He found replenished food and drink supplies in the coolest crevice he'd already walled off with uneven planks for a roughed-in cooler. Though not exactly hungry, he needed fuel to rebuild both his physical and magical energy. He ate some dried meat and fresh pineapples. The cool coconut and pineapple water he found in the cooler desperately made him wish it contained the energetic juice of the wild citrus fruit he'd discovered up island last week.

He downed the fruity drink, wiping the back of his hand across his mouth. A shuffling noise at the entrance set off his defensive radar, and he reached for his short spear, fire magic vaulting to his hand in a spray of sparks. The foal poked its head into the cave, allaying his jagged nerves. It crept along the walls, casting wary glances at Ryan and urgent stares at Morgan.

Ryan scowled. "You may as well come in." He extended a pineapple wedge and coaxed the little beast into the darkening cave. The winged horse sniffed the fruit, chomped down on it, nearly taking Ryan's fingers with it. The foal licked Morgan's hand, and then settled down between the fire and the bed, watchful as a pit bull.

Flames devoured the firewood, and Ryan added more logs to the fire. He changed his filthy shorts and washed up. Skirting the winged horse, he crawled into bed and curled around Morgan, lending her his warmth. The velvet skin of her legs against his legs sent barbs of fire to every nerve ending in his body.

Ryan stroked her beautiful sun-freckled cheek, once again amazed she was flesh and blood. Not a dream. Drawn to her charm, her spirit, and courage, her determination and strength of will humbled him. That he wanted her, and may very well love her, he didn't doubt. Nothing else explained the unfamiliar feelings welling up in his chest or his heart stopping anguish when WindWraith captured her. Never before had he experienced such fierce jealousy as when that bastard shadow seduced her. Or the inconsolable fury when Ryan believed he'd lost her.

When she accepted his star power, euphoria had almost done him in. Only a few on Earth—at least in his time—possessed the strongest element. Ether didn't naturally occur in sorcerers or witches of the twenty-first century, and the few who ruled it were revered. The powerful element could easily kill someone able to draw it from another who possessed it naturally. When the island opened up and infused Morgan with its earthen power, he knew she was capable of accepting any pure elemental magic. No element was as old and pure as ether, the grandfather of all. Natural, pure earth magic was a close second.

Morgan's lips parted and she moaned, seemingly lost in a dream. He rested his hand on her dry forehead, checked her steady neck pulse. Satisfaction unhitched the restraint on his heart another notch. Ryan placed his mouth on her lips, tasting the sweet life she exhaled in a uniform rhythm.

Disoriented and groggy, Morgan stirred, unable to move her sore, stiff body. A heartbeat later, she realized she snuggled in bed with Ryan. Her head rested on his chest, and his arm cradled her against his side. She felt his hardness pressed into her thigh, and sharp desire flared in her lower region. Knowing that he wanted her even in sleep was a heady feeling. Morgan inhaled the jungle's loamy richness from his skin. She feathered her lips across his bare chest, wondering why she didn't remember falling asleep in his arms.

Fragments of information jostled in her head, ending her blissful moment. She took a sudden sharp breath and felt for her powers, ensuring that WindWraith hadn't caused any damage. Air, fire, and earth magic spooled together weakly, but intact.

It all rushed back to her. WindWraith had filled her mind with its needs and wants, stemming from a sadistic, violent history that began the day the Sluagh demon betrayed him. Morgan squeezed her eyes shut, and the prophetic visions she'd endured in sleep swept WindWraith's evil aside. Trepidation cinched her chest as she concentrated on the visions.

A man similar to Ryan stood upon a deserted beach under the shadows of a steep natural sea wall. Entranced, he stared out to sea, watching the white-tipped waves roll ashore and recede. An air of desolation shrouded him. He shared Ryan's muscular frame, height, and features. He wore his fair hair short. Identical blue eyes shimmered with sadness.

The man glanced down, studied his right hand, and his expression flitted to triumph. One corner of his mouth pulled into a slight smile. A large gold ring with an onyx center stone glittered on his finger. A ruby-eyed, golden dragon overlay the onyx, bordered by an engraved fist on one side of the band and a lightning bolt crusted with diamonds on the other. The familiar dragon tattoo on his arm flexed.

Was this Ryan in the future? Disappointment spread through Morgan like a fungus, insidious and encroaching. Again, she concentrated on remembering the vision.

The ocean curled and crashed on the beach, rolling within inches of the man's bare feet. Water ebbed, leaving dusty-white foam spotting the sand. Seagulls screeching disturbed him, and he pivoted toward the figure that startled the birds into flight. A smile as intimate as a kiss spread across his handsome face. He extended a tanned hand. "It's done." He beckoned to the woman. "Come here, my love."

Lauren Blackwell.

The blond woman looped her arms around his neck. She rubbed her body against his seductively, possessively. A tall woman, she was lithe and small breasted. A sensuous, sulky smile stretched her thin, berry lips.

"We did it," she purred and pressed her lips to his. His large hands held her face, and his mouth covered hers hungrily.

The long kiss ended and Lauren quirked her eyebrows. "The covens are united. The pact is signed. Power is ours."

"Not completely."

Lauren fluttered her hand in the air. "You didn't waste the last year scrounging the dead countryside for ingredients for that damned potion just for grins. It will work."

"It'll have to. Otherwise, we'll all surrender to Fomorian control." He eased her closer. "I love you." He buried his face in her neck, his lips caressing her honeyed skin.

She stiffened and a blank mask descended over her face. "Alexander's coming." With a confident toss of her head, she swept her windblown hair out of her face and smiled radiantly at the approaching man.

Tall and lanky, Alexander dressed head to foot in black. Long ebony hair framed a cruel, bloodless face.

Lauren's lover shook hands with Alexander. "The game's in play."

Pale, full lips pursed in a grimace, and Alexander's whiskey eyes gleamed intensely. "Lauren." He kissed her on the lips, his mouth lingering longer than acceptable on another man's woman.

She slipped one arm around Alexander's waist, the other around Ryan's waist. Sharing a good-natured laugh, the three trod across the sand toward the cliff path.

Morgan pressed her fist to her mouth. Somehow, Ryan would leave the island and return to Lauren Blackwell to lead and restore balance to his people. She gnawed on a knuckle, stifling herself.

Had Fate willed that Morgan live her days on this island alone? Slapping her hand on her stomach, she realized she must accept the inevitable. Once they destroyed WindWraith, she'd cast the charms in the sea for the other star-crossed sorcerers. The bereft and lost Druids would have a newfound joyful life. They needed her magic and intervention, and she refused to deprive them of a gift so easily given. Not that she had any other recourse. Many people depended on her—and on Ryan. It was nigh impossible to ignore the reality of her destiny, all the sacrifices made by her father and herself, for the strange new existence granted her.

Wrapping her fingers around Ryan's amulet, her nails dug painfully into her palm. She rubbed her cheek against his chest, and his arm hugged her closer, although he remained asleep.

Another vague vision lumped like clay in her mind. WindWraith's purpose had become evident while it held her in thrall. What had it meant by its final words to her? The Fomorian tried to warn her of something. Would Ryan betray her? Did he want her only for her power? She strained her mind until her head pounded. For hell's sake, what did the forsaken bastard mean? Why had it shared that story with her? Goddess, how had she ever gotten embroiled in such a world of desire and terror?

Morgan's arms and legs draped around Ryan like a fire warm blanket. A frisson of desire spread upward from his groin to his chest. Her head rested over his rune brand, lips parted slightly, her breath fanning warmth across his skin. Her heart beat steady and strong against his side, and the knotty fear between his shoulders evaporated. Morgan's magic dusted the air, and her eyelashes fluttered.

"Morgan?" he whispered.

She hid a yawn behind her hand. "How long have I been asleep?"

He glanced at his watch hanging on a wooden peg embedded in the stone wall, grateful it had survived the squall. "Almost half a day. Are you okay?" Ryan twirled a loose strand of her silky hair around a finger.

"Sore, weak." She pulled the furs over her bare thighs. "Thank you for saving me." Dark circles ringed her eyes, but her color had normalized.

"You would have done the same."

"I do not have star power," she accused feebly.

They had a lifetime's worth of history to unearth about each other. It was time they put their brains and considerable powers together and determine how to tackle his plan. WindWraith would reform, if it hadn't already, stronger and craftier than ever. Because now it knew what magic Morgan and Ryan possessed—except for one hidden gift. Smug satisfaction oozed contentedly inside Ryan's gut, smooth as century-old brandy.

Reluctantly, he eased away from Morgan's enticing body. He perched on the edge of the bed, staring at the dead fire. The foal had gone outside during the night and hadn't returned.

"It's not something I tell people. I'm probably the only person alive with ether magic. Because of the element, I was the best demon killer, Fomorian assassin, in the twenty-first century." He bunched his shoulders, flexing his stiff muscles. "Only you and my mother know—knew."

"I need to know everything about your powers," Morgan's voice demanded.

"As I do of yours."

"You know what magic I possess. Earth, air, and fire, which enable other sundry innate powers." She sat up and scooted beside him, a careful distance between them. "I don't know yours."

"You know now," Ryan replied cagily. Averting his face, he rose and snagged a log off the wood stack. Embers glowed beneath the ashes in the fire ring and he stirred them, adding the log in a shower of sparks.

"You're lying," she replied with quiet vehemence. Heat rose up her neck practically putting her own deception on the table.

"And you're not?"

Emerald fury blazed in Morgan's eyes. "Why would I lie when it is my life—and yours—in jeopardy? And the lives of a multitude of others."

Ryan reached over her head and snatched her amulet from the alcove. He dangled it in front of her face, gripping its twin around his neck. "What kind of magic did you dump into me? It's nothing I've ever seen before."

After WindWraith's ominous warning and her morning's vision, she didn't know what to tell him. She didn't know if the vision was a dream, a foresight, or neither. The island had changed everything.

Her gaze followed the amulet swinging from Ryan's hand. Obviously, he hadn't touched the crystal, and he was careful not to touch it now. If he had invoked the magic, she would experience a burning in her heart, an enmeshed drawing of her powers to pinch and poke her insides, and an overwhelming yearning for solace. If the ritual didn't progress, the feelings would intensify until he voiced the words to bind his magic to her. Or death. Death certainly didn't appeal to her, which left her with no choice.

Stalling, she said, "I must relieve myself."

He caught her wrist, his fingers inflexible. Morgan struggled, but his grasp grew ironclad. She refused to waste magic to fight him, even though she wanted to whiplash him into submission with an air flog.

"Give me the amulet." She curled her fingers around the charm. If he touched it, they must complete the ritual, the last thing she wished to happen now.

"Why are the charms identical?" he demanded. "What did you mean when you said it was a temporary spell?" He tapped his healing brand.

She rubbed her free hand over her face. "When I was a child, I found the crystals washed in with the tide on Avalon's shores. I assume the earthquakes here may have loosened them from the island's barrier and they followed the trail of magic to Avalon. There were many matching pairs. I had ridiculous and fanciful notions of love as a young girl when I fashioned each pair into twin amulets."

Ryan strengthened his clamp on her wrist. "And?"

"You're hurting me!" she squeaked out.

He loosened his fingers a hair.

Despite her anger, his touch engulfed her with the all-consuming need to confess everything. She refused to hide from him any longer. She hated lies and hidden truths that always managed to cause more havoc than outright confession. Since he hadn't offered up much information about himself or his world, maybe her tales would start the flow of communication.

Something tight unwound in her belly. "I imbued the charms with ancient Druid magic. They draw destined lovers out of their final moments of despair, to beckon one to the other. Without my knowledge, my father added more magic to them." An ember shot from the fire, crackling onto the ground. Ryan stomped it out, giving her pause to form her next words. "He cast your amulet into the sea some time ago. It landed where you were expected to find it."

Comprehension dawned across Ryan's face. His mouth parted, and he appeared ready to speak, but shook his head. Absently, he touched the rune tattoo on his chest. "Did these spells cause us to share our dreams?"

"I believe that stemmed from the magic my father added to our charms, a means for us to become acquainted and to bolster our bond."

"So the spells are permanent?" He slanted his head, picked at the crusty brand.

"Yes," she whispered. Ryan hid matters of great import from her, and she felt it like a vise on her heart. "Who is Lauren Blackwell?" she asked defiantly.

Ryan released her wrist and dropped her pendant as if both were rancid. He reeled backward and proceeded to stomp a ditch around the fire.

She sent him the first image of Ryan and Lauren announcing their pact, then making love to seal their promise. An image she hated with all her might.

Hands fisted at his side, Ryan halted. Approaching her slowly, he hung his head avoiding her loathing. "She's my intended pact mate. Our covens enacted a law to prohibit marriage. There were too few women left to tie down to one man. Eventually, we wanted to find a peaceful, secure place to start a new life with the hopes of having children to rebuild the human population. But Lauren and I—" Abruptly, he stopped rambling, shuffled his feet over the ground.

Even though Morgan already knew the woman's identity, the spoken truth sent her world spinning awry. "Are you to be exclusive and rule together as if wedded?"

she whispered.

Ryan lifted his head, his misery aging his face ten years. "It's not what you think."

Gooseflesh sprouted on her bare arms, and she rubbed her hands across her prickly skin. "In spirit, you are to wed?" she demanded.

"Yes."

"Do you love her?" Morgan twisted the braided rope around her fingers.

"No. It's not like that," he snapped, his face pinched tight. "I told you I was born for duty. Love isn't—"

"You made love to her," she accused, then realized how foolish she sounded. *They* had shared similar intimacies. He didn't love her, either.

"We had sex. There's a difference."

"You said you would find a way home. When you do," Morgan wiped at her watery eyes, "will you enforce your... pact?"

He stood stone still then walked to the cave's entrance. "I don't know. I don't fucking know." Without a backward glance, he disappeared around the bend.

A feeling of doom swept over Morgan, worse than having her life nearly wiped out by WindWraith yesterday. Death had taken her mother and left her abandoned at birth. She'd seen further death take its toll on her family and people, had been terrorized and lost in the forest, and forced to leave her beloved father. Despite her losses, nothing matched the grief she felt at that moment. Tears slipped down her face, and she let them flow.

Morgan pressed her palms over her scars, her amulet falling and striking the top of her foot. She gulped down the bitter desolation rising in her throat. Leaning her head against the wall, she willed her heart to stop breaking. Why had she fallen in love with a man she could never have? Loathing for Fate made her blood run icy.

CHAPTER 20

Dusk descended, dimming the chinks of light in the ceiling. Morgan returned from investigating the other caves behind the waterfall and watched Ryan prepare supper over the fire. A cautious smile quirked his lips in acknowledgment of her return.

The foal's cold nose bumped her leg. She had all but forgotten about the winged horse. He bobbed his head in excitement, tail swishing wildly.

"Hi, baby." Wrapping her arms around him, she buried her face in his neck. Morning dew clung to his fur. Fresh new life. Hope existed in that, even if Morgan never recovered from her emotions leading her astray, or whatever else Fate promised to serve her on a tarnished, dented platter.

"Morgan?" Ryan called gently. "You need to eat."

He brought her a hollowed coconut filled with flavored water and fresh stew in a carved wooden bowl. Fragrant steam wafted from the wild stew. Her stomach rumbled, whether from hunger or distress, she didn't know. However, she needed to restore her strength after draining her magic reserves. First, she wanted to wash WindWraith's evil filth from her flesh before she crawled out of her skin.

She elbowed aside the burrowing foal and snatched up a fur. "I'll eat in a moment."

Once again, Morgan left the edgy atmosphere and strode outside to the waterfall. She slipped off Ryan's T-shirt, letting it slither down her legs to the ground, and tiptoed into the cold spray. Water sheeted over her, sluicing away the scum of evil and her own tangled agony. She lathered soaproot mixture in her palms. Heat sailed through her as she scrubbed herself clean, renewing her ache for Ryan's touch. *Stop!* She dunked into the waterfall, numbing the need seizing her body and heart.

Torn between passion and practicality, she knew she'd never rest without his touch a final time. Even if he belonged to another, he'd always carry her brand upon his chest, stamped into his soul. If not for his duty, he might love her one day.

"I'd never live with myself if I forced his actions and he held it against me," she whispered. Morgan knew all too well what responsibility and dependability meant in a leader's life. Escaping near death engendered newfound apathy for it. Her damp hair cascaded down her back in a cold blanket, enhancing her cold dread.

Clean and resolved, she returned to the cave. A fire snapped brightly, the atmosphere inviting and homey. Ryan had set her food on an upper ledge out of the foal's reach. Waving his arms like a madman and hissing at the foal, he tried to shoo the winged horse outside the cave, relenting when the foal trotted to her side. The baby horse lay next to her with a deliberate wag of his head at Ryan.

Ryan tossed it a wild carrot, kneeling beside her. "I'm sorry," he said in a gravelly voice.

A sob escaped before she had a chance to choke it down. He slipped his arms around her waist. Her scars burned as he pressed his lips to her moist skin. The fur spilled around her feet as anguish puddled at the bottom of her heart.

First to break the silence, Ryan began, "You were all I believed I wanted from the dream we shared. You're all I want now." Grief spilled across his face in the downturn of his mouth.

Hope pricked her heart. She wanted to smooth his sorrow away with her hands but sat on them instead.

"I realized once I signed the pact, I'd no longer have freedom in any aspect of my life. It galled me even when it shouldn't have." His fingers skimmed across her stomach, his touch blazing a trail over her skin. "Then I dreamed of you, wanted you and everything you represented." Expectation pooled in his eyes, a swirling expanse of ocean blue. "I want to take you home with me."

His words churned in her stomach. "For what, Ryan?" she asked acerbically. "To live in Lauren's shadow?" If escape from the island was even possible after they destroyed WindWraith.

"That's not what I want." Ryan sighed, gliding his hands over her taut skin to her hips. "Lauren is...was the Eastern High Druid. Both the Eastern and Western covens have long planned unification, first with our arranged marriage—" He appeared to war with himself before he released her and rose with the fur in his hands. He draped it over her shoulders, a muscle in his arm protruding tensely. "Everything's changed. Fomorians have destroyed Earth."

Calmly, face devoid of emotion, she said, "My father foretold your devastated future. He told me as much before he sent me here. His Sight is rarely wrong, but I had a difficult time understanding it. Can you tell me what happened?"

Ryan snorted. "Would have been nice to have a seer like your father in my coven to prophesy the end of civilization. Maybe we could have prevented it. As it was, the Druids and other pagans tried their damnedest to kill as many of the Fomorians as possible from the moment their population exploded five years ago. They'd walked among us, looked like us for so long."

Morgan rubbed the silky fur between her thumb and

finger. "How did their masses grow so plentiful? In our time, we were able to recognize and defeat them easily when they slipped into our world, except for rarities like WindWraith, which required more ingenuity."

"Throughout the years, the Fomorians found a way to shield their true nature from easy detection. They hunted the world for unshielded magic to steal, leaving pagans depleted until they died a quick, painful death. Or they marked sorcerers as controlled minions, expanding their ranks. Witches were the first targets, being the weakest. Fomorians became so powerful they craved more magic, stronger magic. One of the Fomorian Cabals, Alasoron, discovered a way to absorb human energy to increase and prolong their power. They alone were able to steal the souls of humans and animals along with our magic. They're part descendants of a demon race called Sluagh." Ryan grabbed a flagon of flavored water and drank deeply.

Chills skittered up Morgan's back and she tightened her arms over her chest. She didn't want to interrupt him now that he'd finally opened up.

Ryan stirred the stew. "The other Fomorian Cabals wanted the secret. Instead, the Alasorons used it against them. They triggered the Horde Wars and the Cabals began battling each other. The Alasorons prevailed, but not before wiping out most of humanity in their thirst for absolute control."

A thread of horror tightened Morgan's chest. "I'm truly sorry." Unspeakable sadness rode the air. She wanted to give him back everything taken from him and his people. If only she had such ability.

He paced the cave, sorrow masking his face. Halting in the cave's entryway, he stuck his hand in a trickle of water and scrubbed it across his neck. "Look, Morgan, you have to understand. Merging is necessary to strengthen the Druid people and repair the rift between us caused by years of enemy attacks. Lauren and I rule the last two Druid covens. Even though we have a united cause fighting the Fomorians, we're warring against each other for control. It needs to stop. The pact signing was critical. Our people counted on it."

"I don't understand why you and Lauren needed to...be together for the pact merger. Why it couldn't be someone else?"

"I'm stronger than my brother Michael. Michael and Lauren aren't strong enough to lead and defeat the Fomorians. My coven expected me to marry Lauren before the war. They expected us to merge for strength. Together, we make a force more powerful than the Alasoron leader, Alexander."

It *was* Ryan on the beach in her vision. *Why is Fate playing such a cruel trick on me?* Morgan bowed her head, letting a niggling doubt rise to the surface. "But—" She hesitated. Didn't Ryan wonder why he possessed a tie to the stars? What secret did he hide from her? He couldn't merge magic with Lauren without killing her, unless she was also a descendent of an Ancient. Maybe the sorcerers of his time didn't unite magic through their bodies like the Ancients. Maybe he meant controlling external magic together. Or were the sorcerers of Ryan's era all descendants of the Ancients?

Standing, she huddled into her fur wrap, pressing her hand against her chest. The fire's heat spooled across her bare legs but didn't rise upward, leaving her feeling like a half-empty vessel. If Ryan held starfire in his blood, he must not understand WindWraith's intent. Surely, Ryan knew the consequences of ether in his blood. She had to tell him before they ventured out again. WindWraith's nightmare hold on her caused a cold claw to drag gooseflesh down her backside.

"I'll find a way to make the covens accept you." Ryan

studied her carefully veiled expression. "You're much stronger than Lauren. They'll accept you. We'll figure out another way to repair the discord. I won't marry...mate with Lauren." He smacked a fist into the flat of his other hand, signifying his dominance over the fractional Druids. Over his decision. Over her heart. "I can't."

Two strides toward her and he held her face in his hands. "I will have you or none other." His lips brushed hers. "If that means I step down as leader, I will. Once my people are secure."

Ryan's eyes reached inside her and touched a spot only he'd touched. Hope jolted her soul, and her body responded with joyful tingles. She threaded her arms around his neck. "You would do all that for me?"

"You did something to me, Morgan. You opened my locked heart." Ryan folded her into his embrace, his arms solid and welcome. "You're in my blood." He kissed her forehead, his hands slipping down to massage her buttocks. "All my life, I've had an emptiness, but it wasn't a hunger in my stomach. It was in my heart." She opened her mouth to speak, but he silenced her with a brief kiss. "When I finally touched you, breathed you in—" His hard body trembled down to her toes.

Morgan stroked his shoulders, loving his solid strength, the fire burning beneath his skin. "Oh, Ryan—"

His mouth closed over hers, their kiss dripping passion, spoken and unspoken. Their tongues met, reticent at first, then greedily, twining around each other like island vines in the sun. Their bodies curved together in a perfect mold, and Morgan thrummed with pleasure from toes to scalp. Their kiss turned tender before he eased back.

Ryan lifted her chin with one finger, his light-hearted smile stealing her breath away. "I want you." He kissed her lightly on the lips. "Only you."

She hugged him hard, never wanting to let go, but her

head stomped on her heart and she pried her arms off him. "We'll have time for more..." She peeked at his bulging loincloth and beat down her mounting arousal. "Later. I have much to tell you first."

He groaned in mock annoyance. "Eat first. You need your strength."

She perched on a crude chair constructed of leather straps and a rough log frame. Ryan handed her a fresh bowl of steaming stew. Wild carrots, potatoes, onions, and a beefy meat renewed waves of hunger in her stomach. Fresh herbs and ocean salt added a tangy spice to the scrumptious meal. Surprised, Morgan praised him between bites. "This is delicious."

Ryan lounged on the bed, leaning against the wall, his arms folded loosely across his chest. "I've learned to cook out of necessity from survival training."

In companionable silence, Morgan finished her meal, washed it down with fruity water. Ryan's gaze clung to hers as if she might disappear if he shifted his eyes. The winged foal licked her bowl clean and resumed resting against the inner cave wall.

"Even he likes it." She laughed.

"I don't think he likes horse food." Ryan rubbed his head and grimaced. "He wouldn't eat the grass I brought him, and he loves your juiced-up water."

The foal growled at Ryan, as if he knew Ryan spoke about him. Ryan and Morgan laughed, an edgy, provocative silence piggybacking along. Disorder in Morgan's mind caused her head to thunder. She massaged her temples.

"Are you okay?" Ryan asked.

"My head aches with knowledge that belongs to others."

"Do you have herbs for headaches?"

"I'll survive." With a flutter of her hand, she waved his concern away. "My mind is stuffed to the brim with ages of information. It's all there, but scattered."

"I'd rather hear your scattered knowledge than dwell on my bleak world."

Morgan touched his hand and he linked his fingers through hers. "We have similar lives." She crossed her ankles under the stool. "My mother was a High Druid Sorceress, my father an equally powerful sorcerer." She was afraid to tell him her father was a descendant of Merlin, the mage responsible for their plight. "Although they loved one another deeply, they wished to create a powerful child to unite the people and bring peace to our lands. They expected me to breed the next generation to keep the Druid magic alive, to carry on Avalon's legacy." Morgan swallowed the sadness welling up from her heart. "I never knew my mother in the flesh. She died giving birth to me." Head bowed, she fought the crick in her heart that always threatened whenever she recalled the mother she knew only through her father's loving words. Now, her sorrow included the father also lost to her.

Morgan heard a rustle and Ryan sat beside her, eased her against his body. "I'm sorry you didn't get a chance to know your mother." His thumb caught the tear sliding down her cheek. The tear for the father she missed, the mother she always wanted to touch.

"I know her through my father. She's always with me." She patted her heart. "In here."

Ryan kissed her temple and hugged her tighter. A sob rose in Morgan's throat and she gulped it down. She must accept her lot and quit sniveling over the family now lost to her. At least her father still lived, when Ryan's family was probably dead. "My father gave everything to me. Once born, it became apparent that I could never take my rightful place as High Sorceress. Our magic threatened those around us. We were the last Druids born with ties to the *Tuatha dé Danann*. With the demise of the general Druid population through repression and conquest, and a declining sorcerer population suffering great magic loss from WindWraith and others, dissenters found ways to kill off our people one by one. Those left on Avalon feared they would be murdered if they revealed themselves away from the sanctuary of the isle." Ryan released her and settled his back against the earthen walls. It felt right telling him her life's story. How could she not trust the man bound to her magic, possibly her destined soul mate?

For now, she concentrated on her story, sorely trying to ignore Ryan's solid body tempting her frayed emotions. "My father believed it best to raise me as a simple Druid descendant. He forced me to hide my magic to the outside world, even though he taught me to use all my talents. Regardless, he schooled me in the ancient magic, and I learned the history and legends of the great sorcerers who lived before me."

She plowed onward, leaning forward as if to press her words upon him. "While WindWraith held me in thrall, it filled my head with its sordid past. Things no one most likely knew about it."

Ryan shoved away from the wall, and sat rigidly on the bed. His knuckle cracking competed with the fire's pops and snaps. "What did the twisted freak do to you?" Veins in his neck stood out in livid ridges.

Morgan held up a placating hand. "It's not so terrible." She sipped the tepid water to loosen her clogged throat. Setting the coconut shell aside, she continued. "It's just a muddle of thoughts and emotions. It's similar to the knowledge my father infused me with." She wanted to sort the Fomorian's words before she shared them with Ryan. A thimble of doubt remained and she had a peculiar feeling that WindWraith had warned her about Ryan. Not that she trusted the abomination or its manipulations, her qualms refused to die.

"Infused?" Ryan's blond brows drew together in a single

stripe.

"Gwilym made me drink a potion steeped with knowledge. I can't explain how he accomplished the spell." She smiled with fond remembrance. "He's a powerful sorcerer and knows secret magic passed down from our ancestors."

"We'll deal with your father later." He blindly picked at the crusty scabs around his rune tattoo. "What did that bastard dump in your head?"

Morgan worried about Ryan's reaction to her words. She squirmed and pressed her legs against the chair frame. The creaking wood sliced through the tense hush. Ryan waited expectantly for her to continue.

"WindWraith needs fire magic to complete it, to regain a corporeal form. It already possesses air and water elements naturally. It has been draining earth, air, and water magic from the island, which enhances its natural elements."

"I get that. Plus it's stealing fire magic from us."

She nodded. "Once it has its fill of all elements except ether, it can possess a body with ancient Druid blood. Any other person of lesser magic is useless to it. They will die from the transference, unable to absorb such enormous power." She weighed Ryan's reaction, but his face was a blank palette.

"Then what will WindWraith do?" Ryan's apprehension practically pulsated in the air. Unintended power seemed to escape him and wrapped Morgan in a protective shield.

Longing raged through her for this man of destiny. She fisted her hands, quashing her overwhelming need to touch him. "Once its transference into a human body is complete, it will be able to return to a populated world to seek vengeance for its long banishment."

Ryan pushed off the bed, paced to the fire. Emotions caused his crystal to bloom, bouncing violet light off the variegated walls. "How? Why?" Ryan stilled. "Nothing makes sense on this freak-show island." He stirred the fire, added another oak log. The fire's hisses and crackles edged the silence.

"Wait a minute." Ryan glared down at her. "WindWraith needs power from an Ancient? Then how has the son of a bitch been sucking on me for weeks? What good is my fire to him?"

Morgan tilted her head to the side, frowning at him. "Ryan, you possess ancient Druid blood."

"Because I drank your ensorcelled water?" He laughed grimly. "I don't think so."

"I will mind-send you things my father fed me. He possessed greater ability to see into the future. His potion gave me knowledge of your world, your speech, things I need to do here. It slowly materializes in bits and pieces."

"Okay." Ryan squared his shoulders. "Do it."

Morgan sent images and knowledge of Ryan's heritage into his mind. His head jerked up, his eyes wild. "You received your ether from your blood father, a descendant of an Ancient." Morgan slid her hand over his, linking their fingers. "Only one of ancient blood can tolerate star power once it manifests. It was your star power that I latched onto to escape WindWraith's clutches, wasn't it? I believe those among your people who have both innate magic and ties to the elements may also have descended from the Ancients."

Blood drained from Ryan's face, and the skin pulled taut over the ridge of his cheekbones. "Yes, it was my ether," he whispered. He sank onto the bed, leaning his elbows on his knees, his chin resting on his steepled hands. Morgan sat beside him, smoothed her hand over his trembling thigh.

"My blood father?" A strange smile played across his mouth. "Ian O'Rourke's not my father?"

"No."

A grim chuckle escaped him. "I hated that bastard. I always knew he couldn't be my real father. We were nothing alike. Except for our mutual inability to love, which he taught me well."

"You're not like him." Morgan shook her head sharply. "Your mother loved your real father, James MacFarland. And he loved her." Morgan kissed his dragon tattoo, skittered her fingers down his arm to rest on his wrist. "They gave each other up for duty."

Ryan sobered, straightened his back. "James was my father's—Ian O'Rourke's—cousin. He was like a second father to me." He beat his fist on his knee. "It makes sense why he was always around, why he and my mother were killed together in a car accident. He knew."

"I'm sorry. And I'm sorry you didn't know this while he lived."

"Are you sure?" Ryan swept her onto his lap, and she straddled his muscular thighs. "What about my brother? You seem to know more about my life than I do."

Morgan rested her hands on his knotty shoulders, tightening her legs about him. Electricity floated from the silky furs on the bed, a tickling pleasure crawling across her legs. "I don't know. My seer powers have changed since I arrived here. It's not customary for me to see much of one's past, or to mind link, for that matter."

"This island enhances everything. It's feeding you pure earth magic." Ryan's hands locked against her spine, holding her firmly in place. The pressure of her rear on his groin sent a surge of heat to his hardening erection. "What else did you see?"

Morgan snuggled into him, her cheek resting on his shoulder. Then it hit her. Brother? Was that Ryan's brother in her latest vision? She lifted her head and kissed Ryan soundly on the lips, grinning wide. "Oh! I thought it was you. But it must be your brother. Is he still alive?" She held her breath.

"I hope so."

Delight ripped up her spine, and she clapped a hand to her mouth. "I had another vision this morning."

Morgan sent the image into Ryan's head. His mind revolted against the scene, and she faded it off at Lauren embracing Michael on the beach.

His back hit the wall. "Son of a bitch!" He eased her off his lap, gently setting her on the bed. He leapt up and stalked the small enclave, smashing a fist into his other palm. "They're plotting against me." Ryan stopped, glowering at Morgan. His face tempered, and he touched his fingers to her shoulder. "I'm not angry with you."

Morgan offered him a timid smile. "How could they be plotting against you? They didn't know this island was your destiny."

A treacherous dark veil shifted over Ryan's features. "I hid the Druid ring of leadership in my room in our base church. Fomorians can't encroach on consecrated land. I wanted nothing to remind me of my future while I took my last trip of independence on the safe seas." Crimson rage rolled up his tight neck. "Michael has coveted my powers, my role as the oldest and strongest all his life. My father gave him whatever he wanted, including freedom to do what he wished."

"Because Michael wasn't strong enough to lead."

"Exactly." The heat of jealousy emanated off Ryan's motionless body. "But it didn't stop Michael from competing with me for everything, including," he sent her a tight apologetic look, "women. But I don't get it. He hated Lauren, tried to break off our marriage pact before the wars. He had an idea to rule without the merger, a demon vanquishing potion he was working on."

"It sounds like you two should have traded places."

Ryan flicked his hand irritably. "Hardly. Back then,

he'd rather befriend a Fomorian with one of his love potions than kill it."

Morgan rose, hugging the fur to her chest. "Are you so sure of your brother? Maybe he wanted you to see things his way. To rule with Lauren's coven without a pact."

He pinned a glare on her, his forehead creased in doubt. "If I'd spent more time at home rather than working my ass off, I might've known Michael better. All I saw were the demands Ian and our people placed on me, and the freedoms Michael didn't have to earn." He resumed pacing in taut, awkward movements. Sounds of his cracking knuckles riddled the tension like gunshots. "After the wars began, he fled to the east coast. He returned just before Lauren and her people found us a few months ago. Lauren hated Michael—or so I believed. I'd probably be a floating corpse right now if it wasn't for your father, for fate." He clutched his amulet. "For this." He kicked a log off the stack by the entry. The log thudded to the ground and split in two. "That bitch probably would've killed me in my sleep."

Misgivings overshadowed Morgan's happiness. The rest of the vision bothered her, and she knew she had to share it. A death trap, a life of betrayal he didn't deserve awaited Ryan if he managed to escape the island.

"Ryan." Morgan approached him, grasped his forearm. "You blanked out the vision before it finished. Who is Alexander?" Not waiting for his reply, she passed the vision.

Ryan froze. Again, the blood drained from his face, leaving an ashen tint in its wake. He deliberately peeled Morgan's hands off his arm and eased away.

"It's worse than I imagined," he finally said. "Alexander is the leader of the Alasoron Cabal. Michael and Lauren are setting up the Druids for a fall." Ryan nailed her with a black glance. "You need to help me return home."

CHAPTER 21

Ryan stalked the confining cave while Morgan tidied their improvised kitchen. He tried to help but she waved him away, her face strained with a range of emotions he failed to decipher. It would be forever before he knew Morgan of Avalon's secrets. A lifetime he'd gladly live whether on the island or elsewhere. He sensed her holding things back, just as he withheld information. Trust hadn't come easy to him in many years, especially when he didn't always know if the person in front of him was a Fomorian or Fomorian minion in disguise. Part of him wanted to share everything with Morgan, the other part kept a tight fist around his mind. However, one puzzle he needed to piece together rose above all others.

The mystery of the Druid charm had nagged him from the moment he came to on the deserted beach with it twined in his fingers. The amulet had lured Ryan straight to it during the deadly squall. Forever etched in his mind, the life-altering day surged back...

Sunlight had beat down on him, roasting his body through layers of clothes. His head thundered and his eyes refused to open. He'd sputtered out a mouthful of seawater, coughing up his lungs, salt burning his throat. Sand mashed into his face, gritty and cool. His battered body refused to move, not that his brain signals slunk past his raging headache. He'd wondered if he was in line waiting for the gatekeeper to punch his ticket to hell. Waves crashed on the shoreline and flowed sedately over his feet. Seagulls screeching filtered into his waterlogged brain. Then it all slammed into him like a tidal wave. The freakish storm, capsizing, oblivion.

He blinked back the grit and peered upon a strange new world. Slowly, he rotated his head to the side and eased his left hand up to check for wounds. Seaweed strangled his fingers, and he fruitlessly tried to shake it off. Fire seared his muscles. Biting down his pain, he pushed up on his elbows and lifted his head off the fine sand.

Slack-jawed, Ryan scanned the deserted beach, the rocky, bushy cliffs leading up to a lush jungle. Vibrant and alive, he hadn't seen such ripe beauty in a year. Pristine white sand surrounded him in a wide half oval, not a bone, nor any evidence of death in sight. Contentment washed over him as if he belonged there. It was a sensation he'd only felt on his sailboat, never in L.A. or anywhere else for that matter, before or after the apocalypse.

He leveraged his beaten body into a sitting position. As he lifted his hand to untangle the seaweed, a glittery object knocked against his thigh. Raising his hand in front of his face, he inspected the charm suspended from a twist of leather, silver, and leafy seaweed. A tarnished silver circlet centered a rough-cut amethyst the size of a robin's egg. Rune symbols covered both sides of the flat ring. The stone had vibrated on his palm. Weathered and ancient, it felt as if it belonged to him and only him. His lifeline to something he sensed, but was unable to pinpoint.

Here and now, he knew why the amulet had found him, stolen him from a life hardly worth living. Gave him to Morgan, to the island. Once the charm branded him, and Morgan cast her spell upon him, he'd felt a microscopic change in his power, a conduit to her sparkly fire, her crisp air, and her velvety earth magic. Did she also feel a bond to him?

Frowning, he strode to the wall alcove and looped his fingers through the braid of her pendant. Careful not to touch the amulet, he swung it in front of him. Morgan's wolfish stare followed his movements.

"What magical abilities will we share once I complete the ritual?" He inched his fingers down the braid. "What kind of bond will tie us together? Will it help us defeat WindWraith?"

Morgan's expression mellowed. "You are perceptive. As I explained, the amulets hold archaic magic. It is how I knew you were of ancient Druid blood. I knew it the moment you touched this one." She delicately traced the rune-marked circlet resting against his chest. "I made the charms based on old customs. You feel my powers, sense a hint of my emotions?"

He nodded, fascination riding the anxiety knotting his shoulders.

"Once you fulfill your part of the rite, I'll sense your power, your emotions. We'll share an awareness of each other that will grow over time." She shrugged, her eyes fixated on her charm, as though afraid it would vanish back to Avalon any second. "The amulet magic is meant to bind," she curled her fingers around her pendant, and added shyly, "Druid soul mates."

Heat tripped his heart, and a slow burn of longing crept to his groin. He hadn't expected to hear that—he'd never believed in soul mates. At least not until Morgan seduced his dream. Damned if it didn't turn him on, though.

She told him how she had bound the amulets with spells she didn't comprehend as a child, and how her father repaired them. "We don't have to complete the ritual." Morgan rushed on, placating him unnecessarily. "The moment you touched your amulet, you bound yourself to it. When I touched it, I set the binding spell in motion. I placed another spell on you to diffuse the magic. If I hadn't, and we never completed that part of the binding spell, the magic would devour your insides, destroy your powers, and eventually kill you."

Shock whipped through Ryan. "What happens if we complete the magic binding? What spells complete the entire ritual?" He eased the amulet out of her hands, his fingers a mere inch from touching the charm.

"Do not touch it if you aren't prepared for this." Her fingers dusted his chest. "For me."

Spellbound in the grip of each other's eyes, they stared as though they could see into the other's soul. He wanted that face gazing at him with need and devotion, her lips swollen with his kisses, her body pressed to his the way it did on the moonlight meadow in their dream.

"Prepare me." His voice sounded husky to his ears. His loincloth barely contained his surging erection. He may as well throw the damn loincloth away for all the good it did.

"Ryan, do you understand what you're saying?" Hope stirred in Morgan's face. Her trembling palm flattened over his heart and he nearly melted from her gentle touch. "We will be bound for life. You will have access to my magic and I will have access to yours. But your magic won't fill me, I can only link to it when you send it to me. The same will work for you with my magic. We'll always have that link."

"Will the amulet brand you?" He hated the idea of her satiny skin marred by the runes. She nodded. "That's it? Our magic will be joined?" Ryan narrowed his eyes.

"We will sense each other's strongest emotions. That's one part." Morgan crossed her arms over her breasts, hiding her beaded nipples.

Ryan's erection bucked against his leather sheath. "The next step?"

She coughed, her neck reddening. "If we wish to proceed, the final spell will also bind our souls. We must make love. You must fill me with...your essence." A crimson tide stained her face.

That explained her reticence to let him make love to her. Ah, Gods...he wanted to perform the ritual that moment. Life altering, the idea allowed no outlet for doubt, no return. Did he want this? He tugged on the leather thong around his neck, cupped the warm, glowing amulet in his palm. Knowing that it owned him, it kindled his inner fire, swept a wave of pride and honor through him.

"You will be mine?"

"Yes," she whispered.

His hand slid down her stomach to the swell of her hips. "I will be yours?"

"Yes."

Hell, yes, it's what I want! All he thought about was Morgan. Loving her, protecting her, having children with her, growing old together. After a lifetime of sacrifices, his feelings overwhelmed him, consumed him like nothing ever had.

Raised to believe no place for love existed in his future as a coven leader, Ryan learned that it was a weakness to fall in love. Deep down, part of him had always wanted a normal life with a loving family. The Horde Wars had destroyed even that slim hope. Was Morgan the chance for a future long denied him? A fresh start in life? Was she truly his destiny? Did the ancient spells really work?

After years spent hunting and killing demons and Fomorians, and a year surviving in a post-apocalyptic wasteland, Morgan exemplified his biggest challenge to date. A challenge he'd spend a lifetime conquering if it meant having her in his life every day, holding her every night, learning to accept love, to give love freely.

"Ryan?" Worry compressed Morgan's mouth into a thin line.

He cupped her face in his palms. "Do you want this?"

"It is our destiny."

"To hell with destiny. Do *you* want me?"

"I think I've wanted you from the first moment your dreams touched mine." Standing on tiptoes, she touched her lips to his. "I never believed I'd live to see this day."

Ryan's mouth covered hers hungrily in a long kiss filled with infinite promise. Feathering his lips over hers, he asked, "If we complete the first ritual now, do we follow immediately with the second?" A slow grin spread across his mouth.

"Do you not want to make love to me?" Her sultry British accent teased his skin like a mild Samhain breeze.

"Hell, yes." Ryan groaned. "But I want to get out of here before WindWraith regains strength. There's a safe place I want to take you."

Excitement and hunger melted in her eyes. "I can wait. But can you?" She reached beneath his loincloth and her fingers grazed his steel length.

A tremor rolled up his body. Her hand fisted around him, and she provocatively applied just the right amount of pressure.

"An appetizer?" Morgan dipped her head, flicked her tongue over his left nipple. His nipple instantly pebbled. She shifted to the right side, the barest touch of her tongue teasing it to attention.

Ryan flung his head back and gasped. In the throes of his desire, his hand coiled around Morgan's amulet, the crystal searing his palm. Adrenaline exploded in his hand, jolted into his groin. "Ah, Gods," he cried, his strength draining down his legs.

Morgan withdrew her hand, an enchanting smile touching her lips. "Say the words."

Magic rumbled chaotically inside him, expanded, detracted. "What words? What the hell's happening?"

Morgan touched his cheek, smoothed her hand over the vein throbbing in his jaw. "The words will come. Put the charm around my neck. The pain will subside." She peeled off her T-shirt and stood reticent.

Firelight rendered her pale skin a golden-tawny hue. It took all Ryan had not to glide his body around her nakedness, and replace the fire's warmth with his own. He lifted her hair free and slipped the necklace over her head, then draped her hair like a black shawl over her alabaster shoulders. Her breath was distractingly warm against his hand, and he forced himself to proceed before he lost himself in her completely. Afraid to allow the amulet contact with her peachy skin, he palmed it securely.

"Let it go." Her fingers slid beneath his hand.

Ryan uncurled his fingers, eased the amulet against her skin. The silver ring settled above her left breast. He focused on the unbidden words surfacing in his head. A shockwave hit him full force, and fathomless peace and satisfaction flowed over him. The words bubbled up from the bottom of his soul, into his heart. As they tumbled from his lips, he knew their absolute truth. "I give you the magic of my body, my heart, my soul. I allow your magic entrance into my body and allow you to call upon my magic as if it were your own. Never will I use my magic or yours against you. I will guard your powers as I guard my own. I will protect you to the full depths of my abilities. My magic is one with you, and our magic together becomes one whole. I give you the magic of my body, my heart, my soul, everlasting."

Electricity sparkled in the air like tiny flashes of lightning. Power streamed between them, showering them as though a rain cloud opened up and dripped sparks upon them. Their amethysts glowed in unity. Energy ruptured inside him, and it wasn't his alone. The silver ring scalded Morgan and her chest twitched. He felt her magic churning inside her, as his magic did the same in him, a dam impatiently waiting for the gates to open wide.

Perspiration filmed Morgan's blanched face. She repeated the spell's words, her voice hitching at the end. A tear escaped her right eye, and Ryan caught it with his thumb, tenderly caressing the moisture over her lips.

He kissed her, slid his mouth lower to the brand above her heart. The scent and flavor of her, freesia and passion, drove him crazy. He pressed his lips against the blistered skin, flicked his tongue over it to assuage her pain.

Morgan held him against her breast. "It will heal and turn gold and black, as will yours."

Their magic swirled sweetly inside him, mixing like sugar and chocolate. Without moving his mouth from her skin, Ryan sank to his knees. He laved her left nipple, suckling it into a stiff kernel. Her soft breasts filled his massaging hands perfectly. He released her nipple with a pop and exhaled a frayed groan. He'd never felt such a desperate need for another. He smoothed his hands over Morgan's hips to her luscious, round ass. She buried her hands in his hair, fingernails scraping his scalp, sending prickles down his neck. Her perfume flowed over him, a salve to his savage world.

Their magic meld cascaded like a river of shooting stars within him. Morgan's elation permeated his mind until he couldn't tell if it was his excitement or hers. Ecstasy blasted through him, traveling to the same destination. So incredible, air grew in short supply and he gasped against her stomach.

Morgan clutched his hair, using the strands as an anchor. "Ryan," she whispered.

Her voice returned him to the land of sanity. Night grew long and they had little time to spare to get to the safe place he wanted to take her before dawn settled over the island. The Fomorian shied from darkness, and he didn't want to risk traveling during daylight. He'd rather move now and have a leisurely time to spend with Morgan in safety. Now that he understood WindWraith's magical makeup and its current potency, he'd give it no more than another couple of days to increase its powers. He didn't want to add to Morgan's fear by telling her about his strange altercation with the Fomorian, and aid in her justification to deplete its powers and kill it. Once he convinced her of his plan and how it would save his people, only then he'd confess how he knew intimately of WindWraith's magic.

Reluctantly, Ryan rose to his full height, his fingers shimming up Morgan's naked body, dying to lay her down and make love to her body and soul. Her eyes had turned to the deep color of emeralds. He stood there and let her consume his senses.

No one else would know her touch and her senses. And he'd destroy anyone or anything that tried to take her away from him.

CHAPTER 22

They followed the familiar path toward the quake-ruined cave, Ryan carrying a torch to light their way. Every so often, an ocean breeze dipped into the ripe vegetation, cooling Morgan's face. The salty tang chased the rich jungle odors, clogging her throat.

She hadn't regained her energy from her ordeal with WindWraith. The binding ritual hadn't helped matters either. Ryan's magic twined inside her nearly as useless as her own sluggish power. It was enough to warm her woman's parts in the most disconcerting way. Desire to be fully bound to Ryan roared to life, and fire blazed up her chest to her face. Flying off a cliff to soak her feverish body in the seas seemed like a good idea. Morgan plucked at her damp chemise, and half-heartedly swatted at a nocturnal black and red striped bee buzzing by her head. Torchlight attracted the wretched backward bugs. "Buzz off. Hope you hate my blood." Her legs and arms grew weary with every movement.

Her presence on the island increased the Fomorian's power at a faster clip than they had anticipated. Even the island magic flowing within her had diminished into a trickle, its resonance barely palpable. Ryan alluded to a plan to destroy WindWraith tomorrow or the next day at the latest. He held back more, wanting to share a surprise with her first, but she hoped they'd have the physical and magical abilities to carry out their daunting task.

"Ryan. My father saw that your land is bleak, buildings destroyed, everything crumbling. How did it happen?"

"Fomorians laid waste to the land fighting their wars, burning whole cities in waves of invisible fire."

"How do your people live and eat?"

"Some buildings remain only partially destroyed and we scrounge what we can. Lots of canned and preserved food. The twenty-first century Fomorian is a hybrid from centuries of change among humans and breeding with demons and Sluagh. Salt weakens them now even though the *Tuatha* drove them under the sea where they originally came from. So the oceans are intact and we catch seafood. We've built our strongholds in churches in my hometown along the coast. They can't breach consecrated land. If we eventually don't find a permanent defensible place to live, we're thinking of building out into the water."

"Trading places with them, from land to sea and vice versa," Morgan mused, rubbing her temple. "Are there many humans left?"

"No. Out of billions worldwide pre-war, there probably aren't more than a hundred thousand free humans. We don't know exactly how many are left since the world is a large place. I'm sure there are groups who managed to survive by sheer will just like my people have. As for other humans, the Alasoron Cabal marked many as their controlled minions, draining their energy to boost their own. Once a human is marked, they essentially become a lower caste Fomorian."

"Don't humans die when drained of their souls and energy?"

Ryan knocked a thin branch out of their path and let her pass. "Not if they're marked first. They live as long as their master does."

"Which can be centuries." Morgan shuddered.

"Exactly."

"Do Fomorians need humans to maintain their energy or powers?"

"No. They used the extra energy to increase their potency to overpower the other Cabals. It helped them win the wars."

A cold burst of air whooshed up her neck. "I'm so sorry the people of your world had to endure such a horrific experience." Morgan faltered on a rock, plowed into Ryan's back. "Oof." She pushed off him and gained her balance. "Pardon me."

Ryan stopped in a small clearing, moonlight painting a violet sheen over the glade. "Rest." He slid her bulging bag off her shoulder and set it on the mossy ground next to his full load. He rubbed her shoulder where the strap left a welt. "I can carry this."

"You have enough to carry. I can manage." She was reluctant to relinquish the pouch of charms hidden in her satchel. Without them, the island would forever remain a lonely prison. Shaking off her paranoia, she continued to interrogate Ryan. "Surely the creatures didn't drain all the dead of their energy. How did they kill so many people in such a short time?"

Ryan secured the torch in a bed of loose rocks. "Fires destroyed many. Fomorians infected major water and food supplies. The ground is tainted and nothing can grow. One bite from a Fomorian or a marked minion can kill within hours. One bite is all it takes to send a human on a killing spree. Only a strong human can survive a mark and hide it. Many people were betrayed and killed by Fomorian minions who were once friend or family."

"Have any in your coven been marked?" Wheels spun in Morgan's head. She wished to find a way for Ryan to save his people and bring them to the island, if possible. There had to be a reason why his people had survived, beyond utilizing their wits.

Ryan slipped his warm hand around Morgan's neck. "They can't touch my people with their taint. The ones who've been marked resist the poison." Ryan hesitated, his brow furrowing. "Do you have a clue why that is?"

Morgan's heart tumbled excitedly. Only the Ancients carried the magic to travel to the island, a tidbit her father forced into her head. "It may be your Druids carry the blood of the Ancients." She wrapped her fingers around Ryan's arm. "Yet, the Fomorians were able to drain your people of magic or energy, just like WindWraith does to us?" She hated the idea that Lauren, as an Ancient, may have a rightful claim on Ryan.

"Yes." Ryan cocked his head thoughtfully. "Except me."

Morgan gasped, leaning into Ryan. "Did one try?"

"Three attempted it. They died from trying."

Oh, Goddess alive! Morgan's mind spun out of control. What did that mean? What other magic did Ryan carry in his body? Was it his ether? How would it affect her if they completed the soul mate ritual?

"But WindWraith has no trouble stealing your magic," she said.

"I know. That alarms me."

"It's likely because WindWraith's older, stronger. Because it knows how to unravel your Ancient magic, whereas, your future Fomorians have lost the knowledge."

A crimson-breasted parrot screeched shrilly at them before vaulting into the sky in a flurry of moonlit wings, startling a whinny out of the winged horse. Morgan's defensive powers rose then unconsciously dropped like lead inside her core, leaving her feeling bereft of magic. She loathed having to smother her magic. Trembling, the foal butted between them, tromping on Ryan's toes. Ryan swore at the winged horse. Smiling, she envisioned his scowl the darkness hid.

Torchlight glistened on his hair, a golden halo framing

his tanned face. He linked his fingers through hers, leading her to a fallen tree. Age crumbled the log's ends, the middle left solid. He hunkered down between her legs and offered her the waterskin, which she gratefully took and drank deeply. Morgan patted water on her face, then handed the waterskin back.

Ryan kissed her lovingly, her lips quivering in unspoken passion. His tongue explored the recesses of her mouth. She swished her tongue around his, tasting the sharp bite of coconut. Their passions magnified and her palms grew damp. Without breaking the kiss, Ryan pulled her into the circle of his arms, her toes barely scraping the ground. Fresh energy danced along her skin. She clung to his waist, loving his safe solidness. Ryan feathered kisses across her cheek to her ear, and they remained in each other's arms for a long moment, hands roving, caressing, devouring hungry skin.

"I can't get enough of you."

She chuckled against his bare chest, preferring his mixture of sweat and spicy soap to the mud-thick jungle aromas. "Nor I you." She craned her neck back to gaze adoringly at this man who belonged to her.

He kissed her forehead, her nose, then pressed his lips to hers in a last fleeting kiss. "Let's hit it."

"Yes, taskmaster." She mock saluted him.

Whinnying and tossing his head, the foal chased a gray and green rabbit into a thicket. He nosed at the bushes and stamped a tiny hoof in frustration. Laughing, Morgan coaxed him away from the harmless bunny. Ryan refilled their waterskins in the creek gurgling sluggishly through the jungle. Soon enough, they wrestled with the overgrown vegetation again.

"Ryan, how did you come by clothes and whatnot when you washed ashore?" She slipped in loose river pebbles in a dry arm of the creek. Ryan caught her elbow, steadying her.

They moved inland a few yards to steer away from the natural path alongside the creek that haphazardly altered their course, lengthening their trek.

"The day before the pact signing, I couldn't wait to escape my horrible life, if only for an afternoon." His tread grew heavy. "I sailed out of the bay on a wide-open sheet of aquamarine, not a cloud in the sky. That wasn't surprising since clouds no longer formed. The Horde Wars caused electromagnetic pulses that zapped all electronics, machinery, and much of the world's population. It also screwed up weather patterns." He touched her arm, stopping her. She looked up at him expectantly. "I'd never given up hope that somewhere out in the vast seas I'd find a normal life again. Hope crawled through me like an inchworm, never dying, never growing." Ryan smoothed his fingers down her cheek. "Hope was all my people had."

Morgan touched his shoulder, sliding her fingers down to his dragon tattoo. "I'm so sorry."

He shrugged, gave her a prodding pat on her bottom and they resumed their journey. "It is what it is."

"Was it so terrible to contemplate your pact with Lauren? She didn't appear to be a dowdy, horrible woman in my visions."

Ryan snickered. "It was the whole idea of the pact that I didn't like. I was willing to do my part for our future, whether I liked it or not. Our people expected us to breed a new generation of strong Druids. I don't love her. Love doesn't exist in our miserable world. I had no choice. Either I entered the pact or risked death to both our covens."

"Why didn't your two covens work together? Why did you have to force a merger?"

"There has always been too much infighting and distrust between our covens. Many in Lauren's coven committed treasonous acts during the wars by helping the lesser Cabals trying to overpower us."

"Oh, lord." Morgan shook her head. "You trusted them enough to enter into a pact?"

"Lauren needed my help to rule her people, to whip them into shape. By the time the Alasorons took power, they'd already killed her defectors who'd helped the lesser Cabals. Together, we brought hope and power to the covens."

Wistfully, Morgan stroked a bloom on a clump of hibiscus. Sometimes she missed the future originally planned for her on Avalon. "At one time, my people had similar expectations of me." She sniffed her fragrant fingers, wishing always to experience a fresh, aromatic, and beautiful life. "Go on."

"I must have fallen asleep, which had never happened to me on the open water. I jerked awake feeling disconnected from my body as if I'd been portal hopping like the old days, hunting one demon or another. My fire barely flared inside me. I thought I might be Fomorian marked or infected, after all." The winged foal raced across Ryan's path, nearly tripping him. He cursed, stumbled upright. "The sailboat bucked and dipped in seething whitecaps. Thick clouds had rolled in."

"How far did you sail to encounter clouds?"

"I'd only been asleep an hour. I thought I was hallucinating—that's one sign of Fomorian poison—even more so when the rain moved in. I hadn't seen rain in over a year. Then wind and lightning kicked up."

"Were you excited by the tide of events after a terrifying year?"

"It totally freaked me out." He chuckled, swatted at another buzzing bee. "Hell hadn't changed since the day before, just another tent going up at the circus." He stopped and spun around, touched his fingers to her moist cheek. "Now I know differently."

Overwhelmed, Morgan blushed, unable to voice her

beliefs about fate. He smoothed his thumb over her lips, and she kissed it before his hand dropped away. "How bad did the storm get?" Exhausted, she steered him forward and they resumed walking. She wanted to reach their destination before she wilted under the night's balmy heat.

"I've never seen a storm that bad. Gale force winds, slashing rain. Fog settled in and I saw nothing beyond a few yards. Mist so thick I could hack through it with a machete. That's when I strapped on my backpack, secured the boat, and watched the world spin around me."

Shaking his head as if to dislodge the memories, Ryan thrust into a tunnel of tall fluttery grasses. "Lightning zigzagged across the surface of the water. Waves flooded the deck. The wind screamed a bizarre warning that cut through my chest." He hesitated, slowed his pace. "A voice called to me over the roar of the storm..."

Morgan's breath caught. "I'm here. Come to me. Talk to me, I had said."

"Yes," he replied in a hoarse voice. "I scanned the stormy depths looking for you, unable to see anything beyond a few feet. I felt an invisible tether to you, as if you were real and within reach. Then all of a sudden, the fog cleared, creating a doorway into the deepest black space I'd ever seen. A triple bolt of lightning lit the sky, intersecting on a sparkle below the water's surface off starboard. I searched for another boat or anything that might make sense out of the nightmare squall. I saw only that tiny light in the roiling sea. It tugged at my heart, called to my soul." Ryan kept moving forward, as if afraid to show the vulnerabilities in his words and voice.

"The boat began swirling as if in the center of a hurricane, making horrible howling, sucking sounds. I lost my footing and my head crashed against the cabin wall. I almost passed out. When I glanced up, water rose above the boat, and it kept rising into the sky. It curled around port, froze in place. Another blinding flash lit the white tip of the curl. Violet light hurtled toward me like a shooting star. The rogue wave slammed over the boat, and flung me into the sea as the sloop flipped over. I thought I was a goner.

"My last regret was leaving my people in a jam they may never survive." He paused for a long moment, smoothing his hand over the foal's mane until the foal shook him off. "I faced death every day, destroying the evil preying upon us, stealing our magic. Then I'd witnessed the war firsthand, saw the destruction of humanity, lived in its desolate aftermath. I always knew I'd die at the hands of a powerful Fomorian. I sure as hell never expected to bite it alone on my sailboat."

Morgan's knees buckled, and she clutched a tree limb. "Fate wields a mystifying sword."

Ryan chucked. "Don't I know it? Before death pierced me, your voice filled my head, hypnotized me."

Leveraging her faltering body, Morgan caught up to Ryan. She lifted on her toes and molded her lips to his, gave him the same breath of life and the light of love she'd given him in the sea.

Shock shuddered down Ryan's torso. He crushed her to him, took her mouth with a savage intensity, rocking her back and forth. Her knees weakened and she held onto his arms, drinking in the sorrow in his demanding lips, giving him back faith. When they drew apart, he said in a husky voice, "Oblivion claimed me as I reached for the amulet beckoning toward the ocean floor. That's all I remember."

"You smiled at me, held the amulet aloft." Morgan smoothed her hand down his chest, inhaled the faint sandalwood soap on his skin. "I dreamed of that moment, but I couldn't make heads or tails of it."

"Seer's Sight?" Ryan stroked her hair. She nodded, planting a cool kiss on his rune brand. "How can you tell if it's your Sight versus a dream?"

Morgan snickered. "It's difficult. This island confuses my magic. Through years of practice, I found a way to pay attention to my dreams. A gut feeling tells me to heed and listen when it's my Sight. When you capsized, it was a foretelling. The other was just a dream. I didn't piece the two together at first."

"I thought I was losing it."

"Did you want to forget about me?" A dragonfly-sized mosquito landed on her arm, and she slapped it away, along with a swirl of apprehension.

Ryan skipped a step. "Hell, I don't know." Fern fronds taller than his six feet blocked the path. He shoved them aside, letting her stride through the slim opening. "You were in my head. I tried to tell myself you didn't exist. But you remained even after the ocean tossed me on the beach. Then we had the one dream and it showed me something I believed I didn't care about, especially in my bleak existence."

The trail tapered to the span of one body. Ryan took the lead, needlessly holding back branches that naturally eased away for Morgan. A half-hidden vine snaked across the path. Ryan stepped high over it. "Watch your step."

Morgan dipped the torch and saw the vine shiver, its leaves fluttering in the stagnant air. It shrank into the ground, buried by mulch. She grinned in amazement. The foal sniffed the spot, stomping a front hoof, trying to dig out the disappearing creeper.

"Fate has a helluva bang. Now that I know it was yours and Gwilym's magic, it all makes sense. Except—" Firelight reflected a deep searching look in his eyes.

"Who believed our magic could reach across time and strange worlds? My father is very powerful, although I never believed him capable of time and space travel."

A seductive smile slid across Ryan's mouth, showing a hint of teeth. "I'd love to thank him someday."

"Maybe we'll find a way." Morgan studied her boots, unable to confess her ability to scry to Gwilym. She wanted to hang onto her father for a time before sharing him.

"I hate that fate split you two up." Oversized magenta orchids grew in profusion beside them. Ryan tugged one off its stem and slipped it behind her ear, fastening it in her braid. "You are one beautiful, brave woman." His lips caressed her neck, sliding down to the hollow of her throat. Her skin twittered along the line of kisses he left behind.

Beyond the cove where they'd spent their first day together, they descended an overgrown, indistinct route to another hidden cove. Secluded on three sides by walls covered by boulders and sea grasses, the water swept onto the shoreline in lazy strokes, the color of gray dawn.

The sun rose from the western horizon. Ginger and gold painted the sky above the water, spreading into a shimmering sheet of gilded crimson that left Morgan gaping in awe. The island's energy seemed centered in the small inlet. It created odd sparks as it danced a jig with her magic. They stood on the craggy shoreline, a tepid mist dripping on them. The bloated northern moon darkened plum like, shadowing the southern moon, casting a violet haze on the white sand. Night's last stars peeked down upon them, winking their goodbyes.

Blinking rapidly, she turned to Ryan, who watched her reaction with a sly smile. "It's raining!" She laughed, holding her palms up to catch the mysterious, cool drizzle. "There are no clouds!" Amazement trilled up her spine.

"This island defies logic." He dumped their bags on the damp ground and clasped her shoulders from behind, easing his chest against her back. "For all I know, we're in an undiscovered dimension."

Morgan knew they were on no documented land. Old Merlin's powerful magic was absolute and far-reaching. Little did he know when he banished WindWraith here that the island contained magic the twisted Fomorian creature was able to decipher and use to poke holes in the barrier. As long as they destroyed WindWraith, the island remained hidden and safe, soon home to those singular lives tied to the charms stuffed in her satchel. Unless they found a way for all of Ryan's people to find the paradise. She certainly would always remain a part of the land. No matter what Ryan believed, he may be stuck on the island forever. He was stubborn enough to want to discover that for himself, so she kept her tongue. Yet, she lived in fear that he'd find a way to leave.

At the right time, she would tell him what Gwilym passed on to her. She only hoped by then he understood that his people must rely upon themselves. Doubts still meandered through her, thicker than the vines growing in wild profusion on the island. Maybe all was not as it seemed and tomorrow falsely proved all the nonsense in her head.

The winged foal trotted hesitantly toward the ocean. A wave rolled in and he scampered back. His ears flattened as he hissed at the foamy froth popping on the white sand.

Morgan laughed. "Silly baby. It won't hurt you."

"The winged horses don't like the ocean. They won't go near it, nor fly over it." Ryan's breath tickled her ear. "Water currents surrounding the island are dangerous, unpredictable."

A loud double wave crashed onto the shore to enhance his point. The raven pair wheeled above, silhouetted by moonlight lending their black bodies an ethereal hue. They swooped in perfect sync. The birds of the seers belonged together. A telling sign, Morgan mused. Of what, remained a mystery.

She leaned her head against Ryan's chest, smoothing her fingers over his forearms wrapped across her stomach. "Did you ever try to leave the island?"

"Hell, yes. From various launching points." He rested his chin on her head. "I built a crude raft. Each time I rowed out, I barely reached the breakers where a riptide swirled me in circles back to shore. No matter how hard I fought, I couldn't row past the breaks. Lunar effects on the tides obviously have strange effects on this fantasy island."

"It is a beautiful, fascinating paradise," she said thoughtfully. The mist kissed her hot face like a balm, doing little to alleviate her fatigue.

"Let's get out of the rain. I want to show you what I found. The earthquake must've opened up a hidden entry into a lava tube."

When he dropped his arms, she staggered without his support. Exhaustion snuffed out whatever energy WindWraith had deigned to leave behind. Ryan caught her before her gelled legs deposited her on the sand.

Concern etched his face. "Did I push you too hard?"

"I'm simply weary." She usually recovered faster after expending magic. More confusing, the island's vibrant energy no longer enhanced her depleted state.

"Can you walk up that incline?" Ryan tipped his head toward a mass of palmettos and pampas grass leading up the cliff.

She nodded. "I'm starving, too. That's probably what ails me." Less convinced than her words revealed, she continued at a slower pace.

They approached the cliff walls. Untainted, crystal energy bristled over Morgan's skin. Ryan peeled away viney tentacles and held back the overgrown greenery to let her slide into an opening along the cliffside. The foal pranced on her heels, and Ryan brought up the rear. A few feet into the interior, the cave deepened into ebony darkness. Tangible energy enticed them forward. Her heartbeat accelerated. "It's very dark."

Ryan found her hand in the tunnel and she grabbed

hold. "Use your other hand to follow the wall. It lightens the farther we go into the interior."

They inched into a tight passageway. Green, amber, and white veins glimmered in variegated granite and lava walls. The air oscillated with life, summoning them forward. Energy spilled into Morgan, feeding her depleted reserves. The farther they traversed beneath the ground, the more gems of every rainbow color guided them onward. The tunnel widened into an eight-foot round illuminated antechamber. Morgan released Ryan's hand and spun in a circle, her mouth gaping in awe.

"Keep going." He patted her lower back. "It gets better."

Water trickled in the passageway, and she heard a waterfall's louder splashes up ahead. They rounded a sharp bend and Morgan stopped, laughing in amazement.

Crystals of every color imaginable coated the walls of an expansive cavern, the size of a large ballroom. Masses of them ranging from several inches to eight feet long dangled from the high ceiling like multihued icicles. Passageways and smaller caves splayed off from the main cavern. In the chamber's center, a natural hot spring bubbled, puffy clouds of steam spiraling up from it. A small waterfall at the cavern's far side poured into a cool water pool. A dawdling stream flowed out of the cavern and seemed to disappear underground.

"This is fantastic." Morgan grinned. She dipped her hand in the hot spring—perfect bathing temperature.

Ryan set their packs on the ground. A low wall of rock encased the hot spring, leaving a two-foot-wide ledge rimming the top. He eased a hip on a smooth spot. A relaxed smile spilled across his face, dazzling against his bronzed skin. His whole face lit up when he smiled now. Eyes full of warmth and promise, dimple curving around his left eye, lips curling up his full mouth.

Morgan lost her breath for several seconds. It was the

first time she'd witnessed such a carefree, happy smile on his handsome face. And no one had ever smiled at her in that way. Flushed, she returned to surveying the cavern to evade his allure. "When did you discover this cave?"

"The cove is where I washed ashore. I felt crystal energy but couldn't locate a source. When I left you a couple of days ago..." He coughed into his fist, a flush working up his neck to his face. "I wondered if the earthquake had opened an entrance."

Dizziness struck Morgan and she swayed, catching her hand on the ledge of the hot spring. Ryan lunged and scooped her up. He carried her into a roomy alcove lined with less radiant, deeper hued gems on one side, offering just enough light to maneuver in the space. Weariness anchored her with the weight of the world on her shoulders.

"You need to rest and eat." He propped her on a flat rock, then covered a sleeping pallet of mosses and wilting palm fronds with a large fur. "I made this pallet for us." He gave her a tender smile as she slid into the softness.

"You wanted to sleep with me?" she teased weakly.

"Hell, yes. Don't ever doubt that." His expression hardened, but his caresses on her face belied his sternness. "Stay put while I get you something to eat."

Lead bogged down her eyelids. The corners of her lips lifted, and she was asleep before he reached their packs.

CHAPTER 23

The foal flapped its tiny wings and trotted back to the sleeping pallet the moment Ryan moved away. "Get!" Scowl lines deepened around his mouth, he waved his arms at it. "Give her a break."

"It's fine." Morgan fingered her bed-tousled hair off her face and scratched the prancing foal's fluffy forehead. "He's tolerant of you because you take care of me."

"Is that what he said?" Ryan smirked. "Little shit. He's tolerant because I feed him."

Morgan giggled. "I told him to mind you because you're good to both of us." She futilely pushed the foal away. "Shoo, RavenStar."

"RavenStar?"

"It emerged in a vision." Morgan traced the crooked white star on the foal's forehead with her fingertip, the foal practically preening at her attention. "I saw him grown into a massive stallion peering off into the distance at a herd of white winged mares. Those maddening ravens were circling overhead, too."

Ryan cocked his head. "He is an aberration. All the other winged horses I've seen are white or dappled grays."

Morgan took Ryan's outstretched hand, and in one forward motion, she was in his arms. "How do you feel?" He locked his hands against her spine, and she reveled in the perfect fit of their bodies.

"Marvelous." She linked her arms around his neck. "I

just needed a little rest. The crystals help—I feel awesome energy here. I could probably assassinate WindWraith myself." She danced a jig in Ryan's loose clasp, rubbing her breasts against his chest.

"I think this cavern is the island's nucleus." Ryan's hands slipped up her arms, his fingers playing with a lock of her hair. "I bet the island draws energy from the crystals."

"Is that so," Morgan murmured. When he didn't respond to her not so subtle persuasion, she feathered her lips over his temptingly.

A muscle flicked in his jaw, and he edged back. "You'll eat first." To her disappointment, he picked up a small sack of fruit.

They settled on a wide stone ledge overlooking the oval inlet outside the catacombs. Water dripped off the plants along the natural sea wall. The mist had left behind a muggy afternoon, the air denser than molasses. By the time they finished eating, perspiration drenched them.

Morgan stood and stretched. "I feel so languid."

"It's more than the heat. WindWraith's been draining our powers faster."

"We are safe here, though?"

"Yes." Ryan packed up the remaining food.

She swung aside her braid, ingesting one last breath of hot, sticky air. They returned to the cool cavern, wiping moisture off their faces. As if he'd been undressing in front of Morgan for years, Ryan stripped off his shorts and strode into the waterfall.

Transfixed by his powerful naked body, she tilted her head to the side to study the various scars marring his bronzed back. "I'll wash you if you wash me."

"I like the sound of that," Ryan replied huskily, not bothering to hide his desire. He approached from behind, hooked the bottom of her shift, and drew it over her head.

His deft fingers unwound her braid and finger combed her long hair one section at a time. Heat expanded in her middle, and she rubbed her arm against his wet chest, needing to feel his skin against hers.

From one shoulder to the other, Ryan trailed tiny kisses, stopping at her right ear lobe. Her skin tingled from his feathery touch. He reached over and dug the bowl of fragrant soap out of his backpack. Fingers twined together, they moved into the refreshing waterfall.

Ryan scooped out a glob of soap and smoothed his slick fingers over her shoulders, down her back. Morgan shivered, reveling in the feel of his large hands lovingly cleansing her from head to toe, his touch so gentle her bones grew watery.

She placed her hand on his wrist, stopping his movements before she melted into a gooey mess at his feet. "My turn," she offered languorously, reaching for the soap.

"Later, love." Velvet layered his deep voice. He rinsed her under the waterfall and then backed her into the cool water pool. His hands cupped her breasts, his thumbs circling her nipples, rousing a new melting sweetness in her.

He returned to kissing her tingling neck. Heat grew fierce within her despite the knee-high cool water. He held her close against him, his rock hard length pressed against her spine. Her head fell back on his chest, his tanned hand splayed on the white flesh of her stomach. The contrast was startling, his touch intoxicating.

When he lowered his hand between her thighs and slid a finger into her wet heat, her knees weakened. His thumb danced on her most sensitive spot, pressing and pulsing. Sensations peaked inside her and Morgan's heat nearly boiled the water in the pool.

Their amethysts glowed vibrantly, glinting off the crystals suspended from the ceiling. Ryan's magic unexpectedly snaked into Morgan causing her to falter and unleash her own magic. Startled, Ryan wrenched back as crackling air swept into him. Their bond solidified, and his fire magic waltzed in flawless sync inside her. Magic tangoed in a sultry rhythm in the air. The insistent press of his desire in her mind intensified her own arousal, and she welcomed him completely.

As his fingers maintained the dance of pleasure on her sensitive flesh, he kissed her neck, nibbled on her ear lobes. His other hand strayed upwards, cupped her left breast, massaging, scorching. Possessing.

Passion spiraled higher, clouded her brain. Hypnotized by his touch, she burned from his expert route to ecstasy. Unable to stand the urgent bonfire rising in her, she cried out, "Ryan! Please...oh Goddess," she almost wailed, biting back a moan.

He chuckled hoarsely, working his magic touch until her release hooked her, pounding waves of desire through her heart, chest, and head. Collapsing against him, Morgan unraveled with one reverberation after another, exploding in a shower of sizzling sensations. Ryan turned her and wrapped his body around her, supporting her from sagging to the ground. She'd never felt so sheltered, so desirable, so loved. Her whole body took on an awareness she'd never believed possible. Trembles rocked her from their enjoined magic gyrating wildly inside her, sending her into another frenzied, desperate ache of longing.

She felt so wanton for the first time in her life. Morgan kissed his chest, licked off drops of water, planting wet kisses down his quivering stomach.

Dipping her tongue in and out of his navel, she teased the tiny depression until his flesh rippled beneath her tongue. Growls escaped him, and she felt his ecstasy surge through his groin. Inching lower, her damp hair skimmed over his inflamed skin, floated on the water's surface.

Morgan touched his hard shaft with her fingertips, running them along his full length, marveling at the softness hiding the iron beneath.

Ryan's back arched, his hands finding purchase on her head. "Morgan, Morgan! Baby, you feel better than I dreamed."

After a moment of pleasuring him, she lifted her head. "Am I doing this right?" She loved returning the pleasure he gave her and knew it would always be this way between them.

"Yes! Don't fucking stop." Sweat dripped down Ryan's flushed face, and he twisted his fingers in her hair.

Gently, she closed her hand around the base of his hard length. His body swayed against her and he exhaled a frayed breath. Fierce, reckless hunger blazed through her, but she kept up the rhythmic pressure with her hand, while she pressed her lips across his chest.

His back and legs tensed, and she felt his passion reaching its peak, electrifying her. With a bellow, a strong tremor rolled up from Ryan's feet as she brought him to release. Legs unsteady, he locked her in his arms. His feral gaze traveled over her face, searching, probing, delving deep into her soul. Her whole being flooded with desire and she was almost boneless with it. Ryan molded his mouth to hers in a hard, demanding kiss.

He owned her. Heart, body, soul, and magic.

Reluctantly ending the soul-stealing kiss, Ryan carried Morgan to the hot spring and released her into the bath temperature water. She floated to a slate wedge halfway down the shallow depths. He climbed in next to her and leaned back, his head landing on the surrounding wall. Water enveloped Morgan in tranquil warmth. It burst from the floor and tickled her sensitive skin. The spring's sharp mineral odor smelled alive with possibilities. Even the bubbles popping against her flesh promised unnamed potential.

She never believed love could be such an enthralling torture to her senses. Their differing magic complemented each other like kindred souls. All those wasted years never believing she'd experience such a bounty of sweet agony offered by her dream sorcerer. Never believing a proper match existed for her, someone not afraid of her immense power, a soul mate who completed her in body, heart, and magic. Those lost years clearly represented a prelude to her rebirth on this island. Now, she easily forgave Fate for leading her to believe her life ended at the age of twenty-two.

Bursting bubbles tickled her nose. She giggled, swam to Ryan. "This feels wonderful."

"Not as wonderful as you felt." He grinned wolfishly.

The water lifted her up, the surface teasing her tender breasts, hardening her nipples. She kissed him, swiping her tongue over his bottom lip. Goddess, she wanted this man in all ways.

"I think you have a little more to give me," she cooed against his mouth. She straddled his lap, looping her arms around his neck, forming her legs around his hips. Their glowing amethysts created purple embers on the water's roiling surface. He took her mouth in another kiss, his lips hard and searching, tender and accepting. Water swirled around them evocatively, and Ryan groaned in her mouth. One possessive hand caressed her back, the other whispered across her scars. The slow, seductive kiss left her giddy. She leaned into him, supporting her weight on his chest.

Relentless, Ryan's mouth began another tortuous assault on her senses. The rough scrape of beard stubble across her throat was almost more than her delicate skin could bear.

"You are so perfect." His fingertips set her scars alight.

"So beautiful." He placed her hand over her scars, gloving it with his. "So strong and fearless."

The heat of his magic dripped his sincerity into her mind. Ryan claimed another ravishing kiss, tongues tangling, proving his candor. Water lifted Morgan on a swirling current. Dizzy with need, their kisses grew frantic. Her hips moved urgently against him and she let the water raise her over his lap. She needed him now, or she'd die. Lost, completely and unutterably lost.

As she began to lower herself onto his iron shaft, he went rigid, his shoulders coiling beneath her touch. "Morgan, hold on, baby." Ryan gently lifted her off him, leaving her floundering in the water. Frustration tightened his jaw and shadowed the raw lust reddening his face.

Morgan's desire zigzagged downward in the face of rejection. "Do you not want me that way?" She folded her arms over her breasts. "I thought—"

"You have to ask?" he threw back. Rising off the ledge, he stood stock still in the hot spring. He pivoted away, his sleek muscular back glistening reddish-brown from the water's heat.

Misgivings chilled her despite the temperature of the water. "Then what is it?" She rose and twined her arms around his torso, wishing to ward off the tempest infringing upon their bond. "Do not fear. I'm ready to continue with the binding rituals. I've given you everything else of myself." Her tone grew bitter. Was it possible her duties threatened to keep her from a family and love? *Goddess alive, may I have one thing in life I desperately crave?*

Ryan eased her hands from around his waist. He hopped out of the pool and slumped to the ground against a smooth, water-worn boulder. The water pouring into the brook vanquished all other sounds in the cavern. Steam floated off the hot spring's surface, blurring Morgan's vision and her emotions. The water grew intolerable as Ryan took his time to speak. Biting down on her tongue, she feared her world would crash down upon her once again if she upset the fragile balance.

After an interminable time, Ryan lifted his head. The lines bracketing his eyes, creasing his forehead bespoke his inner turmoil. "I'm afraid of inflicting demon hunter Ryan O'Rourke on your beautiful, unsullied soul, your giving heart."

"No. No," Morgan whispered. "Why in heavens do you think that?" She climbed out of the hot spring and walked to him, heedless of her nakedness and her vulnerabilities that no longer mattered. She cleared a spot on the stony ground and knelt beside him. Was he afraid his magic might sully hers once they bonded fully? She rested her palms on his knees, his legs tensing at her touch. "We will be united through a pure, untainted bond."

Two creases of worry appeared between his eyes. "What about my ether? Too much and it can kill."

She squeezed his knees, quelling the electricity that zinged along their minute tie. "Remember, only Druids of ancient blood can tolerate star magic. I am one of them."

Ryan leaned his head against the boulder. He fisted his hands on the ground, his knuckles stretched white. He knew she could handle his ether magic. She'd already proven that during WindWraith's thrall. Whatever bothered him concerned his other magical abilities.

Dank cave air invaded her as noxious as her foreboding. "What innate ability do you hide from me?" she asked frankly. She drew her knees up to cover her chest and linked her arms around them. Squeezing into a ball, she wanted to shield herself from the storm erupting in Ryan's residual magic fluttering in her middle.

He picked at loose crystal fragments on the ground. "How exactly does the final bond work? What will happen?"

"You're stalling."

"Answer me."

"Your magic will fill me, and mine will fill you." Her arms tightened around her legs. "I will be able to draw upon your magic. You will be able to draw upon mine—without a sending. The receiver will have many times the power, while the giver's power will drain only slightly." She paused, pressing fingers to her forehead. "Your magic will not fully be a part of me, nor mine a part of you. You have to consciously draw from the accessible power." The long forgotten ritual arose in her mind. "Except for the power that melds during heightened emotions." A fierce blush rose up Morgan's neck. "My elements will complete you. Yours will complete me."

Silent and somber, Ryan soaked up her words. "Elemental or innate?"

"Elemental. You won't have my ability to prophesize or any of my other innate abilities. I won't have your tracking ability and whatever else you were inherently born with."

A smile tugged the corners of his lips. "Damn, I was hoping I'd be the first Druid of my time who could tell the future."

Morgan gawked in disbelief. "You have no seers in your time?"

"A *true* seer hasn't existed since before my mother was born. They were the first to succumb to Fomorian control. Before the wars, they led us into ambushes with false visions. I was still cleaning up the distrust they created under my father's leadership. I outlawed the last seers from our ranks when I took power." He frowned. "Our magic has disappeared. Fomorians have seen to that. That's why I must go back. I have to—"

She held his angular face in her small hands. "What do you truly fear?"

"Hurting you," he whispered, dropping a soft kiss on her palm. "You hating me."

"That will never happen." Despite the splattering of the waterfall and the boiling hot spring, silence fell in the cave like a soft blanket of snow.

A vein jumped on Ryan's temple. "I have the ability to draw black magic into me and subvert it into my own magic. I can alter it and use it to destroy evil. The black magic stays with me, increasing my powers. I don't know of any other sorcerer who can do that. That's why I'm the best assassin. The reason why the pact was made. That's why my people need me."

Speechless, Morgan collapsed back onto her heels. Outright lunacy! No one alive had such capabilities. *No, Goddess, no.* Dread formed a tight band around her chest as her heart galloped to escape it.

Sundry thoughts and emotions tossed about in her mind. WindWraith's haunting words vaulted to the forefront. He knew. The nasty demon knew Ryan held ether. Did the bloody bastard know about this dangerous talent? Jumping up, she tried to distance herself from Ryan but he grabbed her wrist. She tussled against his firm hold. About to lash out at him, a knife-like pain struck her head. Slowly, she felt her body wilting. Ryan's strong arms offered little comfort as a black void swallowed her mind.

CHAPTER 24

Fluctuating bands of air tied Morgan to a flat stone surface in semi-darkness. She struggled against her constraints using magic that refused to obey. Bleary-eyed, she inspected her surroundings, not recognizing the narrow burrow she lay in. Diffused lights glowed in the space like stagnant fireflies. Where was she? How did she get there? Cotton blossomed in her mind, and she strained to recall the last thing she'd done, but was unable to remember much beyond entering the great cavern with Ryan.

The air bands thinned and she attempted to rise slowly, realizing she had barely enough headroom to sit. The right path out of the tunnel led to an abyss of midnight. A faint glow lit the left path. Distant cascading water hinted that a waterfall resided beyond the glowing tunnel. Was it the main cavern?

The vision was so lifelike she had a difficult time judging reality from her dreamlike state, especially when she could almost feel sweat on her skin. The air shackles finally dissipated and she choked back a frightened cry as she slipped off the raised dais. Fear shivered down her back, and she wished she had something to cover her nakedness. Morgan knew this wasn't real.

An energy force, combined with Morgan's intuition, persuaded her to take the narrowest path on her left. Sticking out her arms, she tested freedom away from the stone slab and found no resistance. To avoid ramming her head into a wall, she inched through the dim tunnel, not knowing if she headed toward the crystal cave or elsewhere. The alluring force coaxed her onward, toward a fountain of power. *It had to be the beautiful, big cave!* Not even her bond to Ryan carried such intense power. Surely, WindWraith hadn't gained the energy to draw her to him, had he?

Magic marched along her bond to Ryan, blossoming into desire. Need ripped through Morgan in a mix of pleasure-pain. She wanted more. Wished it would end. Fire ignited her blood. Flames flicked her thighs, and her nipples hardened into aching pebbles.

"Ryan!" she cried. "Is that you? What's happening?"

Once his name left her lips, the painful erotic teasing withdrew. Fiery ropes battered her backside, and Morgan shrieked against the stinging lashes cutting into her skin. Her external shields vaulted into place. Too late.

A whooshing, gurgling laugh echoed in the cave.

WindWraith.

No! Not again, whoreson! The Fomorian fed off her memories, making her believe it was Ryan. Power vaulted up from her core. Morgan erected a protective barrier in her mind and reinforced those outside her body. The walls disintegrated before she completed them. Shaking with frustration, she tried again and the external pressure shredded her shields. Fury forced another tortured scream from her throat. Fighting the vision and her attack as one, she tried to wake up, but the evil held her under its spell.

As quick as the lashes began, they whipped away as one. Enraged and terrified, Morgan brushed tears off her cheeks. No longer in the tunnel she'd been crawling through, she lay naked on an elevated platform in a larger cave. Invisible belts strapped down her arms, torso, and ankles. She focused within to call her magic, but her powers were imprisoned, unreachable, lost. Sickening waves of terror swelled up from her hollow stomach.

Pools of crimson liquid burned the air. Sounds of water tumbling down boulders, babbling over rocks wafted to her from beyond her vision. The dim light enabled her to make out her prison's features. The first thing she noticed was the deadened crystals plastering the walls. So solidly black, no light penetrated or reflected off them. A pinprick glowed in a fissure in the wall, drawing Morgan's attention to it like a moth to a flame. Shuffling noises at the foot of her dais captured her attention before she managed to investigate the pale dot.

Her bond to Ryan whispered in her mind. "Ryan?" She craned her neck against her constraints to peer beyond her platform. More gray gloom.

"Yes, love." Devoid of emotion, his familiar voice fell flat.

"I can't move or reach my magic."

"I have your magic." He laughed in a smugly sinister manner. "As you wished me to."

Barbed vines snaked around her heart. That wasn't her Ryan. Had WindWraith possessed him? If so, how could WindWraith withstand Ryan's ether?

"What are you doing?" Her voice wobbled.

"It's time to end this farce and return home."

The Ryan replica loomed to her left, his features melting into the darkness. Air swooped over her flesh at his approach, as cold and ominous as a swirl of snow on a winter's gravesite.

Uselessly, she strained at her invisible bonds. Her head felt like dead weight, her fingers frozen in place. "What do you mean?"

Ryan laughed again, the sound grating and vile. This wasn't the Ryan O'Rourke she had fallen in love with.

The monster touched her bare breast, his fingers cold,

bony, and sinister. "I told you I would return home to fulfill my duties as Druid leader and assassin."

Rough fingers smoothed down her stomach, scratched over her scars. Morgan shrank inward, tried to close her mind to the invasion. "You can't leave this island." Her voice cracked and she gulped down her mounting horror.

"Ah. You are wrong." He bent his head and pressed an icy kiss on her stomach. "We will leave the island bound together for eternity, as you so crave."

"How can we get off this island?" Morgan tested his receptiveness.

"My love, you know as well as I that one more earthquake will uproot the crystal barrier. Then we can call Avalon's strong magic and destroy WindWraith. Once we do that, the world is ours."

Morgan cringed. Avalon? *Ryan means to destroy Avalon for his own gain!* "Why do you need so much power to leave the island?"

"*We* will return to my land, filled with unimaginable power."

"You aren't Ryan!" Morgan burst out. "You taunt me, WindWraith. You'll never leave this island. Do you hear me? Not in Ryan's body, not in mine!"

Bright light burst in Morgan's skull. Magic shimmered around her, infused every cell of her being. Light and airy, she floated in a vast ebony sea of diamond stars. Energy blazed in her blood as she zipped through the night sky. The thirteen stones on Avalon's highest ground flitted by, standing majestically in a tempest of lightning. A strong, firm hand clasped hers. She turned to see Ryan floating beside her, guiding her through the winking stars. Welcoming, embracing, his smile shot her full of love and joy.

"You'll come home with me and feed me your magic, little raven. That's the reason fate brought us together.

Without it, we cannot leave the island. Now that we've bonded, I'll have all the combined power I need to save my people."

Her brain floundered. Gwilym said she couldn't leave the island. She had duties to perform here. What might happen to her if they found a way to leave? Would she die? Would Ryan die? What about the people destined for the island?

"All I need is your magic inside me completely. Your body and soul bound to mine." A startling vision of Ryan making love to her swamped her mind and receded as quickly.

Damned confused hell! Ryan could have easily uttered those words. Tears slipped down her cheeks. "Ryan," she cried, "you don't know what you're saying."

He slicked his tongue up her torso, between her breasts. Freezing pockets of air followed the wet trail. She writhed in her shackles, the invisible straps biting into her skin.

"Are you so sure?" A slithery tongue flicked over her lips. "Nothing has changed since you arrived on the island. I want you to help me return home. I need your help to capture WindWraith." His lips grazed her ear. "Together we can rule the world." Exaltation fringed his smirking voice.

"No!" Morgan shouted.

The dead ebony cavern trapped the sound. A vision of WindWraith devouring the body of a vaguely familiar man filled her head. The last thing she saw was the man's skull and bones heaped in a corner of a red molten cavern.

CHAPTER 25

Braced between Ryan's thighs and held firmly to his chest, Morgan felt her body rocking slowly. Her eyelids fluttered open and she gazed into his chalky, scared face. A thunderbolt of memory struck her. Repulsed, she wrestled from his hold and scampered across the pebbly ground out of arm's reach.

"Whoa, Morgan. What's wrong?" Ryan leaped up in a defensive stance.

Morgan situated the hot spring between them. She tapped into her magic, readied it.

Ryan scanned the cavern and gave her a puzzled look. Relief flowed across his shoulders, down his arms. "Are you okay? Your eyeballs rolled up into your head and you passed out."

Was this Ryan? Had WindWraith consumed him? Had her vision already happened, or was it her Sight? It seemed real, unlike her other prophesies. She wrangled with the conflicting chaos. A thudding in her forehead added to the fray, and Ryan stared at her as if she'd sprouted thorns and flowers in her hair.

Stalling to form an answer, acutely conscious of her nakedness, Morgan retrieved her discarded shift and slipped it over her head. She gathered her damp hair and weaved it into a knot at her neck.

Crystal light glistened on Ryan's naked body in rioting dots of colors. Her palms grew moist and she averted her head, avoiding his nakedness. He was too distracting when she needed to wrap her mind around the vision.

He advanced toward her, his emotions masked in his level stare. "What happened?"

Their link had dissolved, leaving a hollowness in her middle. Either Ryan shielded himself or WindWraith had found a way to possess him. *Holy Goddess on high.*

"I'm well. It was inconsequential." She licked her dry lips, hating the vulnerability the island's energies created with her random visions. Morgan spent more time knocked out in a vision or asleep replenishing her magic on this maddening island. She couldn't wait for WindWraith to die and stop sucking the life out of her.

Ryan opened his mouth to speak, shut it. Thoughtful, he scratched his tattoo. The dragon rippled and the ruby eyes winked. Finally, he curled his hands, cracked his knuckles. Pained reconciliation turned to confidence in his expression. "I know how to unravel WindWraith's magic. But I need your help to weaken the bastard and hold it in thrall." His tone both requested and demanded. "I need WindWraith inside me so I can take his magic home with us. His power will help me defeat the Fomorians ravaging my people."

The dread in her stomach nearly made her retch. Was that all he wanted from her? Was that what the doomed vision tried to warn her? Morgan desperately wanted to flee to sort out reality and her vision. However, they had to confront the issue and waste no more time. Avalon and Ryan's people were at great risk if WindWraith succeeded in his plans, whether it possessed her body or found a way to live in Ryan's ether tainted body. Either way, the Fomorian was gaining more power than any creature alive or dead.

"You cannot do it. Not without me, and I won't let you. We have to *destroy* it."

"We'll contain it, then destroy it." Ryan thumped his chest. "Inside me."

"It will change you into a monster if it doesn't kill you first," Morgan spat out. "Moreover, you cannot go home." Her voice escalated into a high pitch.

He spread his legs in a rebellious posture, towering over her. "I'll be fine. I've done it before." Ryan's encouraging tone sounded brittle in her ears.

"With a Fomorian this old and strong?"

"We'll capture it and reduce its powers. Then I'll absorb it inside me."

His gaze was like a cold wind down her back. "Then what? There's no way off this damned island. You said so yourself."

"I've found a way—"

"We will never leave this island. It has been foretold," she said evenly.

"You're wrong. I'll show you." Excitement animated his face.

Ryan stretched out a hand. Inwardly cringing, she took it. A false, compliant smile barely twitched the corners of her mouth.

"Morgan, what's wrong?" He squeezed her stiff hand.

"I feel an odd sense of unease." The dialogue in the vision tangled her thoughts. Was it truly WindWraith? Had Ryan discovered a way off the island? Could he really take her home with him? Did she want to go to that wasteland only to battle evil? And risk Avalon's people? No. She must make Ryan see reason.

"Of course you feel uneasy with everything we've gone through, still have to do."

She let the matter go, wanting to first see the subject of his enthusiasm. He rubbed the small of her back, then led her through a tunnel trailing away from the main cavern. Barely wide enough for them to walk abreast, Ryan had to stoop beneath the low ceiling. Morgan noticed a distinct hum, felt the vibrations against her midriff. It intensified the farther they moved away from the large chamber.

The tunnel widened to the width of several men and Ryan slowed. Palpable energy stemmed from around a bend. It electrified her nerves endings, prickled beneath her skin like flickers of lightning. Felt exactly like the force that lured her from the smooth stone bed in her vision. Morgan grasped her neck with one hand, feeling her pulse drum against her finger.

"Don't cross the entryway to the cave at the end." Ryan's severe tone left no room for objection.

She hunched a shoulder in response. What additional mysteries did this mystical island hold?

They stopped outside a craggy archway into another small cavern. About twelve feet round, radiant crystals covered its every inch. Energy swirled as intense as a vortex. It skipped out of tune to the beat of Morgan's magic, similar to the disjointed sensation of traveling through the Sacred Stones on Avalon. She wriggled her hand out of Ryan's and clung to the rugged tunnel walls, peering into the fascinating chamber.

In the center, a warped pillar rose to the gem-crusted ceiling, appearing to support the cave's roof. Morgan guessed it about twenty feet high. Flakes as brilliant as sunlight on diamonds glittered on the pillar. Studying the cavity, Morgan found pockets of colorless stones embedded in the walls. The clear stones absorbed color from the surrounding multihued crystals, giving them the appearance of color. A thrill shot through her. The distinctly different, intensive energy came from the colorless gems. Wild, colossal, exhilarating.

Ryan's breath warmed the side of her neck. "I knew a portal existed somewhere on the island. It was the only thing that made a lick of sense in bringing us here."

"My father's magic brought us here," Morgan replied sarcastically, hands on hips, inching away from him.

"That's what you said," he retorted. "But I know portals. I've traveled through every known one on Earth."

"But you said we may be in another dimension?" Confusion howled like a ceaseless windstorm inside her brain. She rubbed her aching head, wishing to squeeze sense out of it. Did Father know all this?

"Portals can take you from one to the next. You just need to know what's at the receiving gate. You also need strong magic to teleport."

"How do you get home once you've gone through?" Was the monolithic stone ring a space or time portal? Was WindWraith using it somehow? Not if the crystals weaken him, surely? She pressed on her temples.

"The same way. Knowing specifically where you want to go." He leaned against the rough earthen wall. "I lost my memory once chasing a shape-shifting demon in Scotland. I got stuck in the highlands for two weeks until my memory returned and I remembered where the portals were located.

"We arrived through this one, believe it or not. Ancient Druid magic," he hesitated, "and the amulets may have assisted with the time aspects and the island's secrecy, but the portal facilitated the teleportation."

"Gwilym said there's no way off the island," she murmured to herself.

"He's wrong," Ryan declared in her ear from behind.

Startled by his closeness, she stumbled, her heel landing in the threshold, on the fringe of the maelstrom. Intense power spread from her foot to her knee. Nothingness replaced the bottom half of her leg like a phantom limb.

"Ryan!" She raised her defensive magic and seized hold of his hand grappling her waist.

Wind spun up from the ground, spiraled toward the

ceiling. Morgan's braid unraveled and hair whisked about her face. It felt as if a giant leech was sucking the life out of her. The translucent stones radiated brilliant hues, saturating the room in rainbows. The force wrenched her through the entrance and she struggled against the cyclonic wind.

"Drop your magic!" Ryan tugged her safely out of the cave.

She forcibly constrained her magic, locking her insatiable power inside her core.

"Damn, it's strong. It pulled you in by linking to your magic, trying to control it."

Gasping, she rested her forehead on his chest and hauled in air to quiet her frantic heart. Ryan's embrace lulled her into a false sense of security, and she begged for proof to quash her last vision. Goddess help her if she had to deal with WindWraith inside Ryan.

"We need to leave this site now." She sniffed. The moment she spoke the words, her connection to Ryan sparked inside her, sprouting a renewed awareness along their bond. Pure and clean, a part of her body as familiar as her hand.

Ryan smoothed his hand down her back. Their bond twitched fully awake and sweet relief sailed through her, loosening the tight muscles in her arms. Her amethyst hummed, flared in harmony with his. Joyful tears stung her eyes.

Pieces of the vast puzzle clicked together in Morgan's mind. WindWraith was unable to unite with one who possessed ether. Ryan's ether magic would kill it. Which meant the Fomorian's sole goal was to subjugate Morgan's body. WindWraith didn't want to take her away with him as the vision foretold. The devil wanted inside her! It needed her body to use the portal. And it couldn't subsume her until it sucked Ryan's magic dry *and* stole all the magic from Avalon. *Sweet hell on Earth!*

Ryan's voice interrupted her disturbing ideas. "You wouldn't have gone anywhere. There has to be an activation."

Morgan limped away, combing her fingers through her mused hair. "Activation?"

"I'm still figuring it out. I've never seen a portal like this with all these crystals and power."

In thoughtful silence, they returned to the main cavern. Morgan edged her hip on the hot spring's ledge, staring cross-eyed at the tunnel leading to the electrifying cave. She had to do something lest matters progressed beyond no return. Before she lost Ryan for good to that blasted portal, or to death. She feared speaking her thoughts aloud, possibly giving them away to WindWraith. A hot coil of fear brewed in her stomach.

Ryan squatted between her legs. "You see why we must wait to complete the binding spell...to make love." He took her hand possessively. "I can't put you at risk of taking my ether inside you through our bond."

"But you said once consumed, WindWraith will become your magic," Morgan challenged, the coil in her stomach expanding. "Won't it become pure and innate?"

"I believe so." Ryan feathered his fingers from her knee to her inner thigh, stopping before his touch had a chance to turn intimate. "Do we take the risk? Are you sure innate magic isn't accessible to the other if we complete the bond?"

"We must kill the infernal Fomorian and forget this nonsense of returning to your home! What if the alleged gateway doesn't work and you consume this evil?" Morgan's voice lowered an octave. "WindWraith wants me. Isn't it obvious? It can't touch you with your ether, just like your Fomorians at home can't touch your people. It's gorging on our powers so it can consume *me* and leave this island. It will cause untold destruction to the Druids of both our worlds unless we destroy it."

"How does it maintain a link to both worlds when it's never been to my world?" He tapped his finger on her forehead. "What knowledge is floating in your head about that?" Scarlet frustration blotched his face and shoulders, and his troubled blue eyes were tormented with confusion and indecision.

Much of her knowledge came from Gwilym's tales, but more had emerged over the last day from both his potion and WindWraith. The information had mystified her until her vision and Ryan's revelation of the powerful crystal cave.

She smoothed her messy hair, wetting her hand in the water to pat down the flyaways. "I believe WindWraith has a link to your land through his son, Alasdar." She repeated the story of WindWraith's fall to the female Sluagh. "I saw the bones of a human in a cavern where I believe the Fomorian lives. I think the human came from your world. There was clothing similar to yours."

Ryan raked his hand through his long hair, pulling at the snarls caused by the whirlwind. "Why didn't you tell me this before?"

"WindWraith confuses me. I don't know what's real and what isn't. But that cavern may prove the truth of things he told me in my vision." She left it a singular vision, still unsure how to proceed. She trusted Ryan with her life, but she feared he'd only step up his plans to absorb the black magic of the Fomorian.

"Then the portal works." He grinned triumphantly.

"I don't know!" Morgan slapped the spring's surface, splashing warm water over them. "Strong crystals line the cave. WindWraith cannot get to it in its present form."

Ryan scratched his jaw. "Point taken." He nodded at her to continue.

Victory slithered through the knot in her stomach, and

she fought down a smirk. "WindWraith must have discovered how to use the power without being near it. Somehow, it has forged a link to its son in your world."

Ryan paced in front of her. "Which means he's a member of the Alasoron—" Horror engulfed his face and he staggered. "His son is Alexander. The name Alexander is the modern version of Alasdar." He slammed his fist into his palm. "Son of a bitch."

"Oh my." A wintry hand crept up Morgan's spine. "I never contemplated that. You think that's how the Alasoron Cabal defeated the other Cabals?"

"It makes total sense." Ryan resumed pacing short, stomping steps. "If WindWraith passed on his ancient Druid blood to his son, why can't the Alasoron's touch my people with the same ancient blood, if what you say is true?"

"I think it's the dilution of Fomorian and Sluagh blood throughout the ages. The Sluagh destroyed WindWraith's magic when she turned him. If WindWraith returns to your land after possessing one with the strong, pure blood of an Ancient, there's nothing stopping it." Thoughtful, she swished her fingers through the soothing bubbly water. "It cannot go through the portal without possessing the perfect vessel. And it can't do that until it contains immense magic."

"Perfect. It can have my body."

Morgan wanted to smack him on the head to knock sense into him. "It will fight you to the death if you try to consume it. You know that! If it conquers your ether, it will leave this island and destroy your people, killing me in the process. Is that what you want?" She slammed a fist on her thigh.

"Matters will never reach that point," he replied. "We'll rest a couple of days, restore our flagging power. I have some ideas."

She contemplated their quandary. The cave's air curved around her like a blanket of quills. "Then we will never mate." Her mouth compressed hard. Had she been deceived all along? By Ryan, by Gwilym? By ancient Druid rituals and customs? Even if they killed WindWraith and Ryan managed to leave the island, he'd have the Alasorons to conquer, more tainted magic inside him. Dear Goddess, she was in love with a man she could never have completely.

Ryan knelt and rested his cheek on her knee. His hands shook on her legs. Morgan hated to see his misery. She smoothed back his hair as he kissed the top of her knee, his lips soft on her frigid skin.

"I don't know." He rose and walked away, his back ramrod straight. "I'll clean up and go catch some fish for dinner."

Ryan strode into the waterfall, the spray claiming him. Water cascaded down his bronzed body, obliterating the pain and suffering ransacking his face.

Morgan was uncertain how the soul mate binding spell would affect them in either scenario. No one had ever refused an eternal bond to his or her soul mate. Who wanted to forego such incredible passion? She knew they would always sense the other's power and vague emotions. They'd always retain a piece of each other inside their souls, possibly unable to completely love another. Not that she could ever love anyone other than Ryan. And her heart would shatter in a million pieces if he fell in love with another woman, or Lauren Blackwell.

Morgan pressed on her eyelids as if to smooth out the wrinkles in her troubled mind. *Father, I need your guidance!*

She peered intently into the bubbling waters of the hot spring, concentrating on the spell to call her father. Within moments, the distorted face reflecting off the surface changed from hers to a hazy version of Gwilym. Nearly sliding off the ledge in surprise, she stared in stunned silence. It had to be crystal energy enhancing the island's magic!

Misty-eyed, she whispered, "Father, you're here."

"Beloved daughter." His subdued voice bounced off the hot spring's low walls. "Did you not scry for me?"

Morgan blinked back tears. To stabilize the vision, she smoothed her palm over the water, creating a motionless spot in the boiling spring, and bolstered her spell. Gwilym's wispy face stilled, a telltale amber glow ghosting him.

"Father." She lowered her voice. "Strong magic abounds here. I'm tied to the island. Did you know?"

"That is why you are there. You return life to the isle." Without further preamble, he spoke hastily. "Your sorcerer-assassin is there for the same reasons. He holds ancient Druid magic in his blood."

"How did you know?" Morgan held her fist to her stomach and tempered her anger. Her father never deliberately harmed or deceived her, but he had much to answer for. "Have you been to this island in your dreams, or in person?"

"I am too old to transport to distant, uncharted lands." His spectral face took on a grim countenance. "WindWraith would easily kill one of lesser blood and magic than you two."

Bubbles emerged from the floor of the hot spring, bursting around his face like a boiling stew. Morgan intensified her spell to hold onto him for as long as possible.

Ryan stepped out of the waterfall. Unable to peel her sight off him, she watched him strap on his loincloth. He snatched up his knife and spear, sent her a tremulous smile, and herded RavenStar outside.

Gwilym continued, "As I told you on Avalon, I foresaw your destiny. To remove the veil of evil from the world. To live a peaceful and happy life on the shadowed isle.

Remember, you will never leave that land."

"But Ryan believes he's found a way off. A gateway. He thinks we traveled through it."

Her father pursed his lips, rippling the waters around the white hair haloing his face. "He is partially correct. However, that gateway does not work in the manner he believes," Gwilym said insistently. "Mark my words, Daughter. That portal did not bring either of you to the island. *You* arrived through the Sacred Stones with my aid, and with help of magic from the spells and amulets. Ryan arrived through a storm-gate in the ocean, aided by the spells and amulet magic, and through his bond to you. The evil on the island is too strong otherwise."

Morgan's spine jerked straight. She believed the charms and Gwilym's magic alone brought them there, that the stones merely facilitated the spells. No one had ever used the standing stones as a gateway. Who even knew the stones were capable of such potent teleportation?

"Morgan?" Gwilym's voice grew faint.

Chagrined at her wandering mind, Morgan waved her hand over his cloudy face, smoothing the water's surface. "What about the gateway here? What will happen if Ryan uses it to return home?"

"The isle has always been shadowed to his world. Unchartered. There's no telling where or in what time he will land if he uses that portal, if it indeed works. There's no telling who he will be." Gwilym grimaced, his face pensive. "I do not know for certain. I only know that you cannot go through it."

Irritably, she cut the air with her hand. "I understand that, Father. I know I have duties to perform once again." Slight contempt carried her words.

The water undulated and his face misted over. "You cannot leave the island because you will die." Gwilym shook a finger in front of his face. "Do not attempt it. Your duty will turn to love, to the life you've always wanted. Have faith in your destiny."

Gwilym's words skittered through her head. She was glad to have his aid, to challenge her ideas. The amber light paled, and she hastened on before she lost the tenuous link. "What about the binding ritual we started? If we," a tide of fire washed over her body, "complete the final spell, will Ryan's innate magic harm me, whether or not I draw from his powers?"

"If he subverts WindWraith's black magic into white magic, and you draw upon it, your pure magic may reverse a portion of the spell," he said sternly, knowing her thoughts without her voicing them. "It may harm you both. Depending on Ryan's abilities or the Fomorian's powers, he may be unable to cleanse all of WindWraith's taint."

Dread returned with a vengeance, roiling in Morgan's stomach. Matters were worse than she imagined. Her all-seeing father already knew about Ryan's innate magic. "He must not consume WindWraith," she said more to herself.

"Or you must never mate with Ryan," he warned. The glow dulled to pale yellow, and Gwilym's voice grew somber. "You will never fully love another while bound to Ryan. The binding ritual should not ever be taken lightly."

"What about black magic he has already consumed?" Morgan clenched her amulet until it pinched her palm.

"His magic is pure, cleansed by his ether. But no one is strong enough to scrub WindWraith's taint."

Morgan already knew her choices. It didn't help her much to hear them confirmed. She shook her head and anxiously studied her father's waning face. "I cannot ever love another even if granted the chance," she whispered. She thrust her chin out. "Ryan is the only one I want."

"You know what to do."

"You said if we destroyed WindWraith, we would also destroy the evil shadowing the world. How can that be?

How can we save Ryan's people while he remains on the island where we are meant to live?"

Flurries of bubbles popped on the water's surface and Gwilym's image dissipated. A pale reflection of his face emerged in a bubble, wavering specter-like in the dimming golden glow.

"You are bound to the island, Morgan. The shadowed island of destiny needs you to return it to glory and goodness. It is the only place to unite the lost Ancients from all times. You know what to do." Gwilym's voice faded off as she lost her connection.

That cold hand clawed at her heart. *Did* she know what to do? With much to comprehend, her first task was apparent. She'd use the island's magic to help her destroy WindWraith. Ryan was too strong-willed to listen to reason. How could he forsake their love by not completing the binding ritual if he accomplished his demented undertaking? She would save him from choosing, and he'd thank her in the end. Or he'd leave her...

In the face of WindWraith's extractions of magic from her body, her tie to the island escalated every passing moment. Its heart beat strong within her now, and the earthy, watery energies mated with her magic as if born together. Leveraging off that ultimate bond gave her the impetus she needed. Cold determination inched through her mind, gelled her plans.

WindWraith would be long dead before Ryan found the son of a whore.

CHAPTER 26

Ryan strode from the cavern, his troubles anchoring his shoulders. The skittish foal pranced in the tunnel, waiting for him to disappear before returning to Morgan. Shaking his head, he descended the rugged terrain to the beach. Waves tipped in white curled and pounded on the reef, a relaxing sound to drown out his lousy mood. He headed toward the shallow tide pools, salivating at the idea of a lobster dinner.

In spite of his hunger, his dilemma tore his empty stomach to shreds. Everything he'd believed in seemed not to matter any longer. How could he return to his people knowing they might reject Morgan, regardless of her overwhelming powers? They'd never believe the story of this island and Morgan's origin. They'd probably try to burn her alive believing she was a Fomorian in disguise and had brainwashed him or somehow learned to mark him.

"Damn it." He jabbed his spear into the sand. He was still coven leader, still a formidable assassin. His people needed him to right the wrongs Michael, Lauren, and Alexander committed against them. They needed his strength to destroy the Alasoron Cabal. Ryan could never live with himself if he failed them, especially after knowing about the treachery.

"What the hell am I to do about the unfinished binding ritual?" Ryan kicked at a conch shell, launching it far into the sea. What about the danger to Morgan from sharing his potentially tainted ether? A celibate life with her wasn't even on the table. Duty and his desolate world promised to suck the life out of him, leaving little left for her. He refused to do that to her or to himself either. Not now that he'd tasted her, tasted a time of love, of heaven.

Ryan ached to make love to Morgan now and every day for the rest of their lives. He longed to give her the newfound love in his expanding heart. He wanted them to live a life of enduring love, the kind he'd missed living. He wanted her by his side as he started a new life. Before he left New Angeles, his scouts had found a defensible secluded valley in the ravaged California Sierras. Initial soil tests left them optimistic that they might rejuvenate the land with the alchemic spells his coven was developing. If that proved unrealistic, their failsafe took them to building on the ocean. Hell, who knew where they'd end up? Wherever they made a home, Morgan belonged with him.

He sprinted hard across the sand and dashed into the foamy wake, wishing to hurl his troubles into the receding waves. Briny water sloshed to his knees, and he waded to a tide pool among the smaller rocks. The never-ending sea held his gaze for a long moment. He searched for a sign of his world, of any world. Only the diminishing rays of sunlight reflected off the ocean's surface, as blue and endless as his mood.

Ryan scanned the peaceful cove, the perilous jutting cliffs, and the jungle beyond. Wild and challenging, he found an inner peace on the beautiful isle, a carefree calm he'd only experienced sailing the open waters. Home for a few weeks now, the paradise felt like a fresh beginning, a new chapter overflowing with adventure, and most of all with love. He couldn't imagine living anywhere else with Morgan, or ever living without her.

Thoughts twisted in Ryan's head. He lost himself scavenging for shellfish, scooping up several lobsters.

They'd enjoy a feast tonight before concentrating on their decisions and making a plan in the morning. They deserved one last night in paradise before their lives flipped into another hell.

When he returned to the cavern, he spotted Morgan stirring the contents of a stiffened leather pot. Entranced, he froze in his tracks. She wore what appeared to be a modern dress. Certainly, she never wore such a creation during her time, not if history books were accurate. She must have altered it for the heat. An enormous pang of love jerked his heart.

Fringe dangled from the hem of her mid-thigh, royal blue dress. The sleek material clung to her slender frame, accentuating her lush curves to every incredible advantage. Her sun-touched breasts overflowed the low-cut neckline, the amulet buried between the twin mounds.

Raven-wing hair piled high on her head, loose ringlets framing her honeyed face. Ryan adjusted his loincloth, unable to stifle a groan as his hand grazed his hardness. Morgan straightened, their gazes met. The tip of her tongue darted across her bottom lip, and a shy smile spread her ripe plum lips. Her smile was enough to set any man's heart racing. He dumped his load on the ground and slowly walked toward her, drinking in her beauty with every step.

He held her angelic face in his hands, falling into her exotic celadon eyes. "You are so gorgeous." She placed her hand flat over his rune tattoo, her touch drilling a hole to his heart. Their amethysts bathed Morgan's fingers in lavender light.

He lowered his arms to her waist in a loose clinch. "You are my true destiny. I can't deny that. I can't...I won't live without you."

Morgan buried her face in his chest, muffling a sob. "Do you mean that?"

"Yes." Ryan tipped her chin up. "Tomorrow, we'll decide

what to do. Tonight, let's enjoy our feast...and each other." He trailed his fingers down her satiny neck until they rested on her rune brand. His brand. His woman.

Flames caught the crystal icicles dangling from the ceiling, shooting rainbow prisms around the cavern. The glow diffused the natural radiance of the stones and lent warm contentment to their veined, slab dinner table. Morgan pushed her leaf-lined wooden plate of steamed lobster away, wrinkling her nose. No matter how anyone prepared shellfish, she would never acquire a taste for anything that lived in the water. "Not for me. I'm sorry."

Ryan grimaced teasingly. "I can't believe you grew up on an island and don't like shellfish." He snagged her leftover lobster and began layering it on the other two he'd eaten.

Earlier, in semi-stilted companionship, they'd scrounged the darkening island for wild vegetables and hunted for small game, ever watchful of WindWraith. They spoke no more of their plight. Instead, they regaled each other with stories from their past and their worlds. Morgan lapped up every iota of information about Ryan's former world, fascinated with twenty-first century advancements, distressed to hear of their obliteration. He told her about electricity, computers, and cars, all casualties of the Horde Wars.

"Why aren't you married?" Ryan asked unexpectedly. "I thought people of your time married young. Or *were* you married?" His knuckles whitened around his bowl.

Morgan refilled their bowls with rabbit vegetable stew. "No," she said emphatically, beating off the encroaching wistfulness that had no room inside her any longer. "Many noble women married at an older age. Since Avalon was dying. There was no one for me."

Ryan's face softened. "No men at all?"

She rolled her eyes. "Of course there were men. Like you, I wasn't allowed to wed for love alone. As the highest born woman on Avalon, my people expected me to marry one of noble blood with equal or greater powers. They expected us to return the lost magic. A man worthy of that position did not exist."

"Ever?"

"Not in my time."

Greed zipped across the hope in Ryan's eyes. "Until now?"

"Yes." Fierce desire burst hot between her legs and fluttered up to her heart.

Ryan set his stew aside and closed the space between them in one stride. He caressed her face, his fingers slipping into her hair, framing the sides of her head. "Will you wed for love now?" Emotions roughened his voice.

She rubbed her cheek against his palm. "Considering that I was not expected to live past my twenty-second year, yes."

"Excuse me?" Tension increased the pressure of his hands on her face.

Morgan realized she hadn't divulged her prophecy to him. They had so much to share. Sighing quietly, she eased his hands away, held them in her own, and told him about the prophecy she shared with her mother.

"You see." She squeezed his callused fingers. "This island is a resurrection for me. My mother foretold it, but it wasn't until later that Gwilym knew what she meant."

Ryan brushed his lips over hers. "My gain."

Grinning, Morgan angled her head to the side. "Can you love a woman who wields more power than you?"

He flung his head back and roared in laughter. "That

remains to be seen."

She squinted at him. "Excuse me?" *His shields can't hold me, and he thinks he's more powerful!*

"Until you've had ether magic living inside you, you don't know what power is." His arm muscles rippled in an exhibition of strength. And ego. Ego she dared to diffuse.

Without batting an eye, she wrapped Ryan in invisible bands of air, but not for holding him. Yet. Chuckling, she clinked her bowl down on the flattened boulder top.

Surprise bloomed across his face. He flexed his arms, jiggled his ankles. "What'd you do?"

"You don't know?" She tugged on their bond to show him she controlled it, then quickly severed it. Power luxuriated inside her, a thick sweet cream ready to dip into and taste.

A shadow masked Ryan's face. "What're you doing?" His fingers dug into his thighs.

"What do you feel?"

"You cut our bond." His nostrils flared. "I can't feel you. I don't like it."

"Is that a problem?" Exhilaration whistled in her head. "You want me back?" She stroked his taut arm, her magic lifting the pale down.

"Hell, yes." He snagged her wrist in a strong clench. "I don't like not feeling you, now that I've had a taste." A sea tossed storm of blue smoldered in his eyes.

Morgan dropped her shield, leaving the air ropes in place. He jolted from the impact, releasing her wrist. Air cushioned his elbows from banging against the rocks.

"Okay." He held up his hands in a placating gesture. "I get it," he grumbled. "I don't know how to do that."

"It's not okay. I want you to accept me as your equal, not some inferior woman with whimsical magic."

"Morgan, I do accept your powers. I'm not insane."

His sincerity fell to the wayside in her goal to make a

point. She flicked a finger and his loincloth fell away. Another flick and air caressed him into full arousal.

Sweat beaded his brow. "Little raven?" He licked his lips, gulped.

She giggled. "Let me show you what I can do. I promise I won't hurt you." Delight splashed within her as she used air magic to do her bidding. She longed to love Ryan with her hands and mouth, but this time was for show.

Air pressure forced Ryan on his back and stretched out his legs. He was powerless to resist the slow seduction. Hell, he didn't want to. He'd never met anyone with air magic, never knew such bewitching tricks existed. His bond to Morgan sang to his magic, and her elation waltzed through him, meeting his in an explosive tango.

A mild wind caressed him from his scalp to his soles, leaving him a bristling mass of bones and muscles. Hardened air gently pressed in his ears, around his nipples, circling the tattoo on his chest. Lower. He thrashed on the hard ground, a bed of air cushioning the rocks threatening to cut into his backside and legs. Air fastened around his hard-on, stimulating his length from base to tip with multiple tongues. Erotic. Mind blowing. He nearly lost it in the first thirty seconds. A ragged groan escaped him. "You. Next," he gasped out.

Morgan laughed, sultry, seductive. "I'm counting on it."

Power bloated their bond, fueled his fire and ether magic, creating a cyclone of need. His hands scrabbled on the ground, grabbing onto rocks, anything to redirect the lust preparing to spin his senses into orbit. Ryan's back bowed off the ground as his release rocked through him, his roar echoing in the chamber.

The erotic air dissipated, and Morgan lowered herself into his embrace. He held her tight, but it would never be close enough. He lifted her head from his shoulder and kissed her long and tenderly, loving the feel of her soft, satiny body sliding against his slick skin.

He broke off the kiss, reveled in her warm soft curves comforting his hard angles. "Have you," Ryan cleared his thick throat, "ever done that before?"

She snorted against his neck. "I never knew I could do that until I came to this island. Until you." Her accent thickened.

He laughed his relief, smoothing his hands over her buttocks, settling them into the small of her back.

"Will you do it again?"

Lifting her head, Morgan slivered her eyes at him. "Now?"

Ryan chuckled. "Give me a week to recover."

"That's what I thought." She kissed the hollow where his neck and shoulder met.

"You got me, love." Ryan's scratchy voice cracked. "I'll never doubt your abilities."

CHAPTER 27

The splattering waterfall beyond their sleeping alcove did little to calm Morgan's frayed nerves. Ryan slept fitfully, tossing and turning in the crinkly bed. She wondered how anyone slept on palm fronds and vowed to replace it with something less annoying. Left with no choice, she whispered a sleeping spell over Ryan, ensuring another hour or so of deep slumber.

Nibbling on her bottom lip, she prepared for her colossal task. Her needs and wants were petty in comparison. She would kill WindWraith and keep Ryan safe. If he loathed her afterward, she'd hate it, but after fighting for him with everything inside her, she'd live with it. Never at the expense of Avalon's people or the people who needed him, though.

Misery jabbed at her heart as she fastened her knife belt around her waist. She knelt beside Ryan, smoothed tousled hair off his face, sifting her fingertips in the silky locks. His full lips parted to reveal a line of straight white teeth. Even in sleep with boyish looks, his arrogance was immutable in the set of his jaw.

A smile tugged at her lips, and she feathered her mouth over his. "I love you, my Druid sorcerer," she whispered, branding his face into her memory. "Do not fear, I will return to you." With a faint sound of distress, she turned away and made herself rush past the hot spring, through the crystal-lit cavern. RavenStar followed quietly, aware of the secrecy. His tiny hooves clicked on the ground, his nose nuzzled her hand, rendering her a tidbit of reassurance.

Morgan hurried out the tunnel, incredible memories from last night clouding her resolve. They had rested from her blatant display of air magic, then slowly loved one another with their hands and their mouths. After reaching one half-sated climax after another, they fell into restless sleep. It was for the best once again, that they'd stopped shy of completing the soul mate binding. She hadn't encouraged him, even though her burn for him nigh drove her insane.

With a lit torch in hand, Morgan and RavenStar clambered up the cliff path. The foal playfully practiced using his wings for balance. Waving away the dust cloud RavenStar kicked up in her face, she mind-called to him to settle down. Once she paused at the top of the incline, she pressed her hands on her scars, fighting the thread of fear circling her stomach. Anxiously, she scanned the still, dark meadow and jungle beyond, not detecting a hint of WindWraith. Dawn wasn't far off and she wanted to cover as much ground as possible before alerting the Fomorian.

Bits of plants stuck to her clothing, and she brushed them off. Unable to set one foot in front of the other, she faltered. *Damn the fear trickling through me! I'm stronger than it!* She squared her shoulders, letting her confidence rise and join the buoyant reverberations of the island. It hummed strong in her, wound around her chest, gave her courage a boost.

RavenStar darted off, whipping his head in delight. He stretched his wings to their full width, flapping madly to test them out. Morgan laughed and watched his playful antics while she rechecked her pack.

They headed northward in the opposite direction of the emerald grotto, following the eastern coastline. Earthen magic brushed butterfly wings in her mind, grazed her core.

She slipped past a drifting vine, and it curved over her shin, energizing her. Away from the crystals, she needed all the aid available to maintain her stamina and to battle WindWraith. The damned demon had drained too much of her magic, and she feared her defenses were compromised despite the energy gained in the crystal cavern.

Tree branches quivered as though she were their exalted queen. Like adoring subjects, flora and fauna reached for the barest touch of her. They fed her magical energy, and she fed them something else entirely, similar to bound lovers.

Unnerved, RavenStar beat his wings against his sides. He edged away from the plants reaching for him, scrunched himself against Morgan's side, both protecting and seeking comfort.

Enraptured, Morgan walked on, her soft soles crunching on mulch blanketing the ground. She stopped next to a rocky outcropping where a white orchid grew in a crevice. As she sniffed the rich perfume, the flower grew larger. It stroked her hand and she caressed the stem, leaving her skin tingling with subtle island magic.

Brightly colored parrots peered down upon them from a sandalwood tree, trilling their approval. A similar reaction arose from the monkeys and other small animals she encountered. Nothing deterred her from her purpose.

Foliage guided her deeper into the jungle, shielding her from harm. She felt more energized than she had since she'd landed on the island. A garden thrived inside her, a boon to her senses, earthy, airy, watery. She could survive on the island alone if she failed to change Ryan's mind and he managed to leave. Once she rid the island of its blight, she could easily call the gorgeous paradise home for eternity.

Twisting her torso, she felt for the Druid charms in the bottom of her satchel. Clinks of crystal and silver reassured her. Eventually, she'd toss the amulets by matched pairs into the ocean. When and where to accomplish her task was an ambiguous notion in her mind. In theory, she wouldn't always be alone. The mysterious Druids prophesied to populate the island may stem from Ryan's coven, giving her a semblance of his presence if he deserted her.

Morgan hiked close to the coast where the jungle grew sparser. The tree line provided shade from the rising sun. An animal roared in the distance, instantly reminding her of the bluish beast that had stalked her. Heedless of danger, she trudged along the imperceptible path the island cleared for her. A snapping, crackling skirmish in the shrubs rose to her left. Frozen, she rested her hand over her scars and slowly counted to five the way Ryan taught her. Hibiscus sweetened the air on her tongue, and she focused on it to drive off her apprehension. She plodded through a snarl of vines and ferns concealing a cluster of the magenta flowers. The flowers bloomed before her and her fear fled in the wake of her determination.

From her last vision of WindWraith, she knew it holed up in a dark, sweltering cavern. Intuition hinted that it lived in the volcano on the northern end of the island. Concurring with her instincts, the sentient island led her northward. Every so often, she spied steam drifting in indolent wisps from the top of the towering volcano.

Fortunately, she didn't sense any traces of black magic nearby. Nor did she feel her powers leaking out in significant amounts. The island's magic appeared to help shield her from detection. Would Ryan be able to use his tracking abilities if her plan failed? Shaking her head, she refused to think such dire possibilities. *Too much is at risk if victory doesn't greet me.*

Water gurgling over rocks carried through the close-knit growth. Morgan followed the liquid melody and stumbled upon a narrow creek swerving into the jungle. It provided a good spot for a short rest, and she shrugged off her packs.

The sky had lightened enough to see and she snuffed out her torch. The picture perfect glade held a garden of hibiscus, orchids, and jasmine growing within grassy mounds. Across the creek, she spied a mysterious tree grove. Round balls of faintly glowing fruit hung in profusion from profuse branches. Curiosity crawled through her grumbling stomach. She stripped off her boots and stepped into the brook. Water churned placidly around her ankles, soothing her feet. RavenStar whickered to her left. Several rambunctious squirrels cavorted with him, and she laughed at their carefree fun.

"Would that I might enjoy such amusement soon," she grumbled.

Morgan waded into ankle high water to the other side of the creek. Tree branches grazed the ground with hundreds of ripe fruit. She walked beneath the leafy awning of the first citrusy tree. The globes were the size of large oranges, in chaotically swirling colors ranging from eggplant to red to mint green, perfuming the air in an unrecognizable heavenly wine. Her mouth watered and her stomach gave an appreciative growl. Her languid body perked up as if a magic elixir seeped into her pores. Exhilarated, she loaded her arms with a half dozen of the rainbow balls to take on her journey.

Morgan cleaned the fruit, splashing cool water on her face and neck. Refreshed, she returned to her resting spot and tucked away all but two fruits for later. She picked at the smooth outer layer of one with a fingernail and tried to peel the skin off, but it only came away in miniscule pieces. Morgan shrugged and bit into the fruit, peel and all. Ambrosia teased her tongue, taunted her stomach. She stretched out on the grass, savoring the indescribable treat. She wasted no time devouring the first one. A strange dreamy eroticism spread upwards from her feet. She bit into the second one, and her extrasensory perceptions sharpened.

Wonder ruptured low inside her. She had never felt so aware of all her senses at once. Within seconds, she floated above the glade into puffy clouds skimming the azure sky. Her magic bristled across the outer layer of her flesh, beneath her skin in ripples. She loved the feel of it streaming in and out, leaving the door open to the cleansing air.

Morgan soared in cottony clouds, dreaming of Ryan, blissfully fulfilled as she envisioned him seducing her on a beach, and then making love to her on a bed of silken grass in the center of the stone circle on Avalon. Then she took delight in showing Ryan her home island from the cliff top meadow to the castle and village below.

Standing within the stone pillars, shadows dimmed the colorful glade. Morgan smiled and beckoned, widening the door to her powers, to her lover.

"Morgan," the familiar voice intoned in her mind on an airy current.

"Father, is that you?" Morgan's smile grew, her joy unlimited as her weightless body dipped and rose on pillows of air.

"Love, I am here." He caressed her cheek, his loving, lined face wavering into view. "Come with me. I have found a way for you to end your task and return home."

Fog billowed in Morgan's mind. "But Father, I haven't fulfilled my mission. Avalon's Shadow is alive and powerful."

His booming chuckle sounded off to her right and she turned in his direction. Wearing a new brown wool cape, he appeared decades younger than the man she'd left behind. No white tinted his chestnut hair, and the lines bracing his mouth and eyes were only shadows.

"Indeed, you have fulfilled your task, daughter. Can you not see the vitality returned to us?" He swept his hand in front of his youthful appearance. "Avalon's Shadow shall return home with you. As I had planned. You must open yourself to him. Then all will be right with the world once again. Only then will Ryan and his people be safe."

Agitation failed to reach past the euphoria flowing in Morgan's blood, although questions continued to flounder in her head. "I don't understand. You wanted me to destroy WindWraith in order to return magic to Avalon. You said I couldn't return home."

"Let him in. Everything will be in your grasp." Gwilym kissed her forehead in his loving, comforting way. "You will have the man of your dreams, and live a long, happy life on Avalon. Your dream warrior's people will prevail and grow strong again."

The sentiments seemed clear and precise, sinking her doubt fast. Home. All she wanted was a joyful home with the man of her dreams. Happiness flung wide the gates to Morgan's magic. Power flowed outward in a steady stream, even as the soothing warmth of something unfathomable spilled into her.

"Little raven."

Morgan swung her head to the left. Ryan appeared, tall and broad of shoulder, fair hair flowing free, framing his chiseled, bronzed face. His skin glistened, his muscles rippled.

She held her arms out to him. "My love, everything is in our grasp. You no longer have to absorb WindWraith inside you."

Fury flashed across Ryan's beloved face. Then his expression softened and his darkening gaze drank her in from head to feet. "You are right, Morgan," he replied in a monotone voice. "You need only let him in and you will be mine, forever bound, living the life we deserve on Avalon."

He nuzzled her neck, leaving a shower of shivery kisses from her throat to her lips.

He forced her lips open with his thrusting tongue. Morgan closed her eyes, letting him drive her delirious with his drugging kiss. Their tongues dueled in a fierce tango, and she felt her breasts crush against his iron chest. Ryan's hands caressed her back, cupped her bottom, his knees spreading her legs apart. Her body melted against him, the world filled with him.

She wrapped her arms around his strong shoulders, wanting him closer. When their kiss ended and she opened her eyes, the obsidian depths of the ancient Druid-Fomorian looked upon her. "WindWraith," she exclaimed, her emotions faltering.

Something awful and compelling at the same time appeared in the Fomorian's fathomless features. It seduced and beckoned her into a malignant love. The lure to join the depths, to feel the desire wrap her into its ecstasy was too much to bear. Morgan sank into the hard body, let his magic cushion her fall into heaven.

"I am your homeland, your life, your love. We share the same blood. We belong together. I am your soul mate. Do you accept me?" His shadowy form engulfed her, soft, silken, pressing against her sensitive spots, creating an aching tempest inside her body. Again, adopting Ryan's beloved face and form, he whispered words of love, happiness, and home. "Accept me, Morgan. Let me in and we will be soul mates for eternity." Flowers in full bloom perfumed the air, encircled their bed of soft meadow grass, giving credence to his heartfelt plea.

Joy overflowed her until she thought her heart would leap through her chest. "Yes," she whispered. "Yes, I accept you." Her hands strayed across his feverish skin, following the path her lips burned down his throat to the brand above his heart.

The stone in his amulet lay silent and dark. Dead.

Morgan gasped. She whipped her head back and peered into death, thick with centuries of killing and putrid with evil. She screamed.

White-hot agony seized her internal organs, leaving her feeling split in serrated halves. A dagger of light cut her skull in two, tumbling her to the darkened glade.

CHAPTER 28

WindWraith eased Morgan onto the altar he had purified for her arrival. It had been effortless to encroach upon her dreams in her euphoric state. To read her thoughts, to find evidence of the ideas he had gleaned about the Druid male. He laughed gleefully, and allowed his human form to split asunder as his laughter died. He didn't want to waste more energy than necessary to maintain the shape. Very soon, the Druid sorceress would be ready for him. And he for her.

He flicked an appendage over her abdomen, trickled it up her torso to her sticky, sweet lips. A sigh blew out of him. To have this woman bonded to him would make his days on Earth so pleasurable. He might even grow to love again.

Regrettably, the assassin's rare link to starfire prohibited him from using the man as his vessel. He would much rather endure an eternity rutting with her, her lips pleasuring him, than a hasty bedding before his departure. But that didn't mean the assassin's magic was useless. WindWraith needed it to escape the island. In more ways than one.

Merlin wasn't a stupid mage. They both knew the crystal gateway required Druid magic at both ends to make it work. Once the island's barrier shattered, sending a surge of Avalon magic to the island, he would have it all.

One more quake.

One step closer to reuniting with his son.

WindWraith laughed, a blustering, wheezing sound. He smoothed his fingers over Morgan's naked breasts, flicked a tongue of air at her nipple, tasting his homeland, ingesting the rare mix of Druid essence. The four elements wafted off her, paraded through his form in excruciating pleasure.

A magnificent mate. At least she will be, once WindWraith found the male body, Michael O'Rourke, to inhabit for the rest of his days. Arrogantly, he slipped into Morgan's mind again, digging deeper for useful information he may have missed, until her mind stirred and locked him out.

CHAPTER 29

Ryan stretched out on his stomach, the most vivid dream freshly imprinted on his brain. Seductive freesias, mixed with a vaguely familiar fruity aroma wafted in his mind as he kissed Morgan in a meadow beside a meandering creek. They felt like they were luxuriating on a plush, pillow-top bed. What he wouldn't give to sleep on a regular bed again. Romance deserved much better than the dirty, torn beds from one California sanctuary to another and the hard, lumpy surfaces on this island.

Careful not to wake Morgan on the other side of their pallet, Ryan slowly stretched out the knots in his shoulders. She needed her rest to regenerate her lagging powers. But he was bristling to tell her the agonizing decisions he'd made during his restless night. First and foremost, he wanted to tell her he loved her, and that it'd be an honor if she became his wife and bore his children, created from a soul deep love. He wanted to spend the rest of his life cherishing and loving her the way she deserved. Everything he had to give, everything she wanted, including the magic inside him belonged to her. Such a life of love and family had eluded him for so long, but the life-altering decision felt incredibly right.

Ryan no longer harbored doubts about two decisions. He could not absorb WindWraith's powers to supplement his own. Not if he wanted a life with Morgan. She had shown him last night how much a part of him she was, how much he'd missed throughout his young adulthood serving his people to his detriment, never experiencing the love of a selfless woman, one who completed him. They'd finalize the ritual to bind their souls forever—that day—before his lust drove him mad. He'd make it another special day with good food, firelight, and a perfect mood. To take that final step they both craved—to make slow, passionate love to each other. An aching need compelled him to roll over to awaken his beautiful temptress with a kiss. Only his gaze landed on an empty bed.

An air of foreboding permeated the dim cave and punched him in the gut. The end of the dream whacked him full force. WindWraith had lured Morgan from outside the glade, where Ryan and Morgan lay during their shared dream. "Son of a bitch!" How had WindWraith breached their dreams?

A rush of molten outrage propelled him off the bed. He sensed the threat to her in the blood drumming against his veins, in the buzzing amethyst flickering like a light bulb winking out. Their bond whispered in his pulse, receding with every passing moment.

"Morgan!" *Come on, baby, where are you?* "Morgan!"

Ryan scanned the sleeping alcove only to find empty spots where he'd dumped Morgan's packs. He dashed from every nook and cranny in the maze of caves, calling for her. He sprinted outside to search, but she had vanished. RavenStar was also gone. Fear pooled inside him, threatening to drown him.

He raced back into the cave and tugged on a shirt and shorts. Quicker than he'd ever moved in his life, Ryan stuffed his backpack with supplies and his rudimentary knives. Spear in hand, he snatched an empty leather sack and jetted toward the crystal-lined portal.

The tenuous link to Morgan gave him an inkling of the direction she'd taken, enough to prove she lived. He'd find her using his tracking abilities. Pure hatred for the Fomorian burned through him. In his blind rage, he stumbled in the portal's entryway, lost his footing, and slammed his head into the archway. Pain hammered his forehead. Staggering, he caught his shoulder on the stone wall, balancing against it to remain standing.

"Shit, shit, shit!" He held his head with one hand. Blood oozed between his fingers, and a haze of gray swept over him.

He strained to temper his power, preventing it from activating energy within the gateway. Sharp crystals bit into his skin as he slid to the ground, sidetracking the thumping in his skull. Lifting his face to the roof, he pleaded to the heavens, receiving neither sign nor answer. As his gaze slid down the gem-crusted wall in the crystal portal across from him, a dead spot in a deep crevice rising two feet off the ground caught his attention. Searing light blinded him and he shut his eyes, pressing his temples between his palms to massage away the accompanying throb.

Unable to move, Ryan wasted precious time conquering his vertigo. After what seemed hours, he struggled to his feet, head still aching, but his dizziness had abated. He stepped into the crystal cave and froze. Translucent stones flared to life so brightly, he had to peer through hooded eyes. Crystal energy merged with his ether, an inferno dominating his momentary weakness. Endorphins fed his rushing blood. He gathered loose gems off the littered ground and shoved them by handfuls into the empty bag.

Ryan shot a last look at the dead spot, warring with an urge to investigate. "Screw it. I don't have time." Without looking back, he sprinted from the cavern to find his heart's desire.

Thick heat bogged down the air. The dreamlike effects of the mysterious fruit had retreated, but Morgan's head ached dully in its nasty wake. Her scorching bed scratched her bare flesh with every twitching movement she made. Where, by the Goddess, had her clothing gone?

"Ryan?" she called through a scratchy throat.

Useless gurgling and hissing answered her. She batted her heavy eyelids several times trying to open them. Her arms were leaden; her legs so sluggish they refused to budge. What happened to her? She swallowed, her throat dry despite the broiling humidity. Finally, she focused her vision and instantly wanted to blink away the terror shredding her lethargy and puzzlement.

Unable to lift her head, Morgan swung her head from side-to-side. Invisible fetters bound her wrists and ankles on a stone platform. Peering into the smoky air, she knew she lay in the cavern from her previous vision of WindWraith. Far above her, light slivered down a hole in the cone-shaped ceiling, dissipating near the sky-grazing top. Acid formed in her stomach when she recognized the sources of heat and moisture.

Boiling lava pools bordered three sides of the cavern. Water splashed onto the fiery liquid from several small waterfalls and brimming basins of water. Molten lava exploded in fragments into the water, churning beneath vapors spiraling up from the pools, clouding the air. Lifeless black crystals layered the walls so dark the amber and crimson light from the lava died on their surfaces.

She lay in the nucleus of a volcano. And this time it wasn't a dream.

She wondered how the Fomorian lived in darkness when it seemed to prefer sunlight. Obviously, the liquid fire called to him, enough to burn away the absolute dark of night.

Morgan's stomach lurched violently and she screamed until her voice grew hoarse. With all her might, she battled against her constraints, gaining chafed skin for her efforts. Hard gasps heaved her chest up and down until she thought her lungs would burst. After abrading skin off her shoulder blades on the rough bed, she froze and forced herself to calm down. To think. To plan her escape.

The last thing she remembered after eating the delicious fruit was drifting in the sky, WindWraith gloved around her. He had given her power and taken some of hers in a mutual exchange of need. The former Druid reminded her that they shared the same ancient blood, the same homeland. He told her he loved her and wanted her, that she had come to the island to end his long imprisonment, to unite their powers and their souls. She was his destiny as he was hers. He wanted to love, protect, and cherish her for an eternity. He vowed never to leave her. All the sentiments she desperately longed to hear.

Doubts had zigzagged up her boneless body in a prickling tide, filtered into her fuzzy mind. Wasn't Ryan her destined mate? Didn't they share a soul bond? Hadn't Ryan said similar words to her and shown her how much he loved her? Were WindWraith and Ryan one and the same? In her sluggish state, her mind had fallen into a chaos of rights and wrongs, needs and wants, and selfless destiny. Believing it another dream, she had passed out from the pressure of balancing her life and the world in her head.

Then, she'd awoken here and now. Definitely not suffering a dream or foretelling. The nightmare was real.

Morgan gathered her diminishing magic to access her sparse link to Ryan. Even that effort proved difficult. Volumes of frustration replaced her internal resources. Magic bled out of her like blood from a dozen stab wounds, causing further ruin to her consciousness. Fighting sleep, vivid scenes of Ryan's world crowded her head as her body slackened.

Lauren and Alexander sat in a gloomy room, lit only by twin candles on a table between them. She slicked her fingers through the cracked bowl of precious melted chocolate, and Alexander devoured the scarce treat. He licked Lauren's fingers clean, sucking them into his mouth.

The Fomorian Overlord waved away her next offering. "You are ready to kill O'Rourke tonight?"

Even in her dream, confusion expanded in Morgan's head. Weren't Michael and Lauren planning to kill Alexander? Why were Lauren and Alexander together? Were the two plotting against the O'Rourke brothers and both covens? In fascinated horror, Morgan's unconscious mind watched the scene unfold.

Lauren scooted her chair closer to him, her small hand landing on Alexander's thigh. "Michael won't know what hit him, darling. Then I'll return to celebrate our new pact." She slid her hand up his thigh, circling the bulge in his trousers, her fingertips teasing his hardness.

Alexander cleared his throat, covered her hand with his. "You're sure you don't need my help?" Candle flames reflected in his aroused eyes and his voice held a dual anticipation.

"I can manage that spineless idiot." Lauren leaned closer to Alexander. Her right breast skimmed his arm. With the tip of her tongue, she licked his lips. "You taste divine." Her mouth grazed his and he crushed her to him. His hungry kiss was punishing, and his forceful grip on her arms yanked her onto his lap. Alexander kissed her with a savage intensity, her whimpers spurring him on until he had his fill, leaving her panting.

Easing back, she brushed her fingertips across her mouth. She exhaled a shaky laugh. "Not now, darling. Save it for our celebration."

He caught her chin roughly between his thumb and forefinger. "Do it and get back here." He thrust his hips up, grinding into her, squeezing and kneading her breasts as if they were dough. "It's time to take what's mine."

Halting outside the catacombs, Ryan set his internal tracking mechanisms in play. He sensed traces of Morgan's magical signature around the cave's perimeter and followed her intangible trail toward the singular path that led away from the hidden entrance. The tremors in his tight arms loosened a fraction. Her trail was stronger than any he'd ever tracked. Their bond helped create the robust connection, but the tie diminished with every passing minute.

"Hope to hell I'm not too late." Fear skewered his heart. He had to force himself to quit thinking about her in order to concentrate on his search before he bashed his already bruised head into another boulder, or nosedived off a cliff.

Expertly drawing on his tracking abilities, he shielded his dwindling link to Morgan. Using all his internal and external senses, he scanned one spot to another. Trampled grass here, a broken twig there gave visible evidence of her passage, but she left little damage behind. Morgan's strange, lifelike link to the island prevented her from causing unintentional harm to the land. Since he'd already witnessed it, he knew the island had assisted her journey. He derived small comfort in that, not that it derailed his angry fear.

Even though she was a powerful sorceress with the island as her ally, she didn't possess enough magic to destroy WindWraith. Or did she? Didn't they need his ether? Ryan knew in his heart that she'd left to prevent him from absorbing the black taint.

Frustration shimmied over his skin in a hot breeze. An ankle high vine whipped out of his path. "Thank you," he murmured absently.

If only Morgan had waited for him to tell her of his decision to help her kill WindWraith! He knew he needed her in all ways. He couldn't risk her life or his own by taking in WindWraith's magic. They would find another way to save his people. It was possible that bonding with Morgan would supplement his magic enough to conquer the Fomorians back home. He needed to trust her, like he'd trusted no one in his life. He loved her even more for trying to protect him, albeit with misplaced intentions. With her strong foresight, maybe she knew something he didn't, though. Why else would she attempt to hunt a fearsome Fomorian on her own? He shook his head sharply, wishing to shake off this nightmare as easily.

Surely, she didn't plan to kill WindWraith simply because she wanted to complete the damn ritual. Or to use him. Her entire purpose on the island gave testament to her unselfishness. Ryan wanted to hammer sense into his head for wasting so much valuable time concocting his stupid plans, rather than sitting down with Morgan and hashing out their existence on the island, their destiny. To learn more about the enigma he loved more than life.

Refocusing on the path, Ryan shoved out his troubles. He trudged through the jungle until he emerged in a familiar colorful meadow. A brook gurgled on one side, sea cliffs and the ocean framed the other sides. Magic fluttered in his gut, drew a miniscule sense of Morgan from the glade. "This is where she rested."

Incessant cawing in a tree grove across the creek responded to his mutters. He studied the ravens. Quiet now, twin sets of beady eyes bored into him. The birds launched out of the tree in an explosion of black wings. They circled low above his head. Cawing in unison, they flew north, stopped, and wheeled around, luring him to follow. A barbed vine twisted around his heart, and he questioned what the featherheads tried to tell him.

The sleeping volcano reached for the stratosphere far to the north. Steam spewed from the top in a thin cloud about once a minute. Otherwise, the summit crater remained silent, harmless. Was it possible WindWraith shacked up in the volcano? Had Morgan known?

He stalked the meadow, scrutinizing any tangible and intangible evidence left behind. Along the creek, he found a flattened area where she'd rested. He sifted through the mashed grass, hunting for clues, finding nothing.

Ryan strode to the creek, draining his waterskin. Just as he crouched to refill it, he spotted a half-eaten piece of the punchy fruit. Lunging forward, he seized the leftover off the grass, searched for the peels, but none met his panicked gaze. That explained the vaguely familiar fruity smell on Morgan in his morning's dream. It also explained Morgan's capture.

"Son of a..." He hurled the fruit into the creek so hard it splattered into bits off a rock. "I should have warned her."

In his first encounter with the fruit, he'd eaten two of them, and they'd caused the most intense eroticism. The effects had lingered for hours. In his boredom, he'd discovered the peel was a potent aphrodisiac. The candied meat stimulated a minor feeling of wellbeing and adrenaline, a lesser drug-like effect. The juice had identical effects as beer or wine. Diluted with water, it energized.

He searched the rest of the clearing, emerging clueless. Returning to the invisible trail, he heard a tangle in the bushes. His biceps coiled, and he poised his spear. A whinny erupted behind the nearest bolder, and the winged foal raced toward him.

A smidgen of tension slid off his shoulders. RavenStar trotted over and nosed him, its tongue rasping along Ryan's palm like sandpaper before biting down on Ryan's fingers.

Ryan snapped his hand back. "You little shit."

The winged horse snorted, head bobbing. It backed away and trotted north along Ryan's invisible trail. RavenStar glanced over its haunches at Ryan, waggled its head and whinnied.

The foal was trying to tell him something, too. Ryan tugged a few ripe fruits off a branch and crammed them in his knapsack. He patted the foal's quaking haunches, and they headed toward the volcano.

Morgan's body refused to awaken in the roasting cavern. Another prominent vision scattered the ideas forming in her mind...

Smiling nervously, Lauren walked into the office behind the old pulpit. Michael rose from a scarred cherry wood desk and greeted her with a lingering kiss. She slipped her arms around his neck and encouraged him for several moments. They ended the kiss but remained in a tight embrace.

"I love you so much." Lauren touched her hand to his cheek. "Can you believe it's almost over?" Neat rows of precious beakers and bottles lined the shelves behind the desk.

"Thank the Gods." Michael squeezed her waist before releasing her. "You're here to *kill* me?" His right eyebrow slid up his forehead. "Alexander didn't tail you, did he?" He perched a hip on the desktop.

"Yes and no." Lauren tossed her grubby leather purse beside him on the desk and tugged her hair from its bindings. "I had my usual spells in place to gauge his sincerity and naïveté. He passed. He's testing my loyalty and ruthlessness, so he won't follow. The guards verified I wasn't tracked."

Grim resolve traversed Michael's face, etched lines on the sides of his mouth and eyes. He twisted the Druid leader's ring around his finger.

Lauren caressed his cheek. "You miss Ryan." An undeniable statement of fact. "Will we ever know what happened to him?"

A thick pall hung over the room almost as tangible as smoke. Michael wrenched the ring off and handed it to her. "It's physically impossible for me to wear this if he were alive. It would reject me as the strongest O'Rourke."

A tear trailed down Lauren's cheek. "I admired him so much. I know we could have made it work and been content together." She clutched the ring in her fist. "But I love you and have since I was a metal mouth teenager." A wan smile curved her rosy lips. "You know these things happen for a reason."

Michael exhaled loudly. "I know."

"All the sacrifices we'd planned, and see what it got us." She laughed bitterly. "Each other. Exactly what we wanted since you rescued me on the East Coast." Her somber smile turned tender.

"Was it worth it?"

She brushed a kiss across his mouth. "Not Ryan's loss. Nothing was worth that."

"I love you." Michael pulled her between his legs, his thick arms holding her tight and safe. "I hate that Ryan's gone, that I won't ever get a chance to mend the discord between us. Show him how our father pitted us against each other to toughen us up. All I wanted was to be second to Ryan and work with him, not against him. But our damn father wouldn't allow it. Wouldn't allow me to practice spellcraft, telling Ryan my efforts killed our mother, turning him completely against alchemy." He pressed his hands against her spine. "But I won't ever regret our love. Never." Their lips met, a sweet, gentle kiss sealing his vow.

Lauren drew back in surprise. "I thought your mother died in a car accident."

Michael hung his head sheepishly. "She did." He scrubbed his hand over his eyes. "My father took one of my early demon vanquishing potions and slipped it into James MacFarland's drink. He didn't know how it would affect James or that he'd drive my mother home that night."

"Ryan blames you for it? That's insane."

"He didn't necessary blame me, but it didn't endear him to the arts of alchemy either. If Ryan knew you were involved in useless, unpredictable pansy potion mixing, as he called it, he probably would have nixed the merger."

"That's why you were insistent in working secretly on the East Coast." Lauren hugged him. "Honey, why didn't you tell me?"

"I planned to a lot sooner." He rested his chin on her head. "Then Dad was killed. The wars broke out. You and I didn't exactly see eye-to-eye, at first, both of us strong leaders from opposing covens. Ryan hated me. Then he disappeared."

"Why tell me now?"

"Because I don't want any more secrets between us. We've signed the pact, it's time to put the last few years behind us and create a new life for our merged covens."

"Once we destroy the Overlord." Lauren shivered, tensing.

"Let's go over the plan." Michael eased her aside and hopped off the desk. He walked to a patched cherry cupboard and drew out a small, carved teak box. Reverently, he lifted the container in both hands and carried it to the table. He pulled a large vial of crimson liquid from his jacket pocket.

Lauren flicked up the latch on the box and threw Michael a skittish look.

"Open it," he commanded. "Now's not the time to freak out. If this doesn't work, we'll both bite it tonight."

Without skipping another heartbeat, she flipped the lid open. The sight of the pale human heart nestled in the plastic-lined, black velveteen interior stung her eyes.

"Touch it, hold it. Make it appear as if you yanked it out of my dead body. Your touch and smell must be all over it." Michael's bark belied the angst ghosting his face, deepening the circles under his glacial eyes. He poured half the vial of blood over the lifeless organ. "Smear it all over."

Lauren clasped the table to still her shaking hands, adopted an uncharacteristic arctic mien, and handled her task efficiently. Michael's ensorcelled blood was tepid, matching the newly acquired heart cut out of the corpse of their latest war casualty. Michael's second lieutenant had met the pointed end of a Fomorian minion's saber while walking his perimeter rounds that morning. Gooseflesh broke out on her arms, and she finished quickly before she spewed her breakfast over the gruesome heart. In the adjoining bathroom, she poured seawater in the sink and scrubbed her trembling hands, leaving a few rusty splotches on the backs to show evidence of her perceived assault on Michael.

Together, they invoked the final banishing spell on four vials of perfected vanquishing poison. When finished, she carefully stuck them with Michael's ring into the designated compartments in her purse.

"I'll stand guard outside his house, shielded. Like we planned." Michael guided her to the door, the wooden box clutched in his hand. "If the banishing spell and poison don't kill him, I'll draw from the stars and link our powers, okay?"

"We were meant to be together, Michael." Lauren kissed him, smoothing the lines across his forehead. "Nothing will go wrong. Alexander's led by his dick these days, and I know how to stroke that to my advantage."

Fury colored Michael's face, but he rapidly masked it. "I hate that that bastard has touched you."

Lauren averted her face, shrugged. "My skin's raw from the scrubbing I give myself after every visit with him. I'll live."

Michael had nothing to say to that. Every night she fell asleep shaking in his arms, he agonized over the open wound her forced affair with Alexander left in her heart and in his own. Nevertheless, it had been imperative she gain Alexander's trust to ascertain his vulnerabilities.

Tonight was the beginning of the end. Magic and balance would return to the Druids. They would reclaim Earth and ship the Fomorian scourge to hell forever. Michael hugged the teak box to his side. He swore the heart thumped against the interior in tandem with the heart pumping icy blood through his veins.

CHAPTER 30

After hours plodding through the jungle, Ryan reached the volcano's perimeter. Between his innate tracking abilities and the island's guidance, he knew Morgan was there. Bird cackles bounced off the side of the volcano. He glanced up into a sandalwood tree and saw the stalking ravens land at the top. Instead of flitting to the next northbound tree, they dug into the branch and fell silent. "Suppose you featherheads know she's here, too."

Bracing his weight against a staggered rock formation, he stretched his magic out, seeking the precious bond. With the incomplete spells and their dwindling magic, his link to Morgan was no stronger. He felt her presence, though, a feather dusting his mind. Token relief loosened the knots working across his shoulders, down his arms.

The two moons dominated the early twilight sky and illuminated the withered perimeter of the conical mountain. The volcano appeared inactive, and he guessed it hadn't caused the death of plants and trees that extended out two hundred feet from the base. The island had quit encroaching on the volcano, as if it also detested the evil within. It has to be WindWraith's lair. Where else would it hole up on this forsaken island?

RavenStar nudged a couple of rocks the size of basketballs, trying to reach a patch of island grass sprouting between them.

"Leave it." Ryan toed the foal away. "Morgan's

returning the island to life." He idiotically spoke to the winged horse. Just as crazily, he believed the damned thing understood him. RavenStar gave up on the new growth and watched him, head hung low with soulful eyes.

Ryan returned to the verdant border separating life from death and perched on a boulder. RavenStar butted his leg expectantly as if a snap of his fingers would magically produce Morgan. "I wish." He waved the foal off. "Settle down."

The winged horse sagged to the ground underneath a low-growing palm fern, hidden from view above. Ryan had no reason to hide from WindWraith, since it probably already knew of his presence. The crystals in his knapsack kept him safe, giving him a chance to finesse the plan he'd formulated on his journey.

He ate several strips of jerky, then lit the reed torch he'd made on his hike. Ryan thanked his lucky star he'd found a box of lighters buried beneath rubble in a demolished convenience store in south New Angeles and had stuffed a few in his backpack. He feared using magic to start a fire in case it gave the Fomorian bastard a conduit to grasp onto his magic.

The torch threw off enough light for him to search for an entrance in the volcano's base. Climbing to the volcano top and attempting to enter through the top barely made it on his short list of backup plans. He drilled the spiked pole into the ground, anchoring the torch with rocks.

More stars popped in the diamond-studded canvas above him. Night descended, the moons brightened, encroaching on the starlight surrounding them. Ryan blew out a weary sigh, pacifying the terror that had flogged him since he discovered Morgan gone. Even though his ether magic was always attainable, his link to the visible stars augmented the magic inside him. A clear nighttime sky provided his best opportunity to defeat Fomorians. If ever he needed the glorious ether, it was to find the love of his life. The woman who made life worth living.

And Ryan needed as much power as possible, along with Morgan's elemental magic, to destroy WindWraith. He rubbed his jaw, scratched a mosquito bite on his neck until it bled. If WindWraith had already possessed her, he'd require ether in their binding to scour the evil out.

A fierce tremble rolled up from his feet to his neck. He hoped it didn't come down to that. WindWraith inside Morgan could easily kill him if they attempted the final ritual—if the bastard didn't kill them both beforehand, or if anything existed of Morgan after it seized her body. The emotional rollercoaster twined his intestines into a cement ball. This mess would never reach that gods-awful state. He'd die trying to save Morgan.

After he annihilated every trace of WindWraith.

Stoked with determination, Ryan created an eight-point protection circle on the barren ground using crystals to form the points. Once he captured WindWraith, he'd use the impenetrable Druid circle to contain it, giving him time to reduce the shadow demon with smaller bursts of killing magic while he set in motion his next step of attack.

Satisfied with the circle, Ryan led RavenStar into the jungle. He carved out a burrow in a thicket, coaxed the foal inside, and cast an invisible shield over the bushes. Petting the winged horse's head, he felt numb relief sift through the hardening ball in his gut. Morgan would hate it if anything happened to RavenStar. This small act for her gave him hope.

He reentered the volcano's dead zone, centered his mind on starfire. Magic kindled, sparked in his gut, moved up his torso and down his legs, until his body became a mass of burning stars. Euphoria blew away his doubts, leaving warmth where frost had formed earlier. Ether emanated off him in a pale blue glow, and he commenced his search for an entry into the volcano, hardly needing the torch to light his way.

Power assailed Morgan. Her mind closed against the crawling feel of a water snake on the prowl. Tossing out barroom curses, she fought against her unseen restraints.

"What do you want from me?" she bit out through clenched teeth. The drugged fog had blown out of her mind. Magic dribbled inside her where it usually flooded. WindWraith and heat from the lava zapped her strength. A dangerously thinning air shield protected her. She tried to draw more air magic to thicken her shield, but it felt like drawing energy from a newborn.

Her heart thumped in her throat. *Breathe! Breathe*, she scolded in her head. Frustrated, she quit wasting her might on her impossible shackles and drew in steady, shallow puffs of air. Sulfur and dankness filled her lungs.

Morgan studied the mysterious cavern. Little had changed from her last view, but for one difference. For the first time since she'd spied the constantly undulating shadow her first day on the island, it held stationary beyond her feet as though asleep.

Black as death evil deluged the air, flowed across her skin in both freezing and scalding wickedness. The air burned the taint into her lungs, evil feelers exploring inward, leaving shards of darkness in their wake. She coughed and gagged, attempting to dispel the squiggly fingers. Her elemental earth magic raced to aid her barriers against the exploratory invasion. WindWraith withdrew, whipping away in a tornado, leaving her a shaking heap of limbs and nerves.

The Fomorian had never breached her skin and

muscles, not even when it captured her in the glade. Holy Goddess! After more than a century leeching the island's powers and days feeding upon Morgan and Ryan, WindWraith's strength had expanded immensely. Was she too late, too weak to destroy it? *No, no, no!*

Fear for Ryan chilled her burning skin. Had he awakened? Did he know where she'd gone? Regardless, she must hatch an escape plan without factoring in rescue by him. Their bond had disappeared, but there wasn't a devastating loss inside her heart. Ryan still lived. *I feel it in my soul.* She clung to the feeling, and it fed her efforts to escape.

WindWraith stroked her exposed skin, trying to provoke a response. She ignored it, no longer fooled by its fake arousal. Ryan's passion was born of love and true destiny. The Fomorian's false lusts stemmed from a lifetime of malevolent greed and vengeance.

WindWraith must die that night. No other alternative existed.

Morgan formed a mental sending to Ryan, gauging his receptiveness. The spell sputtered out in her purgatory. Resolve conquered a corner of her terror, and she concentrated her efforts on escape and WindWraith's destruction.

Focusing her powers on unraveling the complex restraints, Morgan surreptitiously studied the fissure on the cavern wall she'd seen in her earlier vision. A needlepoint of light on the deadened crystals called to her. Excitedly, she studied the crack until she found several more glowing pinpricks. She glanced toward her feet to determine WindWraith's awareness. The Fomorian hovered over her, its power less idle than a Druid initiate. No longer trying to breach her, the bastard merely swayed around her. Nor did it feel as malicious as it had earlier. Was WindWraith fooling her into taking rash actions? Or did it bide its time, gaining strength? Was it using her bond to Ryan to lure him here, if it even had the ability?

Carefully, she searched for similar dots on the earthen walls. After a few agonizing moments, she spied a sprinkle of subdued light. Her pulse quickened. WindWraith's form fluctuated, its motions increasing. She hastily buried her excitement and the evil blob steadied.

The longer she laid there, the more power it stole from her, power she couldn't contain, nor regenerate fast enough. Holding her shields in place grew increasingly difficult. Once her body depleted of power, WindWraith gained its prize.

With no time to lose, she studied the dots of light, dampening her excitement. Beneath the dead black surface, untainted crystals thrived. WindWraith must be unaware of the crystals or confident of the protections it derived from the lifeless surface. Morgan maintained her composure even though she wanted to shout in triumph.

As she scanned the walls, the beast awakened, billowing faster, bearing down upon her. Wicked power bathed her, assessed her barriers. It chipped away at her shield, using her own stolen power against her. Morgan lost her fractured calm and shrieked inside her head. She had to make a move! Hating to unleash magic the Fomorian might exploit to break down her walls, she must take the risk, or lie there to die in spirit, if not in body.

Weakening magic crawled sluggishly to her hands, formed amber balls on her open palms. She gathered an extra boost of air magic to enable the toss from her fettered position. Aiming at the crystal spots on the rugged walls, she loosed two blasts.

The fireballs hit the wall and a torrent of crashes deafened her. Ebony slivers and chunks of rock showered the cavern. WindWraith howled and lashed into a cyclonic frenzy. It increased its bashing against her weak shields, a wailing wind of voices and screeches drowning her mind. The attack upon her body, against her barriers was merciless. Coils of her magic unwound in the Fomorian's frenzied assault. She fought to maintain her shields, as WindWraith began ripping out her magic in excruciating barbs of fire. Voiceless, agonizing screams rent her head. Oh Goddess, they were her screams! Horrendous pain flooded her, and she frantically tried to ignore the twin agonies of being burned to cinders and buried alive.

Crystals shimmered beneath the destruction on the cavern's walls. Not enough to affect WindWraith. One more shot might drive the damned devil away. *Please, Goddess, let this work. Give me access to whatever magic I have left.*

Earthy energy suddenly skated across her flesh and she seized it, drawing from the island, turning it into Druid fire and air. Magic barreled through her, balling on her palms in an almost tangible manner. She pitched two more fireballs at the vulnerable wall. Faltering, she lost a toehold on her shield. A tortured scream erupted from her, the sound drifting to a whisper toward the volcano's peak.

WindWraith breached her barrier, a scorching evil zooming past the splinters. Fiendish, dirty power roared over and through her body in a searing swell that kept growing.

Two blasts shook the ground like dynamite exploding in a mineshaft. Ryan halted in his tracks. He sensed Druid magic, Morgan's magic. Was she battling WindWraith now?

"Ah, hell!" He bellowed his aggravated inability to breach the volcano, and sprinted toward the area from where the blasts originated. Sweat ran in rivulets down his chest, soaking the waistband of his shorts. Ryan sniffed for brimstone, the telltale sign of Druid fire. Nothing but dead soil and sulfuric gases rode the air. An odor he'd smelled occasionally in the winds blowing from the north. Volcanic odors.

Another explosion rumbled beneath his feet. The mountain quaked, drawing him toward a glowing fracture in a knoll of black, shiny volcanic rock to his right. Now he smelled distinctive Druid fire and felt a tug on his link to Morgan. Unfettered relief kicked adrenaline into his blood. She was alive and something had cracked open their bond.

Excitement and anxiety fed his clambering steps atop the hardened lava mound. Holding the flame away, he peered into the crack. Crystals blazed, obscuring his vision before his eyes adjusted. Beyond the radiance lining the interior walls, his gaze landed on his treasure, laying naked on a flat stone platform. *Morgan!* Terror knotted his shoulders. He bit down on his tongue to quell his silence.

WindWraith's black form swallowed Morgan's body whole. Her shields held the evil from touching her body but Ryan sensed her fading fast. Her fire blasts had zapped her already depleted power.

Snarling, he flung the torch to the ground and sprinted away from the mountainside. Drawing from his internal fire, he slammed destructive spheres at the weakened fissure until he formed a tunnel large enough to fit through. Ryan crawled into the tunnel, ignoring the razor-edged stones digging into his hands and knees. Crystals cut into his shoulders as he squeezed through the tight tube. He concentrated only on saving Morgan and killing that bastard who dared touch his woman.

Several yards ahead, dazzling light raged in the inner volcano. Had WindWraith absorbed so much power that crystals no longer affected it? Had the ancient Fomorian tricked them all along? Ryan's gut constricted. Suddenly, he felt a wrench on his bond, an infinitesimal slip in Morgan's magic. Rapid-fire evil began sabotaging her dissolving barriers.

Ryan scrabbled through the last few feet of tunnel. Racing against WindWraith, he pitched power to Morgan along their bond, holding nothing back, not even his ether. The Fomorian's strength had mushroomed. At the rate the evil attacked, it may only need minutes to possess Morgan completely.

Her torturous screams reverberated through the cavern and carved holes in his heart.

"No! Morgan!"

WindWraith had completely decimated her shield.

Throat burning with each sound, Morgan's useless shrieking escalated. Ryan's magic surrounded her, but she was unable to feel his power inside her. A hole in the volcano wall caught her rabid attention. She focused on regaining her shield, but the more magic she expended, the more territory the Fomorian gained. The weight of ages pressed down upon her, and her body prepared to implode from the force. She centered on Ryan's ether, breathing in small gasps to keep from passing out from the smothering pain, the scorching evil attacking her from head to feet.

A cautious, earthy force latched onto her air, fire, and earth meld. Thin threads snaked outward, down the platform, to the ground. Rolling trembles belowground rocked the volcano, and ebony stones plopped into the lava and freshwater pools. Unsullied, earthy power burst into the cavern, reaching for Morgan. The island's heart resonated strongly within her once again, working to force the dissonance away. Morgan opened herself to the currents of green power, and prepared for its expansion.

WindWraith battered her relentlessly. It loosed an almost human shout of exaltation that sliced into Morgan's soul, fragmenting her concentration. Her last barriers shattered. WindWraith engulfed her, pinching every inch of her flesh, muscles, and bones until she grew numb. Fuzzyheaded with agony and terror, Morgan heard Ryan yell her name. She felt his torment and his magic thrashing the Fomorian. Without her elemental magic aiding him, his power wasn't strong enough to destroy WindWraith. Once again, her magic was lost to her under the stifling, dead weight of malevolence.

A second wave of tremors beneath the earth shook the cavern. The ground rocked like a ship swaying in a sea tempest. Rocks dislodged from the walls and crumbled to the ground, sizzling in the lava pools, exposing pure crystals behind the black stone. Rubble cascaded down the shifting waterfall, splashing water in every direction. Steam spiraled in vapors, meshed with cloying dust in the air. The tunnel where Ryan's magic stemmed collapsed inward, avalanching debris toward her platform. Another fissure widened in the wall to her left, spraying the cavern with gravel.

Morgan lost sense of Ryan completely, and for all she knew, rubble buried him. Still, she didn't feel the soul deep sorrow if he was truly dead. Yet, as if death had claimed her, she floated in her final moments before her soul ascended. Foggy light penetrated her numb mind. Was it the Afterlife?

Another fierce rumble below the earth's surface combined with several explosions cracked open Morgan's consciousness. Beautiful, amber sunshine replaced the murky light in the cavern. The suffocating weight and agonizing pain dissolved. She sputtered and coughed, heaving in air. The weightless fetters had vanished, replaced by an anchoring exhaustion. Furious howls obliterated the final sounds of the volcano's interior shattering. The island's spirit thrummed gloriously through her veins, awakening rivers of energy, of precious life.

Morgan struggled to a sitting position. Rubble surrounded her in piles, but miraculously, the rock platform escaped damage. The island's magic had protected her like an iron glove. Gems illuminated the cavern as bright as summer's midday sun, providing shelter against harm from WindWraith.

She whipped her head around. "Ryan!" Anguish drove her off the platform, her knees buckling, barely managing to stand upright. WindWraith wailed, huddling in on itself in the chamber's darkest corner.

The island's newly awakened magic saturated her with the might of its power. Her magic flowered, fueled by the earthy gift combined with pure crystal energy. Using the glorious meld, she hauled forth a binding spell. She recited the words and blasted the spells at WindWraith. Magic circled the manic shadow, encapsulating it in a bubble the size of a warhorse. Morgan waved a finger and the seething bubble plunged to the ground.

Knife-sharp rocks cut into her feet, but she didn't feel the pain. She scurried toward the capsule, reinforcing her restraints with every dangerous step. She viciously kicked WindWraith. "You're mine, you son of a bastard's whore!" The action gave her a nibble of vengeful satisfaction.

With WindWraith safely captured, Morgan began searching for Ryan. She scuttled across the cavern toward the area where she'd first spied the hole in the wall, singeing skin on lava puddles, shuffling feet through mud, screaming Ryan's name. Gaining only pain and bloodied feet, she leaned against a mass of dead inky crystals. *Damn my muddled mind!* She hadn't tried to use her link to Ryan. *Fool!* Inwardly, she reached for the bond. At first, she felt nothing. Then a grain of ether manifested. She dug for it and followed the seedling.

Morgan shot regenerative power along the intangible path and felt acceptance behind a mound of loose rocks to her left. Using the island's elemental magic to bolster her own, she chipped away at the rocks, sending bits and pieces flying.

"Morgan." Ryan's hoarse voice was near.

Relief fueled her actions. Within moments, she'd gouged a small opening in the collapsed tunnel.

"Clear the area," he called out, his voice stronger, louder. "Protect yourself. I'm blasting through."

She hid behind a raised basin of lava, throwing up a barrier between them. Fire exploded and rocks sprayed the air, landing ineffectively around her. After the last rock pinged the ground, Morgan released her shield and rushed toward Ryan. No longer trapped, he lay on a bed of stony wreckage, gravel blanketing him. She picked her way over the littered ground, every cluttered tread tearing agony across the soles of her feet.

Ryan lifted his head. The ferocious hunger and love in his magnetic eyes folded her knees from under her and swamped her with the greatest sense of love and belonging. She had finally arrived home after a lifetime away from the man dreams were made from.

Ryan shrugged off the grit carpeting him. She held out her hands, and air currents blew the rest of the dirt and pebbles off his backside and legs. It was no dream.

Nothing felt real until he cupped her face in his large hands, a gesture she had grown to adore. Love blossomed across his face, and he bent his head, grazed his mouth over hers. She linked her arms around his neck, smashing her naked breasts to his dirty, bare chest. His kiss became passionate, drenching her with reverence. It possessed her in every way she wanted it to, relinquishing a lifetime of needs and wants. A kiss to drown in, to live a lifetime within.

CHAPTER 31

I thought I'd lost you." Ryan's voice cracked and his trembling joined hers.

Sympathy and guilt sprinkled holes in Morgan's relief. She had caused him to feel that way, and she never again wanted to see him in such anguish. Tears welled up. "I thought I had lost you, too."

Ryan snorted. "What a pair we make." His iron arms bore her closer to him. Fury flashed in his eyes, and he scanned the wreckage around them. "Where's WindWraith?"

"In that far corner." She flicked her hand over her shoulder. "Don't worry, the wretched scourge is contained."

Ryan exhaled heavily. He released her and pulled off his T-shirt. "How long can you hold it?" He slipped the shirt over her head. "Sorry, it's filthy."

Morgan smiled, tugging the shirt down over her dust-streaked torso. "I don't know where my clothes are, so it's better than nothing."

A sultry grin transformed Ryan's ashy face. "I rather like the naked you."

Morgan leaned forward, touched her lips to the healing tattoo on his chest. "I rather like the naked you, too. I'm sure if you had your way, we'd never wear clothes."

Ryan groaned. "But now's not the time to put the policy in motion." His grin faded. "How much time did you buy us?"

Morgan swept up her loose hair, shook out dust and grit. "I'm channeling energy from the island. It's not going anywhere for a few days." She tossed her ponytail over her shoulders.

Ryan's brows peaked. "Days? Thank the stars we won't need that long."

Suspicion edged through her and she clutched her throat. "You mean to take it inside you now? In your weakened state?"

He hooked a loose strand of hair behind her ear. "My love, if you'd only remained behind. I'd decided the safest thing for the world was to destroy the Fomorian completely."

Morgan's heart leapt. A cautious happiness crept upward from the pit of her stomach. "I thought—"

He touched his forefinger to her lips, then raised her off the littered ground, nestling her in his arms. "Let's get out into fresh air."

Slow and cautious, he carried her through the rubble to a gaping hole in the mountainside. Gems blazed along the newly exposed tunnel walls, the radiant light crushing the dawn sneaking into the volcano's hull. They emerged onto a bleak landscape of dead and dormant vegetation. Scattered young shoots of greenery had already begun to reclaim the brown land.

Ryan set Morgan on a smooth patch, his hands spanning her waist. Her feet were so grimy with dirt and blood, she hardly felt the pain, didn't even care. She loved being in his arms and never wanted to leave them.

A low whicker sounded behind her and RavenStar raced toward them, practically barreling her over. Morgan knelt, burying her face in the soft fur of his neck. He whinnied again, his tail twirling at the speed of a cyclone.

"I had an inkling you were in the volcano, but that little shit led me here. He *knew* you were here."

She kissed RavenStar's nose. "You don't hate him so much anymore?" she chided.

"I never hated him," Ryan said with mock annoyance.

Morgan swatted at him playfully. "You were jealous of him."

"Damn straight. Anything that comes between me and my woman—" Ryan's neck and face grew beet red. "I mean, well..."

Morgan's heart flip-flopped. *His woman!* She adored the sound of that. Tipping her head back, she gave him an encouraging grin.

Dread transfixed Ryan's expression. Morgan held back a laugh. She straightened to her full height and laid her palms flat on his chest, her right hand covering the rune brand over his heart.

"Ryan. I belong to you. You belong to me. That's why we're on the island together. It was our duty." Conviction accompanied her firm pat on his chest. "Our destiny."

"Screw duty." His eyes seethed sapphire darkness. "Fate had something to do with it, yes. We came here to find each other, for each other. Not just for duty. I understand that now."

"For love, too?" Happiness burst inside Morgan. The most incredible mixture of love and passion swirled around her chest, a rush of emotions she never wanted to forego.

"For love." His tongue traced a kiss across her lips. "I love you, Morgan, High Druid Sorceress, heart of the Druids." She drank in the sweetness of his lips that caressed her mouth more than kissed it. "Heart of my heart," he whispered against her mouth.

"I love you, too," she whispered, blinking back tears of joy.

They kissed deeply, a kiss overflowing with infinite love. A forever kiss.

In the grassy glade outside the volcano's lifeless

boundary, they rested in each other's arms, recharging their powers. Ryan explained to Morgan his plan to destroy WindWraith in the Druid circle. Later, she would mull over his need to leave the island and how best to approach the subject. No more withholding, no more mistrust. For now, she wanted to relax and handle one task at a time. Liberation and acceptance chased away her doubts, drifted her into welcome slumber.

Hours later, more refreshed and invigorated than she'd felt in days, Morgan stretched out the cricks in her sore muscles. Ryan stepped away to refill their waterskins. Mouth watering, stomach grumbling, she reached for one of the citrus fruits Ryan had brought with him. She was just about to bite into it when he rounded a thicket.

"No!" he shouted.

Startled, she jumped, her defensive power rising. "What's wrong?"

Ryan scrubbed his hand over his face, chuckled. "Don't eat the skin."

She looked askance at the rainbow fruit. "Why ever not?" Reality dawned and her face flushed. "Oh! Is that what caused my blackout?" She threw the fruit on Ryan's backpack and wiped her hands on her T-shirt as if the fruit was wormy. "That left me vulnerable so that whoreson was able to capture me."

"Sorry I didn't tell you."

Ryan enlightened her about the mysterious fruit and coaxed her into eating a few bites of the sweet meat for an energy spike. He split the rest with RavenStar, burying the peels to keep the foal from eating them. The foal's joy at her return hadn't abated, and she didn't want to create a delirious monster.

"Why did you think you could kill the Fomorian on your own?" Ryan slugged down a cup of spring water, white knuckling the coconut shell.

Morgan swallowed a pistachio nut, nearly choking on it as the moment of truth rapped the back of her hands. Like when her father used to tap his training wand on her hands when she took advanced liberties in her sorcery training and had to explain her motives. Rarely failing at the advanced spells, she might add. Now, she wasn't so sure Ryan would understand her intentions.

She cracked open another nutshell. "With the island's magic bound to me, I held a potent mix of all four elements necessary to imprison WindWraith like I did in the volcano. Then after a recharge of magic, I'd use spells my father imparted to me that joined with air, fire, water, and earth magic promised to destroy it forever."

A muscle throbbed in Ryan's neck. "Then why'd your father say you needed my power if you could decimate WindWraith on your own? Or was that just a ploy to get me here?"

Morgan thrust forward, fingers landing on Ryan's thigh. "Please don't think that. Father knew I was unhappy living alone. He only wanted the best for me and he knew we were meant to be together. He envisioned it, and it all came together—"

"Killing two birds with one stone?" Ryan grimaced.

Morgan laughed and pressed a quick kiss to his mouth before sitting back, sobering. She plucked at the grass, a flush rising up her neck.

Ryan groaned, twined his fingers in hers. "Now what?"

Morgan tossed the blades of grass aside. "Father wanted me to use the alternate plan only if something happened to you." Her voice grew somber. "If I had used the spells to kill WindWraith, they would have drawn all my magic out forever, leaving only my bond to you if you remained alive."

Ryan looked as if a she'd grown scales and a forked tongue. "Sweetheart, why would you have done that?" He closed the distance and pulled her into his arms. "To save me?"

"Of course to save you," she cried, slapping his back with the flat of her hand. "Your bloody plan would have killed us all and sent the Fomorian on his merry way to your land. In my body, no less."

He shook her as if he wanted to shake sense into her. "That wouldn't have happened."

Morgan squeaked out a frustrated cry and pushed out of his arms. "Ryan Almighty knows everything. No, thank you. I'd rather take my own chances with my body and my life. Let's get on with killing it before you have another harebrained idea to turn us into killer toads."

Ryan rose off the grass, his pack clasped in his hand. "Okay. You're probably right."

"Probably?" She snickered, rising to face him.

He held her face and she wallowed in the feel of his hands on her skin, the promises he held in that simple gesture. "I love that you would sacrifice so much for me, for us. I won't ever take your sacrifices or you for granted. Nor will I ever fail to take your intelligence and knowledge into consideration." He leaned in, his mouth a hairsbreadth from hers. "You believe me, my little raven?"

Melting against him, she placed her heart and soul, her life in the hands of this man fated for her. "I believe you. And yes, I would have sacrificed my magic for your love."

The whole of Ryan's joy spread across his face in his smile, in his lively eyes. It stopped her heart. "I'd do the same for you." He clasped her hand in his warm grip and held for a long moment. "Are you ready?"

"Yes." Not wanting to break contact with him, she hugged his arm as they walked into the volcano's cavern. Not so much for his protection and support, but because her entire body tingled happily whenever she touched him now.

He'd fashioned a smaller set of leather shoes from one

of his satchels to protect her raw feet from the spiky rocks littering the ground inside the cavern.

The air shroud encasing WindWraith pulsed frailly in the far corner. The Fomorian's power had diminished since it no longer siphoned magic from them and the island. The grayish shadow had shrunk to the size of a large man. A simple wind spell enabled Morgan to guide it out of the volcano without breaking the casing.

WindWraith bounced fiercely above the Druid circle in futile attempts at avoiding death. Using tethers of shimmery air, Morgan anchored the cocoon a few feet over the eight-point circle and looked to Ryan across from her. He nodded once.

They voiced aloud the spells to invoke their individual magic. Ryan pulled from the first stars in the deepening twilight sky. Morgan drew from her elemental magic, and then called forth energy from the island, fusing it with hers. Immense power swamped her, more than she'd ever wielded naturally. Crackling pleasure burst throughout her body. Bluish-white star power emanated off Ryan, illuminating the ground surrounding them.

"Concentrate on the crystal energy," Morgan instructed. "We say the spell together, sending your power into me, and mine along with the island's power into you."

Sweat filmed Ryan's bare torso. "Are you sure you can take the ether?" Apprehension pulled the lines tight around his mouth.

Morgan blew out an exasperated sigh. "We've been over this, Ryan."

After a moment's hesitation, he nodded. "Do it."

In unison, they spoke the words of the transference spell. Once the last word left her lips, Ryan's power whammed into her, knocking her off balance. She hastily regained steady feet and noticed with amazement the same had happened to Ryan when her power meld crashed into him. His mouth hung ajar.

The three powers gyrated inside her, dangerously close to erupting outward if she didn't forcibly dampen them. The twisted energy showered the air like dry rain.

WindWraith wrestled within its prison. Morgan cut the air tethers and the bubble dropped into the Druid circle. WindWraith's shrieks ripped into the night, sending RavenStar into a noisy, scampering bolt toward the jungle. Birds took flight, screeching and cackling, unable to drown out the earsplitting sounds of rage and terror.

"Now," she shouted over the din.

They spread their arms to the stars, calling down the sky's magic. Together, they blitzed a destructive bomb of ether, fire, air, and earth magic on WindWraith, decimating every cell of evil.

Euphoria roared through Morgan seconds before her knees turned to slippery seaweed, and her world whirled away.

"It's done." Lauren brushed past the gloating Overlord. She strode to the immaculate kitchen at the rear of the gothic mansion and slid the offensive box on the granite counter. Wiping her hands on the silk pants she'd discovered in an attic trunk in the former ritzy O.C. neighborhood, her muscles grew taut with apprehension.

Alexander approached from behind. His arms encircled her waist, tugging her roughly against his solid body. He mistook her tremor of revulsion for lust and rubbed his growing erection against her ass. She knew it wasn't her body that turned him on, but the killing act, the blood and gore, the thought of Michael's death. The power over the Druids he would attain—the only humans left on Earth, he and his soul-sucking minions were able to kill only in traditional physical ways. Bitterness rose in her throat. She plastered on a smile and turned in his arms.

"Don't you want to see what's inside the treasure box?" she asked in a lilting, sweet voice.

"I'm dying to." Alexander planted a sloppy kiss on her mouth then shoved her out of his arms. "I smell Michael's blood." He licked his lips, his eagerness now a palpable fire inside him, glowing through his eyes as if the fire burned behind them.

Lauren wiped the back of her hand across her mouth, avoiding a smear of blood staining her ring finger. She slipped her purse off her shoulders and dug out Michael's ring. The ring signified loyalty and leadership to the Druid who possessed powerful magic to wear it. It hadn't circled the finger of anyone but an O'Rourke for centuries. Lauren studied her own family ring, the cushion set moonstone that denoted the dominance of the Blackwell women for less than a century. Her grandmother had killed off the last Westerfield rival who'd ruled their coven, after they originally stole the power from the Blackwell family.

"It's yours now." She tossed the O'Rourke ring on the black granite. It clinked and skidded against an empty wrought iron napkin holder. "The last O'Rourke is dead."

"You really did it." Rare awe laced Alexander's rich, bass voice. "I had my doubts."

"Why? I thought we trusted one another." Lauren rubbed her arms, chasing gooseflesh. "From one Druid to another." Little did the asshole know she'd pegged him as a Fomorian from day one. The covens had conducted their research before the Wars, and she'd known for two years that he was the Alasoron Overlord. As much as he tried to hide his true form, it was unmistakable when he forced her to give him hand jobs and his eyes went all fiery red. Was he a stupid-ass Fomorian or what? Only the potions her master alchemist made her drink everyday kept her mind and her true feelings hidden. But she had prepared for him to reveal his true nature tonight. After all, he wouldn't be able to put the ring on if he was a Fomorian.

Alexander opened the box and clucked his tongue. Lauren moved to the other side of the counter to witness his smarmy face as he died and released the poor marked humans from demon hell to a miserable post-apocalyptic life. At least those humans would have their will back, if nothing else.

Without touching the box, Alexander leaned down and sniffed the heart, drawing in the bite of Michael's blood. Ebony darkness suffused the whites of his eyes, and his mouth distorted in a cruelly gleeful grin. His face turned ruddy, and she swore he'd spew in his shorts if he took another whiff of the blood.

Lauren's heart sank to the dregs of her stomach. Sweat dripped between her breasts. While he fawned over the heart, she slipped her hand inside her purse and grasped one of the bespelled vials of demon poison. Years of work and testing had gone into preparing the vanquishing potion. Despite the devastation of Earth's plant life, her people had scoured North America for the ingredients obtainable at most of the former herb stores. But it was the combined power of herself and Michael that stirred the brew into the mega potency of its current solution.

"Druid to Druid, you say." Alexander's voice grew throaty. "I do have a little Druid blood in me. Enough to wear the ring, I'm sure." He seemed to grow larger. Was that an illusion, or her mind playing tricks?

"What...what do you mean, darling?" Lauren managed a fake smile. Hands trembling, she uncorked the vial inside her purse.

"Your silly potion won't work on me, *darling*." Alexander's face reddened dangerously. Steam wafted from his collar. "Did you think I didn't smell it?" His straining erection pierced his trousers. His penis had morphed hideously, barbed, humongous. It took all Lauren had not to flee and throw up her guts in the dead flowerbeds in the backyard.

She sensed Michael's hidden presence outside the French doors behind her. He sent a wave of shielded ether to bolster her vast power. Alexander counterattacked with a tainted barrier to thrust the magic away.

With inhuman speed, the Overlord stood beside her. Lauren screamed, a half-animal, half-human sound. She jumped back, invoking a protection shield. Alexander walked through her barrier, splintering it asunder. An arrogant sneer inched across his crimson face. His power engulfed hers and swallowed the entire house, locking Michael away.

"Did you really think you'd triumph with your paltry attempts to fool me?" Long, ragged claws pinched Lauren's shoulders, tearing her blouse into tatters.

Blood rushed from her face, and she struggled to raise her shackled magic.

"Did you think I fell for your subterfuge?" Alexander pressed closer, his body growing larger, burning hot, slapping its evil around her, suffocating her. "Did you think I didn't feel his *shielded* presence outside, even though *his* heart lay in a box?" He clicked his tongue, shook his head. "Wonderful work. You'll have to enlighten me on the magic you used to pull it off. And you will, my love, you will. Once I bond you to me, you'll spill all your little secrets."

"Alexander," Lauren gasped out. "You have it all wrong. I want you. I want to meld my power with yours, rule with you. To grow the ranks of the Alasoron with my people just like we planned." She writhed beneath his powerful hands, straining to hold onto her sanity, reaching for the ties to Michael she no longer felt. "The Druids need *you* to unite them, not that second-rate O'Rourke. I have so much to offer. You know that. Only my people can give you the magic and genes you need to create your new race."

Alexander's head tipped back. His abrasive laughter boomed out, echoing up to the vaulted ceiling, a rumbling thunder along Lauren's eardrums. The Alasoron incubation farm was faltering, the Fomorians unable to procreate among their rank. Not even marked humans and Fomorian minions bore fruit. After capturing one of Lauren's young female guards just before the outbreak of the Horde Wars, the Alasorons discovered the woman was a perfect breeder. After she'd birthed triplets with Alexander's seed, the Alasorons captured a Druid male guard. Using his sperm, they impregnated several of their female freaks, all birthing babies at full term. All the offspring appeared human on the outside, beautiful innocent babies, but they carried the super DNA of a Fomorian and Druid mix. A master race of unfathomable evil. A master race the Fomorians tried to create centuries ago.

The Fomorian dipped his head and grinned at her. "Oh, darling, you will rule with me as will your beloved Michael, if you prefer his outward appearance to mine. I rather fancy his human form, all tied up in a knot in my backyard." His hands moved down to her breasts, and a claw ripped the buttons off her blouse, shredding the material.

Lauren heaved in air that seemed to be diminishing quickly. Her mind spun, searching for a get out of hell card. "I'll do whatever you ask, Alexander. Just let Michael go. I'll serve by your side. We'll rule the Druids just as we'd planned. Michael will be nothing against the two of us. He could even be a useful minion in time. Remember, his gene pool is exactly what you wanted at the incubation farm. He's the epitome of perfect Druid power to compliment your blood stock."

"Perhaps he's too powerful, eh?" Alexander pinched her

nipple hard. "I certainly don't want his blood to dominate any Fomorian younglings." He squeezed her breast. "However, my love, you are the perfect female specimen. Not too powerful, not too diluted. Not too weak to die from me fucking you over and over, birthing one little Fomorian after another." He took her hand and placed it on the bulbous head of his grotesque penis, covering her small hand with his huge clawed paw. "Are you willing to take me in my current form? Do you think you're woman enough to handle me inside you?" He thrust into her hand. "And live?"

Air wedged in her throat and her knees buckled. The implications revolted her so much, she'd rather kill herself and all her people than let the Alasorons touch them in their quest for a master race. The *one* race.

Alexander's hand on hers kept her stroking his disgusting penis. He leaned in and planted sloppy kisses on her neck, his lips hot, sticky. She battled the bile rising up her throat. All of a sudden, his lips grew cool on her jaw, his dick began to soften and shrink. A cold wind blew through the evil energy saturating the air.

Alexander gasped, staggered. "No!" he bellowed. His hands dropped away from her as he lurched backwards. Clutching his head in his hands, he cried out as if talking to someone behind her, "What's happening? Who's cutting our bond?" Confusion marred his expression of evil. Blood drained from his face, down his neck, mottling his crimson hatred. Internally, he appeared to battle something horrific, evidenced by the emotions flitting across his face, the cowering way he wrapped his arms around his torso.

Stunned and unable to move her rubbery legs, Lauren internally searched for a crack in his magic. She found dozens. Without giving it another thought, she scrambled backward and grabbed her purse. Her fingers latched onto the two vials of death. Gritting her teeth, she splashed the clear potion in Alexander's face, across his chest, the last drops glistening on his now deflated prick.

The Fomorian Overlord roared and fell to his knees, clutching his throat with one hand, grabbing for Lauren's leg with the other. Alexander began to dissolve into himself and his shrieks of anger became squeals of agony.

The doors crashed open, glass shattering. Michael raced in, throwing a defensive armor around both of them, and an invisible prison around the dying Fomorian. "What'd you do?"

Air grew in short supply. Lauren waved one hand in front of her face, the other held to her chest.

"Sweetheart, breathe, breathe." Michael shook her, eased her against him.

She leaned her forehead on his shoulder until her heartbeat began to even out and air inflated her lungs.

"Something broke the barrier, distracted him," she finally managed to answer, her shock holding her upright. "Did you do it?"

"No. I felt his magic shatter." He hugged her tighter. "Oh Gods, I thought we'd screwed up when he erected the shield before you used the potion. I never should have let you do this alone."

Mewling grunts and groans erupted from the shrinking Overlord. Michael pushed away from Lauren, his magic engaged and ready to strike.

Alexander melted into a gelatinous mass on the slate tile floors, seeping into the grout until there was nothing left but cracked tiles and black powder. For good measure, Lauren sprinkled the vanquishing potion on the floor, where it fizzed and evaporated. The vials now empty, she dropped them, and tiny shards of glass shattered across the tile. She lunged into Michael's awaiting arms, and sobbed her relief against his chest.

CHAPTER 32

Ryan held a cool, wet cloth on Morgan's forehead. He hugged her fiercely, holding on as if WindWraith might spirit her off to hell any second. "Too much ether?"

She buried her face against Ryan's chest, basking in his familiar texture and scent. Morgan had much to tell him and things she needed to hear from him. She wanted him to stay on the island with her because he chose *her* over his people. Until now, she had a hard time reconciling between the two. How could she prevent him from helping his people if they desperately needed him to survive their bleak life? Matters were different now with both WindWraith and his son Alexander destroyed. However, Ryan may still feel a duty to his people even if she revealed her visions. Air hitched in her throat, her chest constricted.

"Are you okay?" Ryan searched her face.

"I'm fine," she replied. "It wasn't the magic that knocked me out. I had another vision." She touched his rune tattoo, tracing the marks, smoothing her fingers over the amulet. "As the island's power increases and aids me, my visions have become stronger and more numerous. I don't normally pass out, since they usually come while I'm asleep." Despite the absence of evil in the air, she had to ask the question. "Did we destroy WindWraith?"

"Down to the last cell. I don't think anything will ever grow in that Druid circle." He chuckled and patted the grass. "Sorry, island."

Plucking at her twisted T-shirt, she eased back. "We must talk." She had to tell him about Michael, Lauren, and the safety of his people. There was one thing she needed him to know before his hopes rose and he hatched another plan to leave the island.

Ryan's eyebrows knitted together. "O-kay."

Morgan scooted out of arms reach. RavenStar perked up at her movement, butted her shoulder, and she shooed him away. She hugged her knees to her chest, hooking her wrists around them, her dread trampling a slice of her confidence. Ryan stretched out on his side, nonchalantly chewing on a blade of young grass. Anticipation paved his face.

"First, your people are safe now that WindWraith is dead." His eyes bugged out, and Morgan held up a hand to forestall him. "I will explain in a moment. You must also know that I cannot leave the island. I will never join them in New Angeles." The words tripped out. She waited for his reaction, but he kept nibbling on the infernal blade of grass, excitement brightening his eyes.

Finally, he spat out the sprig. "We've done our duty here." He gave her an expectant look as though he required her to agree with him on the spot.

Annoyance rose inside her. She quelled it, realizing they hadn't yet had this discussion. "Killing WindWraith was only part of it. I have other duties."

He flicked his hand sharply through the air. "Gwilym said you can't return to your time, your home. What more can you possibly do here?" He jumped up, towering over her. "Avalon's magic is safe. The island doesn't need to draw magic from it to hold the barriers in place any longer. Your people will be fine."

"I know my people are safe now." She lifted her chin, tossed her hair over her shoulder. "They are not my only concerns."

Ryan shrugged and rose off the grass. "What's left? My people? You'll come home with me. They'll accept you once they learn what we did. Once they learn about our bond, they'll accept you as my wife... mate." His tone left no room for objection.

Ire twisted in Morgan's belly, and she leapt up. Hands on her hips, she glowered at him. "I have more duties on the island. It's the other reason for our being here." A hush spilled over the sound of birds chirping in tandem with the distant crash of waves on the shoreline.

Ryan stroked her arm, his touch warm and welcome. "What are you trying to tell me?"

Sadness overcame Morgan. "I was also sent here to reunite the sorcerers of ancient Druid blood across lands. The Ancients are lost and alone in your world, just like you and I were. Now that the island is free, it will become their haven. They'll find their way here to populate it, thrive, and love."

He circled his arm around her waist. "I thought the barriers hid the island. And why do you need to stay?"

"The barrier continues to hide the island. The last earthquake fixed the holes WindWraith caused when he battled with the island." She placed her palm over his heart. It beat erratically, betraying his frustrations. "My magic will draw them here to safety, to a new life away from your world's devastation."

"Then the portal works?" Ryan canted his head.

"Not in the way you think." Morgan wrung her hands, futilely searching her memory for a hint WindWraith had disclosed to her. She traced the rune marks on her amulet. "My magic will pair the lovers who are bound to the island. The island will aid me."

Ryan scratched his neck. The corners of his eyes crinkled as he laughed. "Others will be tossed up on shore clutching a damned amulet, half dead like me?"

"I don't know for certain how they will arrive. They will all have an amulet. Fate has charted their course. The same as ours."

Ryan caressed her cheek, his fingertips sweeping her windblown hair off her face. "Once you carry out your duties, we can use the portal to return to my home, and I can protect my people. They can sustain for a short time without me."

Heat rose up Morgan's neck and she put her thoughts on the battlefield. "I cannot physically leave the island. If you try to take me through that wretched portal, you will kill me, and possibly yourself. We were destined to remain here. We must not tempt fate. You don't even know if that bloody cave is a portal, or where you will end up if it is."

Ryan's hand tangled in her hair painfully. "Is this one of your visions?" Morgan touched his wrist and he released her hair, clenching his hands loosely at his sides.

"Yes. My father told me the same." She looked daggers at him, daring defiance. "We are meant to lead these Druids once they arrive."

A long moment of silence ensued. Ryan's face gave nothing away before he spun around. "I need a moment. Wait here." Once again, he stalked off, spine straight, shoulders flexing.

Remorse prodded her heart. She had only herself to blame for not being forthright about their destiny, or not understanding it herself. For not trusting him sooner.

RavenStar butted into her leg, shaking her off balance. Suddenly, her memory jogged loose. Something her father had shoved into her head, information that jibed with WindWraith's ranting—the reason why she couldn't leave the island even if physically able.

Ryan refused to leave the one person he loved and cherished beyond reason. Nor this plentiful island paradise he'd begun to love. After spending years putting others' needs and expectations ahead of his own, he'd take the selfish road and put his needs first. The Druids owed it to him, whether they believed it or not. First, he had to attempt to go home, had to know if Michael and Lauren betrayed their people or not. Had to find out if his coven could return to the island with him.

He halted at an outcropping of trees bordering the base of the waterfall he'd passed in his blurred race to the volcano. Birds trilled happily in glittery trees, undaunted by his presence. Ferns and buds grew radiant and larger. The scent of salt and flowers cleansed the dank jungle air. Was it his imagination, or did everything on the island look, sound, and smell new—livelier and happier—now that they'd shipped the evil to hell?

Not much of a religious man, he knew divine intervention had occurred in his life. What else explained his good fortune of finding the love of his life? Or saving his people? Remaining in view of Morgan, Ryan sat on a tree stump and beseeched the Druid Gods to give him wisdom and discernment. He asked for peace and protection, asked the Gods to scrub the evil from Michael and Lauren, which had caused their betrayal. He thanked the Fates for his biological father, James MacFarland, for giving him the blood that enabled him to fulfill this bizarre task, which still left him unsure as to how it helped his people in the short term.

Finally, he thanked Fate for leading him to the island. For bringing him his one true love. He pressed his fingers to the rune marks on his flesh. Immense love coursed sweet and warm through his chest. His bond to Morgan sizzled to life inside his heart, accelerating his pulse.

Ryan rose and wheeled around. Morgan knelt on the ground where he'd left her, arms looped around RavenStar's neck. Even from this distance, her sorrow and disappointment chilled his blood, and he hated himself for making her feel that way. Never again. They both deserved happiness, peace, and everlasting love on this isle of destiny.

He began a fast walk toward her and ended up sprinting the final distance. She rose to meet him, and he scooped her up, spinning her in the air. "Baby, don't cry. I'm not going anywhere." He grinned at her as she brushed her tears away in an attempt to hide her sadness.

"You mean it? You won't try to use that portal to go home?"

"I want a life with you here. Away from that hell." He set her down, curved her precious body into his, loving the feel of her against him, inside him. "I won't do anything you disagree with. Deal?"

"Oh!" Morgan tapped his chest. "More of my father's information came to me just now, making me remember something WindWraith told me."

Ryan groaned. "I'm not sure I want to hear it."

"You'll like it." She jiggled against him in her excitement. "WindWraith also believed the crystal cave was a portal. That was how he planned to escape the island...in my body." She swished her tongue in her mouth as if to wash the taste of evil from her teeth. "Merlin's magic ensured WindWraith couldn't escape the island without one of ancient Druid blood on both ends of the portal."

"So if he'd possessed one of us, then the other had to remain alive on this island."

"I believe so."

"Do you suppose that's why you can't leave the island? Because you're meant to be my lodestone, my anchor here if

I leave?"

"Partly." She pinned him with a glare. "Don't even think about it until we investigate."

Relief whipped through him. There was a way home. He just knew it. Morgan would support it, after they learned what else floated inside her head, and figured out how to work the portal, if the damn thing actually worked. For now, he wanted nothing more than to spend a night or a hundred nights relaxing in the arms of his beautiful temptress without a care in the world. He beamed a smile at her, inhaling the dusty scent of her hair.

Morgan gave him the most brilliant smile, like sunshine breaking through clouds, her eyes sparkling with her inner fire and beauty. "I love you, Ryan O'Rourke, Druid king."

Ryan nuzzled her neck. "I like the sound of that. Druid king." He kissed her neck and she shivered. "Druid king of what? The island?" He chuckled.

"King to your queen and loyal subject, RavenStar," Morgan teased. "And the island." She shrugged and tilted her head to the side. "Shall we name our new home?"

Ryan dipped his head and kissed her, his tongue tangoing with hers, exploring and plundering. Her lips were warm and honeyed on his. She opened herself to him completely, giving back as much as he took. He yielded to the searing need that had been building within him for weeks. Vitality zinged from his scalp to his toes as he breathed her in, a sweet potent drug. Pulling away, he said, "Later. Right now—" He snatched up his knapsack, picked her up in his arms, and headed toward the waterfall.

Morgan's body quivered with anticipation, feeding his exhilaration.

"I have more to tell you."

"Later."

She giggled. "Where are you taking me?"

"We have unfinished business," Ryan said hoarsely.

"You will perform the soul-bond ritual?" she asked tentatively.

"Today, now, and again every day for the rest of our lives." Ryan growled low in his throat. He slowed to a stop, searched her eyes. "Know that I love you with everything inside me." A savage need stormed through him, and he almost laid her down and took her on the spot.

Morgan reached forward, her lips brushing his. "Show me," she whispered. She licked his lips, and he choked down a moan, clamping his jaw.

Amidst Morgan's peals of laughter, he ran the last distance to the waterfall, the starlit sky lighting his path. He dropped his sack and carried her into the healing waters to cleanse the vileness off their skin. He wanted nothing to taint the final ritual to bind him to his soul's heart forever.

CHAPTER 33

A spangle of diamonds in the night sky bordered the twin moons, bathed the lush glade in heavenly light. Unfettered and cheerful, Ryan had tossed a small fireball into a ring of wood they'd gathered earlier. The sultry night didn't need additional heat, but the flames dancing around the logs, and the reflection of the undulating fire glazing the surface of the pond set a flawless ambiance for the binding ritual. Since Morgan and Ryan contained the element of fire, they wanted all their elements present to celebrate their first joining.

They lay on a bed of silky, long grasses, their bodies shimmering from the moisture their foreplay caused. Morgan's cry of ecstasy drifted away on a joyful breeze.

"Are you ready for me?" Ryan lifted his head from her moist flesh, his low voice husky. The reflection of flames flickered in his eyes. "No doubts?" He caressed her scars and she trembled from his blistering touch.

She captured his spicy scent, mixed with the perfume of wild flowers dancing in the air, and locked it inside her senses. "After all we've endured, you need to ask?" Grinning, she sifted his damp hair between her fingers. His body glowed with fire and excitement, lit from within as if stars lived beneath his skin. "Share your ether with me. I want all of you inside me," she whispered.

A possessive snarl rose up Ryan's throat. "I've waited forever for you." He worked his lips and tongue over her feverish flesh, up her quaking body until his body covered hers, and they locked gazes.

Morgan leveled her breathing from the intensity of the spasms Ryan's expert fingers and mouth had already generated. "As I have you." The fierce love in his eyes almost made her weep with happiness. "I never thought I'd love someone as much as you."

He nibbled on her bottom lip. "Heart of my heart." Ryan edged his hard length into her slick heat. "I love you."

"My Druid king," she whispered on a gasp. "All of you. Inside me. Where you belong."

Ryan pushed in farther. "Like this?" he groaned out in a teasing voice, shuddering against her.

Erotic sensations blinded her and prepared to fling her over the edge once again. She reined in a scream, fighting the agony of her restraint. By sheer magic willpower, she forced herself to hold back her release. She wanted to soar free with Ryan together. They *needed* it to fulfill the soul mate binding. Regardless of the bond, she wanted their surrender to each other complete, to feed her crazed need for this man of her fate. Her hands balled and unclenched on his hard buttocks. Her nails dug furrows into his skin as she fought the sensual pleasure threatening to overtake her will.

Ryan inched into her deliberately, seductively, sliding in deep. He stretched and filled her until she didn't think she could take any more. She arched up to meet his firm push, rapture flooding her with liquid warmth. Morgan grabbed his hips, raking her fingernails up his slick back. Magic infused her and lightning seemed to flash along her nerve endings.

He kissed her deep. "I'll never get enough of you." Another sensuous kiss. "Fly with me, little raven."

Morgan instinctively wrapped her legs around him and met every thrust with one of her own. His gaze riveted on her face, soaked up every nuance of sensation she experienced. Their magic joined, whispered to each other. Ryan's pleasure exploded in her blood, and a yelp of blissful surprise erupted from her.

On their fur-covered grassy bed, Morgan writhed beneath his slow, tortuous movements. Bluish-violet light radiated off them, showering them in tingly stars. Morgan flew out of control from the explosive currents ripping her apart. Ryan's thick, hard length stretched her, and she welcomed every inch, wanting more, so much more. She clutched his muscular buttocks, feeling them tighten, dip down, then bow with every drive. He slipped his tongue into her mouth and it pulsed against hers in tune to his hip thrusts.

He began to move faster, as if a fury had taken hold of him. "I can't hold on much longer." Sweat dripped off his face onto her lips.

She licked the drops, savoring his salty taste. His mouth claimed hers in another possessive, melting kiss as he plunged in, withdrew, his body quivering with his need. The fiercest need crested, shoving all other senses out of her mind, body, and soul, burning with a nameless pleasure.

"Fly for me." Ryan's mouth enslaving hers stifled her rapturous cry.

Hot, magical, and powerful, all of him filled her. Absolute and exquisite. She hung on the precipice, tipping over, slipping fast. Tremors of pain-pleasure jolted through her. Starlight burst inside her magic core, showering her with breathtaking joy. Sweet exhilaration washed over her like sunlight on ice. Her release began to rock her to the base of her soul, and she lost control, slicing the last shackles on her magic. Ryan's fire and ether shot molten heat into her every cell, instantly fusing with her magic. Clinging to his shoulders, she dipped her head back and screamed as the elements swamped her, soaking up Ryan's prickly ether as if her insides were starving for lifeblood.

Morgan's air, fire, and earth magic seized the ether and detonated inside his body. Magnetic, electrifying flames lit her up from within. His eyes widened and a convulsion bucked him against her. He tore his mouth from hers and yelled out as his own release hooked him. Energy swirled above them in a dangerous cyclone of light and electricity, joining their souls together. Her heart quit beating for seconds then beat as one with Ryan's heart. They shuddered together, heaving with the force of their mutual release.

Vast power cascaded inside them, electrifying the air, pulsing along their skin in an indigo glow. Their crystals exploded lilac light around them, illuminating the uncontainable power leaking from their bodies.

The invocation came unbidden in the midst of her unraveling. "I dream of you, lover of my body, enchanter of my heart, warrior king of my soul, sorcerer of my magic. You are mine everlasting. Our hearts, bodies, souls, and magic are entwined. Here, now and forever." Morgan pressed her open lips to his, blowing in the last bit of magic.

Slowly moving inside her, Ryan kissed her forehead, her eyelids, her mouth. "I dream of you, lover of my body, enchantress of my heart, queen of my soul, sorceress of my magic. You are mine everlasting. Our hearts, bodies, souls, and magic are entwined. Here, now and forever."

Her heart thudded against her chest, in her ears, on the edge of bursting anew with ether. Renewed ecstasy plunged through her with the perfection of their united magic. Her release went on longer than she thought possible, rocking her body against Ryan. More of her magic spilled into him as Ryan's magnificent magic took its place.

She cried out, dragging in gulps of air. Only the power fuse inside her kept her from passing out. Ryan collapsed on top of her, panting hard. Morgan lay beneath his welcome weight, reaching for the tantalizing power fuse, glorying in the excruciating pleasure of their union. They lay still for several long moments, leveling their breathing and pulses. Their magic danced a slow waltz inside each other, a tantalizing mix of life and love.

"Holy hellfire." Ryan shifted his weight off her. "You just about killed me." He managed a chuckle that turned into a snort. "That's one helluva ritual." He stroked her face, love blazing with the dance of firelight in his eyes. "Your magic is so sweet and fresh inside me. I feel like I've died and gone to heaven with everything I've ever wanted."

"I *am* in heaven." She nestled into his sweat-drenched body. "Your ether magic plays nice with mine, too. I feel invincible." Morgan pulled his head down and kissed him. She parted her lips and released a final taste of magic into his welcoming mouth.

Ryan jerked his head back. "What was that?"

"Another gift. Something I tried to tell you when you stomped away from me earlier."

Ryan hung his head sheepishly. The visions of home hit him and he whipped his head up, landing a wide-eyed look on her. The visions played through Ryan's mind. His expression changed from confusion, to awe, finally to relief when he witnessed Alexander's death scene.

"Michael and Lauren would be dead if not for us," he said in an awed whisper.

She nodded. "We saved their lives."

Moving his full weight off Morgan, he molded her to him, chest to chest. "Killing WindWraith broke his tie to Alexander?"

"Yes, also Alexander's minions who will not survive without him. Those carrying his mark are free." She swept his damp hair off his temples. "Michael and Lauren did not betray you. They love each other. But they first and foremost honored you and your duty."

"Wow." Ryan rubbed his chin. "I underestimated Michael and his potions. I'd been so sucked up in leading and protecting our people, I ignored what was in front of my face."

"I think they'll make wonderful leaders and prove they can guide and love at the same time." Morgan caressed his face. "How do you think they'll fare against the Alasoron Cabal now that the Overlord is dead and the Fomorian ranks reduced?"

"The Alasorons can barely wipe their asses without Alexander's leadership and power. They'll start infighting and their powers will dwindle without ties to Alexander. Eventually, they'll kill each other off."

"What if they don't? What if you're wrong?"

Ryan hugged her tighter, his relief a palpable weight on their bond. "My love, you don't have anything to worry about me leaving you alone now. There's really no need for me to return. Alexander was our greatest threat. Michael and Lauren can take it from here."

She kissed his rune brand, relishing his musky, salty skin on her lips. "Did you know that your adoptive father was the cause of your mother's death?"

"No," he whispered, his voice cracking. "The bastard played it off, made me think Michael forced James and my mother to take a prototype balancing potion to help them focus their magic easier. They'd both had problems with inconsistent casting."

"But didn't Michael refute your father?"

"He tried. I wouldn't listen." Ryan's faced reddened. "Then he took off to the East Coast. Gods, I'm such an idiot."

"I'm sorry you won't ever see Michael again."

A melancholy frown flitted across his features. "Maybe we'll find a way to scry to my world someday so I can tell him I'm alive, that he and I are where we belong. Maybe my people will wind up here. Isn't that the purpose of the island?"

Morgan touched her fingers to his whiskered cheek, glad she'd told him about her ability to scry. No more secrets would separate them. "The magic here is unfathomable. Killing WindWraith opened the lock on the island's door, so to speak. On an isle with two moons shadowing each other in the sky, anything's possible."

Ryan pressed his feverish forehead to hers, his fingers playing with a lock of her hair. "You are the star of my sky now."

Morgan felt the buoyancy of his heart and gloried in the easing of his burdens. Her magic bottled his ether inside her in warm comfort. "I definitely feel like starfire." A tear of happiness slipped down her cheek.

He delicately traced the scars on her stomach. No longer stinging with misery and embarrassment, they melted every time he touched them. No longer evidence of fear and abandonment, she wore her badges with pride.

"What I don't get is how Michael pulled magic from the stars. That bastard my mother married didn't possess ether magic."

Morgan stroked his face. "I have a feeling you and Michael were both conceived in love. Not duty."

"MacFarland is Michael's father, too?" He flung his head back in a hoot of laughter. "Ian's gotta be rolling in his grave with the knowledge that neither of his so-called sons carried his blood. If it wasn't for him pushing me into the life I left behind, I probably wouldn't be here with you now." Ryan kissed her leisurely, lovingly. "I wouldn't want it any other way. He'll see in the Afterlife that love does indeed conquer duty."

CHAPTER 34

Ryan's steps were light and carefree as they returned to the emerald grotto. He was anxious to stop by the crystal cavern to check out the portal. Not that he wanted to test it, but when he'd knocked his head against the wall the day before, he'd seen something that intrigued him. He held a flowering branch aside to let Morgan pass. The limb quivered in his hand, the tip reached to touch Morgan's arm. "It's going to take some getting used to this bond you have to the island."

"As if you need to tell me that." She gently peeled off the lacy moss clinging to her hair, creating a net. They resumed hiking along the narrow path, Morgan taking up the rear as Ryan cleared the way.

"Was the portal cave safe to enter?" Anxiety entered Morgan's voice. "RavenStar!" she yelled at the foal seconds before it bit into Ryan's bulging backpack. "Oh, heavens. He wants more fruit."

Ryan yanked the pack higher on his back, looping the strap on his shoulder. "Get, you mangy beast. If you eat more of the peel I may have to knock you out for a day."

"I'll help." She laughed. "My arm's bruised from his tail whipping me a hundred times. I'm surprised he's not permanently dizzy." As if to prove her point, RavenStar began running in a circle, chasing a rodent the size of a cat around a thicket.

Ryan stopped. "Let him wind down. He'll catch up." He

picked out a flower petal stuck in Morgan's hair. "As for the cave, it appears safe. What you felt before will be all you feel without an activation."

"Whatever that is."

"I'm hoping to find out one day." Morgan's paranoia flitted across her expression, and he added with a chuckle, "Don't worry. I'm not going anywhere. I'll never leave you. Living on this island with you tops every perfect event in my life to date and hopefully will until the day we die."

"Oh, you can count on that." She trailed her fingers down his chest, setting a path of fire from the rune brand to the belt of his loincloth. Her fingers brushed over the pliant leather. Teasing. Promising. "I can promise you many moons of pleasure."

Ryan coughed, adjusted his loincloth. "No doubt." As she whisked her hand away, he grabbed it, bringing it to his mouth to plant a soft kiss on her palm. "I plan to ravish every inch of your body tonight." He licked her finger teasingly.

"That's a promise I'll hold you to." She fanned her face. "After we bathe in the hot spring, I hope."

"I suspect you'll need the energy from the cavern to keep up with me, so we'll stop there tonight."

Morgan laughed, a joyous boon to his ears. "Let's go, master of my heart. My air magic and I have plans for you tonight."

They resumed their trek, laughing and bantering in a way Ryan hadn't ever experienced with anyone. The raven pair joined in, cackling and cawing as they flew from tree to tree, scaring off the parrots and smaller birds. Before long, the odd party of five reached the hidden entry into the catacombs.

When they approached the portal cave, the magic seemed even more alluring than before. "Killing WindWraith and stopping its drain on the island appears to have affected the portal." Ryan wrapped his arm around Morgan, pulling her into his side, her braid swinging against his arm from the wind their presence created. "To be safe, stay here." He felt her nod against his shoulder.

Again, the energy crackled like strikes of lightning, but once Ryan adjusted his eyes and found his balance, he became one with the cave's power. Without wasting time, he dropped to his knees before the staggered crystal wall where the crack running its length widened toward the ground. He peered inside at the crystals lining the crack the entire depth, proving how thick the radiant stones lined the walls. He centered his sight on a dark spot deep inside the fracture.

"What do you see?" Morgan elevated her voice over the wind's whistling and whooshing.

"Not sure. Something's stuck deep inside."

"Can you fit your arm in the crack?"

"Just barely." Ryan inched his hand into the crevice. Sharp stones bit into his flesh as the cleft narrowed. He shoved his shoulder into the wall to dig deeper until his fingers brushed against something pliant. He fingered the edges of the object. Excitement swept through him as he realized what he'd found. "Hot damn."

"Careful. Is it activating?"

"No." He stretched his arm and leveraged his fingers around the harder shell of the object. "It's a book."

"Holy Goddess. The portal works!"

After delving deeply into the fissure, Ryan managed to get a sufficient clamp on the book to pull it out. Aged leather encased the inch thick journal. Ryan brushed the dust off the front cover. The familiar tooling of the gold dragon spewing fire beneath a star-filled sky stopped his heart. He'd seen this journal or duplicates dozens of times for as long as he could remember. They'd been custom made for one man.

"Ryan, what is it? You look like a ghost just walked through you."

"One did." He raised his head, stared at Morgan, wanting to ensure he wasn't dreaming again. "This journal belonged to my father. James MacFarland."

Morgan's hand flew to her mouth. "How could that be? He died in the car accident. How did his journal end up here?" She hugged the walls of the entry. "Ryan, please come out. The power scares me."

Her concern broke the barrier of icy confusion numbing Ryan's mind. Holding the grubby journal tight to his chest, he rose unsteadily, pushing against the energy as he made his way outside the cave. The moment he stepped into safety, Morgan's arms wrapped around him, giving him the fortitude to confront the puzzling possibilities.

They returned to the main cavern and sat near the hot spring, careful to maintain distance lest the bubbling water land on the precious pages of his father's legacy.

"Do you supposes James—your father—traveled between the island and your world?" They sat on the smooth boulders they'd earlier commissioned as seats, their hands linked on his thigh.

"I don't think so." Emotion roughened Ryan's voice. "The car slid down a cliff off the Coast Highway into the shallows of a cove. My mother's body was recovered from the car, but they never found James. The official police report said his body had been swept out to sea. No one questioned it."

Morgan squeezed his hand. "Do you think—"

"He space traveled here? That's exactly what I think." Reverently, he pried open the leather cover, excitement buzzing the length of his body with every word he read. "The journal predates his death." He flipped to the last page. "The final entry was a month after the accident."

"Oh, my." Morgan scrambled closer to peer into the

book. He moved the journal between them for her comfort. "Did he always keep a journal?"

"As a professor of botany, he was always jotting down his findings and experiments. I think that's why he was so willing to believe in Michael and his alchemy. Michael used a lot of plants and herbs in his potions. You know, you have that in common with them."

Ryan flipped through several pages about James's time on the island, stopping on an intriguing passage. "Check this out: *I believe the crystal cave I returned to life in is the teleportation device that stole me from death's claws and catapulted me to this beautiful island of mystery. Without making any guesses as to where I landed, whether heaven, hell or a place in between, I believe there is a greater purpose for my presence here. The plant life on the island is incredible and I will document as much as I can. However, I don't think that's my reason for landing here. I've begun to have visions of such horrible devastation to the world I'd left behind. So much hideousness, death, and destruction. Apocalyptic in nature. I cannot fathom how our people will survive it, but I see my sons in the end, surrounded by many familiar Druid faces. My Sight has never failed me...*" Ryan's voice faded off as the enormity of the words banged off the walls of his gut.

"Did you know he was a seer?" Eagerly, Morgan dug her fingers in his arm.

Ryan snorted. "Obviously he hid it or else Ian would've kicked him out of the coven. It's possible Ian found out and that's partly why he caused James's death."

Morgan tapped a finger on the next page. "Oh, read this."

Ryan skipped ahead to the entry Morgan pointed out. "*I have just discovered fierce evil on this island. I barely made it back to the great cave, which appears to be a safe zone from the invisible creature that chased me throughout the jungle. My magic is weak and ineffectual against the beast, and I will have to remain on guard when I venture outside."*

"WindWraith," Morgan spat out. "Do you think it—"

"Killed James? Hell, yes." An unfathomable rage seized Ryan, his seething muscles protruding along his arms.

Morgan leaned into him. "I'm sorry. I hate seeing you forced to live through James's death twice. Perhaps he's on the island somewhere."

Ryan kissed her temple. "That gives me hope, sweetheart. Thank you. I don't want to count on it, but I'd like to find his remains, at least. Give him a proper memorial."

He fingered the mist from his eyes and focused on James's tiny scrawling handwriting. James had told Ryan once that he wrote so small to get as much as possible in one journal. Crammed with words from front to back, this journal was no exception. Ryan scanned a few more pages until he came to the first section that mentioned the portal.

"Here's where James began to realize the portal was meant to save our people." Exhilaration replaced Ryan's grief, and he read aloud, *"Despite the life-sucking evil on this island, I believe my purpose is to carve out a home for our people here, possibly to avoid the devastation on Earth my Sight foretells. But I am loathe to bring anyone here with such evil, for there appears to be no destroying it."*

Ryan skipped past James's ranting about WindWraith. *"My Sight is greatly magnified here. I have now seen my fate."* His heart pounded in his ears. *"I was meant to be an anchor on this land for people in the old world as I now call what is left of Earth. To that end, I will experiment with the portal and document every last detail. Unfortunately, my Sight has conveyed my true death. In my weakened state, I no longer have the ability to fend off the demon, or whatever evil has plagued this land. My transport to the isle broke my link to the stars. I'll fight death for as long as possible. I have no choice but to accept it. ShadowMoon Island, as I have dubbed the paradise, will become my graveyard. This bequest of my journal to the deserving ones who find it will be my last act in my life's opus. I will ensure it is a superior act."*

EPILOGUE

Groggy and out of sorts, a serendipitous pall haunted Morgan. Already up and about, Ryan had stoked the fire in the emerald grotto's cave. Despite the lack of changing seasons on ShadowMoon Island, the air was noticeably cooler, proof of an approaching electrical storm.

"The cooling before the storm," she murmured, swishing her tousled hair off her face.

She hastily performed her morning ablutions. Later, she'd bathe under the waterfall and cleanse off the lingering traces of their long night of lovemaking. They had marked their first wonderful six months together with a feast, which included pieces of the Celestial fruit. Heat infused her as she remembered the incredible sensations the drugged fruit had created.

Time was of the essence, though, since she sensed the telltale nausea in her gut to fulfill another Beckoning Spell. She locked away thoughts of Ryan and their ceaseless passion.

Having spent months on the island, she'd learned how the weather affected her magic and her tasks with the spellbound amulets. The fathomless ache inside her reinforced the timing. But something was off that day. She normally felt elation and anticipation. Apprehension now tinged her excitement, turning her blood into ice water.

A hidden crevice gouged into the stone wall held her pouch of amulets, and she grabbed it on her way out of the cave. As she walked past the waterfall, she studied the clear sky. Both violet moons had dark amethyst rings circling them, painting the moons almost black. The final sign she needed. "Will it work this time?" Morgan pushed out a shaky breath. "Or am I wasting my time? Maybe we ought to try James's experiments and send the amulets through the portal." She rolled her eyes to the azure sky, hoping to see the answers written in the heavens.

"Morning, love." Ryan called to her from across the pool where he was repairing her herb-drying shed after RavenStar unfurled his wings in the interior.

She held up the amulets, and Ryan nodded. It was her third time. He felt what she experienced each time the electrical storm hit. Their empathic connection saw to that. Ryan always followed, keeping his distance, giving her time to perform the spells. He watched over her, ready to aid if needed.

She waved to him and strode away from the grotto beneath the slim archway Ryan had cut into the vegetation. Wind buffeted her, plastering her tunic to her torso. RavenStar whinnied and trotted to her. The foal nudged her behind playfully, flapping his wings in the wind.

"Not now, little one." Single-minded steps carried her toward the cliff above the cove nearest the crystal cave. She passed by the stone marker at the grave that held James MacFarland's skull. They had found it in the volcano, the likeliest place. Ryan recognized the cut of the teeth and the two gold fillings. Apparently, people used to tease James mercilessly about the gold treasure in his mouth.

RavenStar sensed her determination and sedately trotted behind her, leading her mind back to the amulet rituals. Not sure when, how, or if her efforts would ever produce results, she'd continue tossing the amulets into the sea until her visions told her otherwise, or no more pendants remained.

Maybe my gut feeling is a sign another person may arrive soon. She clung to that idea as she stopped inside a ring of boulders edging the cliff top. As much as she loved her time alone with Ryan, she was curious if the beckoning magic actually worked. Mostly, she wanted others to experience the love and joy she had found with Ryan. And to escape their drab black and white habitation for a colorful land of plenty.

Seawater eddied and frothed over the rocks lining the left side of the cove. A strange aquamarine swirling beneath the water's surface mesmerized her, despite the foreboding knotting her stomach. The wind blew locks of her hair in her face. She hooked it behind her ears, wishing she'd tied it back before she left the cave.

Lightning flashed and crackled between the moons. She propped a foot on one boulder and untied the drawstring on the leather bag. Electricity snapped and popped harmlessly around her. The moons shimmered bright in the darkening sky. The sun faded, and a wintry chill swept over Morgan. Shivering, she looped the ties of the pouch around her wrist for safekeeping. She stuck a hand inside, hooked a twisted pair of amulets on her fingers, and plucked them out.

Three identical amulets twined together. The blood drained from her face as she stared at the jumbled pendants. There should only be two ruby amulets tied together. "Why three?"

She knelt on the grassy mound and opened the bag wider to search for a fourth ruby amulet. Only one lone pendant not attached to another held a pink stone. Stunned, she checked the rune marks on the four amulets. They all matched.

The island's sole pair of ravens flew toward Morgan, cawing in unison. Flapping their wings, they sped by her head, the wind from their wings caressing her face. They circled over the cove like vigilant vultures.

"Bloody birds," Morgan muttered. A sick feeling washed over her. Signifying death and life, the ravens never appeared during an amulet ritual. What did that portend?

She rose carefully, braced against the blustery wind, dangling the four amulets from her fist. She'd throw them all out to sea and let Fate chart their course.

Misery tinged her decision. With little choice, she began untying the three silver and leather thongs. Wind gusted from behind, blowing her against the rocks along the cliff's edge. She cried out, caught herself on a patch of sea grass sprouting between two boulders. The island's magic kicked in and she landed gently. The jolt knocked the amulets out of her hands, and they sailed into the swirling, chaotic waters below. "No!" She glared at the turbulent sea. Usually separated when she tossed them in, this time the pendants remained knotted together.

"Morgan!" Ryan's shout flew away on the wind, lost by a snap of lightning.

She held up her hand, keeping him from approaching, but signifying her wellbeing. He wouldn't stay away for long. He hated her standing so near the precipice, even knowing the island protected her.

Morgan recited the lovers' Beckoning Spell, hoping she wasn't too late. She usually voiced the words before tossing the amulets into the sea, adding an extra dash of magic for their journey.

Pushing away from the boulders, she drew her right hand to her side, and to her dismay, discovered the fourth amulet wrapped around her iced fingers. Not knowing what else to do, she quickly cast the spell again and threw the pendant toward the roiling ocean.

One of the ravens zoomed over her head, swooped down, and snagged the pendant in its beak.

"Hey!" Morgan shouted, stamping her foot.

The raven rose up and circled, its beady eyes scanning

the ocean's surface. A glint of light sparkled off the dark waters and the raven dropped the pendant over the spot.

Swirling waters claimed the pink amulet. Waves battered the boulders along the reef in a final surge. Then the waters calmed, sheeting like glass. The sky brightened, the moons reverted to their normal violet-tinged gray, the air stilled.

Arms gathered around her waist from behind, and Ryan held her close. He made a noise low in his throat, letting her know he wasn't pleased with the ferocity of the storm and her presence in it. She leaned against the solid strength of his body.

The ravens wheeled overhead, diving and swooping like seagulls. One let out a screech, the other answered. They fluttered to the ground at Morgan's feet, strutting, staring out to sea.

"You're shaking," Ryan chided.

She turned and buried her face in his chest. "Something didn't go right."

"Hey." He lifted her chin and gazed lovingly into her face. "Whatever happens, happens. Let it go."

"I know." She breathed him in, tasting him on her tongue. "I could scry to contact Father, ask if he knows what may happen."

His chest rumbled with his laughter. "No. Please. I don't think I can stand to hear another tirade about our binding before we were handfast."

Morgan giggled. Nothing dented Gwilym's pride and happiness in her. He loved and respected Ryan and knew she could not be better protected, more loved, or happier. "Poor Father. He has his hands full lording it over the people and magic returning to Avalon."

Ryan's eyes twinkled. "And the lusty, mischievous initiates chasing after him."

"There's something about those with ancient Druid

blood who love powerful Druid sorcerers." She feathered her fingers over his rune mark, causing their crystals to flare.

Ryan kissed her, clasping her hand in his. "I've cut some Celestial fruit for you. It'll make you feel better."

A slow smile spread her mouth, and warmth curled from her stomach, trailing southward. "With the peel on it?"

Ryan laughed. "Definitely." He claimed her mouth in a searing kiss.

About
Chasing Shadows

One kiss, one touch, one night. It's all she wants to last her forever.

Psychic Juliana Westwood returns home after twelve years and foresees a young girl's abduction. Not only does she risk her life delving into the mind of a dangerous kidnapper, she risks her heart assisting the lead detective and child's uncle...the man she was forced to leave behind. Juliana knows Alex doesn't trust her, but can she endure another twelve years without him?

He deadened his heart against loss. Her return changed everything.

Alex MacKenzie's wary of reconnecting with the woman who broke his heart, but he knows Juliana can save his niece. As they race against time chasing clues, Alex realizes he'll fight to give Juliana a lifetime of forevers...if the kidnapper doesn't destroy her first.

PRAISE FOR
CHASING SHADOWS

"Never faltered from its action and suspense." *Night Owl Reviews, 5-Star Top Pick and Readers Choice Award Nominee*

"A whirlwind of emotions, twists, turns and rediscovered love will keep you breathless!" *~Fresh Fiction*

"The suspense will keep you turning the pages... The characters are complex and well-developed and there is never a dull moment in the story. If you love your romance with suspense, this is one book you need to read! 5 stars all the way!" *~The Romance Reviews*

"This story was masterfully written and illustrates just what a frightfully good imagination the author has to work with." *~Fallen Angel Reviews* (5-Star Recommended Read)

"This book has so many twists and plot turns that a seatbelt should be required. One of the best romantic suspenses that I have read this year and I heartily recommend to any fans of this genre. This book is just incredible." *~Love Romances & More*

DID YOU ENJOY
WICKED PARADISE?

If you have a few moments, I'd love for you to leave a review for *WICKED PARADISE* at your favorite online retailer or review site. Your review is greatly appreciated!

To stay up to date on Erin Richards' latest happenings, including new releases, sales, special announcements, exclusive excerpts, and giveaways, subscribe to her newsletter at: **www.erinrichards.com/connect.htm**

About the Author

After lamenting the lack of young adult books to read, Erin Richards wrote her first novel at the age of eighteen hoping to shift the tide. But the only tide she shifted was moving from high school to college. Then everyday life took its toll on her writerly dreams until 2003 when she couldn't ignore the writing bug any longer. By then, she had immersed herself in reading adult fantasy and romance novels. Writing paranormal & fantasy romance was a no brainer and she went on to publish two adult romance novels. But her muse wanted to give that YA writing gig another chance, and Erin finally realized her lifelong dream of publishing a YA novel with the debut of *Vigilante Nights*.

Erin lives in Northern California. In her spare time, she enjoys reading and re-landscaping her backyard, even though she hates digging holes...unless she's burying fictional bodies! She also confesses to a fascination with American muscle cars and reality TV.

To stay up to date on Erin Richards' latest happenings, including new releases, sales, special announcements, exclusive excerpts, and giveaways, subscribe to her newsletter at: **www.erinrichards.com/connect.htm**.

Please visit Erin Richards online at:
www.ErinRichards.com